Then Chrissa screamed

'DAD! I'M GOING TO
ME!'

Making a supreme effort

'Chrissa, I'm coming!' he roared. 'Don't move!
Keep still!'

Yet even as he found his voice and leapt through
the rain down to the sink that now had her up to the
shoulders, *he's attacked again, for the sight of Chrissa's
desperate mud-plastered face reminds him of a fearful event
in this world of moon and horns where he belongs — of a
sacrifice in a dark underground place, and himself the chief
actor. He shudders to a stop amid cruel laughter; instead of
Chrissa's fear-white face he sees the Red Woman before
him, smiling triumphantly from her bath in the bog of red
mud. Spreadeagled on her back, naked. Showing her
webbed feet . . .*

'*You're not much,*' she whispers, '*but you'll have to do.*'

Clapping horrified hands over his eyes, Sam
screamed.

ARCHON

The First Book of the Watchers

Richard Gordon

Futura

An Orbit Book

First published in Great Britain in 1987 by
Macdonald & Co (Publishers) Ltd
London & Sydney

This edition published in 1988 by
Futura Publications

ISBN 0 7088 3708 5

Typeset by Leaper & Gard Ltd., Bristol, England
Printed and bound in Great Britain by
Hazell, Watson & Viney Ltd
Aylesbury, Bucks

Futura Publications
A Division of
Macdonald & Co (Publishers) Ltd
Greater London House
Hampstead Road
London NW1 7QX
A Pergamon Press plc company

This one's for Pam.

Author's Note

The title of this book, ARCHON, a term not found in the text, means ruler, from the Greek, referring to one of the nine chief magistrates of ancient Athens. In Gnostic lore the term embraces powers which, singly or in multiple, were seen as the false creators of this world, wrathful and hostile rulers who stole the Light and ignorantly used it to their own ends — the Demiurge or fallen angels. Thus, from THE NAG HAMMADI LIBRARY: *For the Archon was a laughing-stock because he said, 'I am God, and there is none greater than I.'* (SECOND TREATISE OF THE GREAT SETH: VII 2: 64); and again: *Then the wrath of the archons burned. They were ashamed of their dissolution. And they fumed and were angry at the life. The cities were overturned; the mountains were dissolved. The Archon came, with the archons of the western regions . . . (etc.).* (THE CONCEPT OF OUR GREAT POWER: VI 4: 43-44). In terms of this tale, ARCHON can be identified with Madame in her various guises, and with the false creator called *Rex Mundi* or *Jehovah* by the Cathars; i.e., with the Watchers in all their manifestations.

Contents

Prologue:
The Burning Man

He's trying to touch her again.

He's straining forward at her from the smoke and roaring flames, his face a peeling ruin, his skin cracked, his eyelids burnt off, his mouth a gaping round black hole, his arms (the wide black sleeves fallen back, blazing) reaching desperately towards her, the already-shrivelled hands like claws. All this she sees with utter clarity.

He's trying to reach her from the flames. She wants to flee, but she cannot move; she's rooted to the spot, so petrified she can't even throw up, though the stench of his roasting flesh (it stinks as terrible as the turkey her dad Sam burned in the oven when he got pissed last Christmas) sickens her to the pit of her stomach. Nor can she shut her ears to the shrieking, the cracked cries and sobbed prayers. For the burning man isn't alone in his agony. Others burn with him, many others, perhaps hundreds, all thrown alive onto the huge pyre lit in the timber stockade. She can barely make out their writhing bodies through the eye-stinging, oily black smoke. It's a small mercy. She can hear them wailing. She can smell the stomach-turning stink of them. And she can see him.

He alone terrifies her. He alone has eyes (bursting, popping eyes) for her, he alone is aware of her. He alone tries to touch her, to reach her before he dies with the message she doesn't want to hear. Yes. She knows there's a message. For out of the ruined black pit of his mouth, strangely audible through the screaming of

*the other victims and the crackling of the flames, he's crying out
... no, SINGING, he's singing to her ... and though the language
in which he sings is none she ever consciously spoke or heard (nor
could he possibly be singing from the heart of such an inferno)
somehow she hears every word (how can it be? she wails silently)
that he sings with such sweet clarity ... and, worst of all, she
knows she knows the song:*

> *Quant lo bouié ben de laura
> Planto soun agulhado
> AEIOU!*

*No! she whimpers, cringing, fearing what she hears, gagging
on the stench as thick black ash whirls out of the smoke to lodge
in her hair, in her clothes, No! she cries, beating the foul stuff off,
Let me be! Leave me alone! What do you want? I don't know
you! I don't want to know!*

*Desperately she strains to turn away and tear her eyes from the
sight of him, to tear her spirit from his terrible dying song ... and
even as she feels the scream welling up she breaks her gaze free ...
only instead to see the hooded faceless ones (scarlet crosses stitched
on their black robes) who stand all round the stockaded pyre, praying aloud, and the cursing soldiers who, mouths agape as they
flinch from the heat, with long poles beat back the pain-maddened
hands clutching the charred top of the timber palisades. With
tears in her eyes she looks up the precipitous, forested peak soaring
above this awful place; she sees the castle stranded like Noah's
Ark on the summit of the great rock; beyond the wind-whipped
plume of stinking smoke she sees birds hurled free and far above
through the grey cold windy sky and wishes she could be up there
with them ... yet even as the scream bursts from her, still, as if
she's there in the flaming stockade with him, she sees the burning
man lurching before her, reaching out for her with his charred
claws, and still his bursting eyes are fixed on her and still she
hears his voice: his voice singing that sweet sad song, impossibly,
from the heart of the inferno:*

> *Planto soun agulhado
> Trobo sa henno al pé del foc*

And despite herself the melancholy beauty of it grips her, draws her into the heart of the terrifying mystery. Again she screams as the burning man embraces her in his sheets of flame like ice. There's a great roaring in her, and another voice that sounds like a trumpet above and below and all through the singing of the song, and his voice vibrates with an utter clarity in the very centre of her; a voice that burns her heart, her mind, her entire being, crying out in her:

CHRISSA, SWEET CHILD, DON'T RUN AWAY FROM THIS! UNDERSTAND WHO DOES IT AND WHY! REMEMBER THE LOST STONE AND THE DARK WATCHERS WHO STOLE IT LONG AGO! BEWARE THE EVIL ONE WHO HUNTS YOUR FATHER! WHEN SHE STRIKES FROM THE EMERALD DEPTHS AND HE FALLS, REMEMBER THIS SONG AND COME TO ME! FORGET, OR FAIL, THEN THE WORLD WILL BURN AS WE DO! THE WORLD WILL BE CONSUMED AGAIN IN FIRE AND FLOOD! SO REMEMBER THE SHINING ONES! THE SHINING ONES!

Then fire consumes her; the tortured face of the burning man explodes, and it's the round world itself that explodes, explodes in sheets of flame, in billowing clouds of black smoke. And the song is drowned by a sudden harsh, enormous laughter. In that instant Chrissa sees, gazing at her from the black void now shrouding her, the vast, mocking, blood-painted face of a raven-haired woman. The woman's beauty is awful, severe ... yet in those gleaming jet-black eyes Chrissa sees not only triumphant hatred but doubt too, and ... fear? This is the face of the Enemy! she screams silently as the worst terror of all seizes her, for those eyes hold no light, and the emptiness in them sucks all strength and hope from her.

Then she's falling, falling, falling, the stench of the burning in her nostrils as she screams ... and she went on screaming and falling until frightened hands were shaking her, shaking her awake in the darkness of the night, and she sat up, shivering in giddy confusion with her mother's hands on her sweat-soaked brow, knowing only that the burning man had come to her yet again in her sleep, come to her as he did every night now.

Breathing harshly, Diane Joyce switched on Chrissa's bedside light as the girl, still shuddering, sat up and stared with startled, frightened eyes at her bedroom in all its familiarity, at the George Michael poster over her bed, at suburban north London rooftops outside her window, and last of all at her mother's white, anxious, oddly unreal face. 'Mum, why is this happening to me?' she whispered when at last she was able to speak.

'Don't worry, dear. The doctors will stop it.'

But Chrissa knew already that the doctors at the Royal Free could do nothing. They didn't understand. They only prescribed drugs. And with a coldness in her heart, a coldness that grew night by night, she asked:

'Mum, does Dad ever have dreams like mine?'

And Diane, feeling an answering chill, could find no answer . . .

Part One
In the Last Days

If you bring forth what is within you
what you bring forth will save you.
If you do not bring forth what is within you
what you do not bring forth will destroy you.

The Gospel according to Thomas
(Logion 45)

Gairloch —
N.W. Scotland

Atlantic Ocean

Lo[ch]
Gairl[och]

▲Tir Nan C[...]
(Red Poin[t])

N.

W.

E.

S. 4

0   Scale
         in Miles
8

(Gardens)
Poolewe

R. Ewe

Gairloch

Cuilchonich

Loch
Maree

Inverness 60m

Sidhean Mór
& Fairy Lochs

Skye

(over the sea)
To Skye

Map 1

1.
In Crouch End

'Sam. Are you asleep?'

'Mmmm. What?'

'Sam, we must talk about Chrissa.'

'Oh for godsakes. Again?'

'Don't you care what's happening to your daughter?'

'Diane, it's weeks since she last had a ...'

'I don't mean the dreams. Sam Joyce, don't you notice *anything*?'

'Look, Diane, I have to be up early. So drop it. Right?'

'Oh. So it's fine by you if she burns down the school or something. So long as you get your sleep. Thanks, Sam. Sweet dreams!'

'I don't dream, dear,' mumbled Sam Joyce, 'Not any more.'

Seven years, Diane thought, and he still blames me.

But that night Sam did dream ...

'... I mean, lately he's been really difficult!' Diane complained next day to Mona Jackson over a lunchtime drink in the uncrowded beer garden of the Princess Alexandra on Park Road. 'He's hardly ever home and when he is his mind's somewhere else.' It was early May — sunny, almost warm — amid yet another day of union action at the Park Road Primary; the two teachers had been to yet another meeting at which the education minister's latest final offer had yet again been dismissed as an insult, and Mona — very active on all the committees — was hearing out Diane's tales of domestic trouble with a thin smile and thinner patience. 'He's a good bloke at heart,' Diane rushed on, knowing full well what Mona thought of Sam but unable to stop. 'In part it's my fault, because he *does* try, and ...'

'Rubbish!' Mona interrupted, cynically blunt as always, the result perhaps of ten years spent 'teaching' at the same inner-city school. 'Face facts. He came back because you were a familiar port and he needed a shoulder. Now he's getting itchy feet again. That's all.'

'That's not quite true!' Diane said in a very cool voice.

'Diane, don't waste your life on a man who refuses to change.'

'He hasn't refused! It took him a year to get onto that training scheme, but now he's really into GRYP, and I don't grill him when he gets home late because ...' — defensively Diane straightened her glasses, touched her wedding ring — '... if we can't trust each other, what is there?' She met Mona's sceptical grey eyes. *She thinks I'm an idiot. A bourgeois housewife serf.* 'Sorry to waste your time with my problems,' she added, too lightly, and sipped without tasting at her vodka-tonic.

Mona seemed amused. 'How's Chrissa?'

'In a political phase.' Diane's tone was pointed.

'Is she still having those ... what was it, burning man nightmares?'

'No,' said Diane, too flatly. 'Dr Isaacs says it was just a phase. A side-effect of puberty.' In a wry voice she added: 'But now she smells burning everywhere. And she says she wants to burn down the school.'

Mona arched her brows. 'Does she know why?'

'Oh yes!' Diane smiled without humour. 'She says: "Nobody cares about us. You lot just want more cash. The government wants us to rot. Nobody cares about the SCHOOL — so why don't we burn it down and have some fun!"'

'Remarkable!' Mona brightened. 'She's ... how old? Twelve?'

'Thirteen in August. Mona, look ...'

'And how do you answer her?' Mona asked intently.

'That burning things down must makes life harder.' Diane faced Mona's disapproval fiercely. 'You just end up with everyone angry and miserable.'

'You'd burn out a cancer that's killing you.' Downing her half-pint, Mona eyed her watch. 'Or would you? What's Sam got to say about it?'

'Sam?' Diane couldn't keep bitterness out of her voice. 'He's too busy with his kids at GRYP. He doesn't have time for his own daughter.'

'Dump him,' said Mona briskly. 'Neither of you need it.'

'Maybe we do.' Diane went cold again. 'We were getting on fine until Chrissa's dreams began.' She sighed. 'You've got no idea. She was waking up screaming every night. That's stopped, but the shadow's still there. Whatever it is. Nothing you can touch. Just ... something very wrong.'

Don't fool yourself, she thought mordantly. *You know what it is. You thought it was dead and buried years ago. But it isn't. It's back.*

Mona's shrug was impatient. Her tight, rational face said: This is nonsense. Again she checked the time. 'I'm picketing with Des. Coming?'

Refusing, Diane walked fretfully home to Berkeley Road. Sam was out: it was a Thursday, meaning he'd be out all evening too, supervising a discussion group of kids on court orders. But because of the teachers' day of action Chrissa was in — upstairs in her room, blasting the house with Wham on full volume. Or was it Duran Duran? Diane didn't care to go up and find out. Lately she hadn't had much success, communicating with Chrissa. No more than with her husband. Both had grown surly and strange. Yes. It was like a shadow. Infecting them all. Tainting everything.

Better noise than nightmares, she rationalised, wincing

21

at the volume as she hung up her anorak in the hall. But in the kitchen she wondered: How do we know they've stopped? She says they have, and the screaming's stopped, but she doesn't look well. She isn't sleeping; she won't talk to us or anyone else; she smells things on fire in here when the stove isn't even on. It's not right. And Sam ... he just doesn't want to know.

God! she told herself wearily, I could scream too!

She didn't. Too well brought up, I suppose, she thought, unhappily eyeing her pinched face in the mirror over the fridge as Prince replaced Wham. You look like a dog's breakfast! she accused the face, hopelessly finger-combing her long, tangled ash-blonde hair. No wonder Sam stays out.

She filled the kettle then sat down. On the kitchen table lay a book Sam was reading. Its cover was black. It was called THE POWERS OF EVIL.

Diane closed her eyes, fighting an old, familiar sense of panic.

It's starting again, she thought. Just like when Chrissa was born. When he wouldn't stop doping and he wore that thing all the time. Did he really throw it away? I never dared ask. I just hoped. Now it's starting again. I don't know if he even knows it himself yet. That look on his face this morning. I'm sure he didn't recognise me. Oh God!

The kettle began to wail in fiendish counterpoint to Prince's mega-decibel blast. Diane sat rigid, digging fingernails into her palms. We must get out of London this summer, she told herself desperately. Devon. Wales. Maybe Scotland. Sam's been on a lot about Scotland lately. I'm sure he feels the same. He *must!* Maybe ... if I put it to him right ...

The kettle went on whistling as she sat there, worrying ...

The dream had shocked Sam. He'd woken in a sweat, unable to face his wife, and gone to work feeling dull and unreal. The feeling hadn't worn off. All day his nervousness persisted; by evening it was worse. And his day wasn't over yet. At eight every Thursday evening he supervised a discussion group of four teenagers referred by court order to GRYP — the Greystoke Road Youth Project — as part of their Intermediate Treatment programme. Now, at one minute to eight, he sat slouched on a stool in a grimy pub, gloomily eyeing his gaunt reflection where it swam in a puddle of beer on the bar. Above a blue denim collar the narrow, rather saturnine face with the shock of grey-streaked black hair gawped back at him, its mouth down-at-heel. 'It's crap!' he told it savagely. 'Keep 'em out of jail, land 'em on suckers like me. What's the use? It's not doing any good and we're losing our funding anyway. It's just dead-end bullshit!'

You chose it, mate, said his reflection unsympathetically.

'Go to hell!' he muttered. The barman eyed him, then shrugged at another customer in a We-get-'em-all-in-here way, but Sam didn't notice.

Ragged today, aren't we? His reflection's dark eyes mocked him. *Must be that dream. As bad as one of Chrissa's ... or one of yours, years ago. Odd how you can't face it. Scotland, eh? That Christmas you were with Grandad when Mum was dying. Remember? At Tir Nan Og. You were eight. He told you about Captain Davey and Madame Pédauque. He showed you the ...*

Screw this! he thought, suddenly alarmed. I put all that crap behind me years ago. Who needs it? In a hurry he drained off his second pint of strong 6X, nodded sourly at the barman, and left the pub. Trembling, on edge with an ugly tension, he strode round a corner into decayed Greystoke Road with its view over Finsbury Park rooftops to the distant City towers where whizzkids made their millions. The evening was sweet, fleecy cloud sailing high in the pale blue sky, the air almost fresh up here on Hornsey Rise, but it gave him no pleasure. He felt ready to explode. Last night, he thought. Oh hell! I should have called her. And it was then that a gang of small kids, black and white and brown, burst out of an alleyway and erupted round him; weaving through bumper-to-bumper

23

parked cars, shouting as they came. One of them, not looking, ran into him then scampered away laughing. A sudden murderous rage seized him. His body knotted. GRAB THE LITTLE BASTARDS! SNAP THEIR NECKS! Shocked, he bit his lip, shut his eyes. Slowly the bile subsided. He unclenched his fists. Christ! he thought in dismay, Where did that come from? They're just kids. Younger than Chrissa. Watch it tonight. Get a GRYP on yourself. Ha bloody ha!

Confused, he reached the decrepit old church that housed GRYP. Pushing through heavy swing doors he entered a large open space, sparsely carpeted and furnished with insurance company cast-offs. Jobless kids hung out here every day but tonight it was almost deserted. He saw but ignored his group waiting for him in a nook to one side. The sense of unreality struck him again. I've been here three years? He felt amazed. Why? For what? And his eyes, seeking a clue, roamed disbelievingly round the flimsy partitions that defined activity rooms, workshops, and the office cubicles he shared with Marge Benson and Ro Walters, the other youth workers, and with Tony Morrison the co-ordinator. Bright primary colours were splashed all over; mellow evening sunlight streamed through the plain glass of mullioned windows onto notice boards and rock concert posters. Yet despite every attempt at cheeriness an aura of Victorian decrepitude persisted.

Oliver Twist could turn up tomorrow, he thought, appalled. *Sorry, kid, we've got no more.* His sour grin faded. What if Chrissa ends up in a dump like this? The way she's carrying on ... is it my fault? I've been ignoring her, true ... but why? God, I think it's that her dreaming scares me ... it's too much like when I used to wear that ... is that why last night I ...

'Sam, a word about the weekend.' Unexpectedly Marge Benson, big and bustling, bore down on him. Shocked out of his reverie by her sudden approach, he flinched at the sight of her. Her red hair ... something to do with his dream ... he scowled, and she drew back in surprise.

24

'I'm not going to eat you,' she said, frowning.

'What is it?' he demanded edgily.

'Saturday's trip to, um, Whipsnade. The zoo.'

'Tomorrow, Marge.' He grinned sharply, falsely. 'No time right now.'

And he left her standing and staring. He came to his group and sat down heavily among them. Bessie, Sean, Julie and Jim. Sprawled in old armchairs donated by the caring insurance company, without enthusiasm awaiting their weekly dose of his adult input to their stumbling self-analysis. Sean and Julie, both fifteen, nicked for lifting expensive designer gear from West End stores. Fat Bessie, suspended from school for truancy and mayhem. And Jim. Who'd brought his dog with him again. Built like a wrestler at 17, punk-styled in torn denim with an emerald-green Mohican quiff, Jim cradled his little wire-haired terrier protectively in his arms, and his hard eyes dared Sam to so much as mention it.

'Hi,' said Sam glumly, 'and how are we tonight? Happy and well?'

Four pairs of blank juvenile eyes stared at him ... and at the sight of their empty faces that sudden inexplicable rage seized him again. Bile — hot, viscid, choking — surged up his gorge. SCREW YOU! PATHETIC LITTLE SHITS! Behind clenched teeth he swallowed with difficulty. *You don't have to take this!* snapped his silent voice, and without realising it he nodded.

'None of you got anything to say?' he demanded in a harsh thick tone. 'I do all the talking this week too?'

Jim shrugged. The others remained blank.

Right! said the voice. *That's it!* And as suddenly as it had struck him the rage receded, leaving him in a sea of extraordinary calm.

'Okay. Fine.' He clapped his hands. 'I don't want to be here any more than you do. We all know it's a waste of time, so ...' — and without planning it he found himself on his feet, beaming genially — '... if one of you doesn't say something *fast*, I'm going home. Any offers?' He met each of them in the eye. They looked uneasy, but none of them said a word.

Sam shrugged. He felt an amazing sense of airy release.

'Wonderful,' he said, 'Goodbye. Enjoy your lives.'

And he turned and started for the door. *Didn't know you could do it, did you?* the voice congratulated him. *You're a free man again, Sam Joyce!*

'Hey! Sam! Mr Joyce!' Jim cried out angrily. 'You can't just walk out on us! Marge, stop him, willya? He's gone nuts!'

'Nuts?' Ignoring Marge's attempt to intercept him, Sam turned on them. 'Nuts for refusing to waste my time and yours trying to turn you into obedient state-approved zombies? You must be joking!' He laughed, his dark face alight. 'Don't worry, I'll sign your attendance sheets. See you next week. Maybe.' And he abandoned them, stalking past Marge, slamming GRYP's door shut behind him. But out on the street doubt struck him.

What the hell am I doing? he wondered. Sure I'm sick of it. Sure, I want to walk out. But into what? Top job in industry? Millionaire Row?

Hating his cowardice, he began to turn back. Even as he gripped the door handle it twisted sharply and Marge shot out. Colliding with him, she pulled back and drew herself up — a boiler-suited pillar of affronted rectitude. He grimaced, unable to hide his dislike. She glared back.

'Sam Joyce, what's the matter with you? Don't we have enough trouble already without you acting like a lunatic? Those young people need you.'

'*Need* me?' He eyed her as if she came from another world. 'We're not helping those kids,' he explained very patiently, 'we're just hanging onto our jobs. My daughter's alone at home tonight, and it's time I paid her some attention ... or she'll end up in a squalid dump like this!'

That's telling her! marvelled the voice.

Marge trembled angrily. 'You're not yourself.'

'You're wrong.' He smiled. 'You couldn't be more wrong.'

He started walking without looking back, ignoring her

26

shouts. he didn't stop until, in the urban gloaming, he reached 15 Berkeley Road.

Home sweet home.

His mood of airy confidence evaporated the moment he entered their mortgaged house and remembered bills, overdrafts, and domestic crisis.

'Oh my God,' he muttered, 'what have I done?'

Diane was out with her women's group, meaning until closing time or after, and Chrissa (he assumed, given the shrill volume of Madonna echoing through the house) was upstairs in her room.

'TURN DOWN THAT BLOODY RACKET!' he bellowed.

His plea was futile. He knew that in advance. What's the matter with that child? he wondered as he stalked into the kitchen. She used to be so quiet. Then these damn dreams. Burning men. Now she's turned into a rude little monster. Maybe it *is* puberty, like that bloody doctor said.

You don't really believe that, do you? whispered the little voice.

As he got the Grant's Standfast down from its top shelf and poured himself a stiff three fingers he noticed that his hands were shaking.

'What is this?' he demanded angrily. 'It was just a dream. Sit down and relax. Watch TV or something. Don't think about it.'

But in the potted-plant jungle of the living-room the bass of Chrissa's stereo sounded like the feet of an entire army on the march. Grimly he located the TV where it lurked behind a giant fern. Switching it on with the volume full up, he collapsed into his favourite chair. The programme was a report on City corruption. The reporter had cornered a reluctant pin-stripe witness. 'BUT WHAT DO YOU SAY TO THE CHARGE THAT YOUR COMPANY HAS MISMANAGED THE FUNDS OF THOUSANDS OF SMALL INVESTORS?' the reporter bellowed, vying with the deafening whirl of Madonna's Material Girl.

Something in Sam snapped. Again the rage seized

him, bubbling up from a foul black gulf. He shot to his feet, face contorted. With rigid care, teeth clenched, he put down his whisky without spilling it, then started upstairs to Chrissa's room, step by step, slow and deliberate, as if he were a grenade and the least shock might jar the pin right out of him.

He knocked on her door. The music drowned his knocking.

He knocked a second time, harder. Still she didn't answer.

Again. No reply. He breathed deep. He opened her door and entered, clearing his throat as he did. But still she didn't seem to hear.

His daughter sat hunched over her desk by the window, her fair hair (Diane had held out against Chrissa's demand for punk styling) sweeping the exercise book in which she wrote. The speakers were so close to her head that Sam (dully he wondered at his fury) thought it amazing her eardrums hadn't blown out. 'CHRISSA!' he roared against the tidal wave of sound.

She flinched and swung round, her pale bespectacled face white with shock. 'Dad!' she gasped, 'You're not meant to be home yet!'

'WELL, I AM HOME! PLEASE TURN DOWN THAT ...'

'How dare you barge in here without knocking!'

'FORGIVE ME, MADAM, BUT I *DID* KNOCK. NOW PLEASE WILL YOU ...'

'No!' she cried angrily, 'I need it to concentrate.'

'CHRISSA! BEFORE I GO BANANAS!'

'Oh, all right!' Pouting, giving him an injured look, she reduced the volume. 'But why be so nasty about it? I didn't know you were in. I'm usually the only one here on Thursdays.' She scowled. Her face was drawn, with dark circles round the eyes. Plainly she hadn't been sleeping well, and through his rage he felt an obscure thrill of fear. She's still dreaming, he realised. But *what*? Then she demanded aggressively: 'So why aren't you with those yobs that get sent to your stupid project?'

'I told you before,' he growled, 'don't call them yobs.'

'But they are!' Her jaw jutted; her blue eyes shone with a hard light that made her face look too old: certainly older than her barely-developed body. 'I hate how you spend more time with them than with me or Mum!'

'I don't like it either. That's why I'm home early tonight.'

'You used to be like a Dad should be,' she went on so bitterly that he felt abashed, 'but now you're a real wally. When I started those horrible dreams you wouldn't listen, you just sent me to that stupid doctor. You're never here, and when you are you just moan all the time, and you only notice *me* when *I* make a lot of noise!' She turned away. 'It's not fair! I'm not here just for you to shout at!'

'Of course not.' Sam really did try to sound friendly, but it came out wrong, and she flashed him a look as if he threatened her. Her eyes grew wide and piercing again; suddenly, shaking her head, she drew breath as if she'd seen something terrible. Her expression baffled and upset him.

'Go away, Dad.' She was *afraid*? 'Just leave me alone, okay?'

He stood just inside her door. 'Is it those nightmares again?' he asked tentatively. 'The burning man? Won't you tell me about it?'

'No.' Again she shook her head, her gaze fixed on him. 'Go away!'

'But how can I help if you won't say anything?' he exploded.

'You can't help,' she said flatly. 'You don't know any more than Dr Isaacs.' And then she blurted out: 'If you did, you'd be watching out for the ... for the ... for something bad ... wouldn't you?'

Sam started. He couldn't face the fearful edge to her question. Nor, apparently, could she. *Watch out for ... what?* She'd begun to say something specific, then changed it. *I didn't tell either of them about my dream last night,* he realised. *She can't possibly know!* He stared at her. She stared boldly back. Yes. There it was in her eyes. Not only fear, but ... knowledge and a sort of hope.

A look, too adult, that knew things about him that he didn't want to see. Abruptly an overpowering sense of dullness struck him; he could not meet her gaze any longer. Sighing harshly he turned away, shutting her door behind him as he started down the stairs ... but halfway down he froze abruptly, again seized by the sudden huge rage. Like a tide of hate it roared over him, this time receding as swiftly as it had come ... but for a moment it consumed him, bringing before his mind's eye a face — the red-painted face of a raven-haired woman — and murderous visions of ... NO! He refused it, locked it out as he stumbled down to the foot of the stairs, more shaken than he could admit.

For the fury had not only shocked but exhilarated him.

And then the phone rang. Shrilling like a bird of doom.

'Yes?' He snatched up the receiver. 'What? Who is it?'

It was Marge. 'Sam?' she asked hesitantly, 'Are you ...?'

'Not now.' His voice shook. 'Sorry. Not tonight.' Cutting her off before she could say another word, he returned uncertainly into the living-room. Now there was not a sound from above. *Chrissa!* he cried silently.

He realised he was shaking. Physically. Violently.

'Don't think,' he muttered. 'Calm down. Watch TV.'

But he couldn't sit. Memories of a mad earlier period in his life were flooding him. Long-buried memories of a time when sanity had all but left him. With Diane's help he'd rebuilt his life so carefully these last seven years, making a virtue out of those middle-class normalities which once he'd rejected derisively ... but now, beginning to doubt everything again, he paced their living-room carpet (wall-to-wall Axminster) like a caged cat. He swallowed the whisky and poured another. It didn't help. *The Red Woman. Madame Pédauque.* All that crazy stuff, like a gaping abyss under his feet. He shut his eyes and sat down, raking his scalp. 'We need a holiday,' he whispered. 'It's stress, that's all. We must get out of here. Go somewhere healthy before we all go up the wall. Let's face it, Diane's a mess, Chrissa's turning into a monster, poor kid, and I'm ...

Yes? asked his voice, *What ARE you, Sam? Who WERE you, before the nine-to-five gobbled you? Want to find out? Why don't we all go to Scotland? Why don't we go to Tir Nan Og, where Grandad showed you everything ...?*

I *am* going nuts, he told himself fearfully. Yet he couldn't deny his excitement at the idea of rediscovering what seven years ago (*remember that night in Algeria, Sam?*) he'd abandoned in terror. Now, shivering, he eyed the fern-thick living-room. Plants, TV set, the walls and windows — all seemed to be pulsating, ebbing and flowing in their distance and density, growing more insubstantial with every passing second. He groaned with apprehension. I thought I'd got rid of all that. Now what? What do I do?

Try the attic, Sam, whispered the crafty, near-subliminal voice. *Your diaries. Don't you remember your diaries? And that ... other thing? That other thing old Roderick gave you? Remember it?*

In a daze he stood and started up the stairs again. He knew he should fight. But the worst thing was he wanted it. He wanted it all back ...

2.
The Enemy

It had been close. Chrissa's heart didn't stop hammering until she was sure Sam was all the way downstairs. When the phone rang she switched off the stereo and listened at the door. When she heard him enter the living-room she relaxed slightly and went back to her desk, feeling hot and faint. Yes, very close. She'd heard his last knock just in time. Now, chewing her underlip, she drew aside the exercise book. Hidden under it was the pencil drawing she'd been doing since Diane had gone out an hour earlier. It showed a bald old man in flames (the flames like angel-wings leaping from his shoulders), his skin peeling and cracking, his mouth a round black O of agony. With him in the timber stockade, against the background of a huge rock with a castle on top, a great many other vaguely-drawn stick-people were burning. She'd given them all round black Os for mouths.

It's not very good, Chrissa decided, eyeing her work miserably. Art definitely isn't my best subject. I don't know what is. Having video nasty dreams? Seeing and smelling things that can't be there? I wish I could tell someone, but what's the use? If Mum or Dad see this they'll send me straight back to that stupid creep who only wants to know what I'm doing with boys. And her face twisted with unhappy contempt.

'You see, Chrissa,' she piped in derisive mimicry of Dr Isaacs, 'you're going through a VERY important change, and it's MOST essential that you don't think of these dreams as anything but hormonal stimuli!'

She puffed out her cheeks and blew a loud raspberry. Then she groaned, threw herself onto her bed under the George Michael poster, and buried her head in her arms. Oh no! she thought, Dad hates me! I saw it in his face!

I can't deal with that, she told herself fearfully, wanting to cry but refusing the tears. Not yet. Not after last night. Did I give too much away? I'm sure the Enemy made him dream of her. I'm sorry, Mum, I don't want to lie but I must. If I told you the truth you'd just make a fuss.

For, an hour earlier, before going out to her weekly yak-yak group, Diane had knocked and come in with her usual mixture of timid severity.

'Chrissa, your supper's in the oven.'

'Okay, Mum. Thanks.'

'Are you sure you'll be all right, dear?'

'Yes, Mum, I'll be fine.'

'But what've you been up to all day?'

'Oh, nothing much.'

'But it's not ... I mean, why have you stopped going out with Jane and Clara and all your friends?'

'I haven't, Mum. I just want to be on my own for now.'

'Chrissa. Are you sure you've been telling your father and myself the truth? Those dreams really have stopped? You're sleeping properly?'

'Yes, Mum,' she said blankly, 'They stopped weeks ago when Dr Isaacs told me they're just ... you know ... hormonal.'

That had been hard. Meeting her mother's searching gaze squarely and telling the outright lie. Telling Diane what she wanted to hear. It made Chrissa very sad, and it made her angry too, because she hated the truth for being untellable. Not only that the burning man still plagued her dreaming, singing his strange song from the flames, but that often now she sensed him while awake. Sometimes, headphoned in bed or at her desk, she saw him out

33

of the corner of her eye, mouthing at her through Madonna. She wasn't so scared of him any more (his look melted her heart), but she was tired of him and still tried to ignore him, shutting her eyes or turning away. At these times there was a whine in her head like the buzz of an invisible insect, and the stink of burning flesh. And two days ago she'd heard voices, apparently from the air outside her window. They weren't speaking English; it had sounded like that language the burning man sang. French, maybe. She didn't think so, but she couldn't be sure. That had been scary. But the stench was worst. The screaming she could control — the dream was still awful, but familiar; now in her sleep she could stop herself from screaming — but the smell of burning all the time ... twice she'd made Mum suspicious by asking if something in the kitchen had caught fire, when in fact nothing had been burning or in the oven at all.

All very scary, but it had been going on for weeks. She was used to it. She didn't like it, but no harm had come of it ... save that she wasn't sleeping, and had to keep quiet or be sent back to Dr Isaacs. She was seeing nothing of her friends: at school she kept to herself and endured the comments. At home she rarely left her room. She had even begun to feel *protective*, as if talking about him would somehow betray her burning man. She was beginning to think of her dream as real. She had begun to wonder who the burning man was. *Where does he live? Why must he die like that?* And the nightly warning — BEWARE THE EVIL ONE WHO HUNTS YOUR FATHER! — what did that mean? Yes, and the images of the world blown up. But most of all, most uneasily, she had begun wondering about the Enemy: the raven-haired woman with the blood-drenched face who glared at her from the void.

Yet despite that it had all become ... almost cosily familiar.

Until last night.

The Enemy had found her.

The dream, as usual, had the burning man groping at her from the fire, screaming his haunting song ... *Quant lo*

34

bouié ben de laura ... and as usual its melancholy beauty had drawn her despite herself into the ice-cold heat of his burning embrace — (that was the bit which most interested Dr Isaacs, the creep: '*And does he DO anything to you when he, um, embraces you, Chrissa?*' he'd asked her during their last session, wet spaniel eyes gleaming, and she, not trying to hide her contempt, had replied: '*How can he DO anything when he's burning to death?*') — and then the great voice (vibrating, it seemed to her, from the heart of a shining sphere of living light) had as usual steeled her with warning.

But last night the warning was changed:

THE ENEMY'S COMING FOR HIM! SHE CALLS FROM THE EMERALD DEPTHS AND HE ANSWERS IN ANGRY IGNORANCE! LISTEN! SHE HAS POWER, BUT SHE NEEDS MORE FOR WHAT SHE MEANS TO DO. BE READY NOW! WHEN YOU CALLED US, WE WERE READY! NOW, SWEET CHILD, IT'S YOUR TURN! DON'T BE SCARED! GET READY!

Then again the world exploded in sheets of fire, in clouds of roiling black smoke; again she'd found herself hurled into an endless void, a mere pinpoint of light amid the horrible laughter, and she'd seen the Enemy again. Grimacing hatefully from the walls of the abyss with those empty jet-black eyes like blank spinning saucers amid the bloody beauty of its face. And as usual then she'd plunged, falling, falling, her screaming silent now as she fell all the way back to wakefulness in her midnight bed at Number 15 Berkeley Road, London N8.

Yet as she'd sat up in sweat-drenched relief, ignoring the familiar burning stench, it was immediately clear she wasn't yet fully awake.

For, facing her from the bottom of her bed, at the centre of a core of darkness like a great enveloping wing, the Enemy stood.

She didn't look like an Enemy — she wore an emerald robe, and no blood disfigured her smooth olive complexion — but Chrissa knew her.

Appalled, unable to breathe, Chrissa stared even as the poison stench of burning turned into a sweet fragrance of

35

wild rose. And the raven-haired woman smiled at her — gently, peacefully.

'*Don't ever listen to what those Weak Ones say about me, Chrissa,*' the awesome woman said in a voice like a summer breeze. '*I've come to help your father — and you, if you'll let me — and all the world. Listen to those stupid martyrs and you'll make a mess of everything . . .*'

But then Chrissa, sitting up, saw the Enemy's feet.

They were wrong. They were not human feet.

They were the webbed feet of a waterbird — a goose, perhaps.

Chrissa drew fearful breath, which must have broken the spell, because suddenly the raven-haired, goose-footed woman had vanished, and the night had been calm again, save for the wailing of a police siren over on the Broadway. But it had been hours before she'd dared to sleep, and all today she'd hid in her room, playing music loud so she couldn't think. Too scary. Just another dream? Maybe. Yet now Dad had charged through her door, and in his congested face she'd seen it. The ugliness of the Enemy. His eyes so dark and dreadful. Yes, something evil had got into him. She'd faced him out, but . . . oh please! she implored now, rocking back and forth on her bed in a sudden attack of terror, why is this happening to me? Why won't it leave me alone? What does it mean: *She's coming for him?* Who is she? What does she want? Is it because of what happened when I was a baby? But they never told me anything! When he came back to us they both pretended nothing had happened? So how can I talk to him about it now?

Suddenly, where she lay with her head buried in her arms, she heard Sam's feet on the stairs. Quickly she turned to the desk and hid the drawing again. What's going on? Why isn't he at his stupid job?

There was a thumping outside her door.

On no! she wailed silently, I can't stand it!

She sat on her bed, shivering, hugging her knees.

More thumps. The sound of something heavy, dragging. Abruptly she realised: He's going up into the attic!

There was a crash. It was followed by a curse, by the sound of her father's feet stumbling on the creaky attic floorboards above. Suddenly angry, she opened her mouth to shout a protest, but she had no saliva.

She smelled burning. The stench of roasting flesh. Fatalistic in her waking dream she turned ... and there, through her closed door, as if at the end of a long dark tunnel, she saw him. The flames leaping up from him and the round black O of his open mouth, and he wasn't singing, he was talking to her, and she heard his voice deep in her mind:

'Sweet child, its starting now! You must be brave!'

Dad, Dad, what are you doing up there? she cried in silent panic, unable to take her eyes from the hideous, agonised face of the burning man. I'm seeing him, and I'm hearing him, and I'm wide awake! Dad, help me!

But already she knew that her father needed her help, not the other way round. And not a sound escaped her lips as she stared at the burning man, as Sam tramped overhead ...

3.
Moon and Horns

Nobody had been in the attic for months. It was no more than a box-space, three sides sloping with the roof. Only under the ridge by the web-thick and never-opened window was there room for even a small man to stand upright. Sam was tall and gangling, with awkward feet and elbows. From the stepladder on the landing he pushed up the hatch, pulled himself up into darkness, and immediately banged his head against the unseen edge of a wooden box. Cursing, he scrambled up into a dusty mess of lidless tins, scattering them as he reached over a stack of suitcases to feel for the light switch. 'This is crazy,' he muttered, his hand coming away sticky with cobwebs, 'Why am I farting around like this?'

He tried again, knocking over a hat rack, but this time found the switch. Behind him the bare 40-watt bulb flickered reluctantly then steadied, throwing his stooped shadow forward over the jungle of junk. Breathing hard, he looked about. *Those diaries!* I put them up here, but where? His eye roamed past a pile of broken up-ended chairs to a battered yellow chest of drawers standing under the worm-eaten window ledge.

There! In there! It's all in there, Sam!

In that instant a sensation of great danger struck him, as if a voice he couldn't hear cried out subliminal warning. Faces flashed before him. He saw Diane. He saw Chrissa, and his heart missed a beat. And then there was another face; a face of terrible bloodsoaked beauty that gazed at him as if through green glass laid over the mouth of a deep black abyss. He stopped in his tracks, shivering and uncertain, but shutting his eyes did no good at all; still the dreadful image persisted in his mind, not letting him (as it seemed) look away ... *and as he eyes her the awesome woman is ever more substantially revealed as the ikon of all his desires: he drinks her in with rising heat; his nostrils flare at the lustrous raven hair pouring over her shoulders and down her back, at her deep dark breasts, her belly and thighs, and ... her hairy legs that diminish, impossibly, down to scaly ankles and the webbed feet of a goose. Despite all that he feels familiar heat begin to pulse in his groin; desire floods him despite the blood that runs dripping from her nipples and soaking the thatch between her thighs; he groans as uncontrollable giddy spasms ripple through him, fully aware of the danger but unable to fight as her eyes, flashing in dark demand, fasten on him; as her slender long tongue snakes from her mouth to lick her bloody lips as she reaches out her arms to him ... not in invitation, no, but in command. You're my creature! her cold eyes tell him; you're my Fool! I sent you to the Last Days; now I want you back! And her voice is a stormwind, a hot wind beating in him like the wings of great birds as a violent dizziness of ancient fears attacks him.* Almost too late, he fought. With a wrench he tore his eyes open, dismissing her, and looked instead round the dingy, dusty clutter of the attic, breathing in gasps as slowly — so slowly it appalled him — his erection subsided. His brain fumed with a sulphurous fire; he imagined he heard a cry of disappointed fury. Oh Chrissa, he thought in agony, is this what you meant about watching out for something bad? Have you seen her too? God, what am I doing! Why provoke all this again? What if I find that thing again and put it on? It destroyed Grandad, he thought feverishly; it nearly destroyed me before I learned better. Yes, you idiot! You swore to Diane you'd never wear it or look at those diaries again, never ever again! You *swore!*

Then why didn't you burn them when she asked you? the little voice asked him slyly, *And why didn't you throw it away while you could?*

He had no good answer. He stood shivering, vacillating, divided. Yet almost without his being aware of it his feet began to carry him through the attic clutter towards the yellow chest of drawers. Reaching it, with an unsure finger he drew shaky spirals in the thick dust that covered it. He knew exactly where he'd put the diaries: in the top left drawer. 'Open it,' he muttered, 'and there's no going back. I don't really want to do this, do I? I can't be so crazy! Just because of a dream ... am I so bored with my life? Is it so bad? This is absurd!' Yet again, as he shut his eyes, he seemed to see her, waiting greedily in the abyss, and even as the fear swept over him the hunger of an ancient addiction overcame his fear. His blood began to pump again; feverishly he licked his lips, remembering the last entry he'd made in his diaries, seven years ago at Ghardaia in the Algerian Sahara. Yes, I really did run away, didn't I? he realised, filled with a sudden haunting shame. She wanted me to go through to her, through the Gate, and I could have gone — I *would* have gone ... but ...

He cut it off. Breathing deep, he stared through the web-thick window at the ordinariness of the road outside. Night was falling: the streetlights had just come on. Yet what he saw was not Berkeley Road but himself on that last night seven years ago ... storm-maddened, doped up to the gills, scribbling by torchlight under a blanket in the cane shelter below the holy city of Beni Isguen. Smoking dope in *Algeria?* Crazy! With ... *what was his name?* He shook his head in irritation. God, he thought, the bloke saved me from ... well, from suicide. I'd have gone through, I really would, but he got that thing off me at the last moment, he tore it off my finger and stopped me ... and I can't even remember his name!

Then he snapped his fingers. 'That's it!' he exclaimed, 'Trucker Dave! That's right! The Watchers were after me and he ...'

Dizziness seized him. *The panic storm. Her voice wailing in the wilderness, drawing him out of the shelter. Sand, lashing him from every direction, drumming his flesh, slapping him, taunting him, talking in tongues and numbers, spiralling him into the emerald abyss from which she called him, reached out to him, needing him to . . .*

'No!' He shook his head furiously, 'I don't need it! I'm in Berkeley Road, I'm Sam Joyce, I've got a life to live, I've got a wife and kid to look after, I'm going to work tomorrow! Don't fall for this! Not again! I escaped once, so why tempt fate again? Come on!' he scolded himself, forcing himself away from the window, from the urgent and greedy demand of his reawakened desire. 'Leave it! Forget it! Get back downstairs NOW!'

Goodbye, Sam! sang the almost-subliminal, sweetly-mocking voice. *Bye-bye dreams! Hullo Death-in-life! Crouch on your fat End for ever, Sam!*

'Hell!' he shouted, tormented by a sudden huge sense of cowardice, of missed opportunity. 'What have I got to lose?' And with an impatient jerk he turned and yanked open the top left drawer. It came shooting out so fast that instinctively he dropped it and jumped back, bashing his head severely against a joist. It crashed to the floor, spilling pencil stubs, old biros, pieces of rock, several moth-eaten blue exercise books and . . .

And something else.

Something he had not let himself name or think about directly.

Even as his eyes blurred with tears at the blazing pain in his head, he saw it. Gleaming dull bronze, brighter emerald. Flying out on its own arc, hitting the floor beyond the drawer's crash, tinkling and rolling away through the dust to a shadowy stop.

For a moment everything stopped.

For a moment 15 Berkeley Road was silent and still . . .

Then the front door opened and Diane came in even as Chrissa ran out of her room onto the landing and cried in a terrified voice:

'Dad, will you stop it! Will you stop it now!'

Diane groaned. She too had come home earlier than usual. Her group had been discussing (arguing?) whether to join a Mothers Against Cruise march to the American base at Molesworth, but during the evening she'd developed a splitting headache. For a moment she leaned wearily against the doorpost. She rubbed her brow and breathed deep. What now? she wondered. Heavily, she entered the hall and started upstairs.

On the landing the stepladder stood up against the open attic hatch with Chrissa beside it, flushed and distraught. 'Dad's up there and he's bringing the house down!' she told Diane, almost sobbing. 'He came home early in a foul mood and there's something wrong with him but I don't want to go up there on my own!'

'All right.' Diane sighed. 'Sam?' she called tentatively.

There was no sound at all from the attic.

'Sam, are you all right up there?'

Nothing. Not a stir. It was then that Diane began to prickle with the fear, the old fear she'd never quite laid to rest. 'Stay here,' she told Chrissa in a thin cold voice. And slowly, very slowly, she mounted the stepladder, reluctantly raising her head through the open hatch. She took a deep breath. Through the clutter she looked. After a few seconds she spotted him, under the window, by the yellow chest of drawers.

Sam was on his hands and knees.

He was bleeding from a gash on the forehead. His face was covered in blood. She gasped, but he didn't hear her. He didn't see her. He was totally oblivious to her, to his wound, to his surroundings.

He had no eyes or ears for anything but the scintillating object he held in his hand. He was holding it up to the light, staring into the depths of it, and even before she saw it she knew what it was.

'I thought you'd got rid of that thing years ago,' she said dully, knowing even as she spoke that she'd never believed any such thing.

Sam still didn't hear her. He was gladly lost in the

emerald depths, faraway in the dream he'd had last night, spending Christmas with Grandad Roderick in the croft called Tir Nan Og near Gairloch in north-west Scotland. He was eight years old, and 'that daft old man' (as his father always called Grandad) was showing him something very important ...

'My mother, whoever she was, must have been a remarkable woman.'

Aged 73, Roderick Moses Joyce still sat as stiff and straight as a poker. His weathered and aquiline face, deeply furrowed under the white mane of his hair, was dominated by pale blue eyes that always seemed to be staring at something beyond the edge of the visible world. His presence was commanding but also dreamy and remote as he gazed into the glowing peats. Sam was not a little in awe of him. Yet they'd eaten well and now sat in comfort by the fire, which sparked brightly each time shutter-rattling skurries of Atlantic gale burst down the chimney. And Sam, who after a week in this remote place had overcome the worst of his initial homesickness and fear for his mother (she was ill in an Edinburgh hospital) felt rich anticipation as Roderick eyed him sharply. For he liked Grandad's tales; he felt sure that one was coming. And he was right.

'You've heard the story? About Madame Pédauque and my father?'

'No.' Shaking his head, Sam grinned. 'Will you tell me?'

'Why not?' And the old man grinned back. 'Of course you haven't heard it. I've never told you, and your daddy's not the sort for stuff and nonsense. But maybe I am, and maybe so was my father, Captain Davey. Maybe you are too, Sam. Who's to tell? Let's find out.'

There and then the old man stood and from the age-dark mantelpiece took down a little carved walnut box. Sam leaned forward, an odd expectant anxiety fluttering in him as Grandad opened the box. And in it, on a couch of faded green velvet, sat the emerald ring.

'This,' Roderick murmured, 'is the only proof I have — but for my own existence, of course — that my mother even existed. Take it out, Sam. Hold it, feel it. But don't put it on. Not yet anyway.'

43

The ring itself was of bronze, heavy and warm and plain. The gem was set in a raised oval boss. Cut in five facets, it shone in the firelight, sparkled with its own mysterious inner flame. Laid into the topmost facet was a strange bronze sigil that consisted of a tiny sphere flanked by two slender crescents. So there on the boy's uncertain palm it lay, and as he gazed past the sigil into those hypnotic green depths, Sam felt the storm's skirling music run wild in him, anciently familiar and exciting.

Roderick watched him. 'What does the circle remind you of, Sam?'

Sam came out of his trance. 'The full moon,' he said slowly.

'It could be the sun, or an abstract circle in your geometry lessons.'

'No.' Sam was absolutely sure. 'It's the full moon.'

'And the two crescents? What are they, do you think?'

'The horns of a fighting bull,' said Sam instantly — and as he said this, something dreadful happened inside him — a sharp pain, a sensation of utter terror. He gasped, and his face twisted. The sensation passed quickly, but the old man was staring so hard at him that his unease was compounded. 'Why are you look-ing at me like that, Grandad?'

'When your father was your age,' said Roderick slowly, 'I showed him this ring, and the sign in the emerald, and asked him what he saw.' The old man shrugged. 'He saw a zero in brackets. That's all. I knew then he'd make a lot of money. But you and I, we're not the sort to do that.'

'Why's that?' Sam still felt pierced, but fascinated too.

'Because we see the moon and horns where others see pounds and pence.'

There was a mischievous lilt in Roderick's voice, but the remote and steely look in the old man's eyes told Sam what he knew already: this was a serious business. 'Stay there,' Grandad said then, rising to his feet.

With his heart beating hard and the ring warm on his palm (its green depths speaking to him with messages only his blood could hear) Sam waited as, with priestly reverence, Grandad brought out the Talisker. Drams of the dark, smoky malt were carefully measured into two of the cut crystal glasses the old man kept for special occasions.

Then, gravely, Roderick toasted his only grandson.

'Your health, Samuel David Joyce,' he said. 'The ring and this stone that it holds will be yours when I'm gone, for you see the moon under whose sign it was cast, and the horns of the Bull in which time it was made.' He grimaced and added: 'And it may be that one day you'll wear it in the place it likes, which is not far from here. Maybe I'll show you sometime.' And again he paused, thinking what to say. 'Myself, I've never dared wear it in that place ... or maybe it's that I've never felt myself fit. For in the emerald lies a power not to be abused, as perhaps you'll begin to see when I've told you the tale of how it was found, and how it came to me.'

And, after this strange benediction, the old man told his tale ...

Diane never knew how long she stood on the ladder, staring through the broken chairs at her husband where he crouched on the attic floor, his wet shining eyes lost in the gem's green depths. Perhaps only seconds, half a minute at most, for Chrissa, waiting below, soon interrupted anxiously.

Yet to Diane it seemed for ever that she stared at Sam, silently, unable to say a word for fear of alarming their daughter. Though utterly dismayed by his madness she too became spellbound; for as she gazed at him she saw (as if in a glass) their ... is it *fifteen* years? ... spinning from meeting in Marrakesh *back when hippies weren't old* to mid-seventies summers in Wales at Nantgewydd (*outside Elsan and no hot water*) when Chrissa was born, and their *difficult* years when Sam, ring never off his finger, had gone crazy.

You know I never believed it, she told him in sad silence. What crap! Reincarnation and planetary doom! And that ... *thing!* Your gateway to the bloody stars! What a joke! But it just got worse and worse. You couldn't face yourself, you couldn't handle Chrissa, you couldn't even see me as I am. Women scare you: that's the real reason you ran off. *'By the way, I'm off to Africa tomorrow!'* And look what happened! A year later you crawl back sick as a parrot, and I took you back! But you blamed that thing for all of it; you swore it was finished and you'd throw it away, and I believed you! So I was a fool! But it was for Chrissa too. She needed you. She needed a father. Yes, and you really did seem to change.

Seven years, she thought blankly. You even got a job ...

Now she looked at him and saw their life falling in ruins.

Perhaps, she told herself with dreamy fatalism, there's a curse on us. Chrissa's nightmares started it again. Where do they come from? God knows. It's in the family. In *your* family, I should say. She's your daughter, it started before I met you. Maybe your mad black isle story's true, and maybe there *is* power in that damned ring, something hypnotic, God knows what ... but why make it an excuse for being a shit? *Sam, wake up!*

But Sam remained unaware of her. There he crouched, a bleeding beast on all fours. Look at you! she thought, her disgust and sadness growing. Giving up your choice, your humanity. Letting that thing have you again. *That thing!* Amid her fatalism she felt a huge rage. That bloody thing! That bloody woman in your poor stupid mind! she thought, frantically calm.

Oh Sam! she implored silently, Sam, *please!* Can't you see me? I'm here! Chrissa's here! Won't you stop and look at me?

But she knew already: it was no use. For Sam was far away, deep in the emerald depths, deep in an ancient sea ... and, as she watched him during those endless seconds, Diane had the strange sensation that her head had just turned into a gigantic time-clock, pounding its way back to zero ...

4.
Madame Pédauque

By the age of 62 Davey Joyce had become a lonely man.

Born to Godfearing farming stock in 1820 near Troon in Ayrshire, he'd got in trouble over a girl and run away to sea at 15, working on off-shore drifters. He'd rarely set foot on land again. At 35 he held a master's certificate in the Queen's Marine, and for over twenty years captained tall ships, turning both Cape and Horn half a dozen times under sail.

In 1875 he retired to Gairloch in Scotland's remote north-west to marry and raise a family while he still had time ... but his wife Sophie, thirty years younger, died in labour, and the child (a boy) soon followed her.

Much later Davey told his son Roderick he'd have gone stark mad if the company he'd sailed for — Wheel and Waite of Threadneedle Street in London — hadn't taken him back, offering him five more years ... on steamers.

Now Davey didn't like steamers; he had a sailor's scorn for messy, stinking metal tanks that just wallowed through the sea instead of riding the waves, but it was better than nothing. He had a lot to forget.

The five years passed too quickly. On a coal-fired tramp steamer of 1,800 tons, the SS *Heaton*, he went back and forth across the Atlantic with cargoes of this and that, and he knew his way, so he didn't have much trouble with his crews or even from the sea, but he had plenty of bother with himself as the years slipped by and his memory of Sophie refused to die. And then his time was all but up: he embarked on his last voyage out of London, to New Orleans and back via the Mediterranean.

This time there was trouble even before the *Heaton* docked at Messina in Sicily. Disputes simmered, some carried over from previous voyages, most of them between the deck crew and the engine room's black gang. But Davey was too distracted by his impending retirement to notice or care, leaving all discipline and the running of the ship to First Mate Pierce.

Dick Pierce was a steady and experienced man who appreciated Davey's problems but lacked a heavy hand. He needed support he didn't get from the other officers. Second Mate Platt, a self-opinionated would-be rake and youngest son of a wealthy family, was much happier dreaming of women than maintaining order; while Third Mate Leigh, once at Messina, went ashore and promptly fell prey to a disabling 'flux' of the sort that would clear up as soon as the *Heaton* left port. To replace Leigh, the First Mate hired Joseph Josephs, a black-bearded Welsh Nonconformist whose mouth was full of the Bible — and soon nearly as full with the Chief Engineer's fist.

An Aberdonian, John McDermott was sufficiently famous in fifty ports to have created singlehanded the cliché about fighting-drunk Scots engineers who give their engines the love their women never get. If not for his undoubted mechanical skills he'd have been out on his ear long since, for whenever the *Heaton* docked he invariably led the drinking and spoiling on shore, leading his black gang into battle like a balding marine Rob Roy. And most times before, when things got serious with the local carabinieri, Old Davey had waded in and sorted things out, for in no way was Davey a small man and he had even the Chief's respect.

But in Messina, where they took on a cargo of dried

fruit, Davey would not stir from his cabin. Even when reports came of Chief McDermott at the heart of trouble in the taverns, Davey stayed on his bunk, brooding over a daguerrotype of his dead wife. So Pierce went ashore, to find the Chief and his gang in a vast smoky sailors' dive. A black American sailor called Chattanooga Chuck mocked Pierce's limey accent — 'Ah do lahk to heah thet fency talk!' — and McDermott went for him with an enraged whisky roar. In the brawl that followed Pierce was knocked cold. Next day he woke up, head pounding, in his cabin to find that McDermott and his gang had carried him tenderly back. 'Aye, we pit ye tae bed, Dick,' grinned the Chief, bruised and black-eyed but happy. 'But furst we showed yon Yankee bastards ye cannae insult an English gentleman — that's fer the Jocks, eh?'

'Thanks for getting me out, Mr McDermott,' Pierce managed. 'Now will you return your men to work and get those lines cleaned!'

'Aye, aye, we're about that a'ready,' said the Chief in a wounded voice. 'Wi' a lady on board ye winnae expect us tae ...'

'With a *what*?' Pierce sat up, and immediately regretted it.

'A lady, Mr Pierce,' said the Chief solicitously. 'The skipper's brung a lady on board wha's giein' tae New Orleans wi' us.'

She gave her name as Madame Anna Pédauque, a widow of Toulouse. She approached Captain Davey Joyce on the quay as he supervised loading at dawn on the day the *Heaton* cast off for New Orleans. The day was dull and his mood was poor. He saw a striking, raven-haired, olive-skinned woman who held herself proudly. The antique style of her ground-length hooded cape of green velvet, faded and here and there patched, suggested a person of means who had fallen on hard times. Also he noted her scant baggage and the fact that she had no male companion or guarantor. Nor was he reassured when she offered payment for passage in local bills of dubious value. Yet her gaze was clear, and her English — inflected by many cultures — was excellent. 'Captain,' she pleaded, 'I must go to New Orleans. I will pay well, and work if you ask — but understand: I am a respectable woman.'

Uh-oh, he thought, and perhaps his pulse quickened just a little as he stroked his bushy white beard. I've met your sort before. Like a queen without a country, and look at those big dark eyes ...

'Sorry, ma'am, but company policy is we don't take unescorted lady passengers, for reasons which I'm sure are obvious. Ma'am.'

He tipped his cap and began turning away, but she laid a light, lace-gloved hand on his uniformed arm. He felt a mild shock run through him, tingling in his blood. It was surprising rather than pleasant or unpleasant, and it stopped him. 'It is mal chance I know,' she said quickly, holding him with her look, 'to have women on a ship, or so sailors have it. But surely your rules are satisfied if *you* agree to be my escort, Captain.' There was quiet intensity in her tone. Davey frowned. She dropped her hand but held his gaze. *Such deep eyes!* He stared at her. reluctantly fascinated. 'You must excuse my boldness,' she continued. 'I have no option. I must reach New Orleans by the end of the third week in March.'

'It's almost March now, ma'am,' he said in a rush. 'This old tub'll only make seven knots. Try Marseilles. You'll get a faster vessel there.'

'Too late.' Her eyes had grown bigger. They seemed to spin in his head. 'For me it is here and now — or never. You must take me.'

'Why?' he growled. Giddy currents ran in him, currents for which he had no charts. He felt unsteady. 'If it's so urgent, why start so late?'

'I have only just learned of a private matter that must be fulfilled by then.' Again, urgent, she took his arm. 'My happiness rests on it! Don't fear I'll provoke or enflame your crew.' Her laugh was light, but her gaze was not. Davey felt transfixed. Ah Jesus! he wondered, Who are

50

you? 'Be assured,' she insisted anxiously, 'I'll be as quiet as a mouse, Captain!'

Davey made an effort. He tore his eyes from her face and turned to the ship. 'Stop gawping and get those men back to work!' he roared up at the Second Mate ... but he felt the fire die out of his blood as she took her hand back again. 'Ma'am,' he muttered, swinging violently back to her as if trying to shake off an invisible weight, 'mouse or not, your presence will make you provocative. As for myself as your escort, I'm supposed to keep order on this vessel, not destroy it. Anyway ...' — he paused, for again her great dark eyes held him, and through the wharfside stink of oil and fish a strange, tantalising scent of wild rose distracted him, so that he finished lamely — '... if the owners hear of it I'll lose my pension ...'

She smiled, very slightly. He breathed deep. His heart was thumping. What is this? he wondered. What am I saying? Turn away, man, turn away! And maybe he was about to break free when (perhaps it was a little breeze) her hood slipped ... and the movement she made to catch it back snared him with the memory of his lost loved one, his unlaid ghost, his dead wife.

That's just how she'd have done it! he thought in fascinated horror as Madame Pédauque plucked back a wayward strand of hair like gleaming jet.

'Is your pension worth more than your soul, Captain?' she asked very quietly. 'Would you refuse a woman in need on your last voyage?'

To the end of his days Davey insisted he couldn't remember actually agreeing. But there she was. And even before they left the Med there was more trouble, though none of it could be blamed on the mysterious Madame Pédauque. True to her promise, like a mouse she kept to herself in the portside cabin, aft of Davey's, which Second Mate Platt gallantly gave up to her, instead imposing himself on the new Third. 'Don't mind doubling up, do you, old chap? For the lady, you know. I'll swing my line up here and be snug as a bug.' But the new Third glared so furiously that Platt immediately doubted the wisdom of his choice. Soon he doubted it even more. Only hours out of Messina, with Tunis far to port, the clogged-up oil lines overflowed and flooded the deck, just as Mr Pierce had feared. McDermott's black gang hadn't done their job, and since casting off Davey hadn't been out of his cabin to see that they had. Dispute broke out between the engine room and the sailors who'd have to clean up the mess. Mr Josephs the new Third tried to establish his authority by going in among the men with his biblical manner, laying down the law in his high-pitched voice. The Chief, who'd been at the bottle, mocked him.

'It's a fine wee voice for the Lord's wee man!' he bellowed.

Josephs cursed him. McDermott cocked his fists. The sides squared up, and Pierce was hurrying down from the bridge ... when Davey at last appeared.

'Stop that!' he bawled. 'There's a lady on this vessel!'

The fight was nipped in the bud. But the tension didn't diminish as Davey went straight back to his cabin, leaving Pierce to sort it out. Mr Pierce resented this. Why in the name of God did you let her on board? he wondered. But he said nothing. The crisis was conquered, for the time being ... yet not a man on board didn't have his mind on that closed portside cabin, and Steward Perkins was eagerly questioned after he'd taken in her supper. There was little he could say. 'She took it at the door. There's no light on at all. I didn't even get a good look at her.'

Later, with Sardinia astern, Mr Josephs came off watch and kept Platt awake for hours praying aloud at his bunkside. *'Come out, my people!'* he cried, *'Come out from her! For her sins are piled up as high as heaven, and God remembers her wicked ways!'* In vain Platt protested; the biblical exhortation continued until at last Josephs retired to sleep, replacing loud prayer with louder snoring. So Platt lay sleepless ... and as he lay there he began imagining that she was calling him, from *his* cabin. He tossed restlessly, and all night hot and lustful visions disturbed him ...

Davey couldn't sleep either. For hours he lay on his bunk, brooding amid clouds of pipe smoke, wondering how she'd done it and what she was.

He wanted to knock at her door. But he didn't.

On the third evening, with Melilla to port and Gibralter approaching, Madame Pédauque for the first time consented to dine in the wardroom with the Captain and officers of the SS *Heaton*.

Throughout the meal (the cook went to great lengths to overcome the limitations of an Anglo-Saxon maritime cuisine) the mysterious Frenchwoman (if in fact she was) maintained a charmingly demure, high-collared, speak-if-spoken-to manner. She complimented the cook and kept her eyes downcast while Second Officer Platt, speaking appalling schoolboy French, tried to monopolise her conversation. He had the gaze of a starving spaniel, but she showed an equal if remote interest in everyone else at table, save Captain Davey, who kept directing piercing looks at her which she would not meet or return. But the Captain remained correct and the talk frivolous:

'You speak excellent English, Madame.'

'Merci, mon capitaine. I command several tongues.'

'May we ask where you acquired your command of ours?'

'You may, mon capitaine, but the tale is much too tedious.'

And so on, minor coquetries all, if coquetries at all, but her mystery remained complete, with many men on board who'd have given up more than their pay to know, so that tension on the *Heaton* was not decreasing as, during the night, Gibralter slipped behind and the continental shelf fell away beneath the pounding of the engines to a deeper gulf.

Dawn saw all land last. A stiff breeze hurried high white castles of cloud through the vastness, and at last Davey seemed himself again, barking and booming, face ruddy and beard snow-white like an angry Santa, shouting at the crew to get the brass cleaned and the decks chipped … and though from his brooding he looked thinner, somehow less solid, they knew him and were reassured. Then the Frenchie woman (some said she looked more Jewish, or perhaps Levantine) came out of her cabin and promenaded, modest in green velvet, with every man anxious to show her his work and how essential it was to the safe passage of the *Heaton*. Even the Chief, who had little respect for the fair sex, was conquered. 'Yon ane's a bonny wee quine, even if she willna smile,' he bellowed at his gang 'an' I'll brak the neck o' the furst chiel tae pit his fulthy fingers on her. An' nae gabbin' aboot her, mind — she's Auld Davey's business, an' guid luck tae 'im!'

But Pierce saw how visibly relieved Davey was when Madame retired to her cabin 'for a siesta' … and what happened when, later in the day, they were overtaken from the south-east by an elegant Bordes windjammer. In her full suit of thirty-five sails, lee rail awash and green seas hissing past her quarter, the white-and-grey *Charlotte* slid rapidly past the port beam of the racketing tramp. Davey blew three long blasts of acknowledgement on the steam whistle, and Pierce saw how sadly the Old Man stared after the beautiful ship as, its colours dipped in reply, it receded like a mirage.

'When my lot's gone there'll be no one to tell you that brute mechanics is for soulless men alone,' Davey muttered with a wintry eye.

'But sail's holding its own,' Pierce insisted. 'The French plan an entire new fleet, with government money for construction *and* voyages.'

'Government money!' Davey spat, slapped shuddering brass. '*This* holds the candle now — racket and stink and smoke. But I won't be around, thank God, to see it conquer entirely.'

Yet that night, at dinner in the wardroom, Davey surprised them all. He appeared in his dress uniform, with all the braid brushed and buttons polished, and his beard was combed too. Mr Pierce and Mr Platt and the

Steward eyed him with astonishment as he sat. He noted an empty place. 'Where's our glamorous guest?' he demanded jovially. 'Scared her off with your French, Mr Platt? Or is it the way you watch her like a sick dog?'

Platt scowled as Davey laid his big red hands on the table.

'Well, boys,' the Captain announced, 'I've not been myself. It's hard, knowing you're near the end of the way ... but that's in the hands of the Lord, and now we're out on the open roads again, and this is my last time on them, so ...' — he rapped the table — '... Steward, issue an extra ration to every man, and be generous with it.' More quietly he added: 'And ask 'em to drink a toast to the Old Man, if they will.'

So it was amid an acute silence that Perkins, ferret-quick, rose and went to do as he was told ... even as Madame made her entry.

The Steward was not famed as a man sensitive to feminine attraction, but as he almost collided with her at the door he jumped back and stared, mesmerised for a full second before, with an audible gasp, recollecting himself and, ducking past her ample décolletage with an incoherent apology, fleeing about his business.

The *Heaton*'s officers were each in their own way equally taken aback. In fact they had stood so suddenly that two chairs were still rocking as Madame came to her place on swift, light feet. She wore a full moss-green robe, low-cut and fitting her like a skin, the swish of its hem on the deck audible through the throb of the engines. Her jet-black hair fell to the smooth olive fields of her shoulders; her slender neck was made to seem very vulnerable by the encircling blood-red necklace of what not only appeared to be real rubies, but large ones too. They glowed in the lamplight as, smiling very slightly, she seated herself ... and it was only then, too late, that Platt recollected himself and sprang behind her chair.

'Sit down, you idiot,' growled Davey, deeply affected.

'Thank you, Monsieur Platt,' she said quietly, and smiled at Davey, who glared at her as he too sat down.

'Mon capitaine,' she went on, her irony delicate, 'you look at me as if I sin. But tonight I wear my finery, such as it is, as you wear yours — and, I think, for much the same reason.'

Davey grimaced. He couldn't take his eyes off her.

'What reason is that, ma'am?' he demanded suspiciously.

'Now we are out on the deep.' Her smile faded. She clasped her hands before her. 'Who knows what lies under us? Here we enter the Mystery.'

'Profonde,' uttered Platt, 'Trés profonde!'

'I see you know about the Mystery, Captain,' she went on as the cabin boy, goggling at her, brought in bowls of steaming broth which somehow, with Pierce's aid, he managed to set down without disaster. 'If not, you would have turned me away from the pier when I first approached you.'

Davey Joyce scowled. Her gaze was hard to face. 'Ma'am, I don't know one mystery from another. I'm not a curious man. I can't afford it.'

'How sad for you.' Her shrug rendered the mystery of her bosom more achingly prominent. 'It is not true, though, that you suffer alone.'

What's come over her? Davey wondered wildly.

'You have suffered, Madame?' he barked.

She said nothing. She sipped at her broth, made a face, then quickly smiled as if to conceal her disgust.

'There's something wrong with it?' said Davey quickly.

'You have never had a good wife to cook for you?' she asked.

Davey looked strangled. 'Madame!' interrupted Pierce urgently, cutting through the sudden chill, 'Don't you realise that our curiosity about you exceeds anything you could possibly want to know about any of us?'

'A gentleman doesn't ask a lady personal questions!' Platt objected, stoutly chivalrous, but Davey, his face brick-red, ignored him.

'Mr Pierce is right!' he growled at Madame. 'You haven't told us one damned thing about yourself.

Nothing at all. Ma'am!'

Madame sighed. She laid down her spoon and looked uncertainly round the table, biting her lip as if in great anxiety. At that moment Josephs entered the wardroom. He saw her and turned crimson. Only Pierce, moving up to give him room, sensed his embarrassed hostility. Neither Platt nor the Captain even noticed him, and if Madame did, she gave no sign. 'Very well,' she admitted at length. 'You have accepted me among you. Perhaps you have a right to my tale. For what little it's worth.'

In a low and resonant voice, with her eyes fixed on the table, she told them how she'd grown up in the Saint Sabran quarter of Toulouse, by the banks of the Garonne. 'I had twelve brothers and sisters, she murmured. 'We were not rich. My father was a weaver.' And she went on to tell how at the age of sixteen she'd run away with her sweetheart, Roger, whose gods were two Germans, Marx and Engels. In Paris he'd fought on the barricades. Mortally wounded, he'd died in her arms. 'I loved him, not his ideals,' she said sadly, shaking her head, 'but after that I could never go home.'

For seven years she'd wandered wretchedly, suffering great poverty until, sick, she'd found her way to Lourdes. There, by the healing waters, she'd met a wealthy man, an American called Jourdain Lafayette. 'He was wounded in their civil war battle called Bull Run,' she explained, her voice barely audible. 'My Roger would not have agreed with his politics, but perhaps they would have admired each other's spirit.'

Jourdain ('A fine, fine man!') had fallen passionately in love with her, and she with him. Yet when he asked her to return with him as his wife to his estates in Louisiana, she had foolishly dragged her heels. 'He told me it is not all cowboys and indians, but I said: "Mon cher Jourdain, I doubt if ever I will live with one man again, for in my experience it can lead only to sorrow." He protested, he swore his undying devotion to me, but ... I was foolish.' She fell silent before adding: 'And so we parted.'

Now again she frowned at the table, brooding on her memories with such intensity of feeling that Mr Platt was staring at her open-mouthed, and Davey looked unwillingly spellbound. But Mr Josephs was glaring at her. Beside him, Pierce could feel the man's loathing and disbelief. Then she looked up and met each of them in the eyes, and only Josephs looked away. The rest of them, Pierce included, felt their breath quicken.

'In the years that followed,' she continued slowly, her tone ironic, 'I came to regret my decision deeply — very deeply indeed! I lived on, yes, as we must, having nothing better to do ... but it would be true to say that my life became an empty shell. Until not a week ago!' And her eyes now came to life with sudden excitement. 'I was in my pension at Messina when a letter is delivered to me! It is from Jourdain, this letter!' Abruptly her radiant smile faded. 'But over a year since it was sent. In it he said to me: *"On the 21st day of March in 1882 it is five years since the day that we met by the healing waters. We have until midnight of that day. If you do not come to me by that time, then all is lost!"*'

She shrugged tantalisingly. She heaved a sigh.

'Yes, gentlemen. Then I knew hope again! A man who will wait five years! — is he not a treasure?' Her face clouded. 'That's my tale. But it is March the first already ... and there is so little time left.'

'We'll get you there, never fear!' Platt assured her, alarmed by her despondency. She seemed not to hear. Again she eyed each of them in turn. Her gaze lingered on Mr Josephs, who flushed angrily. She seemed troubled by him, looking away with a shake of the head. Davey grunted.

'I've known men who've waited nearly a lifetime,' he muttered, 'but I doubt the waiting made them no sweeter when it came to it.'

'Mon capitaine, you think of yourself as an old man,' she said sadly, but her look was provocative, and Davey's bearded jaw thrust out.

'Ma'am, I don't believe a word of your tale,' he told

58

her abruptly, 'and I'll not be driven to tell mine just to satisfy your curiosity!'

She flinched as if slapped.

'But you cannot be much over sixty!' she declared tartly, and of a sudden again Davey saw in her eyes those depths which had drawn him at their first meeting. 'In Georgia by the Black Sea they remain gallant at over a hundred years of age — some of them, anyway. But you are not from the Land of the Golden Fleece,' she went on scornfully, 'just as I am not a liar!' And abruptly, without preliminaries, she stood, her eyes flashing. 'Now I will go to my cabin and keep my own company because I am called a liar by the Captain of this big, important ship! I am very, very upset!'

Too late Davey tried to call her back; she had swept out already, slamming the wardroom door and leaving behind her the aching sensation in all the men but one of a void, unfilled, that longed to be fulfilled. And in his cabin that night Davey could find no rest, for his body felt like a sack of old bones, and his mind could no longer find a purpose. At length an uneasy sleep fell upon him like a stifling weight, bringing dreams that made him toss and turn until in a chill pre-dawn hour he started up awake, blaspheming, soaked in a cold sweat. And in another cabin, while the Third Mate prayed aloud all night (in a terrible droning monotone calling down God's Curse on the Great Whore and all her foul works), Second Mate Platt in his hammock groaned silently and just as silently played with himself, seeking both to ease and maintain the exquisite torture that his heated imaginative visions of Madame's voluptuously naked body were causing him.

Three nights later they came among the shoals of dead fish.

5.
The Black Isle

Under increasingly cool and hazy skies the *Heaton*
steamed on until well west of Madeira and south of the
Azores. Since the disagreement at dinner Madame
Pédauque had kept to her cabin, incommunicado behind
shuttered ports, and Davey had grown morose again,
infecting the general mood, so that it seemed almost
appropriate when late one day the rolling seas grew
strangely muddy and brown. Soon after that the ship
began passing through shoals of dead fish, their white
bellies up in the turgid waters — thin shoals at first, but
soon thick and continuing hour after hour in the ever
muddier ocean. Fetched out for a gingerly examination,
the dead fish showed no signs of disease, but were not
even rotten and still hard, as if somehow cooked in the
sea itself.

These inexplicable shoals continued unabated until,
just before last light, Davey noted a trail of smoke on the
western horizon.

'Steamer,' he muttered into his beard.

Doesn't look like steamer smoke to me, thought Pierce.

The night was unusually dark and still. No clean
waves broke against the bows; everyone felt sluggish and
stiff. Even down in the engine room there was a sense of

foreboding; foreboding that proved well-founded. For at dawn next day the sky was overcast and the shoals of dead fish more dense than before, millions of them belly-up amid opaque brown mud. And it was seen that the smoke glimpsed the night before came from volcanic peaks on a large black island directly to the west.

Madame Pédauque appeared on deck in her green hooded cape. Pale, oddly tentative, looking more like a nun than a temptress, she joined Captain Davey on the bridge. He stood gazing at the sharp raw black mountains.

'What's the name of that island, Captain?'

She spoke in a whisper. Davey shrugged.

'It has no name,' he told her harshly. 'It shouldn't be there. The charts show open sea ... to a depth of one hundred fathoms ...'

She drew sharp breath. She muttered inaudibly. He judged they were about twelve miles offshore. Ignoring her, he ordered the anchor let down.

It hit bottom at seven fathoms.

'Will you stop here?' Madame appeared agitated, her gaze continually switching from the isle to the dead fish all about. 'Surely it's no part of your business to linger in this ... in this horrible place?'

Davey gave her no more than the edge of his eye.

'You're telling me my business ... ma'am?'

Ashen-faced, apparently deeply depressed, she retreated to her cabin. Pierce and Platt and many other men watched her go; Davey did not. Her door shut. Then, amid silence so profound that nobody found it easy to speak, Davey called his officers to the chartroom. He felt oddly calm. The appearance of this isle that shouldn't exist threw his doubts and fears into sharp focus. It seemed to him that his tortured emotions of the past days and nights had been premonition of the cata-strophic event which had driven this jagged, smoking ridge of black rock up from a huge depth to the surface of the sea. The muddy ocean, the dead fish — there must have been a huge subterrranean explosion, a violent upheaval in this region where the seabed was, after all, notoriously restless.

That he could accept.

More disturbing was his irrational conviction that *she* had somehow caused it ... by her presence, by her will ... who could tell? For in his dreaming lately she had appeared to him in a primal, instinctual form that his reason rejected but that his Celtic blood understood all too clearly.

The *badb*. The raven-goddess of furious violence and death.

Now he seized the chart and thumbed the island's position so hard that Pierce thought: He's trying to push it back under the sea!

'Thirty-one twenty-five north. Twenty-eight forty south. It's just come up. Maybe it'll just go down again. What d'ye say we do, boys?'

They were all stunned. Platt objected feebly that islands don't just appear and disappear, but the Third Mate corrected him. In a voice that shook, Mr Josephs mentioned Sambrina in the Azores in 1811. 'It was even charted before returning to the deep!' Most agitated, he turned on Davey. 'Captain, this place is ungodly!' he insisted. 'Under no account must we land here!'

But Pierce interrupted, stating that as British officers it was their duty to land, plant the flag, and claim the territory in the name of Her Majesty. 'We have also a duty to Science,' he added, at which Chief McDermott, who'd been unusually subdued, suddenly grinned.

'Mebbe we can dae oorsels a wee bit o' guid, Captain,' he said, and winked. 'Could be they'll hae ye up tae the Royal Geographical Society tae pin the Gold Medal on yer breastcloth!'

This the Third Mate immediately denounced as Satan's counsel.

'Aw, shut yer trap, wee man!' roared McDermott, but Mr Josephs persisted, speaking of the risk to their souls.

'Long-drowned evils need only the spark of our misbegotten interest to revive them!' he piped. 'To land on that place is to put our heads into the mouth of Satan himself!'

Davey, very thoughtful, nodded gravely at this, then sought Mr Platt's opinion. The Second Mate was against a landing. He advised that Davey's first duty was to the safety of ship and crew, the profits of the owners, and — he coughed — 'the speedy arrival of Madame in New Orleans, sir.'

'But don't you see, man,' Josephs burst out, unable to contain himself, 'that it's this she came for?' Impassioned, he flung his arm out at the smoking and eerie isle. 'Look at it! A black Eden, for a black-souled Lilith! For what else is she, to have you all so enchanted?'

'Mr Josephs!' roared Davey, 'That's enough!'

But it had been said, and it hung in the air as Davey added:

'There's no harm in taking a look. We're going ashore.'

With the *Heaton* anchored a mile offshore the nine men drew the skiff up through sharp black shallows onto the desolate land. Before them lay rock, rock and more rock, lumped and littered with volcanic slag, stretched and heaved into extraordinary forms, split by chasms and buckling gradually up to a plateau beginning some miles away, beyond which rose to three or four thousand feet a range of bare, precipitous mountains, their smoking peaks mostly lost in the ashen haze that permeated the sulphurous air and made breathing a heavy trial.

They were appalled. There was nothing alive at all. Nothing green, nothing growing, nothing moving: no sand on the beach, no weed on the slick bare rocks, no life in the pools, no gulls screeching round the crags. The entire isle was so silent and still that even McDermott found no humour in it as he splashed ashore. 'Aiberdeen on a Saturday nicht's got mair life thin this dreich dump!' he observed grimly, giving Davey a hand onto the rocks, followed by the Second Mate (there under protest) and six crewmen.

Once ashore a paralysis seized them, an unbearable sense of weight, as if by rights they should have been rooted by thousands of fathoms to the bed of the sea. On angled shelves of gleaming black rock they stood and stared blankly — at each other, at the island and the crumbled cliff above them, at the *Heaton* — their will gone, their memory lost, unable to move, numbed by the sense of a huge, still-echoing disruption. Indecipherable visions preyed on their sluggish minds, vanishing before they could be known or identified. Second Mate Platt began weeping, imploring his mother to forgive him; a seaman called Barnes crawled in circles on his hands and knees, making baby sounds; McDermott later swore he'd heard ringing silvery voices that spoke a tongue he'd never heard but felt he ought to know. And Captain Davey ... he stood aghast, his mouth open, taken by a vivid hallucination: for, as if he hovered bodiless before her where she lay in her dark cabin, he saw Madame's eyes fixed on him. Her face was pallid, beaded with feverish sweat, and the intensity of her stare burned holes in him. *'I am La Reine Pédauque!'* he thought he heard her cry. *'Here you'll find a key to what's lost — but be quick: I cannot endure this weight for long.'*

McDermott's harsh laugh broke the spell. 'I'll no stond here wi' Mr Platt greetin' like a bairn!' he bellowed. And so gradually, encouraging each other, they shook off the phantoms, then set out to find a way inland. A sudden contrary mood of hilarity had them babbling jubilantly at each other as they started eagerly over the initial obstacles. This mood did not last. Up one slope they went to find a chasm at the top. Starting again, they scrambled over naps and nubs of rock and round a corner, only to meet a sheer cliff. A third time they set out, crawling up a rising field of little knife-sharp ridges set in perfect curving parallels, but the sole reward for the slicing of their hands and knees was another uncrossable chasm. Cut, bruised, breathing hard, they slid back to their starting point under the crumbled cliff where, gloomily oppressed again, they sat resting at the foot of a slide of loose stone and gravel.

Platt, detailed to keep a log, took this rest as his chance to scribble down some observations. Shakily he eyed the crumbled rock about him.

'Well, it's no paradise,' muttered Davey, wiping his brow.

'Her Majesty wouldnae want a place like this,' McDermott agreed.

Platt saw something in the rubble at his feet. He bent and picked it up, frowning with mounting disbelief as he turned it over in his hands.

'Captain,' he called cautiously, 'I think I've found something.'

Davey turned without enthusiasm. McDermott, who was closer, saw what the Second Mate held. 'I'll be damned!' he exclaimed, his eyes widening. Taking the flake of flint from Platt's trembling fingers, he inspected it before handing it on to Davey. 'An arrowheid! See? It's bin wurked!'

Feeling the huge weight on them again all the men crowded round Davey. With the utmost delicacy he held the arrowhead — if such it was — between a horny finger and thumb. Slowly he nodded, then turned to scan the gravel-slide. His expression was dazed. He eyed Platt, McDermott and the others doubtfully. Mr Platt looked terrified, ready to crack. 'We'll need picks and shovels,' said Davey, his voice thick and dragging, as if his tongue had swollen too fat to fit or move in his mouth. 'Mr Platt, get on board, take over from Mr Pierce. Tell him ... bring the flag, but ... Madame stays where she is. Chief ... you too, and ... come back with Mr Pierce ...'

When the skiff had pulled away Davey set the two men left with him to dig barehanded in the rubble. Chewing his pipe, he sat on a rock gazing at the smashed cliff. Soon his imagination ran amock: a sly voice babbled greedily in him. *Davey boy, this is your big chance! Miss this and you'll never get another! There's treasure here to make you rich and famous, and maybe they'll even give you another five years! It might not be your last voyage after all, not if you play your cards right!* Yet at the same time he seemed to see Madame again, tossing feverishly on her bunk ... but she was naked, and worse, she was caked all over in a slimy red mud that dripped and coagulated on the cabin floor like blood. And her feet ... with a shiver he realised: *They're not human feet!* The fear in him grew so great it was all he could do not to shout at the skiff to return; to carry them all away from this dreadful place and never come back. Mr Josephs is right! he cried silently. She's a Lilith! A *badb!* She's here to bring destruction on us all! If we don't escape now we ...

'Captain!' One of the men, bending to pull an object from the rubble, called out in a high, strained voice. The object was heavy and round: the sailor cradled it uneasily as if it were some monstrous baby and then, with a curse, dropped it. Shamefaced, he picked it up again and brought it to Davey, setting it down with a gasp. It was a large round stone with a bulging, pop-eyed face carved into it in low relief. Below the face were represented, in rudimentary style, pendant breasts and pregnant belly. In huge unease Davey met the cold stone stare, and felt his heart chill.

Here I am! the head told him. *Your big chance, Davey boy!*
'I seen 'em like that before,' he growled. 'In Yucatan.'

Discipline broke down as soon as Pierce left the ship. 'Keep the men working,' he'd told Mr Platt. 'They're scared; don't give them time to think or let Mr Josephs start ranting. Keep Madame in her cabin. We've not had a squeak from her — let's keep it that way.' He'd eyed Mr Platt's dazed face with grim premonition. 'You know where the revolver's kept.' But Platt had stared blankly through him ... and as soon as Pierce left in the skiff with the Chief and the four men who'd been on the isle (all as dazed as Mr Platt), the crew abandoned any pretence of work. In anxious groups men gathered on deck, their eyes fixed on the black isle, on the departing skiff, and on the closed door behind which Madame had remained since dawn. Mr Josephs soon tired of bawling at them. Warily he joined the Second Mate on the bridge. Platt stood like a zombie. 'You found an *arrowhead*?' the Welshman demanded jerkily.

Platt didn't answer. He was gazing at the black shore.

'Mr Platt, for the love of God! On your knees and pray with ...'

Then commotion broke out. Ned Royston, a big gingery stoker backed up by three others, began hammering on Madame's door. His dreams in nights past had been invaded by fear and lust: arrival at this isle had fuelled the fear; so had the dazed condition in which Platt and the Chief had returned from that bleak shore. Independently Royston had reached the Third Mate's conclusions about Madame's origins; now, determined to act, he struck her door repeatedly with his fist, not sure if he wanted to bed her, kill her, or both.

'Yer in there!' he howled. 'What's yer game? Come out an' ...'

Then everything happened at once. Mr Josephs jumped out from the bridge, shouting, even as the entire ship shuddered ... and a gun went off by the Third Mate's right ear, deafening him. Ned Royston, shaken almost off his feet by the strange tremor, looked up and saw Mr Platt standing above him, behind the Third Mate, aiming a revolver down at his chest. 'Get back!' said Mr Platt firmly. 'Get back or I'll kill you.' His eyes gleamed with a wild light; Royston snarled and backed off and the others followed as Platt came down among them, the revolver cocked. His grin held no humour. Watching them, he knocked at Madame's door. 'You all right, ma'am?' he called, 'This is the Second Mate. Everything's under control.'

Very slowly the door opened. From the inner darkness Madame Pédauque peered out in the ashen light, pale and discomposed, her black hair in a tangle, sweat-sodden nightgown clutched tight against her body.

'What is this?' Her voice was weak and hoarse. 'Are we still in this dreadful place? When will we leave?'

Platt saw the fever-dew on her brow. Shocked, forgetting the men behind him, he lowered the gun.

'You're not well!' was all he could think to say.

'No.' Her white teeth showed in painful grimace. 'And made no better by brutes brawling outside my door.' With an effort she drew herself up. 'What do you want?' she asked the staring crewmen. 'If we don't go ...'

She slumped, exhausted, and would have fallen if Platt hadn't caught her. He felt the heat of her body, the thrust of her breasts. 'She's sick!' he shouted angrily, with a self-assurance he's never known before. 'Tell the Steward to get towels, water, quinine, whatever he's got! Quick!'

Utterly taken aback, Royston and the others watched him carry her into the cabin and shut the door in their faces. Minutes later, when the Third Mate and the Steward knocked on the door, only his hands emerged for the supplies they brought. 'You risk your soul!' hissed Josephs. 'Be warned!'

But Platt slammed the door in their faces.

This left the entire crew thoughtful. They noted that so far Mr Platt was the only man back from the island. They stared at the shore, but the poor light showed nothing. 'Wot if they all comes back like 'im?' asked Ned Royston fearfully ... while up on the bridge, to Steward Perkins and others, Mr Josephs thunderously recited from the Book of Revelation. The passage concerned the Whore of Babylon and the Great Beast, and the Third Mate's delivery was so powerful that nobody was watching the devil's shore when the skiff returned again ... this time with a fatal casualty ...

Upon landing, Pierce, like the others before him, found himself buried under a huge weight of hallucination and lost will. Like a sad dumb stone he sat with head in hands while Davey stamped about with a hot and greedy look that nobody had ever seen before. 'Keep digging, boys!' Davey kept roaring. 'We'll all be richer for it.' And each discovery plucked from the rock-slide — fragments of bronze swords, mallet-heads, an intact narrow-necked vase, stone carvings of birds, animals, and the pop-eyed goddesses — passed through the Captain's big broad hands and under his fearful, half-believing eye. 'My God, Mr Pierce!' he bellowed after time had passed. 'Aren't you with us yet? Get on your feet, man! Start logging these items!' So that soon Pierce found himself scribbling furiously amid the ring of shovels, the shouts of nervous discovery, Davey's interruptions and McDermott's continual curses. Some men were singing shanties to hold off the horrors, and Pierce realised, even as a violent physical shudder rippled through him: *This is nightmare! We're all terrified!* His vision blurred and shook as, with a thunderous roar, a section of the rock-face detached and came plunging down. *It's an earthquake, not me!* he realised stupidly as the diggers, howling and swearing, leaped clear ... all but for an older man, Mick Doyle, who moved too slow. For a rock plunged and struck him, knocking him down: before he could drag himself away, and even as the tremor ended, a larger slab hurtled down and struck him square on the head and upper body.

From the *Heaton* came a gunshot, but nobody heard it. Loose stones kept on falling with men jumping and whooping in pure fear. 'Stop acting like rabbits!' Davey bellowed. 'Help the Chief!' For McDermott was already under the cliff, trying to drag the rock off the crushed man. Davey, with Pierce and two others, started forward ... then he saw something and stopped. Nobody else noticed as, with a heave, Pierce helped shift the huge slab.

Pierce groaned at what he saw. McDermott pushed back his oil-stained blue cap and scratched his balding scalp.

'Aye,' he told the frightened men, 'nae a braw sight. But the puir auld loon nivver kent a thing aboot it.' And carefully, stripping off his grimy jacket, he laid it over the dead man, wrapping the mangled head.

Pierce realised that Davey was paying no attention.

'Captain,' he said sharply, 'we have a dead man here.'

'Yes,' murmured Davey, his gaze distant, 'that's their price.'

'Whit's that supposed tae mean?' McDermott demanded angrily.

Davey pointed dreamily past them. 'Look. See there.'

Pierce felt the blood congeal in his veins as he followed Davey's finger past the tumble of fresh-fallen rock to the ... oddly-regular lines of an inner face now revealed. McDermott whistled softly.

'It's a bluidy massive dyke! *Inside* the rock?'

'Mmm,' Davey grunted. 'Now see there. Under the overhang.'

They looked. One by one, unwilling, they recognised.

'A door.' Davey nodded grimly, his eyes haunted. The look on his face was something Pierce had never seen before. Almost, the First Mate told himself, as if he's *possessed*. 'We're going in there, boys. They've taken a life of ours. They owe us.'

His logic was not persuasive. There was loud dissent, several men agreeing they were damned if they'd move an inch closer. 'Captain, that tremor was only the first,' Pierce objected. 'Let's call it a day and go!'

'Chief?' asked Davey, his gaze hot with eager demand.

McDermott shrugged. 'Ye ken I'm nae one for the heroics.'

'I keep nobody here against his will,' Davey said coldly. 'Anyone that wants can go back on board. It won't be held against them.'

Small stones still pattered down. Nobody moved. Scowling, Davey seized a pick and began scrambling over the rubble. 'Ach, I'll nivver learn,' McDermott muttered, bending for a shovel. Two of his stokers followed him, leaving Pierce with three men and a corpse.

Momentarily Davey paused. 'Mr Pierce, see to it!' he called back. 'See to it, and return with new men and the hurricane lamp! As fast as you can!'

Daylight was fading an hour later when Pierce reluctantly returned. The ashen haze over the isle had partly lifted: smouldering black peaks stood clearly etched against a flat lemon band of sky low in the west. In the stern of the

70

skiff Pierce couldn't stop trembling. Through Madame's closed door he'd spoken with the Second Mate. What if Platt's right? he wondered. A disease in the air making her sick? Will it get us all? But maybe it *is* a conspiracy. Mr Josephs says they planned it in Messina. But why? And who is she? Oh Christ, this is madness! What if they strand us here? The whole devilish place could blow up any minute!

He bit his lip hard as the skiff slid in under the black cliff. Clumsy with fear the new men shipped oars and beached between rocks as sharp as teeth. Carrying the unlit lantern, Pierce scrambled unhappily ashore in the gloom, not daring to tell the sullen oarsmen to wait in case they decided on the opposite. And he was in such a state that he was halfway up the rockfall before he realised the utter silence that lay ahead. He called out, but the echo of his voice was the only reply. With a leaden heart he passed the spot where Doyle had died, and paused to call again, his gaze fixed anxiously on the ramparts of the unstable cliff above.

'Mr Pierce ... we need that light ... now ...'

Pierce looked wildly through the murk for the source of that slurred voice. Against the wall a shadow moved, and he sighed with relief as he made out first Davey, then McDermott and the two stokers. Just feet away they leaned exhausted against the wall. And what a wall! Even amid his fear he felt awe as he took in the huge blocks of close-fitting basalt. How on earth did men ...

'Get up here!' McDermott snapped. 'We dinnae want tae be here firever!'

Awkwardly Pierce joined them. As he did he made out beside them the greater darkness of the doorway they'd excavated. The height of a man and the width of two, it tapered slightly in and up to a broad lintel stone which, jutting from the wall, was incised with spiral carvings that reminded him of pagan maze designs which ...

'Wake up, Pierce!' McDermott's hand jerked him forward; the shadow that was Davey stirred to take the lantern. Soon he had it lit. 'Now,' he said, his voice thick

71

with that slow, hypnotised note. 'Let's go to it.'

Pierce lingered. 'But ... what have you found?'

'Anither door inside.' McDermott followed Davey into the passage.

'There's trouble on board,' Pierce said sharply.

'Trouble here too, mate,' muttered one of the stokers.

'Madame's sick,' Pierce insisted, and at this Davey's shadowy bulk stiffened. 'It's a fever. And Mr Platt ...'

'So the faster ... we work ... the better,' Davey interrupted grimly in that dragging voice. 'Come on, boys ... let's get to it.'

Light was failing fast over the awful land. A mile out to sea the *Heaton* still waited. Unwilling to lose sight of it, Pierce lingered by the broken-in outer door in an agony of nervousness. Inside, by lantern light, the stokers with their picks attacked two diagonal cracks running across the slab that sealed the far end of the short passage, with every blow fearing they'd bring the unstable roof down on them. So, with clenched teeth they struck harder and harder and each in turn until suddenly, with no warning, the stone seal gave way. The slanting central section between the two cracks broke and fell back into the space beyond: immediately the now unsupported upper section collapsed with a crash. One of the men, flinching instinctively, trod back onto the lantern and put it out even as a stupefying waft of dead air enveloped them. Davey cursed; the other stoker shouted in fear at the abrupt and near-total darkness. 'Where is it?' Davey demanded. 'Get it lit!' But nearly half a minute went by before the lantern was located and relit. Davey snatched it up with a dreadful impatient anxiety, knowing from Pierce that it had not been hallucination; his seeing Madame sick and feverish. '*I am La Reine Pédauque!*' It rang in his head over and over again. '*Here you'll find a key to what's lost — but be quick: I cannot endure this weight for long.*'

And as Davey clambered over the remaining bottom section of the stone seal into whatever lay beyond, again he saw her fever-drenched face, saw her clearly, and her eyes were starting out like hot coals, full of hope, and fear as well. For a moment he paused, listening to her voice crying desperately across the centuries, and again he wondered (though distantly it seemed to him he wasn't thinking clearly at all) at what exactly had possessed him and brought him here. In that moment he recalled how, earlier that day, he'd seemed to see her dripping with red mud, or maybe blood ... and he'd seen her feet that weren't human. This is my last chance to go back, he told himself coldly ... but he knew it was already too late. It had been too late from the moment she'd approached him on the quay at Messina, and perhaps even before that. It may have been too late since Sophie died with my son, he realised grimly. Or even since the day I was born. I don't care what happens now. This is what I choose.

So he cast the light before him and entered the inner space.

And he saw them.

He saw them only for seconds, for they were crumbling away in the fresh air even as he laid eyes on them, the three of them, seated at the round stone table in their once-gorgeous feathered robes, seated on stone benches in the small and neatly corbelled chamber which, apart from them and their furniture, was utterly bare and featureless. In the final instant before their disintegration was too far advanced Davey saw in their faces and forms the suggestion of two men and a woman; the men seeming older, the woman very much younger — than their features dissolved, their bodies fell apart, their robes swirled away into dust ... and there was a flat dull tinkle as something metallic fell from one of them to the flag-stoned floor.

'Sweet Jesus!' cried McDermott, who had seen them too.

Davey felt he weighed a ton as he forced himself into that place and round the table to search in the dust of those who'd sat there so long, sealed in at the bottom of the ocean, dead but waiting. With the lantern held low and his fingers like thick cold worms he stirred their dust, a sick faintness in him ... until he saw the sparkle and found the ring, the emerald set in bronze, which had fallen from the finger of one of them.

It seemed so heavy, that ring, that he could scarcely lift it.

But he did. And as he did, he knew that Madame's fever was gone, and that he'd found what he'd come for. Then, for the first time, he looked into the emerald depths that lay beyond the moon and horns ... he looked, and he saw ...

6.
The Fog

... *How in the attic at 15 Berkeley Road over a century later his unknown great-grandson Sam crouches on hands and knees, ignoring the blood streaming down his face, ignoring Diane watching and Chrissa fearfully waiting as he stares past moon and horns into the emerald depths ... into depths where he walks the black isle; from which soft voices — her voices — caress and tantalise him with half-remembered vision. For like Davey and Roderick before him he serves a force beyond his understanding that both entrances and terrifies him with its promises and threats; a force that operates within but also beyond the limits of his self-consciousness; a force which, when he lets it seize him, brings ecstasy that makes everyday life seem pointless and dull. Yes, he knows Diane watches him; he knows his head pounds from its crack against the roof joist; he knows that normal daily adult responsibility demands that he tear his gaze from the emerald and take up his burdens again ... but all that's unimportant. For SHE's in him, in the shining depths, just as she was in Davey, in Roderick, and he belongs to her as they did. For in the depths now he walks more closely with HER and all the other ring-guardians than he'll ever do with his wife and daughter. He smiles fearfully, groaning with the weight of the ring: he's old Davey in that chamber on the black isle, and nothing else really matters ... but perhaps for one thing, a thing*

he can't quite define: a sense of interruption, of another entity watching, an entity who does NOT belong to her and who opposes her in all her purposes . . . an entity who was once a man burned to death. An entity who burns still, yet no longer with merely ordinary flame . . .

But the intrusion's peripheral. The most important thing . . . I've found the emerald! I've relieved her pain! As for the rest . . . time will tell. And as he crouches there in the dust of the ancient ones he knows she has plenty of time. What's a hundred years to her after so long? he wonders, and also wonders at his sensation of simultaneously being someone somewhere else altogether. Then, dazed by the knowledge flooding him as he kneels, gazing into the dizzy green depths, he realizes: Time is limitation! The Fire and Flood return soon . . . and even those like her who remember centuries are anxious. The Shift means the death of this world where she's trapped! Yet, he thinks, staring at the dusty floor and feeling increasingly sick, increasingly caught into a dizzy confusion about his identity, before that happens — maybe in a hundred years or so — there'll be a descendent of mine, a man she'll call through one of the gates, to come to her and help her in her plan. Because she has a plan. Yes, of course she does! But first — and he shut his eyes as the pain grew in him — but first . . .

Then the confusion grows too great and he loses consciousness, the emerald ring clutched tightly in his fist.

It was all they could do to row back to the *Heaton*, numb and utterly spent. Every man was lost in the mad spin of his own mind. Pierce felt like a dreamer, but still he noted how Davey's hand stayed in his pocket, clutching whatever he had in it. Whatever it was, it seemed very heavy, because it dragged his body to one side even as he sat. Nobody else knew what it was, save perhaps the Chief, for nobody else had been into the stone chamber to see anything but the bare table, the unoccupied benches. Nor had they lined up to enter. Everyone, Davey included (once he'd recovered consciousness), had wanted to be gone quickly. They'd loaded the last of their finds and cast off even as night fell, a white freezing mist settling. Davey's drawn pale face grew more haggard even as the oarsmen put thankful distance between themselves and the island. And Pierce's first clear realisation, even as he scrambled clumsily back on board the *Heaton*, was that they'd forgotten to plant the flag.

None of them were in a mood to deal with the near-panic on board. The crew's fears had not been soothed by the earlier return of one of their number dead. Since Pierce had gone ashore again the men had waited, with nothing to test the silence but their own halting talk and the abominable sound of Madame's fever cries. For over an hour she'd been at a peak of delirium, her shrieks audible throughout the ship and punctuating the Third Mate's increasingly fervent prayer meeting. At one point a gang of white-faced deck hands had tried to invade the engine room, demanding that the stokers fire up and get them the hell out. The stokers had refused; amid the subsequent brawl someone had realised that Madame's cries had ceased. Soon the entire crew, saving those onshore, was gathered nervously on deck, their dispute temporarily forgotten. It was darkening by then, the black isle looming ever blacker above the white mists forming and coiling on the chill, motionless water, and their strained imaginations had many of them groaning with fear. They persuaded Mr Josephs to knock on Madame's door, at which the Second Mate emerged, looking like a man who'd been bled.

'Something's happened,' he croaked hoarsely, his eyes quite mad and staring right through them. 'She's asleep, or ...'

It was then a flare went up from the shore, signalling the landing party's return. Minutes passed as night thickened; Mr Platt returned to Madame's now-silent cabin; the crew waited until the muffled splash of oars was heard. Amid speechless tension they lined the rails as the skiff, like a ghost in the fog, grew solid and merged with the side of the ship. Then, men entranced, the landing party returned on board, to be met with such fear and suspicion that Davey would have faced mutiny had

77

not his own desire been the same and as strong as everyone else's.

'Mr McDermott ...' — his voice was faint, and he had trouble standing — '... get us out of here. Mr Pierce, get the skiff up, see the artifacts stowed and secured with a guard. Someone tell the cook ... we're famished. Right. What are you all gawping at? Get moving.'

But for a long moment the men just stared at him.

Then they moved. With alacrity.

Only Pierce lingered dubiously.

'Sure you're all right, Captain?'

Davey gave him a fierce, feverish stare. 'About your business, Mr Pierce! The sooner we're gone, the better!'

Only when Pierce had obeyed did Davey turn and limp, as if his right side weighed much more than his left, to the closed door of Madame's cabin.

He found the Second Mate standing before it like a guard.

'What's going on here, Mr Platt?'

Though pallid with exhaustion, Platt would not stand aside.

'She's asleep, sir. There was a crisis. She seems better now.'

Davey made as if to enter. Platt moved as if about to stop him. Davey sighed and fell back. 'Well,' he muttered obscurely, 'it's done, anyway. There's time later.' And with pain-filled eyes he assessed the Second Mate. 'You don't look so good yourself, son. She's taken it out of you. Believe me ... I know. So go and get some sleep.'

Then the Captain of the *Heaton* turned and went slowly, like the old man he was, up to the bridge. But Platt went back into the cabin where now she slept peacefully, her face blank and smooth and young, and as he gazed down at her his mouth twisted in agony. Tears sprang to his eyes: he made as if to tear himself away but got only as far as the door. Weeping openly, he sat on the cabin floor, waiting, and throughout all this she did not stir at all. It was not until the engines roared and the *Heaton* began to throb and rattle its way to the north-west, clear of the black isle, that the Second Mate was released and allowed to leave ... and only after he had closed the cabin door behind him that Madame Pédauque sighed, and stirred, and awoke with a sleepily contented smile on her ageless face ...

Dinner that night (for those who could face it) consisted of cod and red snapper taken dead from the sea. The day before some men had sampled the free fare without ill effect, pronouncing it excellent; that morning before landing Davey had speculated that the fish must have been cooked by the volcanic heat generated when the island rose.

Of course Madame was not at dinner, but Mr Platt was. To Pierce the Second Mate looked almost as drained as the Captain, his face whey-white and oddly pinched as if he'd lost vital energy nursing Madame through her sudden, incomprehensible crisis. That power with which he'd outfaced Ned Royston and protected her from the crew was gone, along (it seemed) with his interest in her. Now his sole concern appeared to be where he'd bunk down for the rest of the voyage. Under no circumstances, he declared in an exhausted whisper, would he continue in Mr Josephs' cabin. 'Use mine for now,' offered Pierce, and very soon Platt went to do just that, having said nothing at all of what had happened while he'd been with Madame. What did she do to him? Pierce wondered, appalled. Suck out his soul or something?

Davey picked without eating. He looked very unwell and was no more willing to talk than Mr Platt had been. In a whisper he set the watches then retired to his cabin, limping heavily, waving off Pierce's concern with a shaky left hand — his right hand hadn't left his pocket. Pierce stayed behind with McDermott, who wasn't drinking. The Chief told him of the three figures in feathered robes and how they'd crumbled to dust, and of something that had fallen from one of them, tinkling, for which Davey had scrabbled on the floor before passing out. 'But I didnae see whit it wis,' he said, yawning wide, 'an' efter

I've haud a wee sleep I winna care.' Then Mr Josephs came in, and Pierce and McDermott both left.

So the fog lay thick as the *Heaton* left the black isle, as Davey lay on his bunk in a sleepless fever, torn by storms. Once a shudder went through the ship; a swelling force twisted it briefly off its axis; the sea sighed; seconds later a dull rumble caught them from the quarter they'd left. From the bridge where he took the second watch Pierce saw the fog-shroud shimmer yellow-grey as the watch lamps swung. He shivered, beating his arms round his chest, fearing for Davey, for all of them, and tempted to believe that maybe the Third Mate's religious zeal wasn't so far off target.

Mr Pierce was not phantastical by nature, but what happened during his watch, amid the fog, led him to turn his back on the sea thereafter.

For Davey's state was dangerous, and Davey knew it. He'd known what risks he ran that moment he'd paused before entering the chamber. Had he turned back, he knew now (though not how or why) Madame would have died. Now, instead ... stretched out on his bunk with fear knotting his gut and the emerald ring clutched in his sweating hand, he felt sick and hallucinated. Somehow, he knew, he'd taken on her illness by picking up the ring. Now as he lay there he heard voices bellowing in unknown tongues; he felt torn apart by huge soundless explosions. The cool calm faces of the three in the bird-feather robes gazed on him with a sweet severity ... and of the three it was the woman who sat amid the two men who most attracted his attention. Her blue-eyed face, framed in flowing golden hair, seemed familiar to him, though he was sure he'd never seen her in his life before ... or not, at any rate, in this present life of Captain Davey Joyce. For again, as he faced her, he was caught in a confusion of multiple identity, as if he were not only Davey but someone else too. This confusion caused in him a sickening dizziness, amid which the flame-haired young woman was suddenly transformed into Madame

80

... Madame, enthroned in power and glory in a great hall filled with dazzling emerald light. She too wore a feathered robe; her raven-haired beauty remarkable, and she seemed in good humour, but her feet ... her feet were the webbed feet of a waterfowl. And on her finger she wore the ring. It flashed in his eyes ... and it was then, not realising what he did, that he slipped the ring onto his own little finger.

Then without warning the confusion became intolerable. Into the endless bright depths he fell, past the moon and horns, to be overwhelmed by a nauseating flood of clashing images, black and red, of raging war and violence; of tortured bodies, a charging red-eyed bull, an upraised, gory knife ... until, out of all this, *her* face swam. *Sophie's face.* His *wife.* And through the emerald he was seized back to that awful night five years before. Helplessly he heard her shrieks; uselessly he watched as their son killed her and died with her. He saw her cheeks, her hair, her lips, her eyes; he felt the chilling sweat. Then in horror he saw that her face was only a mask, perched grotesquely atop a broken yellow skeleton clad in mummy wrappings. Even as he watched he saw the skeleton crumble into dust, and from the dust fluttered a cloud of green moths that came and settled all over him, scratching, rustling. He panicked like a child and with weak hands tried to bat them away even as he heard Madame cry: *'You don't get something for nothing! Pay the price! Pay the price and come to me!'* And he saw her beckoning to him from the far side of an emerald abyss.

I'm old, he thought then, and an unexpected calm flowed through him like a soothing river. I'm tired and I'm all alone. All I have is gone. Why should I want it back? Why live longer? It'll be the same slow slide whatever happens. Go to her; it's best done now. Yes, he told himself, greatly relieved to find the struggle over, this is it. Now.

The engines sounded smothered and indistinct amid the fog as Davey rose from his bunk and pulled on his boots. For the first time he realised he was wearing the ring. 'You're heavy and old too,' he told it, caught in its depths, 'but you'll take me back, and Old Davey'll sleep at last.'

And on the way out of his cabin he laughed, not loudly, but enough so that he failed to hear another door opening nearby.

On the bridge Pierce had grown so depressed that he'd begun reciting stanzas from that poem by Coleridge which never before had he allowed on his mind when at sea — 'O shrieve me, shrieve me, holy Man!' — when he heard a laugh, apparently to port and below. He dismissed it as a ghost, then heard it again. Peering down into the thick fog (its clammy swirl partly penetrated by light from a nearby lamp) he sensed rather than saw the bulky figure standing by the port rail. Then with a shudder he knew who it was and what was up. He was about to call out when he sensed a second, smaller figure joining the first. So he stayed where he was, listening.

Davey was halfway over the rail and ready for the deep swim, a vision in him of that beautiful swanlike windjammer which had passed them on their first afternoon out from Gibralter, when her hand lightly touched his arm.

'What?' he asked wildly, flinching. 'What?'

She didn't grab for him. She left her hand where it lay until he recognised her touch and came gradually to his senses.

'I can't bear the weight of it,' he told her harshly, not for a moment doubting that she knew exactly what he meant. 'I know it's why we came here, I know you lost it long ago and you couldn't get it yourself ... but why me? Why must *I* die for it? *And* Sophie! Why did she have to ...'

'We didn't come here for you to die.' Her voice, though soft, carried well enough for Pierce to hear. 'One death is enough. Two would be self-indulgence. So give it to me now. Some things a man is not expected to bear. Some things are not possible.'

'I should throw it away,' muttered Davey. 'Then it'll bother nobody.'

'That would be a great waste.' She sounded very cool. 'You think this is the end? No. It's only the start. There's more to be borne ... but the weight's of a kind that'll make you happy yet ... if you'll give it to me. You're not as old as you think, *old man*. Give me what I ask, and in return I'll give you what you long for and lost ... five years ago ...'

Pierce heard Davey gasp.

'I never told you what I lost!'

'It's well known,' she said carelessly. 'All your crew knows it.'

Suddenly Davey was alert. 'If I agree, then what?'

Her laugh was throaty. 'Time and blood alone will tell. But rest assured, I'll make no more demands ... on you, at any rate.'

'Who are you?' Davey hissed, so low Pierce could scarcely hear.

'You know already,' she countered. 'Now, let us agree!'

Davey said nothing. Pierce could understand why. We all know what Mr Josephs thinks, he told himself anxiously. What if he's right? *Lilith?* Adam's first wife who wouldn't lie under him? She who sucks men's blood — look at Mr Platt! — and kills mothers, and children in the cradle? But that's superstition, like believing in witches! It's totally absurd!

Even so ... his flesh crawled, and maybe Davey didn't find it absurd. For at last, very wearily, Davey muttered, 'How can I agree? Today I've seen impossible things. How can I tell who you are or what you really want? I've seen you in forms that ...'

'Don't let fear overwhelm you!' Her voice was sharp. 'So you've seen some of what was and will be! There's not long now! You must do as I ask if that's to be avoided! This is a beautiful world, and you shouldn't ask too much about me, for I care for more than you'll ever know! Nothing that's happened is frivolous — nor is this last little thing I ask! Now give to me, and I'll give to you, and perhaps all will yet be well!'

Then Pierce heard Davey sigh, and knew the old man did as she asked. What is it? the First Mate wondered, fascinated, as dimly through the fog he saw them leave the rail together. What did he give her? What did he find in there? What in the name of heaven is she up to?

But he received no answer, then or later. Only the sound of Davey's cabin door closing behind the pair of them. Soon a breeze rose and blew the fog away. The stars came out, and the sky and sea were clear again as the *Heaton* continued to New Orleans ...

7.
Holiday

One bright Saturday six weeks after Sam found the ring again they left for holiday in Scotland. It was during the long drive north that Chrissa first saw him wear it ... and he told her the tale of Madame Pédauque.

As far as Chrissa was concerned, this honesty was overdue.

'Sweet child, it's starting now! You must be brave!'

But she hadn't felt at all brave that night. Sam crashing about in the attic as the burning man mouthed warning had been bad enough. Worse had followed. She'd sensed the rush of huge dark wings as the Enemy swooped on 15 Berkeley Road, darkening the house with a pall of hate, a stench of blood. Then Sam roared; there was a final crash from the attic, and her nerve snapped. Even as Diane came home Chrissa rushed onto the landing in a panic. 'Dad,' she screamed, 'will you stop it! Will you stop it now!'

So up the stepladder went Diane, then to mutter something which, in her distress, Chrissa didn't remember till later. *'I thought you'd got rid of that thing years ago.'* Before long there came another thump and — even as Chrissa felt the atmosphere lighten — Diane's hiss of pain.

Chrissa breathed deep as the worst of the terror left her.

'Mum? Mum? What's going on? Is Dad all right?'

'Your father's ... hurt himself.' Diane, looking down with shocked wide eyes, spoke with difficulty. 'Go to the ... medicine cabinet, and bring the bandage roll, surgical tape, and scissors. And ... the Dettol.'

In a daze Chrissa obeyed. But once in the neat clean ordinary kitchen, rooting about in the cabinet, she slowly realised: Mum doesn't want me to see what happened! She doesn't want me to know anything! But I *must!*

Quietly she climbed the stairs; even more quietly she mounted the ladder and peered into the attic. In the dim light, through the broken chairs, she saw Diane bending over her father's prone and bloody form. Her mother was gasping with effort and shock as she tried to pull something from Sam's closed fist. Quietly Chrissa descended the ladder then, clearing her throat, mounted again, noisily. She heard her mother groan as she clambered into the attic with the bandages. 'Mum, here ...!' Pretending more shock than she felt, Chrissa stared down at her father. Sam lay unconscious, eyes closed, blood matting his hair and seeping down his cheek to his collar. His left fist was still clenched. 'Oh no, Mum! What happened?'

'Must have cracked his head on a joist.' Grimly, not meeting her daughter's eyes, Diane began to clean and bandage the wound.

'What's he holding onto? What's in his hand?'

'Nothing, dear. His fist's just clenched, that's all.'

Sam groaned. His eyes flickered open, fixing blankly on Diane.

'Chrissa,' she said hurriedly, 'get downstairs now!'

'But, Mum, don't you need me to ...'

'Do as I say!' Diane snapped.

Chrissa flushed ... and then used her wit. Muttering, she retreated down the ladder and at the bottom slammed her bedroom door. Then, as quietly as before, she tiptoed up the ladder again and peered cautiously.

And to her horror saw Sam shuddering, his eyes like wet glass, nothing familiar in them at all as Diane desperately tried to shake him back to his senses.

And she heard his awful dragging voice:

'Never try taking it from me again, Diane. Understand? Never again!'

Chrissa shivered. It sounded like a snake slithering over gravel.

'You swore you'd got rid of it!' Her mother's whisper was edged with hysteria. Chrissa clenched her teeth to stop them chattering.

'I did! But it's found me again . . . hasn't it!'

'Give it to me, Sam! Please let me get rid of it!'

But the creature in Sam just chuckled. Then again he shuddered.

'You know I can't do that,' he said in a bewildered voice . . . and moaned as at last the fit left him and he returned to his ordinary senses.

'Let me finish the bandaging,' Diane said faintly. 'Then put that damned thing away and come downstairs with me. And *don't tell Chrissa anything!*'

'Okay, okay!' But Sam felt terror. As if through green mists he saw, he remembered . . . and in his fist the emerald pulsed; inside his mind the cold voice laughed. *Don't let her see where you hide me!* it whispered.

Chrissa slipped quietly down the ladder and back into her room . . .

Later that night Sam and Diane argued low-voiced in the kitchen. They thought Chrissa asleep or at least beyond hearing. In fact she was hiding in the bathroom above, listening by way of the pipes. She felt no guilt. I have to know! Their voices echoed up hollowly and she heard every word. It was scary but fascinating, for they were going on at each other about that time they never told her about, her mother in a tremulous, weepy voice, and her father sounding angrily confused, put-upon, playing the innocent as usual:

'You can't have forgotten what it was like when you

wore that thing all the time, Sam!' Diane was stalking about. 'Don't you remember Nantgewydd?'

'Come on, we were all crazy then,' Sam muttered. He sounded very depressed. 'It was too much dope, not the bloody ring!'

'*I* believe that, but I know *you* don't! Whenever you went over the top you always blamed it. What about when you kidnapped Chrissa?'

'I did *not* kidnap her! I just took her to the zoo!'

I remember that! Chrissa realised fearfully. *I was three!*

'But you said the ring made you do it! God, Sam, I'll never forget how you went on with your stories about it and how you're it's ... I don't know, *guardian* or high priest or ... or something mad! Sam, you should have seen yourself tonight! It was just like ... just as bad as when ...' — and Chrissa heard her mother crying; it came up the pipes and she felt furious. *Dad, you're a sod!* Her lips tightened. *But it's not you, is it? It's the Enemy.* And for a moment she seemed to see that face of terrible empty beauty glaring at her from the void, and she heard the burning man again. *'Sweet child, it's starting now.'* Oh NO! she wailed silently, WHY is this happening?

'Diane, dammit, stop crying! I didn't *mean* to find it!'

'No! You never *mean* to do anything! *Go with the flow,* eh? Sam, it's been so good since you grew up! Why start it again? Oh God, I knew this would happen! I just hoped we'd get Chrissa through her problems first!'

'Trying to make me feel guilty again?' he barked.

'Sam, don't you see? It's starting again!'

'What's starting again, for godsakes!'

'IT! Oh Sam ... we need a holiday ...'

And Sam gave out that horrible laugh again:

'A holiday? How about in Highgate Cemetery?'

'Don't be morbid! I mean it! A real holiday.'

There was silence. Chrissa sighed. *Please, Dad! Please!*

'I was thinking that myself,' she heard Sam agree in his normal voice. 'We're all going up the wall. Maybe that's all it is. You know I walked out on GRYP tonight? A holiday.' And he asked: 'Got anywhere in mind?'

'Not really.' Mum sighed with relief. 'Where would you like?'

'You tell me. Where do you want to go?'

Again a pause. Then Mum said, hesitantly: 'Scotland?'

'Scotland?' And Sam laughed. And though this time it sounded like his normal laugh, Chrissa didn't like it at all. For even as she heard it she seemed to hear another voice — a light and giggly voice that gave her the odd sensation that it came from nobody human; from nothing that, properly speaking, was even alive. 'Scotland!' Sam repeated. 'Great idea!'

Ahhh! breathed the giggly voice. *Tir Nan Og! That's the place I like!*

Nothing dramatic happened during the following six weeks. Sam returned to GRYP without wearing or mentioning the ring; Diane acted as if nothing had changed, and Chrissa pretended to be fooled.

'Dad, what happened in the attic?' she asked some days later, and Sam shrugged.

'I just banged my head. How did you get on at school today?'

In reply to the same question Diane shook her head. 'I've forgotten, so it can't have been anything important,' she said vaguely, then eyed her daughter. 'You were restless last night. Sure those dreams have stopped?'

'Sure, Mum,' said Chrissa. In fact this was the truth. The burning man had left her entirely alone since that horrible evening, and so had the Enemy. Yes, she'd dreamed, but nothing unusual. It was as if the tension of months had built up to that one evening and then overflowed, releasing itself, leaving nothing behind. Chrissa certainly hoped so, and lately she'd felt much easier, going out with her schoolfriends again ... but maybe her caution showed, because her mother eyed her with a sharp, unhappy look that betrayed her own continuing doubts.

'You *are* telling me the truth?'

'Yes, Mum. When are we going on holiday?'

Anticipating the holiday became an important game. Together they pored over maps and time-share brochures. Chrissa wanted to camp; Diane vetoed this ... but it was late in the season to book accommodation. Sam rang a dozen agencies, specifying 'anywhere in the north-west', yet without luck until, the last Saturday in June, one of the agencies rang back. A house called Cuilchonich near Gairloch in Wester Ross was available for a week from the first Saturday in July. *Gairloch?* Sam took it on the spot ... and his suspicion grew into certainty that made his heart pound when he got out the map. Cuilchonich was not five miles from Tir Nan Og! *That's the place I like!* Fear gripped him. He nearly rang back and cancelled on the spot. But he didn't. He'd been waiting for something like this since that night in the attic; a fatalism had him despite his apparent return to normality. Now, as if it had never left him, he felt that exhilarating terror tingling in his bones. *I ran from it seven years ago,* he told himself, his mouth dry, *But now it ... she ... wants me again. And maybe I want it too ...*

So he didn't cancel, and he didn't tell Diane about the coincidence. But next time the house was empty he stole up to the attic, removed the ring from its hiding place, and put it ... not yet on his finger, but in his pocket. In doing this he felt oddly like a thief ... not in any material sense, but in some more subtle way. And in the days before they left for Scotland he carried it everywhere, not wearing it, struggling with his conflicting desires, for in his dreams it laughed and sang. If Diane noticed any change in him, she did not mention it.

One thing that Chrissa later recalled did happen during those weeks. On a night early in June the main TV news was of a violent police attack on the hippie 'peace convoy' at Stonehenge. Even 'balanced reporting' could not conceal the ferocity of this attack. It put Sam in a fury. 'Here we go!' he raged. 'The same old shit for anyone who's different. Religious persecution masquerading as civil law defending private property! Christ, it's all coming back — ayatollahs and fascist gurus and born-again nutters everywhere! Reason fails, mere superstition's unleashed! Hah! Soon it'll be as bad as it was in the Middle Ages when the bloody Inquisition was burning thousands of Cathars and Waldensians and anyone else who ...'

Chrissa gasped and turned pale. *Cathars?* For at the sound of this name, which she was sure she'd never heard before, she was suddenly back in her dream ... of the burning man, ablaze amid all the other blazing victims, straining to reach her from the pyre in the stockade under the castle on the great rock, and all about the faceless ones, the hideous hooded ones with the scarlet crosses on their black-robed breasts ...

'Sam, stop!' Diane snapped. 'Chrissa, what is it?'

With an effort the girl regained her self-control, as best she could ignoring the stench of burning. 'Dad,' she asked with difficulty as Diane dug her husband fiercely in the ribs, 'what are Cathars?'

But Sam took the hint and changed the subject.

At least, until he wore the ring on the journey north.

He hadn't planned it. But as they left Berkeley Road that warm bright Saturday morning a sudden impulse told him to wear it openly. So suddenly there it was, in full view, sparkling emerald in the sun, prominent on his index finger against the Volvo's wheel. With her mouth open Diane stared at him. Why did I do that? he wondered, as appalled as she was. *Because it's time you did!* Yet her gaze spoke with bitter sadness of the gulf instantly opened up between them. And of course, from her back seat space amid the luggage and holiday gear, Chrissa immediately saw it.

That's it! she knew. That's what he found in the attic!

'Dad, what's that ring?'

She's innocent! Let her be! And he felt guilt that had him clenching his teeth as he geared through dense traffic. But the voice laughed. *You see? She has to know. She's a Joyce too! You can't hide her from me! So tell her!* And even as he obeyed he sighed, feeling the moment of possible rebellion pass. 'Something my grandad gave me long ago,' he said heavily, hating the ring. It seemed almost to grin at him! Don't look so bloody happy! he told it silently, savagely. And in a daze he heard himself add: 'The grandad who lived at Tir Nan Og. Near Gairloch.'

'But that's where we're going!' Diane was now doubly aghast.

'Yes. Quite a coincidence.' He shrugged. 'I didn't realise it myself till I checked the map. Luck of the draw. Odd, though.'

Diane felt the fatal clock slam back another notch. For right on cue Chrissa demanded: 'Does it have a story, Dad?'

'No, Sam,' Diane objected fiercely. 'I really don't think ...'

'There *is* a story, isn't there, Dad?' Chrissa today seemed brighter than she'd been for months, but brittle too, with an expectant anxiety in her voice ... almost, Diane thought fearfully, as if she knows all about it already. But that's impossible! 'I *know* there is! Dad, tell it!'

'Why not?' Sam breathed deep. 'It's only a story, Diane.'

Why does it scare me so much? Diane wondered, grimly watching suburbs slip behind as they started north up the M1, as Sam began the tale of the black isle. It's just a bloody silly story, she told herself, already tasting the ashes of defeat. It's all fantasy. Absurd. But I wish he wouldn't. Why must he act like a shit again? She glared at him. Sam, she's disturbed enough already without you feeding her this junk! Oh hell! She's just lapping it up. Chrissa, why do you want to hear it? I wash my hands of the pair of you! I just plod along, but you two, sometimes you don't seem to belong to this world at all. Well, I don't have to listen!

So for a long time she brooded silently on the ripening countryside as London fell behind and Sam told the tale, and Chrissa did not interrupt at all. But at last, bypassing

Birmingham an hour or so later, he reached the point where Madame stopped Davey going for the deep swim. Then he paused so long that Chrissa leaned eagerly forward and demanded:

'That's not all, is it, Dad? There's more, isn't there?'

Still Diane held her tongue as Sam, concentrating on the traffic, shook his head without looking round. 'No, that's not all.' On his finger the emerald sparkled brightly in the sun. 'There's quite a bit more.'

'Good!' Chrissa announced, her gaze fixed on the gemstone's depths. 'You can't end a story like that. And it's very confusing. I mean, who *is* Madame Whosername? Why did she get sick? Who were those dead people Davey found? And if your ring's the same, why doesn't it do anything bad to you like it did to him? If it's so magic ...' — Diane was alarmed by the rising edge in Chrissa's voice — '... why doesn't it make you drive into the back of that bus in front of us, or something horrible like that?'

'Chrissa!' Diane flinched. 'Don't tempt fate!'

'The ring's just a ring.' Smoothly Sam overtook the bus, his face unreadable. 'And the story's just a story.'

'Then why bother telling it?' Chrissa demanded angrily. 'Dad, I'm not a total idiot! That ring's what you found in the attic when you bashed your head, isn't it! What Mum thought you'd got rid of! Isn't it!'

'That's right,' Sam agreed after a pause. 'Do you ...'

'Sam, I wish you'd stop this now!' Diane snapped.

'You can't go on treating me like a child and not telling me things for ever!' Chrissa cried passionately at her mother. 'Do you think I don't know Dad went crazy and left us and all that? I'm not an ...'

'Do you want the rest of the story?' Sam asked, sharp.

'Of course I do!' the girl agreed grumpily, keeping her thoughts to herself. 'Just don't make it so complicated. And don't *worry*, Mum!'

8.
To Tir Nan Og

'Okay,' said Sam, clearing his throat, 'we were on the *Heaton*. Now I'm going on from another angle — it'll become clear why. Anyway. My grandad, Roderick Moses Joyce, spent his boyhood at a Poor Clare orphanage at Biloxi on the Gulf of Mexico just east of New Orleans. The nuns called him Moses because, they said, he was found newborn in a basket in the reeds at the edge of a bayou — that's sort of like a river swamp. He was swaddled in clean cotton with a note in French pinned to the basket. The note said: THIS CHILD IS NOT ABANDONED. SEE HIM SAFE AND THE REWARDS OF FATE WILL BE YOURS. So he was brought to the nuns, and they took him in. That was in early 1883, about nine months after the *Heaton* docked at New Orleans.

'Nobody knew about that then. Nothing more was known about him for another eight years. Then a parcel arrived at the orphanage, postmarked New Orleans. In it was a letter, a bank draft for $5,000, and a little walnut box with a ring in it — *this* ring, as it so happens. The letter was anonymous, again in French, and in the same neat hand as the original note. It explained that the boy had a father, a retired sea captain in Scotland called Davey Joyce. It said: HE AWAITS THE RING AS TRUE TOKEN OF HIS SON! — and gave an address, c/o Wheel &

Waite, Threadneedle Street, London.

'The nuns found this all very odd, just like they found Moses himself pretty odd, but all the same, they wrote ... and months later they got a reply from Gairloch, in Scotland. In his crabbed old hand Davey said he wanted his son — *Roderick* — sent to him, along with the ring. But Mother Jeanne, who ran the orphanage, wasn't happy. She had the kid in her care and she smelled rats, big rats ... so she placed ads in the press from New Orleans to Baton Rouge, begging the boy's mother to come forward. No result. So next she hired a Pinkerton agent to track down the anonymous letter-writer ... but all the trails ended in walls of what looked like big money protection. Nobody would talk. The bank on which the draft for $5,000 was drawn refused information. So Mother Jeanne reached her own conclusions, and when Davey wrote again months later, she called young Moses into her office. "Do you know where Scotland is?" she asked, and when he said he didn't, she rapped him over the knuckles with a ruler she always carried. "Silly boy! Don't you listen to the geography lessons? Well, soon you'll know. You're going there with Sister Maria to meet your father! He says if you don't want to stay, you can come back here. And he says that your *real* name — the name *he* gave you — is *Roderick*."

'"*Roderick?*" Moses — he was a sharp little kid, though inclined to be dreamy — felt horrified. "What kinda name is that?"

'So. With Sister Maria as his escort and the five thousand bucks as his bond he went by ship to Glasgow, then up the west coast to Gairloch. There they arrived on a cold wet winter day, and old Davey met them on the pier. He demanded to see this ring, and Sister Maria showed it. Then at last the old boy relaxed. "You're my son!" he said. "I've lived for this day!" And he took them by trap to Tir Nan Og — the name, Chrissa, comes from the mythical Celtic isle of everlasting youth — so he called the croft where he lived, where his wife had died and he'd known so much despair.

'So far as Grandad was concerned it was a miserable hovel in the middle of a miserable wilderness. Grandad hated it at first! He was used to the heat of the delta, but here it was winter, cold and wet and bare, nothing growing anywhere. Just rock and sea, moor and giant sky, and long black wailing nights amid poor empty nothingness! What a fate! Suddenly stuck with this gaunt and wifeless old man who clammed up every time Sister Maria mentioned the subject of the boy's mother! Ah yes, a bad beginning, and nothing much to say for it ... but time passed, the nights grew lighter, and one fine spring day Old Davey took the boy out fishing, way out on the sound looking over the sea to Skye ... and that night they returned not only with a fine catch but with good friendship, laughing together, and Roddy who'd been Moses had at last the admiration in his eyes for his wizened and weathered old dad! Then Sister Maria (who knows what had been going on in her mind?) declared it was time she went back to Biloxi.

'And so she did. Both Davey and Grandad did their best to dissuade her, for she'd kept house well, but she served the Sacred Heart first, she was not to be moved, and so after six months she left. Even so, until she died in 1926 she wrote every year to Grandad, though he never replied but twice with Christmas cards in all that time. So he told me, with regret.

'So Grandad grew up at Tir Nan Og. He got to like it, in time. But for years he learned little of his past and less of the ring he'd brought home. Old Davey was no great talker; he was not to be drawn, and didn't say a word about Madame Pédauque or the black isle until the year before he died, 1901, when Roddy was eighteen already and at work stalking deer on a local estate for a southern manager ... and even then he said only just enough so, when he was gone, Grandad was driven to find out more.

'He went to London to see Wheel & Waite, the owners of the *Heaton*. But they weren't at all helpful; in fact they insisted there never had been the voyage Davey described. This only made Grandad more curious. It took him months, but at last he tracked down two contacts. Mr McDermott the Chief Engineer had retired, to Peterhead near Aberdeen, and First Mate Pierce — he'd never gone back to sea after that voyage — now worked in Purley as the commercial rep for a soap company. In 1902 Grandad visited both of them. He showed them this ring and told them his tale. And both of them, once they got over the shock, told him a lot ... more than Davey'd ever done. Which is why the story's so detailed. It's not just a dream, you see.

'Anyway. The rest of that voyage? Well, after Madame persuaded Davey there were better ways of doing things than jumping overboard, everything seemed to go just fine. There they were that night, all bunked up — come on, Diane, there's no use pretending about it — and on the following days they were quite lovey-dovey, so Pierce and the Chief assumed Madame had lost interest in reaching New Orleans by midnight on March 21st. And the weather was fine, so almost everyone forgot the black isle as best they could. *Almost* everyone. One exception was Mr Platt. For the rest of the voyage he stared at the sea and wouldn't talk to anyone, except Pierce. At New Orleans he disembarked, never to be seen again. Another exception was Third Mate Josephs, who finally had to be locked in his cabin, where for the rest of the voyage he could be heard calling down the Lord's Wrath on the Great Beast and the Whore of Babylon. He was such a pain that when the *Heaton* docked in New Orleans — minutes before midnight on March 20th — Mr Josephs was first on shore, paid up and encouraged to leave quickly.

'And Madame left too. Surprised? Pierce and the Chief both told Grandad they saw the man she met on the quay — a tall, well-dressed gent with a limp and an ivory cane. Yes! Jourdain Lafayette himself! But before he bore her away into the sunset she brought Davey to meet him, umpiring a talk which nobody overheard and which Davey never mentioned. Yet it seems when he came back on board Davey wasn't too sad ... and later, on his way back to London and retirement, he seemed easy, with no trouble on his mind that anyone could see. He just collected his pension and retired to Gairloch, leaving a mystery ... and a son, it seems ... behind him.

'As for the isle and what they found,' Sam concluded, 'Well, make of it what you will. The isle wasn't seen again after the *Heaton* left it, though at least one other ship saw an unknown isle at the same co-ordinates, and dozens of ships went through the mud and shoals of dead fish. The British Institute of Oceanography estimated that the dead fish covered 7,500 square miles of ocean. And when the *Heaton* got to New Orleans, Davey invited the press to examine his finds. Yes, really! When I was a kid Grandad showed me a cutting from the *New Orleans Times Picayune*, all about the black isle, and the door, and the weird crumbling people ... though not a word about the ring ... and Davey saying he'll give everything to the British Museum.

'Later he told Grandad that's what he did, but there's no record. Both Grandad and I've been there, to Russell Square, but his finds aren't in any catalogue. So who can say? As for the *Heaton*'s log, which the company wouldn't let Grandad see, it seems that was destroyed along with Wheel & Waite's offices in the 1940 Blitz. So nothing's left ... only this ring ...

'One other thing.' Sam looked round. 'You know what "Madame Pédauque" means in English, Chrissa? No? Well, guess what! It means something like "Mrs Goose-Foot" — or, if you prefer — "Mother Goose".

'Now what do you make of that?'

Chrissa didn't know what she made of it. But she'd listened carefully. And on their fourth day at Cuilchonich she found her special place, by a waterfall where an unnamed burn cascaded down to the sea. There her dreaming came alive, with enormous consequences.

Cuilchonich, with all mod cons at ninety quid a week, was a two-up two-down farmhouse with harled grey walls and a new kitchen-bathroom extension. A sagging dry-

98

stone dyke straggled round the house which, though its Gaelic name meant 'Mossy Corner', was exposed on rough descending pasture under steep birch woods. Above these glowered the bare gneiss brows of a vast high moor, wrinkled and glacier-scrubbed, that ran for many empty miles east to Loch Maree and south to the Torridon hills. A quarter-mile north ran the wooded southern shore of the sea-loch, Gairloch Bay, where small yachts lay anchored near shooting-lodge hotels and hundreds of holiday cottages. At this time of year in the north-west wilderness it was a toss-up whether tourists or midges were more numerous, but at Cuilchonich the Joyces were spared too close contact with their fellow beings. The house, quite isolated, was hidden from the little winding road out to the ocean at Red Point (where lay Tir Nan Og) by decrepit farm steadings. Newly-sheared sheep grazed amid rusting old Fordson tractors abandoned on the pasture. House, land, steadings, sheep and dead tractors were owned by Mr Ian Macgregor; a gnome-like old man who dressed like a tinker and lived with his massive wife in a modern double-glazed bungalow by the water's edge.

When the Joyces arrived that first evening, tired from their 500-mile journey, it was Jean Macgregor — yes, massive, with a kind red face and an amazingly soft voice — who gave them the keys and showed them how things worked. But later, in the midge-infested cool of the otherwise sweet long twilight, it was Mr Macgregor who just sort of happened by the front door, black-and-white collie to heel and carved rams-horn crook in hand, so that Sam felt bound to invite him in for 'a wee nip' which Mr Macgregor, gravely and after due consideration, decided to accept.

'So ye'll be up from the south, then?' he commented.

'We live there, yes.' Sam was apologetic. 'But my father's father lived near here all his life.'

'Oh aye?' Mr Macgregor nodded his polite interest.

'His name was Roderick Joyce. Roderick Moses Joyce.'

Mr Macgregor sipped ruminatively at his Whyte & Mackay's.

'That would have been out at Red Point,' he agreed.

'You knew him?' Sam asked eagerly.

'I remember him right enough.'

'I used to visit him here, from Edinburgh!'

'That must have been a while ago,' said Mr Macgregor obscurely, and he turned to Diane, whose expression said she disliked Sam's fawning. From a pocket of his filthy tweed jacket the old man produced a yellow aerosol, which with a courtly gesture he presented to her. 'You'll be finding the midges the chief bother,' he said, 'but this'll take care of them.' His grin was almost sly. 'Paraffin in the hair is best of all, but I doubt you'll not be wanting to try that.' Then he drank up with a wink for Chrissa, who'd been staring at him so openly that Diane, without success, had been nudging her to recall her manners. Now, to the amazement of both her parents, Chrissa gave their temporary landlord a sudden radiant smile. Mr Macgregor's eye twinkled as he stood. 'Well, I'll be off to see to the beasts,' he said. 'Call down the way if there's anything you're needing.'

Chrissa, watching this little weatherbeaten old man, had felt something warm and friendly spread inside her. That evening the foul mood which had possessed her for months began to dissipate a little, leaving all three of them smiling after a light meal and a late walk down to the shimmering bay. Sam still wore the ring, but Diane felt so — dare she think it? — *content* that she felt it didn't matter. Maybe no harm would come of it. Maybe it was all in her imagination. What counted was the improvement in Chrissa's mood, and for once Sam agreed, so that later, with the clear summer night glowing through their open window, they forgot their differences and turned gladly to each other for the first time in ... was it weeks?

In her own crooked little room Chrissa lay abed, tired but unable to sleep. The silence of this first night outside London was alarming, yet through the window the soft northern night glowed with stars like a field of daisies, and she breathed the clean tangy sea-breeze with a smile. For a time she tussled with the tale Dad had told in the car: when she closed her eyes she kept seeing that funny green ring he was wearing. It sparkled and kept thrusting itself at her active memory — and when she saw it plain and clear the voice from her dream leapt into her mind ...

BEWARD THE EVIL ONE WHO HUNTS YOUR FATHER! WHEN SHE STRIKES FROM THE EMERALD DEPTHS AND HE FALLS ...

Emerald depths! Suddenly wide awake again, she sat up. That's it! she thought with a chill. Emerald depths! The ring! And Madame Pédauque, she must be the Enemy, the evil one! Old Davey saw her just like I did, with those horrible feet. Dad must have seen her like that too, or he wouldn't have told me what her name means. But why's he so helpless with it? Dad, you *must* know what she is! Don't you care? Can't you help it?

Too many questions. Too few answers. At length she fell asleep, and despite the questions she felt quite relaxed, so that when the burning man visited her she wasn't angry or afraid. It was the first time for weeks, and he was no longer horrible. She floated as he blazed and sang his haunting song from the flames ... *Quant lo bouié ben de laura* ... and as she listened in her sleep *she walks in strangely familiar gardens.* And next morning she awoke gently, well rested, the sweet sad melody of his song running like a nourishing brook in her mind ...

For two days they avoided Tir Nan Og.

On Sunday, they toured the lush Inverewe gardens ten miles up the coast. While admiring azaleas and giant Himalayan shrubs Sam and Diane both noted Chrissa's introversion: she said nothing of her dream's return, not a word of her poor burning man and his song, and less still about anything else. And for her part she noted that Dad still wore the ring.

On Monday, Sam drove them north through the timeraddled wilderness of Sutherland, almost to Cape Wrath. He was full of facts all the way, like a talking guidebook.. 'Cape *Wrath* comes from a Norse word, *Hvarf*, meaning "turning-point",' he explained brightly, and Diane was quite happy to let him go on like this, so long as it kept his mind off the darker things she sensed hovering about him. But Chrissa wasn't. 'Why are we just driving around all day like a bunch of wallies?' she complained at lunch in a pub at Scourie. 'There's nothing but bare rock, and I'm sick of it!'

So next day (the destination taken for granted by Sam and Chrissa), they drove the few miles west past the hamlets of Port Henderson and South Erradale to picnic on the sands at Red Point. In the warm sun they sat looking over the water to Skye's Trotternish peninsula. Black cormorants cried from the stacks; fulmar petrels glided above the great green sea; distant ferries glinted to the north, crossing the Minch between Ullapool and Stornoway. But Diane, awaiting the inevitable, could not relax.

Soon it came. 'Let's walk a bit and see what happened to Tir Nan Og,' Sam suggested. Chrissa agreed eagerly, but Diane felt the time-clock tick back yet again. She said she'd pack away the picnic then follow, which she did, though reluctantly and some way behind. The two of them were soon out of sight over a grassy, windswept ridge: by the time she'd climbed it Diane saw them already down at the roofless, thistle-thick pile of stones which was all that remained of Tir Nan Og. The ruin lay in a hollow carved out by a peaty stream, just fifty yards in from the high-water mark. She stood unmoving on the rise. This is close enough, something told her.

'Aren't you coming down?' Sam called up.

'In a minute.' She gestured vaguely. 'There are some lovely flowers here.' And she stooped as if examining the cranesbill and silverweed, the harebell and thyme. But covertly she watched them poke about, feeling like a fool, unable to tell what she feared from the tumbledown stones.

Father and daughter shared a knowing look, a moment of sympathy.

'Maybe she just doesn't like ruins,' said Sam. 'They're too sad.'

'Your Grandad really lived here all his life?' asked Chrissa.

'He hardly ever went away.' Thoughtfully Sam toed the rusted springs of a long-abandoned mattress. He shivered, wondering: Did I sleep on this once? That Christmas? He shook his head impatiently. 'Except when he was in the Argyll and Sutherlands during the First World War.'

Chrissa, perplexed, pushed wind-blown golden-blonde hair back under her blue anorak hood. 'But what did he *do* all his life?' she demanded.

'The same as everyone else round here.' Sam gazed out to sea. 'A bit of this, a bit of that. Stalking in the stalking season, fishing when the weather's right, laying up peat when it's time for that. There's never been money here ... but there's freedom to know your own mind.' And Chrissa saw how, as he spoke, Dad was twisting the ring round and round his finger, apparently without knowing it. 'He had a horse called Fionn.' Sam nodded at another pile of stones from which nettles sprouted. 'That was Fionn's stable. Grandad took me riding once, up to the moors on Christmas Day in 1956. Up to the ... the Fairy Lochs.' He seemed puzzled and nervous as he said this, as if troubled by some newly-returned but still vague memory.

'So?' Chrissa sensed a shadow. 'What happened there?'

But Sam, still playing with the ring as he eyed the vast bare moors, shook his head distantly. Chrissa sighed. She sat on a rock and changed the subject with Diane still hovering on top of the flowery rise.

'Dad, what did you mean about Madame being Mother Goose?'

'What?' Taken aback, he stared at her round, earnest face.

'What you said in the car! About Mrs Goose-Foot! Mother Goose!'

Sam tried to gather his wits. The afternoon was brisk and bright, but suddenly he felt thick, clouded by the past. That ride up to the Fairy Lochs ... *Yes! To the place I like!* He shook his head and, squinting at Chrissa as if not sure of her, sank slowly to his haunches.

'It's nothing much,' he said, staring at the ring as he twisted it round his finger. 'Remember on the black isle how Davey twice thought he heard Madame from her cabin call herself "La Reine Pédauque"? And he saw her with ... goose-feet? And she said she came from Toulouse — in the south of France, right? Okay,' he went on in a slow, troubled voice, 'this might bore you, but stick with it. In French "La Reine Pédauque" — the Web-Foot or Goose-Foot Queen — sounds like "La Reine du Pays d'Oc", meaning Queen of the Land of Oc, which is what that region was called eight hundred years or so ago, before the French did it over like the English did to these parts. The Pays d'Oc had its own language, Occitan, and it had the ... I don't know, the finest culture in Europe, probably. Full of troubadours and poets and freethinkers of the Cathar faith ...' — remotely then he noticed how Chrissa turned pale at this — '... all damned by Rome as heretics.' Why tell her this? he wondered. 'And Toulouse, the greatest city in the Pays d'Oc, was *her* city. The city of La Reine Pédauque ... the Goose-Foot Queen.'

'Do you mean ... like in a fairy tale?' Chrissa whispered, herself now caught in the emerald, staring deep past the moon and horns. In her head the strange singing had begun. 'Was she *real*, like ... like you and me?'

Be careful, she was telling herself. Don't get him suspicious.

Sam shrugged uncertainly. 'Hard to say. Maybe based on someone real, then turned into a myth, like King Arthur or Robin Hood. Or maybe ... maybe there are powers and entities we've denied and forgotten. Maybe ...' — he bit his lip, alarmed by his own words — '...

104

she's the name for another way of things; the queen of a knowledge that church and state have spent two thousand years trying to kill with fire, sword, and derision ...'

'A way buried in the depths? Like on the black isle?'

Chrissa sounded frightened. Sam scowled. I shouldn't talk to her about *fire*, for godsakes! But light flickered beyond moon and horns: his thought was driven out by another. *Tell her! What the hell!* 'Something like that.' His voice dragged as he looked up. Diane still paced up on the ridge, unable to approach, as if prevented by an invisible wall. 'A buried way!' he went on in a flat, hypnotic chant. '... a buried way, for today ... for fire and flood and knowledge of blood ...'

Chrissa flinched. Her head began to sing. She smelled smoke and hot roasting flesh. She saw flame flickering in the emerald depths.

'But ... what happened in the Paydoc?' she asked breathlessly

'Oh,' murmured Sam glassily. 'Her way got too popular. Nobody went to the Pope's church any more. This bothered him so much he made a deal with the King of France. Together they grabbed the land. The armies poured in, the Inquisition was set up by "Saint" Dominic and his black friars, and ...'

'All the goodmen and goodwomen were burned!' Chrissa cried bitterly, loud enough for Diane to hear.

Blinking, Sam looked up. 'What? What did you say?'

Fighting for calm, Chrissa tore her eyes from the emerald depths. 'I don't know!' she yelled — and then her panic increased, for there before her she saw, not her father, but ... *him*. The bald old man in flames, his face a peeled ruin, his flesh bubbling as he stretched his shrivelled claws at her, and in his eyes that desperate appeal. She gasped and shrank from the oily black smoke, retching in pure fear as the whine in her head became the singing, *his* singing, the sweet sad song he sang — *'Quant lo bouié ben de laura'* — and amid her fear she knew then she'd always known it. *'When the herdsman comes home from work'* — yes, in some secret shining recess of her soul that remained untouched by this horror, she knew. It's the *Song of Joana*, and I must not forget how to ...

Then with Diane running down the hill she reeled, dizzily caught in different worlds; she swayed as Sam moved to catch and hold her; she knew fresh horror as at last the burning man actually touched her, and ...

'No!' Diane was there between them. 'Sam, let her be! You've done enough damage. Chrissa, calm down. Come on, both of you. Let's go!'

Nobody said a word as Diane drove them back to Cuilchonich. Both Sam and Chrissa were dazed; the long evening was awkward with unspoken argument and the sense of oppression. Chrissa wouldn't say what had happened, but later, alone in bed, she wept silently. I don't even know who I am! Why is this happening to me? Then, more practically: Is that who he is? A — what? A *Cathar?* From the ... Paydoc? Eight hundred years ago ...? But she was too tired to think, too tired to stay awake. In time she slept.

Meanwhile Diane had persuaded Sam to walk by the shore with her ... but still he refused to remove the ring and throw it away. 'Why are you doing this?' she kept asking. 'Destroy yourself if you must, but leave Chrissa out of it!' Sam couldn't explain. With hands sunk in pockets he shook his head and walked on, staring west into the ruddy midsummer night sky where flame-tinged clouds fought over the ocean like wrathful dragons. Fire and flood! He couldn't contain his dark ferocious glare. Fire and flood! It comes soon! Eternal return, death and rebirth! It's why I'm here, why SHE led Davey to find *you*, he told the ring with a wolfish grin ...

Yes, I know the place you like! he told it as he danced over the dark pre-cambrian shoreline boulders. I wasn't ready before. Now I am! Sam Joyce, you're just a vehicle! There's wider business in the universe than your little ego, so don't shit yourself! And don't worry about Chrissa — it wasn't you she saw, but someone else. Somebody dead a long, long time! But *she* isn't dead, and she won't die at all if you do it right. Fire and flood comes; it always does, but there are ways round everything . . .!

He had no idea what he was on about. For miles along the shore that night he walked through the shadows, yet when at length he returned to Cuilchonich he found Diane long in bed but still awake. Not a word passed between them as he joined her. Next day both he and Chrissa nearly died.

9.
Tide Rising

All night the weather fidgeted. An old moon rose and sulked in cloud; squalls rattled Cuilchonich's windows. Sam and Chrissa slept fitfully amid broken dreams, but Diane slept hardly at all. For hours after Sam came in she lay beside him, her thoughts spinning too fast to seize. Once, when the window rattled, he groaned and shifted in his sleep so that his left hand fell over her belly. She felt the warm hard weight of the bronze and the cooler emerald digging into her; her flesh shrank as if from something radioactive. Maybe that's what it is! she thought fearfully, then mocked herself. Don't be stupid, Diane! It's just his psychological crutch. But Chrissa's beginning to believe it too. Look what happened today. Try it again, she encouraged herself. Get if off him. Throw it away.

She trembled, remembering what had happened in the attic.

Can I do it? she wondered. Could I really? Now?

Then the moment was lost. Sam shifted again, sleeping on with his left hand tucked under his body. In time, despite her dread, she slept too.

Sam awoke first in the morning. His body felt like rusty armour. He ran a bath; as he climbed stiffly into it he began tugging the ring off his finger, then stopped.

'Wear it if you're wearing it!' he scolded himself. 'The problem's in you, not the ring! You moron! You stupid sod!'

An hour later he walked the shore under ragged grey skies, torn by hope and doubt and by an urgent desire that had him looking continually up at the hills. He walked like his feet were trying to go two ways at once. On the way back to the house Mr Macgregor met him and thought him drunk.

'I bid him a civil good morning,' the old man later told his wife, 'and the miserable sassenach just looks right through me. On my own land!'

'But you like the wee lass well enough,' observed Jean Macgregor.

'It's true I wouldn't see harm come to her,' he observed grimly.

'Ian Macgregor, are you saying he's dangerous?'

'No.' He shrugged. 'Maybe just a little fey.'

Meanwhile Sam had returned to Cuilchonich with his mind made up. He found a strained atmosphere in the kitchen. Diane had been trying to get Chrissa to talk, but the girl, staring into a bowl of shredded wheat, would answer only in monosyllabic grunts. With his tight face Sam marched in and straight to the fridge. 'I'm going up to the moors today,' he declared in a surly voice, his back to them. 'On my own. If nobody minds.'

Diane's heart sank, but she refused to show it.

'Let him do what he wants,' she told Chrissa. 'We don't care.'

'Mum,' Chrissa said promptly, 'I want to be on my own today too.'

'Is that such a good idea?' asked Diane in a huff.

'You never let me do anything on my own! Dad ...!'

'I don't like it, Sam,' Diane appealed dangerously.

'Why not?' He slapped sliced ham into sliced bread. 'So long as she's careful.' He half-turned, speaking to Chrissa without meeting her in the eye. 'Don't get caught by the tide or go near edges. If you're up on the top then watch for black peat-hag and places with bright green moss. Avoid them like the plague. Just be sensible, and you'll be okay.'

'This is absurd!' Diane exploded. 'She's much too ... too ...'

'You could go and do some sketching.' Sam shot his wife a dark, lingering look before turning back to making sandwiches. In that look Diane saw disaster approaching. She felt helpless and unreal. Staring in disbelief at her husband and daughter she told herself: I should do something, but what? Scream? Make a fuss? Jump up and down?

In the event she bowed to the situation. Later that morning she watched Sam and Chrissa both set out on their separate ways, though Chrissa wasn't allowed to leave without a supply of sandwiches, a compass, and a map with Cuilchonich clearly marked.

'Don't get wet, and don't be back late,' Diane called unhappily after her. 'And don't do anything silly ...'

Poor Mum! thought Chrissa as she started along the ferny slope above the house. Don't you see I have to be on my own today? I can't stand any more of this! And so she left Cuilchonich, more upset than she'd let on, her face pale, her movements clumsy. Since Tir Nan Og she'd felt detached, like a stranger in her own body. Almost, she thought fearfully, as if really I'm someone else. And for a moment she paused, looking up the slope. Already high above her she saw her father climbing through silver birch scrub towards the crags that fronted the moorland. 'I don't understand any of this,' she muttered. 'Dad, what *are* you up to? Where are you going?'

But soon the twists and turns of her path began to absorb her. The weight that oppressed her gradually lifted: instead a sudden glee filled her. It burst into her as if from nowhere, but she was in no mood to deny it. She shouted at the fresh strong breeze and up at the grey, fast-moving clouds; she began running through ferny glades and over heathery banks, arms spread wide in imitation

110

of a hawk hovering high above. Soon, crossing a broad open slope above the widening bay, she encountered a rowan-fringed burn bubbling down from the moors. Liking this cheerful little stream, she followed it down its steep rocky gully until it plunged under an old stone bridge carrying the Red Point road. Before crossing the road she paused, gulping brisk sea air, finding it hard to believe how her parents and herself had been carrying on. She shook her head impatiently. Not now! Forget it! So she straddled a mossy dyke and continued down the burn's steep banks, the wind rushing through her hair so that soon, caught in a vast exhilaration, she was skidding down the wet black soil with such abandon that she lost her feet. Too late, caution tempered her sense of reckless freedom. Frantically she grabbed at the flaking trunks of stunted silver birches overhanging the burn, but succeeded only in pulling free a streamer of bark as she launched into a terrifying free fall ... to fetch up with a bone-jarring thump on a brief grassy ledge some feet below.

This ledge lay on a spur of rock jutting over a deep dark pool which dreamed under a foaming cascade. Down a long slaty shelf the burn water poured like crystal; below her the pool glimmered with its sun-hidden secrets ... and soon, with the laughing waters to soothe her injured pride, Chrissa knew she'd found her special place. Regaining her breath she sat up and saw how the trees hung all about, the breeze sighing through their topknots as they nodded at her, gossiping among themselves. 'Can I stay here?' she asked, only half in play, and they whispered back: *Well, of course you can!* — at which she smiled and with a sense of perfect lightness, all fears forgotten, she cast herself forward full-length with chin in hands to gaze over the mossy primrose edge down into the pool.

And there he was.

Her burning man, gazing calmly up at her.

She caught her breath ... then slowly relaxed. He was hideous, yes, and maybe she'd gone mad, but she no longer feared his appearance. It wasn't how he looked that scared her now; it was his fate and whatever he wanted from her. So that after a second or so she knew she wasn't even surprised — no, she was delighted, as when something works out unexpectedly right — to see him there, apparently floating just under the surface of the water, his horrible wounds healed by it, and the gown he wore was not in flames but lay placidly round him like a lily. And he was smiling at her.

'*My child,*' he seemed to say softly in her, the wounds of his suffering body like blossoms of blood, '*my sweet child, I bless you.*'

'Who are you?' she asked aloud in a wonderment, again seized by the disturbing sense of inhabiting two worlds simultaneously, 'I mean, I know who you are in my *dreams*, but ... I think I *know* you ... I mean ... *you* know?'

'*So you do.*' Still he smiled. '*But the lower worlds are thick, and it's hard to remember clearly. Soon you will. Start now, if you like!*'

'Remember what?' asked Chrissa reluctantly, for at this talk of memory the fear seized her again, savagely. 'Do I have to?'

'*I suppose you do,*' said the image, '*since you already did.*'

'But that doesn't make any sense!' she exclaimed angrily.

'*I can call you only because you told me how to. Now look!*'

Then despite herself Chrissa looked past him into the deep green depths of the pool ... and abruptly, with no time to wonder what was going on, found herself falling through blinding light into ... into another world.

She's herself. She's not herself. WHO AM I? *Gasping she runs through smoke and dust amid the screams of wounded men; in her tattered and bloody dress she runs under high walls through a crowded courtyard, in her haste slopping water from the wooden bucket she carries. There's a roar and a crash; stone splinters spray her as she throws herself behind a mangled door ... but soon, unhurt, she continues past cursing soldiers and a bearded man shouting about holding the eastern barbican; panting she climbs wooden steps to a covered place where women nurse wounded men. The women wear dirty dusty ankle-length black dresses like hers; they're as tired as she is, but there's no time to complain. Ignoring the hail of small stones flying continually over the walls she kneels, tears another strip from her dress (she seems taller and older) and begins tenderly cleaning the pulped head of a soldier struck by a rock. A tall grey-haired woman calls her by name, and her name isn't Chrissa, it's . . .*

'Look again, child! Look again!'

A shift. A change. In horror she watches, and it's from another place she watches; what place she can't tell. She sees a wild grey mountain dawn. She sees her friends all chained together, herded out of the castle like cattle, forced down the face of the great rock to the stockade at the bottom. They're driven by soldiers in chain mail with the scarlet cross on their white surcoats . . . and there at the bottom wait the faceless ones, robed, hooded in black, holding crosses, begging her friends to recant. Begging begging begging! She feels anguish and fury. Dogs! Swine! Spawn of Jehovah the false creator! But none of her friends answer, and from the dark place where she watches [WHO AM I? WHO AM I?] *she knows it's all part of the plan, though the dogs don't know that! Her friends pray as they're forced into the faggot-high, tinder-dry stockade; as the hooded ones (*You poor deluded slaves! *she tells them icily, silently,* Think you serve God but the Enemy owns you!) *advance behind their crosses, chanting their foul hypocrisies even as flaming torches come looping over the stockade walls.*

*Then she sees him. And he sees her. With his loving eyes he gazes on her even as the flames begin to crackle and roar about him; with his great voice he begins to sing that sweet sad song even as (*I'M BURNING TOO! I'M BURNING TOO!*) she shrieks with horror — but he cries back:*

'Use this, daughter! Use this pain, use this fire, soar on its wings to the Starchamber Gate! See through her night and bring back her day; find your father to kill the Lie; wear the Stone to free yourself; sing the song to quench the fire! Go where the Shining One waits! Go NOW!'

Then everything blazes up through violent flowers of flaming pain into a brilliant whiteness that sings a song of pure creation,

113

and she's in that whiteness, dissolved in it with many worlds and faces swirling round her. And among the faces she sees is Sam's. Screaming. Pleading. Falling.

Then a black abyss. Chrissa passed out above the pool.

'From here you can smell the place the ring likes.'

From Cuilchonich Sam climbed rapidly, following a sheep track through stunted silver birch and dense green bracken, angrily waving his arms at the midges. 'Why's she so upset?' he demanded, but he knew very well, and so on and up he went until the trees were below him and only the bare brows of the wilderness loomed above. The wind stiffened, dispersing the midges and cooling him down. At last he stopped for breath and looked back.

Far below, like a sheet of rippled green glass, the sea-loch widened out to the Atlantic. To the north, beyond the shoreline tourist sprawl of Gairloch village, age-old sandstone crags marched and tumbled in endless fractured waves over the empty land. The view was overwhelming, and Sam sighed, hating the obsession that held him. Biting back his anger he looked for Cuilchonich, but the house was hidden by the trees and by the curve of the slope he'd just climbed. Yet for a moment he glimpsed, down by a stream near the sea, the sky-blue of Chrissa's anorak. She was just above the winding ribbon of the road to Red Point. 'She's not going back to Tir Nan Og after yesterday, is she?' he muttered uneasily. 'Where the hell did she get all that about the Cathars? From her burning man dreams? I don't like it. I don't like it at all.' Distracted, he began twisting the ring round and round his finger. 'Diane's probably right,' he scolded it. 'I shouldn't be wearing you again. I must be mad.'

Yet as he gazed past moon and horns into the emerald depths he was taken again by the old familiar excitement. For a moment he seemed to see Diane in those depths, sulking alone at Cuilchonich, and pain gripped him. Then, remembering his intention, abruptly he turned and continued to the top, wading through fields of springy heather to a long pitch of shattered grey rock.

114

Grimly he trudged up it to a sodden gully until, silhouetted against open sky ahead, he saw something that would have surprised him if he hadn't known where he was going. A rowing boat.

The Fairy Lochs! The place I like! Yesss!

In a turmoil he reached the boat and scanned the placid dark little heart-shaped lochan at his feet — first in a moor-top group of trout-rich tarns locally known as the Fairy Lochs — and the vast moor that opened up beyond its further banks. For mile upon mile the bare, featureless waste ran, all the way to the peaks of north and east and south — An Teallach, Slioch, the steep tumult of the Torridon hills. And as he stared the wind burst into his lungs, exhilarating him ... but bringing memories too. With a frown on his thin dark face he climbed a low eminence and sighted west over the moors to the sound dividing this mainland peninsula from the Hebridean Isles. Storm was moving in on Skye's northernmost ledges from the cloud-black hills of Harris, fifty miles out on the ocean horizon. But he wasn't looking that far as a sudden inner voice made him flinch. *'From here you can smell the place the ring likes.'* Grandad! Breathing fast, he gazed towards Tir Nan Og, hidden five miles away under the western lip of the moor ... and, turning the ring on his finger, he found himself caught back thirty years. Christmas Day 1956! Heart pounding, he examined the bald, fissured rock he stood on. 'Yes,' he muttered, 'It was here! Fionn carried us here. Right here. And Grandad told me ...'

The place the ring likes? He shivered, sensing the abyss he'd feared most of his life. I'm dreaming! he thought as he gazed into the emerald. But I'm here to find it. The place you like. With a disbelieving laugh he pulled a map from his pocket. 'Now be logical!' he told himself crossly, beating the sheet open to locate his position amid the tumbled contour lines. 'First, where are we?' He squinted past the lochan to a crag lying due north. The map called it Sidhean Mór — the Large Fairy Knoll! And right next to the Fairy Lochs! 'That fits,' he said. 'It must be here.' He laughed bleakly. 'You idiot! Running around for years and all the time it's here, like Grandad said. Well, here I stop! But how do I ... *smell* it out? Do you know?' Shakily he tapped the ring. 'I know it's not *you*, it's the ... dowser in me. You just amplify my unconscious biological response to some ... I don't know, natural electro-magnetism which ...'

He shook his head, dismayed by this jabber. Still, he fancied he felt a pull. *Over there!* Yet doubt froze him before he moved a step. This is crazy! What in God's name am I doing? Talking to this ... *thing* ...?

Then rage seized him and sent him muttering into the empty land, his feet taking him where they would. Round about the lochans he strode; in place after place he stopped to gaze into the emerald, but ... nothing. No visions, no message, no thunderclap. Just bare rock, wet wind, endless moor, until in time he was back where he'd started, on the rock above the heart-shaped lochan with rain beginning to spit from fast black cloud above. 'What did I expect?' he demanded, glowering at the approach-ing storm. 'Dad was right! Grandad was full of it! So am I! It's rubbish! It always was! Now back to Cuilchonich before you get soaked, idiot!'

But he couldn't go back. Not yet. There was a tension in him that demanded release — an ancient tension, nothing to do with Diane or his empty present life. It throbbed in him, wanting to burst. He stared into the emerald. Still its depths were vacant. In despair he shook his head at its innocent emptiness. 'Why have we let you obsess us?' he burst out. 'You've driven us mad! For all I know Davey just picked you up in some Moroccan bazaar, but look what's happened! Grandad was crazy, and Dad is too! Wouldn't touch you, no — just withered and made money instead!' Sam nodded wildly. '*And* froze Mum to death because he was already dead inside himself, the cold bloody bastard!' Nodding even more vigorously at the ring, he added: 'He tried to freeze me too! So I was always nuts, you're just an excuse, but was I crazy when Grandad died and ... you got me? I don't think so! I was a model student!' He laughed derisively. 'With Mum out of the way Dad saw to that! Diane,' he cried, for suddenly in the depths he saw her, sleeping under a tree, 'don't you know the curse on the men in this family is a double curse on the women? Roderick's wife was the only sensible one — she left him! And I know you think my Dad's a sweet old man and I should love him, but ... God! You should have seen him whip his only son and heir into shape for the world! *Edinburgh lawyers!* Polar bears have more heart! And he thought he'd done it. So did I, till I got to Durham. Me, an architect! I could have been earning a fortune by now, but the only degree I ever got was a BA in Cosmic Bliss!' He scowled at the ring. 'Is that because I started wearing you? Diane hated you from the start. And when Chrissa came along ...' Falling silent, he realised he'd begun walking inland again, beneath the black spitting sky. I wasn't fit to be a father, he thought morosely. I ran. Maybe I should've stayed away, but I didn't! What I ran into scared me worse than what I ran from.

'I've tried my best,' he declared. 'But it's a lie. A bad joke. Mr and Mrs Muesli who read the *Guardian* and hang onto their caring jobs. Is that it? What happens when GRYP folds? More dead-end jobs or no jobs at all! Chrissa knows it's junk. That's one reason she's acting the way ...'

Suddenly, right at his feet as he trudged round the lochan's sodden verge, movement exploded and he jumped in shock as a brace of ptarmigan burst from the heather, croaking hoarse alarm and whirring away in a blur of mottled brown. 'So what am I meant to do?' he cried angrily after them even as the rain got heavier. Away over the lochan they winged into the mists as the storm began in earnest, instantly icing his cheeks and soaking his cheap parka right through. Soon like a black shroud the storm wrapped him as he staggered on, until again he thought of turning back. No! The wet and cold suited his mood exactly! And he assured himself he'd be okay so long as he stuck to the high ground.

117

So he continued round the lochan through the wet grey murk, avoiding a dangerous sink of bog as he started up the rocky height of Sidhean Mór. Soon he reached a shelf of spongy ground on which lay a random spread of glacial boulders. He was already past them when something alerted him. An itch in his bones. A tingling excitement. He stopped, staring at the boulders and the space they defined. Slowly he realised that maybe their placement was not so random. Slowly, as the tingling in his bones (and especially in his left index finger) grew more energetic, he realised:

I've found it! I've found the place the ring likes.

He hesitated, his mouth suddenly as dry as the rest of him was wet. He stared at the place, afraid. On his finger the emerald sparkled.

Come on! Don't hang back now! It's time!

Step by step, storm-lashed, he entered that place.

So abstracted by what she'd seen that she almost left her satchel behind, Chrissa set off up the burn, bypassing the falls, moving from rock to rock in a sort of trance, ducking low boughs without even seeing them and letting her feet choose the best route. For a time after coming out of her faint (hours must have passed: the day was darker, storm approached) her body felt odd, somehow not big enough. This feeling wore off, but her mind remained caught up in the mysterious, dreadful familiarity of what she'd ... not just *seen*, but *experienced* — the pyre, the castle, the brute soldiers, the black-robed beasts like something out of ... where had she seen them before? In a film? On telly? Surely something like that! She felt no terror, rather a dreamlike perplexity that persisted as she reached and crossed the Red Point road. 'But it all happened long ago,' she murmured, 'and I was there, in the Paydoc or whatever it's called, and he was ... oh, it's *stupid!*' And she tossed her head angrily, blonde hair whipping in the wind as she left the trees and climbed the open slope towards a lone rowan tree higher up the burn. 'I dream too much, just like old Miz Jackson always says. That's it, isn't it?' She stopped, gazing down into water foaming down between mica-flecked boulders. 'I'm imagining it, aren't I!'

'Don't you think it odd,' babbled the water, 'that a girl should talk to a stream and imagine it talking back to her?'

'No, I don't! Zillions of people pray to a god they can't even see or hear, and nobody finds *that* odd!'

The water just laughed as it went on its way.

'You think it's funny, do you?' she demanded.

'I don't think,' trilled the water, 'I just join the sea.'

'Oh, all right then! Go and join it, and good riddance!'

But then she turned and saw just how the burn fell through the woods, past her dreaming pool to the wide, isle-flecked loch and the broad ocean beyond, and she sensed patterns of dazzling, dancing whiteness in which all things flowed together ... and vaguely, without definition, she recalled the last part of her experience by the pool, lost in the shining light. She saw Sam falling, plunging into an abyss, his face a scream. She started, and abruptly the wind grew chill as the sun vanished altogether behind the approaching storm.

It's going to pour, she realised. I must get back.

But her feet obeyed another command. On she went ... and as she neared the lonely rowan tree she saw a woman asleep beneath it, curled up against its trunk. In disbelief she stopped and stared.

It's Mum! What's she doing here?

She opened her mouth to speak ... but something made her hold her tongue and continue without waking Diane. In an increasing confusion she climbed on, zipping up her anorak against the rising wind, frequently looking back. 'This is nuts!' she told herself fearfully. 'He's probably back already. Anyway, how would I find him? Come on! I'll go back and wake up Mum!'

But her feet kept moving up as mists of storm — black sheets stretching from heaven to earth — swallowed the mouth of the sea-loch and came feeling towards her as at last she reached the bare high lip of the vast moor. She looked, and its endlessness of water and rock appalled her. For mile upon mile it ran to a dark turbulence of distant peaks. From her satchel she took out map, compass, and sandwiches, then as she ate she fought the wind to open the map, but the contours and unpronounceable Gaelic names baffled her. And the compass wasn't working right; its needle hunting round the dial without coming to rest. As far as she could tell she was near a hill called Sidhean Mór. 'Probably just means Black Rock, or something,' she told herself unhappily ... even as the storm, preceded by a sudden cold gust, reached her. Hastily she put away the map and pulled up her hood as the first heavy drops plummeted. In seconds the rain was torrential. Angry panic seized her. 'Stop this nonsense!' she shouted at herself, stamping sodden trainer-shod feet. 'How'll I ever find him in this? Go back now!'

Then again she sensed that sweet dazzling light in her, bringing calm clarity. Look, it said. And through curtains of cloud, motion caught her eye. Even as she saw their lean grey shapes, the deer scented her and took to flight ... and as they vanished into the storm she knew them for her sign. She didn't question this. In dreamlike mood she followed them until, soaked through, she came to the ridge where they'd been. Now the murk was so thick she could see no more than a dozen yards in any direction. 'I'm lost,' she said in a dazed voice, and dully she trudged on, no longer sure what she was doing — until without warning the ground gave way and she found herself floundering knee-deep in a black mire. 'What *is* this?' she screamed, pulling herself out, turning round and round as panic surged, 'I don't even know if Dad's in trouble, but I am!'

For an instant the wind-driven cloud broke. Through its shreds she saw a rain-beaten sheet of water below her. And more. For, vague above the further bank of the lochan, she saw one particular shape amid what looked like a random tumble of boulders. Motionless, just another boulder. But —

'Dad!' she cried desperately. 'Dad! Sam! Is that you?'

Only the wind replied. Yet as the murk closed in she

began to run with reckless abandon, down and round the lochan, leaping from one half-seen tussock to the next. She was near the spot she'd seen when the cloud again parted and showed it. She stopped dead. 'Dad!' she screamed, now afraid not only for herself ... for there he was, not twenty yards away, standing as stiff and still as the rocks surrounding him. He was facing away from her, but she knew his parka and blue balaclava. And there was something else.

Something vague, indistinct, inhabiting the lower tendrils of the dirty grey cloud. Something like a host of sour thick fireflies, blood-red and dancing with sluggish menace round him so that he seemed to be on fire.

And the rocks ... she saw black-robed figures, glaring facelessly at her.

'GO AWAY, LITTLE BRAT!' she heard, 'GET LOST! DROP DEAD!'

'Dad!' she screamed. 'You're in terrible danger! Wake up!'

But he didn't even twitch as the cloud closed in again.

Abandoning caution she rushed forward. Blindly leaping a bank, she came down feet first into the level mossy sink the other side. Black mud fountained and she found herself swamped, sinking in a mire like treacle.

She struggled. Her feet found no bottom.

'Dad! Dad! Dad! Help me! I'm sinking!'

He didn't hear. He didn't move. She could almost touch him, but he didn't hear! She lunged for firm ground but found it out of reach as the effort sank her inches deeper. The cloud parted again. Now the stinging, darting blood-red lights had completely enveloped him. Drowning, she saw her father transformed into a writhing field of unearthly fire ... and amid that fire she clearly saw the dripping scarlet face, the empty midnight eyes, the flowing raven hair of a woman who smiled mockingly at her.

'I warned you not to listen to the Weak Ones!' crowed the Enemy.

Chest-deep in the mire, Chrissa screamed:

'DAD! SAM JOYCE! HELP ME!'

10.
On the Whole Place

Fearfully, with a sense of fatal commitment, Sam had entered that space irregularly defined by the thirteen (he counted them) weather-worn, lichen-scabbed boulders. Half-buried in heather they crouched round him like bent old men. Shielding his map from the rain, he looked vainly for the glyph designating a megalithic site. But no building or human remain whatsoever was charted up on this moor ... and as he faced his situation a wild humour blossomed in him. 'You're not mapped!' he cried jubilantly at the rocks, emerald light dancing in his eyes as the wind tore at him. 'You're like the black isle! Subversive! Without official reference!' Then, staring into the jewel, he sobered up. 'Is this the right place? What now?'

Can't you feel it? And yes, he could. The rain lanced out of low, fast-moving cloud; by now his parka was a sodden weight ... but it didn't matter. The tingling glow had spread through him as he laughed; now it warmed his bones and sang in his head. He shuddered in its exuberant vibration; began capering a clumsy dance as it moved through and beyond him, tenting him in a green light shot through with wriggling fire-wraiths that steadily increased in brightness. Bemused, he realised that these worms of light were dancing into and out of his body, blurring his physical edges. It was getting hard to tell where his body ended and the exterior glow began. He saw flashes, as if unseen veils were being struck apart by lightning; an exhilaration seized him as bright familiar landscapes (where had he seen them before?) rippled in his mind. So he danced and cheered the storm; he opened his mouth and drank the rain; he spread his arms and rode the wind; he glowed with a fiery warmth ... then, for a moment, at the limit of vision, he glimpsed a line of grey shapes in flight along a ridge the far side of the lochan. Deer, he realised, and his ecstasy faltered.

Diane! he thought. Chrissa ...

WHO ARE YOU? roared a sudden huge voice in him. *WHY ARE YOU HERE?*

It was an utter shock. Savagely struck, he staggered, and as he did he saw that the rocks about him had transformed into a company of shimmering, shining beings. Again the question roared in him. He couldn't answer. He could only stare. About him they stood, unutterably strange, watching him gravely. His eyes fixed on one then another, his reason overwhelmed. And most fearful was that each, though perfectly visible, was also an opening through which he glimpsed the most bizarre and stupendous scenes. *Here*, a stern naked man, hairless and blue with a cockerel head; through him showed a deep rift in the earth with flame and smoke shooting up from it, human faces screaming in it. And *here* an imperial woman (stars on her brow, her hair like coiling green vine) whose gaze made him cringe; and through her he saw some strange vast dance taking place between three great spheres of light, apparently suns in space, golden and violet and silver, whirling and looping in complex spirals and figures of eight. And next to her, *here*, a hairy cloven-hooved man, his slit eyes filled with merry and dangerous lechery as he danced to the tune of the pipes he played, and through him, in colour so vivid and primal that Sam gagged with nausea, a terrible scene of murder and rape on the viridian jungle banks of a vast slow blood-red river coiling under a crimson sky. Then, *here*, a hideous old crone, and what Sam saw through *her* gate he could not, did not wish to, understand. Next to her glowered an angry red warrior, his chest like a furnace and his thighs like gateposts, whose horned and jealous gaze held murder. *WE ARE THE WATCHERS!* the voice of this warrior bellowed in him, *AGAIN: I ASK WHY ARE YOU HERE? ANSWER!* But, still unable to speak, his gaze whirled round them ... until at last he found himself facing Madame.

Madame, robed in the majesty of blood.

He met her midnight eyes and dizziness seized him.

'*I am La Reine Pédauque!*' Her voice sang; her eyes were like black suns; bloody fire dripped from her. '*Here you'll find a key to what's lost — but be quick: I cannot endure this weight for long.*' Then she opened her arms, her legs, and the dizziness swallowed him into a roaring tumult.

He found himself in that dark stone chamber, facing the three who sat round the table, gorgeous in their robes, their faces so bright he had to drop his gaze. Yet he sensed, strangely, that he knew them. '*Who is this?*' asked one, and another answered, '*The great-grandson,*' and the third asked sadly: '*Has it taken so long?*' The first said: '*He rejected us before,*' and the second asked: '*Then how do we show him what he needs to remember?*' The third said: '*We start where he stopped the last time.*' And they gazed on him, too bright to face ... but even as his skull again roared with that violent dislocation he still had the sense that he knew at least two of them, particularly the golden-haired woman who sat in the middle ...

Then abruptly he was somewhere else.

Staggering in the desert night.

He screamed like a beast in pain.

'*Don't flinch!*' Madame cried from the storm. '*This is memory of that night you ran away from me: when your "friend" tore the ring from you and your fear told you I'm only illusion. Now we can start again!*'

But again he screamed, scourged by flying sand as he staggered into the Saharan night, thrashing his arms against the stinging wind, overwhelmed by visions he

124

couldn't face. 'REMEMBER YOUR TASK!' howled the wind, 'STEP THROUGH THE GATE!' Yet whichever way he tried to escape the wind slapped him, tormenting him, driving him to his knees amid darkness redeemed only by the ring's blazing emerald depths. And in those depths he saw her, and her alone. *'Do you know who we are?'* she cried. *'Have you forgotten the whole place, the place of moon and horns? Have you forgotten the Watchers? Wake up! The time of fire and flood is near, the Shift approaches again, and if you Lullu can't rise above it this time then we're lost too. Get off your knees! Step through the gate. We're caught too, the Shining Ones won't listen! Don't you remember? We came down to raise you, but time and gravity caught us, flesh took us and slowed us. And where once you Lullu thought us gods and demons, now you won't even see or hear us any more! You've turned us into shadows in your dreams, you explain us away as mad delusion — do you wonder we prey on you? We have only the substance you give us! We've lost the weight to carry flesh, and flesh is needed to act upon this earth. That's why I need you! If the tragedy's to be averted we must take flesh again — in YOUR age, in the last days! But for this we must meet in the time when I had a body — which means you come through the gate to me. You must witness me in seed and in flesh! I need you to bring me strength; I need you to help me persuade the Shining Ones to relent!'*

'Get away!' he croaked. 'Get away from me!'

'You must remember! Look up and remember!'

In despair he gave in. Cupping his eyes against the storm he opened them and looked up, and through the storm he saw the stars. Hard and sharp and pure they shone, and the sight of them filled him with hate. So serene they floated, while down here the world flayed him. There was a gulf, and himself the wrong side, trapped in time and weight and matter. He glared at Sirius and the Seven Sisters. Oh, you're so fine! he cried silently, remembering without knowing what or how. But what about us? You sent us down here and left us to rot in the flesh we took. You blamed us for your own mis-judgement, you left us here to perish when the Shift comes again. You could stop it, but you won't. Damn you! Damn you! Damn you!

And whether it was his voice or hers he had no idea, nor did he hear another voice that hissed in him: 'FOOL! DON'T LET HER DARK SIDE ENCHANT YOU! LOOK BEYOND THE LIE!' — for even as he shrieked at the sky a great black wing overwhelmed him, sweeping him away as her voice, grown dark with time and melancholy, cried out again. *'Yes, they imprisoned us! They locked us up and condemned us here, and soon the Shift will finish us all! You MUST remember your mission and come through . . .'*

'THE SHIFT?' Was that his own voice? 'WHAT'S THE SHIFT?'

Then another hammerblow, another dislocation.

And he forgot.

He'd forgotten already.

He had no idea what had happened.

Whatever it was, it was on a scale too vast and terrible to comprehend. All he knew, as the wind tore at him, was that the high tide kept rising far beyond its former limits. With the ring on his finger he fled, fled inland beneath the fire-shot, ashen sky, a mad disquietude in his heart as the waters rose steadily behind him. He had confused memories, if that's what they were, of laying low for what seemed for ever in a stony dockside vault as the fire and ash rained down. Now, bent double against the gale, he staggered through the smashed countryside, through wrecked farmyards and burned cornfields, past fluttering birds charred out of the ashen sky, kicking his way through the hot grey ash that lay a foot deep everywhere. Once, crossing a dried-up stream bed, he kicked into a rotting mass, half-buried, that gave way sickeningly. With a shudder he pulled back his foot even as he knew what he'd kicked; the remains of a man and a woman, melted together. They must have retreated to the stream when it still held water, and stayed there by preference even as the steaming water began to boil them into one flesh. A true marriage! Perhaps they'd perished already; he hoped so. And so on and on he fled through the growling uproar of a world in chaos, running from the loudest sound in all that catastrophic bedlam; the hungry bellow of the ocean's no longer bounded waters. In time he reached an open, cindered slope, with the suggestion through the bloody murk of high hills ahead; he began climbing and didn't dare stop until, choking and sneezing and cursing, he met what once had been a rushing cold mountain torrent. Now there was no more than a trickle of warm mud. Yet it was liquid, so he stripped off his rags and bathed, soon drowsing into an exhausted near-sleep, and as he lay there he looked back the way he'd come and saw how, for hundreds of miles, the sea was overwhelming the low places, slowly surrounding and smothering the land, or pouncing quickly up river beds in a foaming welter of black water. Far to the south a great city burned, but as the sea continued rising, that wide isle of flame divided into a multiplying archipelago of many lesser fires which in time were put out, extinguished into watery blackness ...

He could no longer laugh or cry or feel anything at all. He stared into the emerald depths of the ring he wore, and from it she eyed him with chill sardonic humour. *'THAT'S the Shift, my friend!'* she whispered. *'That's the early days of fire and flood to come — unless we do something about it. Do you want to live to see it happen? Then do nothing! Ignore me, dismiss me as delusion, go back to your wife and daughter, lose the game and live to regret. For you'll live, that I promise! The vision is true! My power may have declined through time and weight, but I know what'll happen. For those who order worlds have reached a decision about THIS world which isn't to your advantage, nor to mine! I didn't go to all that trouble with your great-grandfather for nothing! It was difficult possessing Madame, and it almost killed her. But the isle came up just as I'd seen — and there we are with the ring! It proves we'll get to the Starchamber just as I've planned! So come through now! Join me! Remember the whole place? No? Yes? Well, make up your mind, don't keep me waiting! It's time for the Horned One to rise! Isn't loving better than losing? Come through, NOW!'*

And so then, sighing amid the fire and flood, he submitted at last to the blazing emerald depths, and ...

It's time. Soon, very soon, the Horned One arises from Her vulva that the Children newly carved in Her eastern hills. On the high whole place he stands alone, naked, ready, waiting. He has eaten the vision-food that dismisses flaccid fear. He is painted in the black-and-silver. He wears the horns of Bull-That-Roars. The equinoctial evening is chill up here, but it's not that which makes him tremble. The dusk is falling, and far below many of the Children also wait. Some were birthed in this new land, but most have come great distances — across the Narrow Sea and along Her rivers, over Her mountains and through the depths of Her thick tangled woods. Along Her myriad green veins they've journeyed here to take part in this high rite of the year's rebirth. They've come to acclaim the rising of the fire in Her depths below this holy whole place, they're here to celebrate Her annual fertilis-ation by the Horned One. Yes, He'll rise, and She'll receive, and so She'll come to bless the year ... if all goes well. If. Always if. Thus in a great circle through the woods round the base of this place they wait, and though some are calm in deep trance, others are nervous, looking anxiously up at the lone naked bull-horned man who stands atop the rocky whole place — the man chosen to play His role tonight. What if he fails? Certainly he wears His horns, he has eaten the skin of the spotted toad to banish all weakness and fear ... but disasters are not unknown; fate is unreliable. Do not fail! many men of the Children beg him silently. We have enough troubles already, what with Her war against the Old Ones and Her cruel new mood of sacrifice and greed.

And where he stands he hears their thoughts, for the vision-food has sharpened his senses, and it is atop Her place he stands, above Her waiting fires, at the centre of a vast web of earth-heat — trembling, shifting and ever-alive. Through him shivers the anticipation of the hills; he feels the eager stirring of woods and deep lush valleys; he's aware of all Her life that lives and moves and breathes, from the hot slow rocks below to the airy skies above, for he is in Her and he belongs to Her; his fate is spun and fixed already ... but he has eaten the skin of the toad to make sure that he doesn't think too much about it ...

As for the Red Woman who takes Her part, the priestess who even now climbs to the whole place with her maidens, she too belongs to Her.

Only ... it is different for her daughters. Very different. And what might have been a prick in him of doubt or fear is banished by the great heart-cry that rises as the Children greet the Red Woman's arrival. Just in time too; as much as anything their cry is one of huge relief ... for the silver glow in Her vulva heralds His imminent appearance.

The Red Woman leaves her ornaments with her maidens and comes to him. Hot and dry, he stands up straight and hard, his fire ready to burst, for she wears only the blood of the Mother, dug from deepest earth-womb. Her great strong body is coated entirely in it. Only the smooth olive oval of her face and the jet-black flood of her hair is free of the red ochre. And now with her great dark eyes fixed on him she stands before him ... yet it was then, as the new moon began its rise, that he felt sudden disquiet, a sense of otherness, of unholy resistance ...

'O Horned One!' cries the Red Woman, facing past him towards Her distant notch where the silver glow rises. 'My fields are ripe for seed! My woods are ripe to bud! My waters are ripe to spawn, and My heart will surely burst if I'm not fulfilled! O Horned One!' she cries, raising up her dripping red hands, offering her breasts from which Mother's Blood runs. 'Now You rise! Now You're born again! Ride through My gates and fill Me with Your silver seed! Bring sweet life to My loins! Lift Your high proud head, O Horned One! Pierce Me with your point; stamp and roar and charge; pour Your horn of plenty into My depths!'

Then with her ebony eyes on him the Red Woman lays herself down on the hard black rock of the whole place; she opens her thighs and shows him her gate even as the tip of His shining-bright horn slids up above Her crack in the east: his own horn awakens and rises to the invitation of Her fire as the song of the Children swells up the height. And shivering hard he roars at the sight of Her, but —

He starts to move to Her, then stops, frowning. Something is false; something's wrong; he's taken by the inexplicable sense of being in two places at once. Her eyes flash angrily at his hesitation. 'Quick!' she demands. 'What keeps you? He has risen!' And yes, the Horned One's fire is ablaze in him, silver and hard, it's time and past time, the moment's nearly over-ripe

— it's time to act! Roaring again, he —

'Dad! You're in terrible danger! Wake up!'

He turns, startled. Only a whisper, but sharp, stabbing with urgent familiarity, reminding him what happens to heroes who plunge through Her gate. And the song of the Children falters at the terrible sight of the man in the god-mask doing nothing, just standing there high above them, the epitome of ill-omened limpness.

'What's the matter with you?' *She beckons urgently, angrily, for He has almost left Her eastern notch.* 'You'll bring disaster upon us!'

'Dad! Dad! Dad! Help me! I'm sinking!'

And everything shifted. For an instant the world fell dizzily apart. He found himself in a bare land, standing soaked and frozen amid a violent storm in odd thick clothing of unknown material. All around old boulders eyed him blankly, confusing him with the sensation that —

Reaching furiously up, the Red Woman seizes him by the wrists and pulls him down to the heat of her thighs. 'Will you spurn Me now and listen to false weak voices?' *she demands furiously, her black eyes blazing.* 'Charge My gate, you Bull, you Thief, you Fool! Will you deny Me? Come through!'

'DAD! SAM JOYCE! HELP ME!'

Shuddering stiff and afraid in his sodden clothes he turned. *The Red Woman howls in frustration as* he saw through a rent in the cloud how, only yards away, there was a girl ... drowning in a mire. A girl? CHRISSA! MY DAUGHTER! *Amid the wailings of the Children and against Her fury he tears himself away from the whole place, from that ancient time, and in him is huge relief (for what is to happen after the rite?) and frightful regret.* 'Chrissa, don't struggle, you'll only go down faster!' he tried to shout, *but She won't let him go so easily*; only a croak came out; he felt unseen fingers nipping his throat, his wrists, his feet; he felt the emerald trying to pull him back to Her; he felt the thirteen ancient Watchers hemming him in as agitated blood-red light-wraiths whirled round his head.

130

Then Chrissa screamed again:

'DAD! I'M GOING TO DIE! HELP ME! HELP ME!'

Making a supreme effort, he burst out of the prison.

'Chrissa, I'm coming!' he roared. 'Don't move! Keep still!'

Yet even as he found his voice and leapt through the rain down to the sink that now had her up to the shoulders, *he's attacked again, for the sight of Chrissa's desperate mud-plastered face reminds him of a fearful event in this world of moon and horns where he belongs — of a sacrifice in a dark underground place, and himself the chief actor. He shudders to a stop amid cruel laughter; instead of Chrissa's fear-white face he sees the Red Woman before him, smiling triumphantly from her bath in the bog of red mud. Spreadeagled on her back, naked. Showing her webbed feet . . .*

'You're not much,' she whispers, 'but you'll have to do.'

Clapping horrified hands over his eyes, Sam screamed.

It was then Chrissa came closest to losing her reason. There she was, drowning inch by inch, and there was her father, only feet away . . . but so far from pulling her out he was on his knees at the edge of the bog, rocking back and forth with his face hidden miserably in his hands, whimpering like a scared child. Yet flickering over his head in the rain were those foul writhing blood-red lights, and even in her extremity she knew: It's not me he saw at all! She's still got him! 'DAD, IT'S ME, CHRISSA!' she wailed. 'PLEASE HELP ME!' But her exertion sank her deeper, to her neck. The mud filled her nostrils with its stench. 'DAD, IT'S ME, NOT WHAT YOU THINK YOU SEE!' she cried in despair. 'GET ME OUT OR YOU'LL NEVER GET OUT YOURSELF!'

Through his terror he heard her. Jerkily, fighting hard, he tore his hands from his eyes. He saw her, and his eyes widened. 'Get away!' he hissed, but not at her, and his body tensed, his back arched; his pupils rolled as he showed his teeth. 'FUCK OFF!' he bellowed, ripping the ring from his finger, aiming to throw it far away . . . but then he shuddered and thrust it into a pocket instead.

131

Chrissa moaned. I'm dying, she thought incredulously. I'm dying! 'Okay!' Sam cried then, rocking dangerously far forward on his half-sunk knees. 'Keep calm! Give me your left hand slowly and I'll have you out!' And he laughed , eyes glittering as he stretched out his right hand, shaking with the effort of a fight he hadn't yet won. *Blinding black wings beat in his head; angry voices shriek in him and he shrieks back* as Chrissa carefully inched her slimy left hand closer to his clutching fingers, the motion sinking her up to her chin ... but still their fingers didn't quite meet. 'You want me alive!' he howled as he rocked forward on sinking knees, 'then help me get her out or I'll go too.'

Their fingers touched, tried to hook, slipped apart.

Again he lunged. His knees slipped deeper into the mire. 'Careful, Dad!' she gasped, and mud slimed into her mouth. Gagging, she heaved herself sideways, and this time he caught her by the wrist, grunting with effort, teetering over the bog as he grabbed backwards with his left hand and scrabbled, and clutched, and finally held onto wiry heather. 'You're NOT my owner yet!' he roared, a mad grin on his face as he began to pull his daughter to safety. 'You can't have it all your own way!'

There was no reply. But the ring was still in his pocket.

Soaked in filth and freezing they staggered away through the storm round the heart-shaped lochan to partial shelter under a dripping moss-thick overhang of rock. There for a time they lay, exhausted, eyeing each other in sheer disbelief. Sam, still unsure which world he inhabited, was now further confused, for Chrissa's mud-caked face displayed not only utter relief but pity too. 'Dad,' she hissed through chattering teeth, 'you'd *never* have got out if I hadn't been drowning, would you? I was *screaming*, and you didn't even hear me! She wouldn't let you, would she? She ...'

'*She?*' He glared in terror. 'What do you mean, She? Who?'

Chrissa bit her lip and stared silently into the murk.

'What were you doing up here anyway, Chrissa?'

'Looking for you!' she blurted out.

'What do you mean?' Fury and fear and pain all flooded him at once. 'How could you know where I was?'

She burst into tears of exhaustion. 'Dad, promise me you'll never come here again! I nearly died, and so did you, because ...'

But suddenly she clamped her mouth shut and stared away with a frown, heeding an inner voice that told her not to say too much. Sam matched her frown, but his bones ached and his weariness was too great to be worrying about what she knew and how. Aw ... Christ! he thought.

Tired? asked a sympathetic little voice. *Cold? It's easy!*

But even as his hand crept into the pocket where the ring lay Chrissa sensed it and grabbed his wrist. 'Come on, Dad, let's get back before we both catch horrible colds,' she whispered hoarsely, again disconcerting him by the pity in her gaze. And more than pity. In her pale blue eyes shone a light he'd not seen before — a knowing light, as if her ordeal had proved her in some test ... and there was something about the shape of her face, the jut of her jaw, that ... She tugged at him fiercely. 'Please don't put it on your finger again!' Again she pulled at him. 'Take me home! Please?'

Badly shaken, he let her lead him away from the place the ring liked. In him was a feeling of amputation, as if some important part of his mind and being had gone astray. His feet felt like lumps of concrete; his sense of direction had vanished. With their heads lowered Chrissa led them on, and as they trudged on down to Cuilchonich through the gale his hand went surreptitiously into his pocket and found the ring. After a while he cleared his throat and like a scared child asked his daughter:

'What are we going to tell Mum?'

11.
The Watchers

Diane never recalled much about that day. After Sam and Chrissa left she got in the Volvo and drove the narrow twisting road to Gairloch with bitter speed, until a near-collision with a Range Rover sobered her up. More carefully she continued over the moors to Poolewe's tropical gardens, where she fled the dollared accents and sought refuge in a fragrant cool rhododendron grove. But soon enough self-disgust had her up on her feet. This is absurd! she scolded herself. I'm hiding here! Why? They just went out on their own. Why should anything happen?

She returned to Gairloch to shop in the general store, then walked the white sands a long way out. Yet the fresh offshore wind didn't exorcise her sense of catastrophe, and when at three o'clock (*only three?*) she got back to Cuilchonich, she found the house empty. Of course.

After an hour of domestic fidgeting she forced herself out for a walk. The uncertain sun was playing hide-and-seek with dark ranks of advancing cloud as she started, climbing a track which led her through bracken and birchwood and then, unexpectedly, into a grove of old Scots pine. It was peaceful there, but still she couldn't relax. On she went, eyes skinned for any sign of Chrissa. Sam Joyce, you take care of yourself! she told him angrily, wounded inside as she emerged onto a wide bare slope, but the view of the western sea began to unknot her. With the wind getting up she came to a burn, its water foaming down the rocky gully it had carved out over many centuries. Here grew a solitary rowan tree, bent but not defeated, and with a sigh, telling herself she'd rest just a little while, she flopped down under its sparse foliage, her back to its smooth grey trunk. Only then she realised how tired she was. It's London, she thought. You live on your nerves and don't realise what it does to you. And for a time, reassured by the tree's lonely strength, she gazed out over the cloudy western sea. Her thoughts dissipated into that vast distance. With a slow long yawn she exhaled her tension, forgetting the gathering storm as she lay in that sheltered hollow ... and soon she was asleep, glasses drooping on her nose, her worn face at last peaceful. And when Chrissa came up past her she knew nothing about it at all.

Hours later she awoke.

She awoke shivering, soaked to the skin, utterly disorientated.

In a panic she got to her feet and faced about through the pouring rain. The murk was so thick she could see nothing but the rowan, ghostly above her. Wild-eyed, teeth chattering, she tried to calm down. Where am I? Remembering the burn, she slid down the bank and almost into the water before she saw it. It'll get me down to the road! she realised. I'll be all right if I follow it. I hope to God they're back!

Thirty minutes later her relief at getting back to Cuilchonich turned to dread when she found the house still empty. They'll be back soon, she persuaded herself. She laid and lit the fire, stripped off her clothes, towelled herself dry. By the time she'd put on clean clothes and poured herself a drink it was almost eight o'clock and as black as night outside with rain lashing the roof and streaming down the windows. Don't panic! Do something! So she began making a shepherd's pie. An hour later it was ready, but neither of them was back to eat it. Dull before the fire she sat, staring into the merry flames, twisting hands and biting tongue to stave off the horrors

... Chrissa mangled at the foot of a cliff ... Chrissa drowned, slack with seaweed in her hair and crabs at her eyes ... Chrissa lost in the storm and stumbling into a bog ... 'Sam Joyce, what have you done?' she cried, unable to bear it, squeezing her head between her hands as she muttered: 'But it's my fault too. I shouldn't have let her go. I should have been firmer. But how can I be what I'm not!'

It was nine fifteen. She struggled into mac and wellies as the mad rattle of storm-black windows told her the clock was almost back to zero. She put the guard on the fire and turned down the oven. She scrawled a message on the telephone pad. PIE IN OVEN. BACK SOON — D.

Outside she could hardly stand against the wind and rain. With bowed head she staggered down the sodden track to the Macgregor's bungalow.

Ian Macgregor was locally known as a sound man, discreet, and not one to broadcast other folk's problems. That night and not for the last time Diane had cause to be grateful. For when she knocked and he opened his door, he saw her distress and made no fuss; he just put on his boots and waterproof, got a lamp and his crook, whistled up the dog, and saw her up to Cuilchonich. 'We'll see,' was all he said ... and he let nothing show when they got there to find her husband and daughter in the kitchen. Safe back. Both exhausted. Both plastered head to foot in stinking black mud, both wolfing platefuls of steaming pie as if their lives depended on it. Quite a sight. 'Where have you been?' cried Diane, relieved and angry and embarrassed all at once. Without a word and all but unnoticed he left them to it. Yet for a moment as he went he caught the girl's eye and what he saw disturbed him. 'A look I did not like at all,' he told Jean later. 'That lass knows things she shouldn't. Ah, but maybe that's the South for you. Who can tell?' And Jean eyed him sceptically. *Maybe it's just your hot old eye she saw too much about*, thought Mrs Macgregor.

But neither he nor Jean told anyone about it, and

when some days later the press came knocking and calling they said as little as they had to on the subject of events they were rumoured to have witnessed, maybe.

They ate like hogs, dripping black mud on the floor, on their plates, everywhere. And their faces! Appalled, she paced helplessly. 'Look at the pair of you!' But though neither spoke they eyed each other with looks she could not read, and that ... thing was still on his finger. Something burst inside her; she rushed upstairs to run a bath into which, a half-hour later, she directed Chrissa. The girl was already asleep at the kitchen table and had to be woken up; she didn't protest as Diane washed her like a baby. 'But what happened?' Diane asked. And with closed eyes Chrissa mumbled something about Dad saving her life. With that Diane had to be content: soon Chrissa was in bed and out like a light. Steeling herself, Diane went downstairs again. But Sam, who'd merely eyed her blankly as she chivvied Chrissa up to the bath, was no longer in the kitchen.

She found him asleep in the living-room. Still wet through, he lay sprawled in a chair by the fire, his left hand dangling, fingers slack and open. She saw the emerald, flashing in the firelight. Her heart came to her mouth. *Now!* she thought. He's completely out! And very carefully, watching his face, she got down on her knees in front of the fire. She touched his knee. He didn't stir. Tentatively she lifted the fingertips of his left hand. Still he didn't stir. She drew breath. She eyed the emerald depths, then shook her head and looked away. Bolder, she gripped his wrist firmly. There was still no reaction. Feeling giddy, she drew quick breath ... and then took hold of the ring.

Sam bellowed. He shot to his feet as if electrified, throwing her hard against the fireplace, stunning her as he lurched across the room with arms waving over his head. Then he stopped. He turned and glared at her, his eyes bloodshot and strange. She didn't recognise Sam in them.

He's going to kill me, she thought, curiously unafraid.

'Sam,' she said from where she lay on the hearth, 'don't you think you should get out of those wet clothes and take a bath?'

The fury left him. Puzzled, he shook his head.

'Yes,' he said quietly. 'A bath. I fell asleep, Diane.'

She led him to it. He took it. Soon he was fast asleep in bed, right hand curled protectively round the ring on his left. For a while as the storm died down she sat beside him, watching him as he slept. She sighed. Poor man, he doesn't know what he's doing, she told herself. Should I be sleeping with him? But soon, habitually, she joined him in bed.

Near dawn she awoke. He was shouting in his sleep. Apparently waking, he sat up, staring at her in the semi-darkness. 'Fire and flood!' he said in that horrible dragging voice. 'Fire and flood! She's in the mud! In the mud!' Then, chuckling, he fell back again. Soon he was snoring.

Diane spent the rest of the night on a sofa in the living-room.

Next day both Sam and Chrissa slept late and woke up with streaming colds. Diane quizzed them separately. Their stories agreed, more or less. Sam had come across Chrissa drowning in a bog; he'd pulled her out in the nick of time. That was it. That was all. 'Why were you up there anyway?' Diane demanded. 'I got lost,' Chrissa sneezed. Go on! Diane thought sceptically. Tell me another! Dismayed, she realised: They're both hiding something. Whatever it is, it's worse here. We have to go. Quickly.

So at supper that evening she announced, in a flat voice that brooked no argument: 'We're going home. Tomorrow.'

'Good idea,' Sam agreed unexpectedly, his eyes downcast.

'Dad,' Chrissa cut in, 'get rid of that ring before we go?'

Diane stared at her. 'Yes!' she heard herself say. 'Yes!'

Sam said nothing. He blew his nose, gazed at the wall, and went early to bed. That night, making his cold her excuse, Diane again slept in the living-room. Once she woke up to hear him shouting. In the morning they packed and left, a day early. It was Friday. The journey south was a nightmare. Sam kept forgetting how to drive. It was as if he'd never been in a car before. Twice in the first hour Diane had to grab the wheel. At last she made him stop and insisted on taking over. Sam just shrugged, not caring at all. His mind was somewhere else. In the back, Chrissa stared out of the window and said not a word all the way back to London. Her face had grown thinner, and Diane feared for her.

As for Sam, he was due back at work the following Monday morning.

Back at Berkeley Road, Diane overcame her doubts and slept with Sam again. On the Friday and Saturday nights nothing happened: he moaned a little, but that was all. On Saturday and Sunday he seemed normal, but spent hours clearing out the attic. 'I need somewhere I can go and be on my own,' he said. Fair enough. But still he wore the ring; still he refused to tell her what had happened. As for Chrissa, she was not to be seen. As soon as they got back she shut herself into her room: for two days she hardly emerged save for a visit to the library and brief trips downstairs to eat, which she insisted on doing on her own, with nobody else in the kitchen. And her face was pale, haunted, not happy at all.

Late on Sunday night the uneasy peace was broken.

In bed, Diane was at last growing drowsy when, from the depths of his sleep beside her, Sam began muttering and shifting. 'Okay, okay,' she heard she mumble, 'I'll do it! Just don't look at me like that!' Then without warning his elbow dug her hard in the ribs as he sat bolt upright. 'Chrissa!' he roared. 'I'm coming! Don't move! Don't struggle!' And before Diane could gather her wits he screamed piercingly, covering his eyes as he did ... and that awful dragging voice came out of him:

I don't let the Weak Ones steal what's mine!

Crying with fear Diane snapped on the light and shook him, hard.

'Wake up, Sam! For godsakes snap out of it!'

He sees the Red Woman before him, smiling triumphantly from her bath in the bog of red mud. The sudden light and the shaking confused him utterly. 'Chrissa!' he moaned, tangled up in something white, unable to move.

'Sam, it's Diane! Chrissa's all right, you got her out, we're back in London!' The shaking went on. 'Wake up! You're dreaming!'

Huge wings and a raucous scream of disappointment beat in him. *Don't think you'll escape me!* For an instant then he saw a giant, terrible bird receding into a black void, drawing him so magnetically that nearly he plunged into it himself. For a moment he teetered on the edge. *If I go now I'll never come back!* But, shaken hard again, he awoke with a shudder. His eyes fixed on Diane's taut, fearful face. Slowly, soaked in sweat and tangled up in the sheets of their bed, aided by the recognition in her eyes, he swam back to himself. Berkeley Road? he wondered, and looked dazedly round the room. It was all so familiar it made no sense at all — the Laura Ashley curtains, the wide-open summer night window, the streetlight glow, the burned-out floodlit shell of Alexandra Palace up on its hill beyond the rooftops. A motorbike revved up in the street; police sirens wailed over in the east towards Tottenham. A muggy London night in July. 'Jesus!' he whispered, and in him the sense of many times and places overlapping with him at home in none of them. A sense of things he dared not recall. *The whole place.* On his finger the emerald glowed. Lost, he gazed at Diane.

'You were screaming.' Her voice was under tight control. 'Sam, we must discuss this. How can you cope with work in this state?'

'Work?' Then he remembered GRYP. He groaned and swung his legs out of bed, still hearing the beat of huge wings. 'It'll be okay,' he muttered.

'What do you mean, *okay?*' She laughed in nervous disbelief. 'You were babbling like a lunatic. First about Chrissa, then in that awful voice; *"I don't let the weak ones steal what's mine!"*' Diane breathed deep. 'Sam, who or what is that voice? I want to know. Now!'

140

Okay, Sam! Tell her! Go on! Tell her you're chased by a naked woman caked in red mud who lived five thousand years ago! Tell her you're needed to save the world from fire and flood! Tell her you'd have gone already if not for your stupid daughter spoiling everything! Go on! Tell her!

'Sam, will you please talk to me!'

'Forget it, okay?' he snapped. 'For your own sake drop it!'

'And what about Chrissa!' She was stridently sad. 'Don't you care?'

'Who pulled her out of the goddam bog? Of course I care!' He turned with a fierce, pleading look. 'Why do you think I've spent the last seven years doing my damndest to be what I'm not?'

'That chills me,' she murmured, looking and moving away.

'Diane, what ...' Exasperated, afraid, he tried again. 'Look. Hiding from the truth just makes it worse, and ... oh God!' He threw up his arms. 'So something crazy's going on, and it scares me shitless, but ...'

'So *talk* about it! If not to me, then a doctor!'

'Which kind?' He laughed joylessly. 'Valium? Shock? Analysis? If you know a good witchdoctor we might start getting somewhere!'

'The truth is you just want to run away again!' she flared suddenly, 'You won't remove that ring because you don't want to face the world!'

He didn't answer, and when at last she could bring herself to look at him she saw a nakedly baffled and terrified man. Don't fall for it! she told herself coldly, but despite herself — maybe *for* herself — she found her eyes brimming as she reached out for him. 'Oh Sam,' she murmured, 'please let us solve this!' And then he was crying too and they were in each other's arms, seeking a vanished comfort. 'I know you've tried.' she whispered, softly pressing. 'Now please try a little harder and tell me what really happened up there. On the moor. Sam, get it off your chest!'

'There's a place up there the ring likes,' he muttered brokenly, his tears mingling cheek-to-cheek with hers.

But her heart chilled to hear him on about the ring again. 'It's like a gate, a way through to … I don't know what or where. And if Chrissa hadn't …'

And how did Chrissa know where to find you, Sam? Who exactly do you think told her? The Weak Ones, that's who!

He stiffened. Diane hugged him tighter.

'Go on, dear, I'm listening. Don't stop!'

'No.' And with a shudder he pulled away, roughly breaking the embrace, averting his eyes as he left the bed. Yet in him a small boy wailed as he reached for teeshirt, briefs and jeans. With her heart like cold stone she crouched on the rumpled bed and watched him. 'Maybe you're right,' he told her jaggedly, speaking not to reassure but only to fill the awful silence, 'I should talk to somebody. First, I've got to work it out myself. Don't worry. Get some sleep. We'll sort it out, Diane. We really will!'

'I hope so,' said a listless voice, and it was only as Sam left the room without looking at her that Diane realised: I said that?

Chrissa felt the Enemy lie thick on the house. Silently, only seconds before Sam emerged on the landing, she returned to her own room. Behind her door she waited as he went down to the kitchen, and there she stayed, listening. Five minutes later he came up the stairs again. She smelled a waft of fresh coffee; heard the scuff of his feet on the stepladder, then thumps as the attic hatch was lowered firmly in place behind him. Only then, with his feet padding over the creaky floor above her ceiling, did she leave her post, nodding with slow, dreamy concentration as she picked her way back to bed past the books spread out on the floor. In the last few days her face had developed a brooding, bony look; her hair was a mess, she still had the sniffles, and there was a stiffness in the way she moved. But in the blue brightness of her eyes was something new — a knowledge, a determination, a look that went beyond her not-quite-thirteen years.

It'll be soon, she told herself remotely, eyeing the ceiling as silence came to the attic above. She won't let him go now. But what's so special about us? Is it accident? Or just that we don't remember yet?

Back in bed under the George Michael poster, she put on her glasses and took up the library book she'd been studying before sensing the Enemy near, before hearing her father scream. It was an illustrated history of the Dominican Inquisition, graced with a cover so lurid that the librarian had given her a *very* suspicious look as if she were some new kind of juvenile pervert. Now she had it open at an imaginative nineteenth-century engraving which showed, in detail, a terrible event. She wrinkled her nose, scowling as she eyed it. The black friars. The faceless hooded ones! In the picture their hands were clasped; they were on their knees and their cowled heads were bowed in prayer as they presided devoutly over the mass immolation of two hundred men and women. The victims were shut in a flaming stockade on a wooden slope at the foot of a great rock with a castle on top. Under the picture a caption identified them as Cathar *parfaits*, or *perfect ones*, burned alive for their faith after the fall of the castle of Montségur in March 1244. In the Pays d'Oc. In the northern foothills of the Pyrenees.

Gazing at this fearfully exact version of her dream-vision she began feeling sick again. Of course it wasn't quite like that, she thought faintly. The stockade wasn't there, it was lower down the slope, and . . .

Suddenly it was all too much. The terrible oppressive weight of it, the sadness and stench! Hurriedly she set aside the book and shut her eyes. I was never there at all! SWEET CHILD, DON'T RUN AWAY FROM THIS! I'm just imagining it! It can't be anything else! GO AWAY, BRAT! GET LOST! DROP DEAD! Then through closed eyes she saw the black-robed ones turn on her, rising from their prayers, facing her with their faceless faces. No faces! Blank white slugs in black hoods! But they can see me! They're looking at me! Stop! Go away! She shrank back in bed, her terror rising, for with utter certitude she knew that they actually were coming for her; she could feel them closing in on her, on her mother, on her father, on

143

this safe normal suburban house of 15 Berkeley Road; closing in, chanting in Latin, bringing the poison stink of death to her room, bringing — even as she opened her eyes — a darkness that dimmed the light of her bedside lamp to a feeble glow. She felt this darkness like a great black wing swooping; she sat up straight against it, teeth clenched, nails digging hard into the palms of her hands. REMEMBER THE SHINING ONES! But there was nothing shining at all, nothing but the green depths in that terrible ring her father wore and into which, she knew, at this very moment above her head he was sinking, sinking, sinking ...

'Why are you scared?' asked a gentle voice from the foot of her bed as the poison stink turned into a fragrance of wild rose. 'You're not seeing straight. Your conscience must be bad. Look! I've sent them away.'

Unwillingly Chrissa looked. And there by the curtained window, as solid as could be, raven-eyed and raven-haired in her faded green gown, stood Madame Pédauque, her gaze gentle and kind, but troubled.

'Why bother with those Weak Ones, Chrissa?' Madame asked sweetly. 'All they do is moan about how evil the world is and how any kind of action is wrong. But if we don't act now — if I don't get your Dad to help me — then soon there won't be any world left at all. That can't be right, can it?'

Chrissa braced herself. 'Why do you want my Dad anyway?' she asked out loud. 'What's he to you? He's nothing special. So leave him alone!'

'To hear a daughter speak of her father like that!' Madame sighed. 'But what else can we expect in these last days? It's part of what brings the Shift — this evil, disobedient thinking!' Her eyes flashed with anger, and Chrissa gasped. 'Thinking!' cried Madame as if the word were a curse. 'Too much thinking! That's part of the trouble! Too much thinking and not enough feeling, turning paradise into the pit, bringing the fire and the flood! That's why I need your father — to help me free the world from the curse of too much thought! I need a witness to go through the Starchamber Gate and plead for life before those who can stop the Shift! I need ...'

Overwhelmed by this fury, Chrissa shook her head, covered her eyes, and turned for help in the only direction she could think of. 'Where are you?' she cried aloud to the burning man. 'What do I do?'

'*Don't you dare!*' hissed Madame, but there was alarm in her voice. '*I warn you, if you get in my way again I'll ...*'

'Get out! Get out!' shrieked Chrissa, half-scrambling out of bed as the poison stench returned ... but even as it did, something inside her shone and told her what to do. And she did. '*Quant lo bouié,*' she began to sing in a soft high voice, not at all like her normal singing voice, '*... ben de laura, planto soun agulhado ...*' — then tears filled her eyes and a great violet light suddenly blazed in her as she cried out, '*AEIOU!*' This sound — for it was not a word — came out of her like an explosion, and even as it did she expanded, became gigantic, filling space, inhabiting the singing fields of light and looking down on the sorry dark planet so threatened by the coming Shift; looking down to the pale glow of London, to Berkeley Road and into her room where a terrified girl in her Marks & Spencer nightdress confronted a ... a whirlpool of dark red hate, rapidly fading and falling in on itself under the pressure of the shining. Then Madame cried in fury:

'*So embrace your stench of stupid martyrdom! Drown in your bog, burn at your stake and die! What do you think life is? A playground for the saintly to prove their contempt for flesh? I warn you, if you don't keep out of my way, soon I'll give you another chance to die stupidly!*'

Then Chrissa was back in bed in her shivering body, alone in her room with the 60-watt bedside lamp shining steadily as it should; but her head was whirling and her stomach heaved. She ran, clutching her mouth, and got to the bathroom only just in time as Diane, alerted and now doubly alarmed, rushed out onto the landing under the tight-closed attic hatch. 'What is it?' she cried, arriving at the open bathroom door. 'What is it?' But Chrissa was too busy throwing up to tell her anything, then or later ... and meanwhile from the attic there came not a sound ...

12.
Mark of the Owl

Shivering by the dusty yellow chest under the cobwebbed window Sam distractedly sensed trouble, heard Chrissa scream and Diane cry out ... but none of it touched him. With his diaries open before him he was trying to think. He felt like an empty house, all his doors and windows wide open, banging and rattling as gales of ghosts and dreams rushed in and out. For godsakes THINK! he ordered himself feverishly as the toilet flushed below. Step by step! First, that night in Ghardaia. It wasn't the dope. It only stopped when Dave pulled the ring off my finger and I rejected it. I was scared shitless! Wasn't I? Yes, I was! Now ... second ... (he paused to gaze into the emerald depths) ... now I'm wearing it again, and it's going further than before, maybe because I've stopped doing dope. Dope just got in the way, blotted it out. Third ... (for a while he lost focus and sat with glazed eyes) ... What? Yes! I'm wearing it again, which means ... I choose to wear it. Right? No, maybe not, because if ... if she's coming through my unconscious, then how ... (confused again, he stopped, gripping his aching head) ... how can I be sure if what I'm thinking is *me*? It might be *her* making me think her thoughts are mine, so that means maybe I'm not who ... I think I ... am. Oh shit! No! I'm doing it because I choose! Maybe in a way

146

Diane's right: I put it on again — not to run away — but because I'm sick of the shit. Seven years I've tried this crap, and it's ... well, meaningless. That's what's really sick — no meaning. That's it! I won't take any more! I'd have gone through already, and good riddance, if ...

But gone through into *what*? he asked fearfully. The world of moon and horns? Isn't is just a crazy way of committing suicide?

And if you don't go through? demanded the flashing depths. *Then what?*

He sensed the abyss. There's no house! I'm not here at all! In a dizzy hurry he stood, remembering at the last moment to duck and avoid the non-existent joist. In a sweat he sat again. 'But *what is she?*' he asked aloud, in agony. 'The Watchers? Like in Enoch? The ones who fell because of their lust? That's lunatic! And this Shift thing, it's all ...'

He couldn't articulate it. The moment he began trying to think at all logically his head began to spin and the abyss opened up. For a while he flipped through the diaries, reading one neat, insane entry after the next, but he couldn't make sense of what he'd written seven and eight years earlier. The Sam Joyce who worked at GRYP rejected it. Yet the Sam Joyce who'd been in the place the ring liked, who wanted to return there ...

The Watchers. The Nephilim, the rebel angels of the Elohim, the Shining Ones. As described in the apocryphal Book of Enoch they'd been punished for lusting after the daughters of man, locked up in time and matter ... ludicrous superstition and myth, yes, but ...

All night he sat in the attic, staring through the window at Crouch End rooftops, hopelessly twisting the ring round his finger as he tried and failed to rationalise the mad tide mounting in him. He pulled blank paper towards him ... but by six thirty on Monday morning, with the city waking up and just three hours before he had to be back at work, he had written down precisely four words and a question mark:

HAVE I GONE MAD?

Leaving the house before seven he trudged up Shepherd's Hill to the fifty acres of Queen's Wood. The day would be hot, but under the dense beech canopy it was cool. To start with nothing went wrong. For a time he watched the squirrels scamper. A dog barked, a voice called out. It was as quiet as London could get. Soon he found a root and sat down, but as he did he felt it was in a wood elsewhere and elsewhen. A sweat broke out on him; he gripped the root tight and dug his heels into the yielding earth. I'm *here!* he insisted fiercely. I'm *now!* He tried to relax, but the weight of the last week lay too thick on him. *Face it*, whispered the crafty voice, *you can't trust Chrissa. She works for the Weak Ones, she stopped you going through, and if they win, it's fire and flood for sure!*

'Lies!' he muttered. 'Lunacy!' And he thought: It's Monday morning, I'm back at work, and this is Britain. God Save the Queen!

The Queen, yes ... *her voluptuous, mud-caked body ...*

'I'm sick of this!' He glared at the ring. 'Leave me alone!'

But what are you going to do about Chrissa?

He groaned. Their return to Cuilchonich that terrifying night ... at no time since had they discussed it. In fact he'd done everything he could to avoid his daughter ... for whenever he caught Chrissa looking at him he saw that intolerable pity in her too-blue, too-bright eyes. As if she knew better than he did what was happening to him.

So who are the Weak Ones? he wondered savagely. Her burning man?

Yes, sneered the voice. *Cathars! Liberals! Freethinkers! Many in many ages. They try to fight by not fighting.* WEAK *Ones!*

'You mean people like me!' he snapped, abruptly standing. He started walking. For over an hour he circled the wood, chased by doubts and ghosts and unwilling to return to the streets. But in time he left the cover of the trees and found himself amid a flood of office workers on their way to Highgate Underground. He saw charred and rusted automata marching. Get back to work, he told himself uneasily, it'll all straighten out.

Ring on your finger! giggled the voice. *Stones on your bones!*

He came to Archway Road. The roar and fumes dazed him. I didn't know how to drive on Friday; now I can't cross a road! Shaking, he let Sam Joyce's memory lead him along the old railway track to Finsbury Park, but after a mile along this woodland strip he had to return to the busy roads. Flashes of other landscapes began imposing themselves: he started over busy Hornsey Lane not knowing where he was. Horns blared, voices cursed, he jumped back in a sweat. 'Concentrate!' he shouted. 'You're back in London, fool!' So with inch-by-inch care he went on to Greystoke Road through decayed streets and damp-stained high-rise estates but several times doubt stopped him taking familiar turns. The visions were intensifying. His fear mounted. *He wades through ash a foot deep, through the fiery murk of a smashed land. Burned corpses all about him grin with ghastly humour.* He stopped dead. Blinking, he stared south from Hornsey Rise, saw how the City money-towers clustered like tombstones under the hazy poached-egg sun. *The entire city in flames but the sea rises, rises, rises, booming black laughter, hurling sodden mountains of charred stock-market print-outs before it.* In near-panic Sam continued through the streets with the sensation that he walked on a thin shell which at any moment might crack.

Just before nine thirty he reached the blackened old church where GRYP lived. *She squats upon its leaded roof, pumping herself upon the spire, grinning at him even as the blood of her wound gouts down.* He shut his eyes to this vision and forced his way into the partitioned interior. Nobody was about in the main space. Tensely he let Sam's memory lead him across to the offices. *Smashed concrete and rusted girders; nothing but cockroaches left.* Faint, he opened a door and saw *charred bones whitened by the sea* Tony Morrison the project co-ordinator. Gulping back nausea, Sam shut his eyes, opened them again. Tony, busy at his desk with a lot of paper before him, frowned. In his crumpled denim suit he had the look of someone who'd been *dead for years* at work for hours.

'Sam,' he said coldly. 'Back, are you? How was Scotland?'

Sam stared. *The skeleton scowls back. Fire and flood.*

'This is Tony,' Sam muttered aloud. 'And I work here.'

Tony lit up an Embassy. 'Are you okay, Sam?'

Sam tried to smile, but it didn't work.

Soon enough he learned how much had gone wrong at GRYP. Jim Rogers (he of the little dog and emerald Mohican hairstyle in Sam's Thursday night group) had vanished off the street. He was reckoned to be the guilty party in a newsagency hold-up which had put the shop's Pakistani owner into the Whittington with a fractured skull. His referral sheet, which Sam had seen last, was missing ... and his probation officer Bill Powers, an active enemy of GRYP, was due at ten thirty. 'It won't be fun,' Tony assured Sam with cool fury. 'He wants our guts. Find that referral sheet, fast!'

'Oh?' Sam stared. *The ocean's crushing weight.* He had no memory of Jim Rogers. Behind him the door opened and Marge Benson came in, brushing back her red hair with Monday-morning lassitude. Turning, Sam *sees the Red Woman, beckoning, dripping blood, open-thighed.* He flinched visibly, the colour draining from his face as he stared at her.

'What's wrong?' Alarmed by his look, Marge stopped. 'Is my head on back to front or something?'

That was bad enough. An hour later the meeting between Sam, Tony and Bill Powers from Probation was worse. Still Sam remembered nothing about Jim Rogers, let alone the missing referral sheet, and every time he looked at Bill Powers *he sees a yellow lizard with a flickering tongue* smoking a soggy Hamlet cigar. He left it to Tony to carry the can. 'Yes, Mr Powers, of course we'll co-operate with the police, but it doesn't help if we just sit here slanging each other, does it?' And Bill Powers removed the soggy stub from his mouth long enough to nod at Sam and suggest grimly: 'No, and I suggest to you it doesn't help when you put kids like that in charge of prats like this. What's the matter with him anyway? Is he qualified?'

'Don't ask me.' Tony sighed.

Sam stared at the table, not daring to look up.

Then the final straw. The Monday staff meeting. There was just one item on the agenda: how to attract new funding and avoid closure. By then not only was the day sweltering but the trepidation was intense, for Sam was twitching like a badly-connected zombie; his eyes were terrified, he couldn't face anyone, he just kept twirling that weird ring round and round his finger. Nonetheless they tried to get it going, and for a while Sam tried to concentrate. 'Yes,' he muttered, and 'No,' but all the time *he finds himself amid the fire and flood.* She's doing it! he told himself furiously. She's trying to force me! Now come on! This is GRYP! Just concentrate! And distantly he heard Tony droning on about seeking advice from the local co-op development agency, and Ro demanding 'an immediate exploration of the viability of voluntarism' — but none of it made sense. So he just sat there, *drowned full fathom deep*, drowned in the heat, in the rising tide of jargon-babble, his eyes wide in the depths of the ring, and when at one point Marge nudged him sharply he reacted by turning red and gasping as if suffocating, staring at them with such horrified eyes that their flesh crawled. How did I get here? his eyes screamed silently, for in him now was a panic; that *he's trapped in a drowned underground maze with many other fire-shrunken people who, like him, have no idea who they are or what they're doing.*

'Okay!' snapped Tony. 'Sam, do you hear that?'

Horrified, Sam stared at him, *at the drifting corpse.*

'Wake up, Sam!' Again Marge dug him in the ribs ... and this time, turning sharply, he seemed to see her. He twitched. His lips drew back from his teeth, his nostrils flared, his eyes widened. The blood drained from his face

151

and he gestured as if sending her off. His chair crashed behind him as he stumbled to his feet. Panting like a beast forced into the slaughterhouse, he fled the room, leaving his co-workers staring. By the time Marge got through the kids in the hall to the front door he was already halfway down the street, running as if pursued by furies. Utterly bewildered, shaking her head, she returned to GRYP's meeting.

The following hours were such a confusion that most of the time Sam had no idea who or where he was. From GRYP he fled her anger into the broken lands that lay all about, pelting down a hill that stank of burning fumes, narrowly avoiding the gleaming metal beasts that charged him continually. In time he came to a marketplace where hooded victims were strung up naked by the feet from huge butcher hooks built into bloodstained brick walls. Lost, he drifted through the shopping crowds, hearing their strange cries — ''Arf-pound of stewing-steak today please, Sid!' — and watching the ruddy overseers in their striped aprons carving cuts out of the trussed victims. On he wandered, his escape forgotten, sure he'd been sent here to meet someone or do something. At length, passing through a long dark tunnel, he read, sprayed in huge wavery black letters running half the length of the naked concrete wall, this legend: REAGAN IS MAD, THATCHER IS HIS ROBOT, AND SOON WE'RE ALL GOING TO BE DEAD! This, reminding him that he was in the last days before fire and flood, brought him to his senses: he swam out of his haze long enough to realise he was in the pedestrian subway under the Archway roundabout. Emerging by the vast black tower on the upper floors of which the poor queued all day and sometimes longer for their social security, he fled the roaring traffic for quieter precincts. Soon he found himself amid a strange dense scrub-wood, stumbling amid endless ranks of stone slabs bursting up from a wilderness of bramble and mare's-tail. He stared bewildered at a cracked stone plaque on the ground. Writing on it told him that here was the original resting-place of Karl Marx, his wife Jenny von Westphalen, and their grandson Harry Longuet. Vaguely then he realised he was in Highgate Cemetery. *'I'm as trapped as you are!'* a cold woman's voice whispered in his ear, making him jump. *'You must come and give me what I need to help me through the Starchamber. Remember: don't trust your daughter! She works for the Weak Ones; their appeasement will lead to fire and flood again — it's what they want! And now, my friend — just in case you've got ideas about escaping me — my mark!'*

'Oh shit!' Sam looked wildly about, but there was nobody near him save for a courting couple twenty yards away on one of the main cemetery paths. And before he could move he heard the beating of wings and a hoarse, eerie, prolonged shriek — then a crazed white heart-shaped face burst on him, talons tearing at his eyes. He fled, windmilling his arms as the barn owl came at him again and again, by now so confused he couldn't begin to tell if this was really happening or not. With sweat pouring off him he escaped back to the street, whereupon the owl (if it really had been there) broke off its attack. This terror encouraged him back to his daily senses: he stopped in the first pub he passed.

'Double Scotch,' he demanded shakily. The barman eyed him curiously.

'What happened to you, mate?'

Sam shook his head, downed the Scotch, and went to the Gents. In the mirror he saw a mess. Three long diagonal scratches raked his still-bleeding left cheek. He cleaned the wound as best he could, then returned to the bar.

'An owl,' he said wonderingly, 'I was attacked by a bloody owl.'

The barman raised disbelieving eyebrows, but another drinker, overhearing, said: 'Warfarin.'

'What?' Sam downed another double. It helped.

'Rat poison,' the man said matter-of-factly. 'There was a case in Somerset the other day. Saw it on TV. Owl attacked a bloke on a bike. They say it was out of its head on Warfarin. Like that Hitchcock film about birds —

Nature getting her own back.' He appraised Sam with the eye of a connoisseur. 'In the cemetery, was it?'

Sam nodded, pushing his tumbler back for another. The whisky was dulling his fear, deadening the abominable pain of his torn cheek. It was her bird, he realised. An owl. She made it do that just like she's making me see all these things, he thought as the barman refilled him. Maybe if I get really pissed and stay pissed she won't get through so easily ...

'Never heard of no owls round here,' the barman commented.

'Get that cheek seen to, I would,' said the other man.

When Sam left, half-drunk, the London street remained a London street, though too hot for comfort. He bought antiseptic and Elastoplast and patched himself up in the Gents of the next pub down the road. For a while he felt quite calm. I'm meant to be at work, he reminded himself after another double. But I'm in shock. I'd better get home.

Then he realised he no longer knew where he lived.

His calm deserted him. In a nauseous near-panic he walked the sultry street, going through his pockets until he found a driving licence. It said he was *Samuel David Joyce* of *15 Berkeley Road, London N8 8TJ*. But neither name nor address rang any bell of memory at all. He realised he stood by a church. An absurd hope took him into the cool, empty interior. 'GOD?' he bawled. 'GOD? ARE YOU THERE? GOD, I NEED HELP, I REALLY NEED HELP! GOD, SHE'S AFTER ME!' But nothing happened. There was no response. Only the emerald seemed alive, its depths pulsating on his finger. 'Why should God listen to a stupid sod like you?' he mumbled, returning to the furnace of the afternoon, sweating and unsteady. 'You never asked him for help before. Why should he listen now?' And with the last of his self-control he hailed a passing cab, slurring out the address on the driving licence. The cabbie eyed him oddly. 'Had an accident,' he managed to explain. 'Please ...' The cabbie shrugged. 'Okay, mate. Hop in.' But en route to Berkeley Road his head began spinning: *he's trapped in a cage of bones rattling and rolling through clouds of thick choking red dust; the sky above is lurid and behind him the sea is rising, rising, rising.* He managed not to scream, but in despair told the cabbie to stop at an off-licence. He bought two bottles of Scotch. Really think that'll work? he asked himself sceptically. At last he reached Berkeley Road, wanting only to hole up in the attic and hide. 'Who the fuck cares?' he muttered as he paid his fare. But the cabbie just shrugged as he drove off.

It was the hottest day of the year. Thunder was building up.

When Sam returned Chrissa was alone in the house. She sat in the kitchen with books open in front of her, trying to concentrate through a pounding headache. It was only part of the sense of oppression she felt. That morning she'd still been in bed when Diane, pretending to be finding out if she wanted breakfast, had barged in, trying to get her to talk. Chrissa had refused. They'd had a blazing row, and it was Diane who'd fled in tears, slamming the front door behind her. Chrissa, still feeling sick from her encounter with the Enemy, had felt guiltily relieved. 'I know it's horrible for you too, Mum,' she'd said sadly, 'I'd like to tell you, but I can't because it's nothing to do with you.' Then, with the house all to herself, she'd sneaked up into the attic (well, it's not just *his* room, she assured herself) and found her father's old diaries. With her ear skinned for any interruption she'd scanned pages of neatly-written ravings that made little sense to her ... save that Madame was often mentioned, described by Sam in terms of hot desirous fascination and fear, and identified by him by many names — Lilith, Cerridwen, Kali, Inanna, Anath, the Black Isis — that meant nothing to her at all. There was a lot about Lilith and her bird-feet, and the owls that accompanied her on her deadly business of strangling young babes, making women barren, and seducing men in their sleep. Chrissa broke out in a sweat at that. There were also weird notes about the Queen of Sheba's hairy legs and her feet which had been changed into the hooves of an ass, and one remark that seemed important: *In the Christian west the Queen of Sheba has been identified as Queen Sibylla, ancestress of all magicians, who has the webbed feet of a goose rather than hooves. This connects her with La Reine Pédauque.*

All this was too scary and confusing. It left Chrissa wondering what to do next. Leaving the attic as she found it, she sat down, trying to get a clear impression of what actually had happened when Madame had called on her. 'I definitely wasn't asleep,' she told herself carefully. 'She tried to persuade me she's okay, and she told me a lot of funny stuff, then she threatened me when I asked the burning man what to do. But she was scared, and I knew what to do! I sang that song, and it really did work! What happened? I sang *Quant lo bouié*, and when I shouted that sound I . . . sort of got huge, just like Alice, and I was in the middle of the shining light, looking down on . . .'

Abruptly the memory returned, making her dizzy with the vastness of that vision from the heights of which she'd driven the Enemy out.

Thoughtful, she took her library books down to the kitchen. But first from the living-room she borrowed the world atlas and turned to the south of France, to the north-east slopes of the Pyrenees, her finger touching names which, as she murmured them, sounded oddly familiar. *Foix. Ax-les-Thermes. Mirepoix. Albi. Carcassonne.* 'I've never been there,' she told herself, 'but I have!' — and even as she said this, she found it.

Montségur.

Again dizziness seized her. Her ears rang; she smelled burning flesh. The early afternoon air was so thick it seemed like cement. Stifled, she shook her head and went out into the back garden. It was hot. All about, the street sounds of London. Above, the sun was vanishing into a dense and sultry haze. She realised she was sweating. 'Come on,' she told herself as the fear began to mount, 'I *must* find out more.' So back inside she went to the library books — dense volumes, the very titles of which put her off. *The Albigensian Crusade. The Cathars and Reincarnation. The Holy Heretics.* No wonder her mother had been bewildered at the sight of them. (*'But what is all this, Chrissa? Does it have anything to do with what happened in Scotland? Or ... with your ... burning man dreams?'*) Chrissa sighed, her headache getting worse. 'This is nuts!' she told herself unhappily. 'I should get outside and forget it all!' Then she scowled, bit her lip, and opened one of the books, not knowing what on earth she was seeking.

Yet an hour or so later when Sam came back she was still at it, reading (without really understanding) about what seemed the very hard discipline practised by the Cathar priests, called *parfaits* or *bonshommes*. Apparently both men and women were made priests by Cathar bishops in a rite called the *consolamentum* (she wrinkled her nose at that one), and they were bound to vegetarianism, plenty of fasting, and complete abstinence from lying, sex and violence. I don't get it, she thought, rubbing her aching head, they couldn't have had much fun but surely they weren't hurting anyone. Why did the Church want them dead? Why does Madame call them *Weak Ones*? And why is it anything to do with me? Or Dad? Is it ... maybe ... something that we got ... *inherited* ... from Captain Davey when he found the ring? And that shining light I was in when I shouted for help ... maybe Dad doesn't see it any better than I do, because it's bigger than both of us, like a kind of war. But ... who's fighting who, and what do they want from us? Oh, Dad, she thought dismally, it looks like we're on different sides. Dad, I don't want that, I just want to help you if I can. I'm sure you don't want to do what Madame tells you to do, but ...

She heard the front door open.

Heavy feet stumbled into the hall, the front door slammed, and with a cold chill she knew it was her father. Hastily she shut and stacked the books, thinking, what can I do? I mustn't pretend nothing's happening. Soon it'll be too late. But I'll have to be careful. And quickly she decided on a course of action. But when Sam

157

appeared in the kitchen doorway and she saw the state he was in, she almost put it off.

For a long moment she could only gape at him.

His black shock of hair was a mess, his eyes gleamed drunkenly, his face was flushed, Elastoplast taped his left cheek, and under it a thick smear of blood ran to his chin. In each hand he clutched a full bottle of whisky ... and the look he shot her held so much menace that automatically she wanted to shrink away and become invisible. But there was fear in his look too, and misery, and, as he turned away without speaking, the question leaped out of her:

'Dad. What do you know about Dualists?'

'What?' Surprised, he eyed her with rough suspicion.

'Dualists. Do you know anything about them?'

Sam laughed, his face hectic. 'Bored upper-class layabouts with nothing better to do but stick swords in each other over imagined insults!' he declared with drunken volubility. 'Okay? Can I go now?'

'No, Dad.' She strove for calm. '*Dualists*, not duellists.'

What are you going to do about her? 'Are you taking the piss?'

'No! I only want to know about Dualists!' Now she wished she hadn't opened her mouth, but it was too late. Lurching across the kitchen, he leaned over her shoulder and stared suspiciously at the books. She smelled the whisky on his breath; the hate and fear and confusion in him.

'You mean *Dual*ists,' he exclaimed angrily, as if *she* hadn't understood, not him. 'Why do you want to know?' She tried to think, but he slammed his bottles down on the table. 'They thought evil as powerful and eternal as good. They said this world was created by a fake god, a lower entity — Satan, Lucifer, Jehovah — who just pretended to be God.' He grinned, and to her horror his hands descended either side of her neck, gripping her tight. 'They said kings and popes and the rich bastards are all servants of Satan. Damn right too — but what's it to you?' His grip tightened. She felt the cold metal of the

158

ring dig into her neck. 'Why aren't you upstairs playing Wham or Madonna like kids your age are supposed to do?'

'What else did they believe?' she persisted, closing her eyes, for now he was beginning to hurt her.

'Is this a test? You tell me, clever girl!'

'Dad!' Convulsively she jerked away and broke his grip, spinning round to face him, but he wouldn't meet her eyes. He grimaced and looked away, right hand gripping the ring-finger as if wanting to strangle that instead of her. It's moving really fast now, she realised through her fear. What happened to his cheek? It's got worse. I should drop it. But then again she seemed to be gazing down from a brightness far above, down at the pair of them, acting like puppets in a drama that had to be played out. No, she decided, it won't get any better, not until we face it. I have to tell him. Now. And she took a deep breath.

'They believed in reincarnation, Dad.' Don't take your eyes off him, she ordered herself. 'I must tell you. I know who the burning man in my dreams is. He died a long time ago, in 1244, at a castle called Montségur in the south of France. He was a Cathar *parfait*, a goodman. They were Dualists and, just like you told me at Tir Nan Og, the Pope and the King of France called them heretics and sent soldiers to get them. They were all killed, burned alive.' The sweat ran off her, it was hard to breathe, still he would not face her. Now, she told herself, out with it! 'And Dad, *I was there!* I've begun to remember, and ...' — she paused, for Sam had begun visibly to shiver, and now he was glaring at her with a truly murderous light in his eyes. She steeled herself. '... And it was him who sent me up the hill to stop you staying too long in that place where ... *she* almost got you. Dad, you're in real danger! She's still after you, isn't she! I *know* she is! Last night she tried to ...'

'Chrissa, this is bloody rubbish!' he shouted, trying but failing to suppress the whisky fury that flooded him.

'Dad, do what she wants and something terrible will happen, and ...'

'Stop!' he bellowed, thumping the table so hard that the whisky bottles danced, his dark face so tense with rage that fresh blood began trickling down from under the Elastoplast. 'Not another word!'

'And Mum's right about the ring!' she persisted stubbornly. 'Why don't you make her happy for once and take it off?'

'Because I prefer to keep it on!' he hissed, appalled by himself, shutting his eyes as he fought the rage that urged him to ... to ...

'I think maybe you're not able to take it off any more!'

Then something took hold of him; he opened his eyes and watched as his right arm rose, apparently of its own volition; as his hand swept down in a hard flat arc, striking his daughter on the side of her head, lifting her off the chair and hurling her to the vinyl floor. Then the anger left him: immediately he tried to help her up, but it was too late. She pushed him away, her eyes bright and wet as she got shakily to her feet. She stood her ground, clutching her face. 'You never did anything like that before,' she whispered, her whole body trembling. 'She's turned you into a monster! Dad, you *must* throw that ring away so she can't get at you! If you don't, you're lost, you'll go to her and do whatever she wants you to do, and the whole world will suffer! If you love us, Dad, *throw it away!*'

She turned and ran out, upstairs to her room.

In an agony, twisting the ring, Sam tried to pull if off his finger. It wouldn't budge. It was firmly lodged behind the knuckle. 'Soap and water!' he muttered feverishly. 'I can't do this, she's my daughter! I need soap and water!' Jerkily he turned to the sink and squirted mild green Fairy Liquid over the ring. 'I must be mad! Hitting her! What's happening to me? She shouldn't have said all that rubbish, but that's no excuse to hit her!' Again he tugged at the ring on his now well-soaped finger, but still he couldn't get it off. It slithered and skidded about behind his knuckle until, cursing with fear and self-contempt, he pulled so hard that the finger burst out of its socket — but the ring wouldn't budge.

'How do I get this damned thing off?' he shouted.

You could cut off your finger . . . or you could — you could just — step through the gate. It's not too late yet, my friend!

Then he thought about the Black and Decker.

In a terror he rushed out of the kitchen. An instant later he returned for one of the whisky bottles. Soon, up in the attic, he opened it.

The sky outside had grown as dark and dense as lead.

Chrissa, locked in the bathroom, ran cold water. The mirror over the basin showed the huge blue-black bruise forming already. As she sponged it, wincing, she heard Sam bellow from the kitchen below. *'How do I get this damned thing off?'* She listened in hope, but when he came crashing upstairs she knew he hadn't succeeded. She quailed, but he paid her no attention as he went down then came up again. She heard him clamber into the attic and slam the hatch. Now he'll drink himself silly, she knew sadly as she dabbed at the bruise. That won't help. It'll just give her more power. But maybe it had to happen ever since Captain Davey found the ring. She's not going to let go. But neither am I.

But, as thunder rumbled in the distance, she felt more fear than hope. Down into the cool clear water in the basin she gazed, silently imploring her burning man to appear and tell her what to do . . . and there again she seemed to see him, pale and remote. His calm, hideous face gazed up at her. 'What now?' she asked unhappily. 'I mean, what's going on? First I'm nearly drowned; now I'm half-strangled then slapped about . . . and for what? I could start believing that you and Madame are both as bad!'

'The Enemy's in everyone,' she thought she heard. Or was it just her ears ringing from the slap? *'But the Enemy's the Lie, not the liars.'*

'Then why let the liars kill you?' she asked wearily, and it seemed to be more than Chrissa's knowledge that asked. 'Must they always win?'

'Truth dies without witnesses who love it,' sang that soft

faint voice, '*but liars are slaves to the Lie. Calling the Lie true to save the body kills the soul when the body will die anyway. Liars win nothing at all!*'

'That sounds stupid! Why does Madame really want my Dad?'

'*To steal a great treasure. To risk the world for her own ambition.*'

'But she says she needs him to help save the world!'

'*Trust your heart to know the Lie! If you love him you'll be brave, and your Shining One will help you to overcome her darkness!*'

'But why me?' she asked fearfully. 'I don't want this!'

'*Because he loves you.*' The image was fading. '*And ...*'

'But he hit me! That means he loves me? Wait! Don't go!'

'*We did wait,*' she thought she heard, '*And you came. Be ready!*'

'That's mad! What do you mean, you waited and I came? That's as stupid as what you told me in Scotland!' she scolded anxiously. 'If it hasn't happened yet how can you tell me it has?'

There was no reply. The image was gone. Dizzy, disturbed, she splashed cold water on her face then pulled the plug. Her cheek hurt fiercely where Sam had struck it. What am I moaning about? she wondered angrily, thinking of the burning man's own pain. This is nothing. But I'd better be careful. Cautiously she left the bathroom. The air was hot and sticky. Even as she tiptoed into her room, lightning forked down over Highgate; amid gathering gloom thunder growled as she locked her door and lay down on her bed with a sigh. Floorboards creaked in the attic above; she bit her lip. What's he doing up there? And with dread she knew: He'll go back to that place ... and I'll have to follow him. But *why*? Don't I have any choice? It can't have happened already! That's mad!

Yet as lightning seared again she had to admit to herself that it was *all* mad already. So what's a little more madness? Then the thunder broke, rumbling close like a furious dog, and at the height of it she thought she heard a lesser crash from the attic. In that instant the rain came hard, drumming her window. Sitting up, she listened tensely, but heard nothing. What was it? she wondered. Maybe he fell down. He's probably dead drunk. I could take it from him! I could throw it away and stop all this!

Heart fluttering wildly, unaware of Diane's attempts to do just that, she nerved herself to try it. But first she thought of something else to do. That's silly! she scolded herself as, very carefully, she opened her door, you're just trying to find a way not to go up there. And she eyed the closed attic hatch fearfully. Still not a sound. Yes, she decided, he's probably out cold. Stupid man! Oh, Dad! Why? Why?

But it was downstairs she went, down to the phone in the hall amid the storm. The gloom was intense. She switched on the light and found her number in the Yellow Pages. She had almost completed her call when Diane came home.

13.
The Enemy Comes

All afternoon Diane had been pouring out her woes to Mona Jackson, whose repeated advice was that it was high time Diane got herself and Chrissa out of harm's way before the mad male beast got truly bestial. 'You've put up with quite enough already,' Mona insisted firmly, pouring more tea. 'Don't leave it too late. If something really goes wrong you'll be to blame too. You can't go on making excuses for him.' And for the first time Diane found herself in agreement. Her depression deepened when she phoned GRYP to learn that Sam had walked out, behaving very strangely. Oh my God, she thought. Chrissa's on her own! 'I must get back,' she told Mona, giving no explanation, and back from Wood Green she started even as the storm broke. Fifteen minutes later, after a crawl through traffic jams, she dashed from the car to the front door, drenched before she even turned the key. Then she paused, shaking.

I'm scared to enter my own house? Oh Diane, come on!

The storm drowned the sound of her entry, but the opening door caught Chrissa's eye. Quickly she pretended to be talking to a friend. 'See you later, Jane,' she said loudly, hanging up even as Diane came in, dripping wet. And the first thing Diane saw was the enormous blue-black bruise disfiguring Chrissa's right cheek.

She froze, keyring dangling from her fingertips.

'My God, Chrissa! What on earth ...?'

Chrissa had almost forgotten the pain of the slap. 'Oh ... I fell down the stairs,' she improvised lamely, turning away into the kitchen. Why don't I want Mum to know? she wondered. 'It's not as bad as it looks.' And she shrugged casually (she thought) as Diane, staring at her with utter disbelief, hung house and car keys on their hook over the fridge.

'Sam's in, isn't he?' Diane demanded. 'Did he do that to you?'

'He's drunk, Mum.' Cornered, Chrissa sighed. 'In the attic.'

'Chrissa, tell me the truth! Did Sam hit you?'

'I suppose he did,' the girl agreed reluctantly, 'but only because I was winding him up to take off the ring.' A sudden hope inspired her: she looked up, eyes gleaming bright. 'Mum, listen, after he hit me I locked myself in the bathroom and I heard him down here, trying to get it off, but he couldn't. But maybe we can, now! He was drunk already then and he had two bottles ...' — she indicated the remaining bottle of Grant's Standfast on the table — '... that's one of them. He took the other one up with him, and I think I heard him fall down. He's probably right out of it. Maybe we can get the ring off him!' Spontaneously, as lightning lit the kitchen in a blue-white flash, she seized her mother's wet hands, and Diane started with shock. We've all gone mad! Diane silently wailed. Why did I ever stick with him? 'I was going to try on my own but ... well, I'm scared, Mum, and maybe two of us ... please ...?'

Thunder crashed. Diane hid her fear behind a frown.

'Chrissa, are you sure? You mean this? After all the ...'

'Of course I mean it!' Agitated, she pulled Diane towards the stairs. 'I know I was horrible to you this morning, I know I've been strange, but there *is* a reason, and I *do* want all this over! Mum, you're not stupid, you

165

know this is our last chance! We *must!* Come *on!*'

'I'm not sure.' In a daze, Diane resisted. 'Now listen,' she heard herself say, 'I already tried it, twice. That night in the attic, last May, and at Cuilchonich when he was asleep when you two ...' She shook her head. 'But he woke up the moment I touched it. I thought he'd kill me!'

'Yes, but drunk isn't the same as asleep! Come *on!*' Chrissa's eyes were startlingly bright now, so much so that for a moment Diane found herself wondering: Is this Chrissa? My daughter? What's happened to her? What's happened to all of us? So she let the girl pull her to the stairs.

'All right,' she agreed nervously. 'Let's find out.' And soon she was up the stepladder, knocking on the closed hatch, grimly recalling that time-clock which had begun ticking back seven weeks ago. It's come full circle, she realised with sick amazement, standing there as thunder crashed again. 'Sam? Are you there?' But there was no reply. She called again. No reply. It's now or never, she knew, pushing at the hatch. It wasn't bolted; she lifted it easily. No light was on in the attic; nothing could be heard but rain hammering roof slates. With Chrissa behind she climbed warily up into the gloom. There was a stink of whisky. Careful! she told herself fearfully. He's dangerous. I should have brought a ...

She checked the image. It had to do with a blunt instrument.

For a time as he'd sat by the window, swigging whisky and watching the sky curdle into darkness, Sam had tried fooling himself with what he knew was a lie: that his mind was working better because of the drink, and that with just a little logic he'd dismiss this entire miserable mess into the oblivion it deserved. We'll go back to the way we were, he assured himself sentimentally, already so drunk that he felt no pain either from his owl-clawed cheek or from the wrenched ring-finger. Of course I'll have to make an effort. I can't let this go on. Did I really

166

hit her? Oh God, Sam, maybe you'd better see a shrink. Or maybe a group's better. There must be a lot of men like me. We think we're handling it even when it's getting to us. We're so cut off from nature that we think intellectual labels are the same as understanding. But I'll bet a shrink would just call Madame a personification of my negative anima, or some smart expensive bullshit like that. Bloody nonsense! I'll sort it out myself. I'll call GRYP tomorrow and say I need a few days off. They'll understand. They're good people. At least they try. At least they haven't sold out.

He took another swig. The whisky burned down to his gut. He heard pipes gurgling as Chrissa drained water from the bathroom basin. *I really did hit her!* He clenched his teeth: pain shot through his left hand as again he tugged savagely at the ring. Still it wouldn't budge. *Cut off my finger?* He laughed. *That's just crazy! This is Crouch End, not the Texas Chainsaw Massacre!* Of course, he reflected, his head swimming, that guy Dennis Nilsen lived just round the corner from here. Boiling the bits of all those boys he killed in a pot on his Baby Belling, then stuffing them down the drains and complaining to the council about the stink. Lunacy! They'd never have got him if he'd kept quiet. Some people! They just want to martyr themselves. *What is* she up to, anyway? The Weak Ones? Burned Cathar heretics from 1244? More lunacy. It must run in the family! How does her creature communicate with her? Midnight astral orgies? Yecch!

Then as he took another swig the image entered his mind of Chrissa gazing into a basin of water; of the man's face she saw in it — a horribly contorted, blackened face with the hair and skin burned off and gobbets of flesh hanging loose. He grimaced. *They say,* came a crafty voice through the whisky-fire, *that the old cabbalists would gaze into basins of water, trancing themselves to summon up 'demons' who'd prophesy the future. Some say that's how Nostradamus worked. Yet what's a 'demon' but an aspect of the unconscious? And what's the unconscious but everything in darkness? And what's consciousness,* continued the little voice as through the window he saw lightning jag down, splitting the black sky above Highgate, *but very little indeed! Just a tiny flicker of light amid the vast and endless darkness. Here today and gone tomorrow, Sam! Isn't it chauvinistic to fool ourselves that creation is limited to what we glimpse during that tiny flicker of light! Hear that thunder roll? Sam, it's getting so dark! By your own choice you're slipping into darkness. How wasteful, throwing away what little light you have! Did you think that by drinking yourself into a stupor you'd keep me out when I possess you already? You fool, your fate is with me! I'm the only one who can bring your life any meaning now, for you've worn the ring in the high whole place, my bird has marked your outer face and your inner mind — and I claim you, NOW!*

Too late he realised what a mistake he'd made.

TURN ROUND! FACE ME! COME TO ME!

A bolt of blinding light fastened greedily from sky to earth; he felt the fire of it flash through the ring into him, illuminating both his mind and the attic as, in a slow relentless motion over which he had no control, he turned and saw her there, naked on her back on the dusty floor, her dark and bottomless eyes fixed triumphantly on him, voluptuous and terrible with the dripping red mud (or maybe it *was* blood) smeared over her breasts, her belly, her arms and legs and open thighs. And as he stood, shaking like a leaf, and began to fall endlessly towards the gulf of her he knew, with a chill certainty amid the roaring of thunder and whisky, that in going to her he was going to his death.

Yesss! But you'll live again in many worlds, not just in one!

Then Sam plunged into the darkness with a crash that shook the attic floor, jarring the half-empty bottle of whisky off the chest of drawers and alerting Chrissa as the thunder still rolled and the rain began to pour.

They stood unmoving in the dingy murk as rain rattled the roof, neither willing to get too close to the half-seen shape of Sam's body. He lay in a heap on the floor between the pile of broken chairs and a stack of ancient

168

suitcases. The attic stank of spilled whisky, and as she joined her mother Chrissa had the prickly sense of something waiting and watching. Bracing herself, she overcome her fear and knelt down by her father. His position was foetal, on his right side, left hand uppermost and limp against his flank. In the gloom the emerald shone like a hard cold green eye. Chrissa reached out, then paused, her hackles rising. 'Mum!' she hissed, 'I need the light!' But since entering the attic Diane had felt panic begin to freeze her.

'Where is it?' she asked shakily, her mind growing numb.

'To your left,' Chrissa whispered. 'Quick, Mum! Quick!'

Diane's hand crept along the flaking wall, then stopped.

'Won't it wake him up?'

'No! He's completely out! Can't you smell the whisky?'

Diane could. It made her gag. Trembling, now quite unnerved, she found the switch. Harsh light sprang on, gleaming through the chairlegs. Now they saw him clearly: Chrissa sighed and Diane gasped with shock at his taut, horrified expression, at his pallor, at the Elastoplast crisscrossing his left cheek, at the dried blood caking his jaw. His eyes were shut and his breathing was shallow, and on his left index finger ... very tentatively Chrissa lifted his left hand. It was slippery with washing-up liquid and felt boneless. She felt sick as she took hold of the ring.

The moment she touched it his body jerked and his head jumped as if an electric current had run through him. Chrissa flinched.

And he laughed.

It wasn't his voice that laughed.

It was a low, throaty, woman's laugh, and both Chrissa and Diane jumped back in horror as his head slowly twisted up over his left shoulder, the rest of his body not moving at all. His eyes, dark and wet and fathomless, opened and fixed on them, and a dizzy terror seized them, for there was nothing of Sam in those eyes at all. Side by side they held each other and stared into a black and ageless abyss as rich, mocking delight twisted his face. His mouth opened wide like a new wound next to the bloodstained Elastoplast, and Diane shrieked as the wet hypnotic gleam of his eyes brightened. 'Don't look at his eyes, Mum!' Chrissa shouted, searching frantically for the song ... *Quant lo bouié* ... as he licked his lips and began to speak in a tender voice — a woman's voice so soft they could barely hear it over the drumming of the rain.

'But it won't come off, Chrissa. It won't come off until he comes through my gate, and there's nothing you can do about it.'

His face smiled, as white as bleached bone.

'I've been waiting so long,' the soft voice continued, 'I've been trapped and denied by men with brain but no heart, but I'll not see all I love destroyed by fools! If I give up now and wither away then the fire and flood will visit this world again, very soon, because I'm needed, and without me there is no balance! I refuse to see my world destroyed again! I'll take flesh and blood and recover the power I had long ago, for as I am there's little I can do. So Sam must come to me, because I need him to fulfil the ancient promise that the Shining Ones broke!'

'Oh God!' Diane wailed. 'Oh heaven help us all!' — but in that moment Chrissa found, not the song, but an enormous rage that filled her and burst from her; she felt tongues of fire shooting from every part of her as she rushed forward and began shaking Sam's body violently, refusing to look in those eyes. 'No!' she screamed. 'You can't have him! He's my father, and YOU'D BETTER LET HIM GO! DO YOU HEAR ME! I WON'T LET YOU HAVE HIM!'

But even as she shook him the voice remained soft:

'Keep on listening to those weak fools, Chrissa, and the Shift will come and kill you and everyone else. *Now look in my eyes!*'

'NO, I WON'T! GET OUT OF...'

Then she stopped, for (inadvertently, it seemed) she found herself gazing into those depths, into those gleaming and bottomless pits, and her own eyes widened as her mouth fell open, and she plunged into ...

... *The huge wave, curling high above her head, high above the ruined skeletons of fire-blackened buildings around her, its frothing lip filthy with debris seized in its march already, and its roaring the worst sound in all the world, louder even than the shrieking storm-wind which already wrought its own huge calamities in the wake of the fire that came in the night. So very high in the blood-black sky towers the wave; it crashes on like an unstoppable horseman, and any second now it will crash down on her, on all the poor charred corpses that lie stinking in the ruined streets; it will plunge and wash the entire world clean, so clean that nothing will live. Terror seizes her then, mixed with brief amazement at how she's survived this long, and a huge sense of futility as, with the wave's wild curling lip already plunging, the wind that rides before it hurls at her a flapping thing, a face that has her howling with instinctive fear before she recognises it as a half-burned poster from the lost world before the fire and flood. And in dreamlike awe she reads — SOON! MADONNA AT THE HAMMERSMITH ODEON! Then too late she turns to run ... but even as she does there is a light, a shining light, a shining, burning face that ...*

'... HIM!' With a shudder Chrissa tore herself out of those depths, the shining fire inside her. 'GO ON!' she screamed, shaking him. 'GET OUT!' And at this Sam's face snarled as the dark heat faded from his eyes; his body began to flex and tense with eerie subcutaneous ripplings as if worms writhed under his skin; thick white drool gathered at his lips. 'Chrissa, stop!' Diane behind her wailed, but Chrissa only rocked him harder so that his head lolled back and forth, gaping at her with those awful but now empty eyes, broken sounds frothing and gargling from his mouth. 'I'M NOT SCARED OF YOU!' Chrissa yelled, panting and red-faced, 'I KNOW WHAT YOU ARE! YOU'RE THE ENEMY, YOU'RE A LIAR, YOU'RE SCARED OF PEOPLE WHO SEE WHAT YOU ARE AND YOU TRY TO KILL THEM OR DRIVE THEM MAD, BUT I'M NOT

SCARED, SO GET OUT, GET OUT, *GET OUT!*' And Sam's body shuddered and twisted against her hands as Diane, moaning with fear, tried to pull her off, but Chrissa would not let go. 'Dad?' she cried now in a different voice, sensing a change. 'Dad! Sam! Sam Joyce! Come back! Wake up! Wake up NOW!'

Sam surged up, his fists clenching, but still Chrissa went on shaking him ... until suddenly the voice howled in fury and outrage. Then Sam went limp. His eyes closed and his face relaxed into stupefaction. 'Whaaas goin' on?' he slurred, 'Lemme sleep ... jus' lemme sleep ...'

'Okay, Dad. You sleep now.' Chrissa sank back, exhausted. The rain still beat down but the storm was dying. For now. *Fire and Flood.* She shuddered; seemed to see the black-robed faceless ones who wished to kill the world ... and from the heart of the light inside her she knew it would come, just as she'd seen in the Enemy eyes, though not necessarily for the reasons the Enemy gave. Unless we beat her, and the rest of them, she thought, feeling quite empty. 'He's okay for now, Mum,' she said dully.

But Diane, mumbling quietly to herself, was in shock.

Chrissa sighed. I'll have to be the adult, she realised sadly. Very slowly and stiffly she got to her feet and took her mother by the arm. 'Come on, Mum. Downstairs now. We'll let him sleep it off.'

Yet he still wore the ring, and she had not the energy to try again.

14.
Test Match Special

It was after ten that night when Sam awoke. He had not so much as a headache, but his body ached abominably — particularly his left cheek and one of his fingers — and his memory was gone. He had no idea why he awoke on the attic floor so stiff and painful, nor why Chrissa sat watching him, her strangely gaunt face disfigured by an ugly black bruise on her right cheek, her blue eyes so piercing that for a moment he didn't know her. My God, he thought, is that my daughter?

'What happened to you?' he grunted, blinking up at her.

'Nothing much.' She didn't smile. 'How do you feel?'

'Sore.' *She sounds just like a nurse!* 'What's going on?'

'Can you get up?' she asked as if she thought he couldn't.

'What do you mean, can I get up?' As he sat up his gut rumbled. 'God, I'm hungry!' he exclaimed, and Chrissa seemed taken aback.

'You don't remember? You don't even feel sick?'

'What is this?' He winced, seeming not to see the ring at all as he touched first his index finger, then his cheek. 'I feel like I've been through a meat grinder! And what in hell happened to your face?'

'I collided with a wall.' She seemed somehow too

calm. 'Dad, come downstairs and I'll get you something to eat.' Eyeing him dubiously she backed down the step-ladder. *Madame's trying something new*, a voice in her whispered quietly. *So can we! Get him in front of the TV set.* Startled, from the landing she said: 'Are you *sure* you don't remember anything?'

'About what?' Uneasy now, wincing as he followed her, he racked his brains, trying to remember. But nothing came. 'Chrissa, what . . .'

'You've been ill,' she told him carefully, keeping her distance, her too-bright eyes resting on him. 'I'm glad you're feeling better, but I want you to go straight into the living-room and stay there while I make you something to eat. Mum's in the kitchen, she's very upset, and if she saw you now it wouldn't help. Will you do it, Dad? Please?'

'Chrissa!' Confused by her adult presumption — she sounded as if *he* were the child, not her — he floundered for words. 'I'm not a bloody invalid, you know, and if you think . . .'

'Can you tell me what day it is, Dad?'

'Of course! It's . . .' And he stared at her.

'You see? Now. What do you want to eat?'

Sam shrugged. 'Anything! But what . . .'

While he was still bewildered she shunted him into the living-room, turned on the TV, and sat him down in front of it. She had to push him into his seat, but he accepted the pressure as if not really aware of it. She felt exhausted, as if she'd been wading through treacle for hours on end. But worst of all was having to treat her father like an idiot.

'Stay there,' she ordered him. 'I'll be back in a minute.'

She went into the kitchen, shutting the door behind her. Diane sat at the table, pale, staring at nothing in particular.

'He's awake, Mum. He doesn't remember. I'm making him something to eat.' Chrissa sighed. 'Why not go to bed and get some sleep?'

'I'm not leaving you up with him!' Diane shivered. His

174

eyes were slightly glazed. 'I think it's best if we stay with Mona tonight.'

'Oh, Mum!' Wearily Chrissa opened a can of tomato soup. 'He's quite harmless at the moment.'

But why in front of the TV? she was wondering.

Sam found himself watching *Test Match Special*. Chrissa had switched on BBC2 just as *Newsnight* (on the Geneva arms talks) was followed by Peter West and Richie Benaud reporting with edited highlights of the fourth day's play of the Third Test between England and Australia at Edgbaston. Cricket bored Sam silly, but during the calypso credits sequence he hardly noticed: he was too busy wondering what in hell was going on. I've been ill? he asked himself dubiously. Okay, so I don't feel great, but nothing's wrong with my mind! Does it matter if I've forgotten what day it is?

Yet as Peter West smiled from the screen it began dawning on him that the day of the week wasn't all he couldn't remember. Alarmed, he touched his taped-up cheek. 'WHAT — IS — GOING — ON?' he demanded through clenched teeth ... and the fear began to rise in him like an unstoppable tide.

'Well, we had a splendid day's play here at Edgbaston,' Peter West told him cheerfully. 'There was some cloud early on, but that cleared up before lunch, and we had three full and uninterrupted sessions. Not often we can say *that* this summer — eh, Richie?' And he grinned from the screen as Sam, distracted, leaned forward with the intention of turning him off. 'Don't do that, Sam,' he said casually. 'I suggest you sit back and watch, or you might miss the next over. It affects everyone, not just you. Doesn't it occur to you that your, er, *Red Woman* might just be bowling you a googly you haven't picked up?'

'Wha-a-at?' stuttered Sam, completely disbelieving his ears.

'You heard,' said Peter West briskly. 'Sit back and listen, Sam. You haven't played the game with a very straight bat recently, have you?'

'What — is — this?' Sam demanded yet again.

'Australia's tail-enders were dismissed for the addition of only seven more runs this morning,' the commentator told him innocently. 'Robinson and Gooch opened England's second innings and made a steady start against some — I'd call it *wayward* bowling, wouldn't you, Richie? — taking twenty off the first four overs. We join play in the fifth over at the Berkeley Road end, with Sam Joyce facing Mother Goose bowling to three slips and ...'

Sam, bemused, managed to switch to Channel Four.

'... so if we're to understand this phenomenon of pole-shift,' said a golden-haired young talking head, identified on the screen as Tony Wilson Roberts Ph.D. of Berkeley, California, 'then we have to stop acting like ostriches and start facing the facts. For example: fossil amphibians and reptiles the size of deer have been found in Antarctica; there have been icecaps in India and the Sudan; not so long ago the North Pole was located at Hudson's Bay.' Dr Roberts grinned engagingly. 'Corals have been found in Spitzbergen, whales in Michigan, hippopotami in York-shire, England, coals in Alaska and seashells at the top of the Andes and Himalayas. We have the Piri Re'is map showing Antarctica before it was iced, and other ancient maps clearly indicating Greenland to consist of at least three islands — a fact only recently established by the seismic studies of Paul-Emile Victor — and of course the curious black isle discovered west of the Azores in 1882 by Captain Davey Joyce, who ...'

With an anxious curse Sam changed channels again:

'... conventions of twentieth-century poetry,' a donnish type proclaimed against a background of cold grey slag heaps. 'Berkeley's metaphysical inquiry ushers in the Industrial Revolution: nearly two centuries later we find Eliot in *The Wasteland* expressing modern industrial man's deep-seated angst thus:' — the don cleared his throat — '*Mother Goose is on the loose, and Sam is on the lam; She's made a noose to cook his goose, and turn him into ham!*' The don frowned. 'Though it must be said that metrically ...'

'Shit!' Sam exclaimed, now on hands and knees in front of the set as he switched again, this time to a movie which he quickly recognised as *The Towering Inferno*. After several seconds of watching people leap from the blazing skyscraper he shut his eyes and turned back to *Test Match Special* even as Chrissa, carrying a bowl of soup and a plate of buttered toast, came in behind him. She paused, unseen and unheard ... and saw him recoil with a hiss from the instantly-recognisable sight (even to her) of Ian Botham hitting the ball out of the ground for six.

But what he saw was the world tumbling over and over through space like a drunken ping-pong ball. 'That's it, Sam,' Peter West told him grimly. 'If you bat for the wrong side then in about fifteen years we'll all be hit for six. You see, there's going to be a new North Pole ... in central China. And this time it'll be more than rain stopped play.' Peter West grimaced. 'More like fire and flood. For ever.'

'When that happens,' Richie Benaud added in a grim Australian twang, we don't just lose the Ashes, we all turn into 'em.'

'True, Richie. Very true.'

'So what am I supposed to do about it?' Chrissa heard Sam demand aggressively as Botham squared up to another ball from McDermott.

'It's not just you, Sam,' Peter West said sternly. 'It's all of us. So we play for money now, but that doesn't mean we can't still act like real gentlemen. If not ...' — he shrugged fatalistically — '... then it's bingo for the pole-shift due to ... what was it, Richie?'

'Our negative psychokinetic interaction with the bio-sphere, Peter. Too much anger and greed literally leads to volcanic eruption and worse!'

'Crap!' Sam snapped.

'Dad!' Chrissa interrupted. She was now so tired she could hardly think. Only later she knew she'd made a mistake by distracting him.

Flinching, he turned, and it took him time to know her.

'Chrissa ... tell me ... what do you see ... on TV?'

'Cricket, Dad. Here's your soup and some toast.'

Doubtfully he turned back to the TV. '... And Botham takes another almighty hoick at that one,' said Peter West even as the action replay cut in with split-second detail. 'This time he doesn't make contact, but if he had he'd have hit the space shuttle with it ... wouldn't you say, Richie?'

'Maybe not *that* far, Peter.'

Sam sighed as he leaned forward and switched the TV off. 'What's happening?' he asked, helpless like a child.

'Your supper.' Chrissa, face a mask, set the soup and toast down by him on the floor. 'What do you think you saw?'

He gestured vaguely. 'My finger hurts,' he said in a slack sad voice. 'And my cheek.' Slowly he raised his left hand and eyed the ring with its depths of moon and horns. 'I can't remember anything,' he said dully.

But *I'm* supposed to be the kid! she thought sadly, struggling against tides of sleep sweeping over her. 'Why don't you sleep in here tonight?' she suggested. 'Drink up your soup and I'll bring you some blankets.'

He nodded without hearing. Back in the kitchen she told Diane, 'I think he's okay for tonight.' She yawned. 'He'll sleep on the settee. You look beat, Mum. Go to bed, please? I won't be long, really!'

Diane didn't object. Since coming down from the attic hours earlier she'd had no clear sense of normality. Whatever she looked at, including her daughter, seemed alien. Vaguely she heard and as vaguely, with the caution of a woman much older, she stood. 'But you will lock your door, won't you, dear?' she said as she turned to the stairs. And step by step, without looking into the living-room, Diane went upstairs to sleep.

Left alone, Chrissa tried to recall what she was doing. Blankets. Making Dad's bed. Arduously she went up to the airing cupboard, got two, and took them down to the living-room. There she found Sam staring at the viscous surface of his untouched tomato soup. He didn't even

178

look up. She couldn't bring herself to speak. Dumping the blankets, she went back to the kitchen to turn out the lights. She saw the car keys on their hook above the fridge. Fleetingly she wondered: Is it safe to leave them there? She was about to remove them when she thought, yawning hugely: Don't be silly! The state he's in he couldn't start a car, let alone drive it.

Her legs felt like ton weights as she climbed up to her room, and she fell asleep on her bed without locking the door or even undressing. The time was quarter to midnight. She'd never felt so tired in all her life before; she knew oblivion as a blessing even as she sank into it . . .

In the living-room Sam was tired too.

He crawled onto the settee and slept.

. . . and gradually he swims out of the great dark abyss to find himself still lost and confused by the gabble of the Weak Ones. He floats through the marketplace where naked hooded victims hang by the feet from hooks in the bloody walls; where blank-eyed gabblers surround him, jostling and shoving, none of them ever silent. Even in confusion he feels contempt, for they have no memory of themselves, no sense that there's anything to remember. Yet his own state is little better. Vaguely he recalls the terror of flood and fiery rain; vaguely he knows he's here to do something, meet someone. But what or who he has no idea . . . until she appears before him amid the crowd. Raven-haired, she wears a gorgeous green robe and her eyes, lustrous and dark, look deep into his. 'Why did you listen to those Weak Ones?' she demands sadly. 'How will you remember anything if you let them confuse you? Now, what have you got to show me you remember?'

Then as if he's always known it he knows he must show her the emerald ring, which he does. Taking it from him, she touches the moon and horns in such a way that without warning, abruptly, they're elsewhere and elsewhen, transported from that doomed city and through a gate into a vast nocturnal forest amid her own mysterious realm. He gapes at giant, vine-laden trees that tower above the mossy, winding, dangerous path. Impatient, she urges him to follow; in time under the bright hard moon they emerge from the wood at the base of a high rocky place. 'Do you know this place?' she asks him eagerly. 'Do you remember the whole place?' But all he can do is grin like an idiot. Sighing, she leads him through a jagged cleft into the depths of the hill ... into the temple and the maze beyond it. Deep beneath the earth she leads him, through twists and turns with never a word spoken, their way lit by the emerald's glow that shines on the slick black walls. And his unease grows — WHAT HAVE I FORGOTTEN? — but his mood is numb, dreamlike, and so on and on he follows, ever deeper until at last she brings him to a rough rock chamber with a floor of earth. This floor is split from side to side by a narrow chasm of unknown depth from which coils a choking vapour. Astride the chasm amid the chamber stands a brass tripod. Upon this sits a carved wooden box. With a smile she gives him a silver key; and with a trembling, unsure hand he opens the box. He pauses. 'Go on!' she urges. Then from the box he lifts out the tiny set of seven silver bells which, even as he lifts them, chime with music so sweet — a music of memory so faraway yet clear — that tears spring to his eyes. For now at long last he remembers, and his tears of loss and rage flow faster, for even this lovely music, he knows, is no more than a faint reflection of the treasure stolen from them, from the Watchers. THAT TREASURE STOLEN FROM US WHEN WE WERE LOCKED DOWN HERE! OUR BIRTHRIGHT! OUR LIFE AND HOPE OF LIFE! THE SHINING ONES DISPOSSESSED US, CLOSED THE STAR-CHAMBER, LOCKED US HERE TO AWAIT THE FIRE AND FLOOD WHEN IT COMES AGAIN! And he groans with grief as the bells chime on ... yet it isn't what he does remember but what lies beyond memory that infuriates him. For even as he weeps at the beauty of the music he cannot quite recall the exact nature of the treasure. And watching him she chants softly, even as the sweet music tortures him and the fumes from the chasm begin to overcome him: 'That is how it is for all of us. For the treasure we lose is what we forget, and the thicker in time the more we forget, until soon we lose all!' Now her voice, vibrant, rings like the bells themselves; he goes whirling into her eyes. 'It cannot be weighed or measured,' she sings, 'it's older and younger than time; more free than the birds or the wind; no word catches it, no hand holds it, no man owns it; the theft of it blights the world! For this treasure is wisdom: without it there's only fire and flood, again

180

and again and again, and every time the disaster's forgotten. But now you come to me, and this time — this time, for I have a plan! — we'll outwit those who stole us from ourselves; we'll open up the Starchamber gate and bring memory back to the world in time!'

With these words ringing in his mind he slept, and in time awoke back to that world which for thousands of years had suffered the consequences of the theft, where every law but that of marketplace and jungle had been forgotten. He awoke on the settee in the living-room at 15 Berkeley Road, he awoke hurting, angry and afraid; he awoke confused by the sense of being more or other than Sam Joyce, by the sense of vast forgotten knowledge now trembling on the edge of recall. Yet he awoke energetic, with the tears still in his eyes from the beauty of the music, and with her voice calling out in his mind, telling him: *IT'S TIME! TAKE THE KEYS! BRING THE RING! COME TO ME NOW! COME NOW, FOR THEY'RE ALL ASLEEP BUT YOU! NOW!*

15.
The Chase

Somewhere an engine revved as Chrissa, subliminally alarmed, stirred abruptly from the depths of dreamless sleep. Even as she sat up on her bed she was thinking, with cold clarity: I made three mistakes. I should have tried for the ring again. I shouldn't have interrupted him when he was watching TV. And I should have taken the car keys from ...

It hit her. She scrambled to the window, parting curtains just in time to see the Volvo pulling away from the kerb in the street below.

'Dad!' she screamed. 'Dad! Come back!'

Maybe it isn't him! Maybe it's just someone stealing it! Oh please let it be that! Why did I let her put me to sleep! Oh, Chrissa!

She hurried down to the living-room. Sam wasn't there. Into the kitchen. The car keys were gone. 'He'll kill himself!' she cried as she ran for the front door, remembering how he'd driven on the way back from Cuilchonich. *Oh no he won't*, came the quiet voice. *She'll get him there*. And then she was out on the street ... but the car was gone, and Sam with it. On bare feet she stood under a streetlamp, gazing uselessly along the empty road, not realising that Diane watched her from an upstairs window. Back inside she limped and flopped down

182

despairingly at the kitchen table.

'How could I be so stupid?' she scolded herself, unaware of Diane coming quietly down the stairs. 'I *knew* this would happen!'. Then again through her fury came the quiet voice. *Maybe you wanted this to happen*, it suggested. *What about that call you made to Heathrow?*

'Don't be idiotic!' she snapped, grinding the heels of her hands so hard against her eyeballs that soon she saw him there, conjured up and writhing amid the bright winking sparks. 'It's you that wants it, not me! I didn't ask for any of this! I didn't want to start being terrified every time I try to sleep; it wasn't me that wanted to walk into a bog. I don't even care if you *did* burn to death! A fat lot of help you are anyway! Why didn't you wake me up or at least warn me? She sent us to sleep, didn't she! And you couldn't stop it! Now I suppose you want me to go after him and ... oh, I don't see why I should, and anyway ...'

Standing tousled and pale behind her in the doorway, Diane saw Chrissa check, startled, as if someone had interrupted her.

'*Sweet child*,' he whispered like a distant wind, '*face the truth. You called for help, and I heard, and at her gate I waited. You were lost — until you heard the Herdsman's Song and called my name ...*'

'But I don't even know your name!' And Diane shut her eyes tight as her daughter cried out, and again Chrissa checked, lifting her head and listening. 'Oh,' the girl said wonderingly, in a totally different tone, and murmured words that made no sense at all: '... *Quant lo bouié ... ben de laura ...* do you mean that ... *ben de ...* Bernard de Lau ...'

'Chrissa!' Diane laughed in sheer disbelief. 'Stop it! You're talking to thin air! And why were you out on the street?'

Chrissa whirled round, eyes wide, mouth open, and saw her mother there in nightie and slippers, hair in a mess, not even wearing her glasses. In shock she tried to recover herself as her insight fled. 'Oh no! Mum, I —

Mum ... ah ... Mum, what ... Mum, he's gone, Dad's gone!' she cried in a rush. 'I woke up when he started the car but I was too late. I shouted but ... he just wouldn't stop! Mum, did you ...'

'I heard you,' Diane said drily. Why am I so calm? she wondered. Automatically she filled and switched on the kettle, then sat down. She breathed deep, eyeing her flustered daughter. She'd woken suddenly, but for the first time in weeks with a clear head. As if a long, dulling fog had been lifted. She thought: People say you feel like this when someone desperately ill has died at last. 'I should be afraid,' she told Chrissa in a gentle, conversational voice. 'I know where he's gone. The place the ring likes.' That's why my head's clear again, she thought. Because he's gone. Flatly she added: 'You realise we may never see him again?'

'What?' Chrissa stared at her in complete amazement.

'Oh, Chrissa.' Diane sighed ruefully. 'I'm not an idiot. You don't have to pretend, not any more. It's too late for that. Maybe soon I'll start screaming, but at this moment I just don't care.' And she asked mildly, 'Who were you talking to? Your burning man?'

Chrissa gripped the edge of the table, hard. She eyed her mother and saw behind the mildness a fierce anger; something Diane was probably not yet aware of herself. 'Yes, Mum,' she said numbly, still shocked and taken aback but deciding to take the bull by the horns. 'But that doesn't really matter, not ... not just now.' Hesitating, she said more sharply. 'I called Heathrow. I mean ... I thought he'd do this. There's a Dan-Air flight going to Inverness at nine in the morning. We could hire a car when we get there and maybe get to ... to Cuilchonich before he does, and ...'

'Maybe *I* could. Maybe *I* will.' Sounding more definite than she had in weeks, Diane got up and switched off the kettle. 'But *you*'re not going anywhere, Chrissa Joyce! You're much safer babbling to your burning man here!' Suddenly she decided what to do. 'Now. I'm calling the police. The state he's in he probably won't even get as far

184

as the motorway, but if he does ...' She shrugged. Leaving Chrissa gaping, she went to the phone.

I've messed it up completely, Chrissa thought miserably. Yet then, as Diane dialled, in her mind she heard that sweet sad song and once again found herself looking down on it all as if from a huge height. Abruptly she remembered the name. *His* name! 'But Mum,' she heard herself say, 'you don't even know where it is. The place the ring likes, I mean. You can't get there without me, and it's no good ringing the police. *She* won't let them stop him ... and she won't let him crash either ...'

Chilled, Diane set the phone back on its cradle.

'What do you mean, *she*?' Diane asked from the doorway.

Chrissa met her eyes, and again Diane no longer knew her daughter.

'You know, Mum,' said the gaunt golden-haired girl with the blue eyes that were suddenly much too bright. 'I *know* you know.'

Father Bernard, Chrissa was thinking. *Bernard de Laurac!*

Amid a cold dark winter night in another age the goodman Bernard, once Chevalier of Laurac in the warm lands that lie between the banks of Ariège and those of Aude, once welcome at all the courts of the Lauragais for his songs sung under the red rose, tosses restlessly in a lumpy, bug-ridden bed in the windy garret of a believer's house in a backstreet of Puigcerda. This shabbily discreet dwelling is open to all exiles from the war north of the mountains. For years the French have been murdering whoever won't bow to the cross of the false god. The garret window is unglassed: the shutters keep banging open: beyond moonlight-drenched rooftops glow high Pyrenean peaks. Slowly, soaked in sweat, the sense of an abyss beneath him, he's alerted by the banging and stirs from the dream that's toremented him since All Saints when his companion Gaillard was seized and burned at Foix — since All Saints when the shepherd Pierre Belot, sent by Bishop Guilhabert at Montségur, came to his hiding-place and led him through the passes to shameful safety here in the Cerdagne. 'Perhaps,' he mutters, needing the reassurance of his

*own voice as he gazes at the pale peaks, 'it's guilt. Why do I live
on with Gaillard dead? Or maybe it's Satan's temptation; a
succubus sent to test me. Why else would I dream every night of a
golden girl with blue eyes that would try a saint! Who is she?
And where's that place she cries out from?' He shudders. That
black, horrible place. 'Every night I wake up in a sweat! My
prayers tell me nothing! Yet if she's evil then why do I also hear,
whenever she cries, that song I found so long ago? That song I
haven't sung since the war began! Over twenty years! How does
she know it? And whenever I ask her who she serves and she cries:
"The Shining Ones!" — could the Evil One claim that? And
how does she know my name, why does she address me as she
does?' And as he stares out into the wild moonlit night still she
seems to cry to him in terror from that awful underground place
which he fears to admit he knows, over and over she cries as,
groaning, he crawls out of bed to pray:*

*'Father! Father Bernard! If you don't come soon it'll be too
late!'*

Exhilarated and terrified, both driver and driven as he
beat time to Brian Ferry's 'Stone Woman', Sam cruised
up the fast lane of the M6 with his mind running wild. To
the east the night sky was lit by the smoky orange glow of
the Potteries; from his sound-blasted cockpit he eyed the
dreamsnake road unwinding ahead. I must be in a video
booth, he told himself, fascinated. I mean I've driven on
automatic before, I've let the robot take over, but never
like this. Didn't Lindbergh feel the same when exhaustion
got him on his solo across the Atlantic, that someone else
was flying? Maybe it's me that's driving ... but it's a me I
never met.

Hi there! Pleased to meet me! Hope I know my name!

He tried to joke, but in truth he was petrified. Since
snapping out of the beautiful music of the bells he'd been
caught in multiple identity so confusing that now he was
sure of nothing. Driver or driven? Yes, it was himself,
Sam Joyce, who'd woken up, left the house, got in the car
and driven away; himself who'd ignored Chrissa's cry
from the window; himself here now groaning through

clenched teeth (*I want to stop and GO BACK!*) with his right foot hard down on the gas (*We MUST get there first!*); and for sure it was Sam Joyce now changing tapes, now tapping his unemployed brake-foot to Dylan's 'Jokerman' (*There's one for you, Chrissa! Think you'll stop us?*) even as the dark satanic glow of Midlands mills declined behind.

HIMself? NO! MYself! But ...

It was different last Friday, he told himself fiercely. The me driving now didn't know how to drive then, we weren't connected to twentieth-century circuits, we knew more about moon and horns than gear-changing ... but now we're acquainted, aren't we? *Aren't we?* Now (*he sees the speedo's emerald worm slide up almost to 100mph as the Volvo shoots past a succession of big Eurorigs barrelling north through the night*) we know what's going on. It's just Sam who doesn't. Drunken, desperate, socially-caring Sam, too scared to admit or remember anything. Tried to keep us out but got too drunk! Now we're in and moving! Hi there, Sam! Enjoying the ride?

His face fell, his mouth opened, his eyes shut. NO I'M NOT! he cried silently as a horn blared and brakes screeched. In a panic he corrected too far right and nearly hit the central barrier ... then something strong and firm straightened him out, pulled him away from the truck he'd almost hit. Yes, of course there's risk! he agreed, strong and firm. But nothing ventured, nothing gained, eh? The connection's mine ... though that stupid girl could have ruined everything. Just as well she didn't try for the ring again ... she'd have had us then. But now we've got a head start, so don't fuck up! Right? *Right?*

As he eased down to ninety a vast loneliness seized him, crowding in from the heights of the night. 'Diane?' he whispered, forlorn and sad. 'Chrissa?' Then he shook his head. 'Nope!' he declared. 'They won't stop us now. How can they? They don't have the strength. They're *weak*. Look how they tried to hit us through the TV with all that crap about the Shift being swayed by human morality, by good or evil thoughts!' And he laughed out loud. 'They're like those morons who call AIDS divine retribution! Oh please, God,' he went on in a scathing falsetto, 'we're all thinking nice thoughts, we're supporting Live Aid and joining Greenpeace, so please don't flip the poles! We'll vote Labour and get rid of nuclear weapons, honest!' He shook his head incredulously. 'Unbelievable! *Weak Ones!* Suckers who don't have the faintest idea! But we'll straighten it out ... once we get Sam here to the whole place ... once we get our bodies back ...'

And with vast vague images surging in him he drove on and on until at length dawn came rising dull over decayed industrial landscapes. Salford, he recognised. He checked his watch. Just after five, and halfway there. Soon he pulled in to an all-night station and filled up. 'Going far?' the pump attendant asked. He grinned. 'You could say that,' he agreed with a conspiratorial wink. Then, his unknown mind balanced on a knife-edge above turmoil, he laughed out loud and pulled away without paying, leaving the man shouting and taking his number as dawn strengthened and he roared off north again. 'Why did I do that?' demanded the Sam in him, horrified. 'Oh, fuck off!' he shouted, remembering other times and spaces, remembering the beautiful music and everything that had been forgotten so long. 'You don't think it matters, do you?'

In this mood of scornful confidence he continued, wide awake and sure now that his driving would carry them safely to the place the ring liked.

Too sure.

For deep in him lay a memory like a scorpion under a rock, poised and ready to sting. Yet for another two hours it held back its barb as, amid an intoxication of vision and speed, the new Sam drove on past Lancaster and the Cumbrian hills to Carlisle and the Scottish border at Gretna, then up the A74 through Lockerbie and the Forest of Ae towards Glasgow. By now the sun was well up in a cloudless sky, and all the time, with the road map open on his lap, he was babbling and laughing in a way that terrified the suppressed Sam in him; all the time, with Radio 2 bringing him the daily news of a world at odds with itself, he went on crying out his sense of approaching triumph.

'Sam, *Sam, SAM!*' he cried as if to a recalcitrant child as he cruised between Hamilton ' and Motherwell to Glasgow's grimy heart. 'Don't you know who we are yet? Don't you understand your part in this? Listen! When the Sometimes Isle last sank, when the Starchamber was closed and the ring was lost we thought *everything* was lost! But she had a plan, and it's working! It began working a century ago when she took the woman you know as Madame, and Madame met your great-grandfather on the quay at Messina! It all comes from that! Your grandad couldn't wear it, your dad's a wimp, but YOU! YOU are the one we needed, and you're doing it now! Why be scared? You're our connection! You're one of us! Why let it worry you, our different voices? Soon we'll go through the gate — then you'll see! Things are not just this and that, black and white, but many and one in the same time! Sam, we have the right to live! Sam, we obeyed orders, and we were betrayed! Should we take that lying down? Would you? The Shining Ones betrayed us! We came down here to do a job with the apes, the near-men, and to do that we had to take flesh, which means passion and conflict! So we got involved — and for that we were punished? Listen! This planet's always been a problem, which is why the Shift mechanism was built into its internal dynamics, so that if you apes get too uppity the Elohim can always press the button that stops you getting out too far — what do you think world history's about anyway? Now come on! Stop worrying! There's not much time, we've got a lot to do, there's a way to go — so which road do we take? Up the M9 past Stirling? Or the Road to the Isles, by yon bonny banks and yon bonny braes? Yes, why not? Cities stink! We'll tak' the high road, right? Sure!'

Sure! he thought, and so in his driving dream he took the M8 through the middle of Glasgow, and at Dumbarton on the banks of the sluggish Clyde turned north to

Loch Lomond, to caravan sites and marinas ... and it was even as the bleak bare Highlands opened up beyond the loch's sunlit waters, even as the road narrowed to snake round blind tree-thick waterside bends, that the scorpion tensed its barb, prepared to strike.

He'd been driving now for six full hours with one brief break, yet even so he took that lochside road at motorway speed: maybe too tired maybe too eager, maybe too sure his fate would take care of everything. Or maybe it was the intoxication of fresh mountain air rushing into the car as vision of what seemed like memory flooded his mind. *Remember that cavern under the whole place where she led you?* *Yes, I do!* And for an instant he was there: the box on the tripod astride the fuming chasm, and the bells, and their beautiful, beautiful music! Oh ... God ..., he thought sadly, letting the Volvo swerve, so that with a sudden shock he had to wake up and pull it back on course. Yet the ... *memory* ... wouldn't let him go.

And do you recall what happened next? The last part of the rite by which we prepared this connection with you now?

Yes! I do! *Driving he finds himself there on the whole place, the Horned One rising as night falls on the deep woods and mountains; finds himself facing the Red Woman, she naked but for Blood of Mother, himself likewise but for the horns of Bull-That-Roars! And no Weak One there to distract us as we couple, as we fuse the seed that ensures our future and marries the past with NOW — Serpent and Earth, Apple in Garden! Yes, and there I fill her Cup, her Grail, her Womb; and we fling our will and prayer through all the heights and depths to find this lost Sam-self, this man of Last Days with his cock that crows, to steer it safe through the gate, to fertilise ghosts back to flesh and recover what's lost! Yes, but —*

That wasn't all. She demanded

(the scorpion creeps out; he shudders at the wheel)

a sacrifice to fire us further on our mission. And — Oh! — I

(the sting trembles above him; he closes his eyes)

was taken; I was grabbed; I was dragged underground to the bottommost chamber and there I was buried up to the neck! Yes, in that same place I heard the bells! Then they opened the gate in the walls; they let it out, and you watched from the gallery; I saw your eyes as they let it out! And it saw me and charged! And you laughed! O Bull-Priestess, drenched in blood, you laughed! Drenched in blood and hope and hunger! You laughed, and it charged, and you laughed! And I saw its eyes, blood-red like you, like Mars in the sky! It was mad and full of lust, and

(the terrible sting whips down)

I DIED HORRIBLY!!!

Sam screamed, flinching from the wheel, scorpion-stung, gored to death, skull crushed, splintered by the mad black bull so that his spirit might be flung free, ravening, and shot into a host ... into Samuel David Joyce ... in this time before the last days, this time before the fire and flood ...

He missed the bend.

The Volvo left the road at over 75mph.

Three hours later the Dan-Air BAC111 landed at Dalcross in bright sunshine. It was 10.30am; the flight was five minutes late. At the Hertz office, Diane picked up the red Vauxhall Astra ordered from Heathrow, and by eleven, with Chrissa map-reading, they were over the Kessock Bridge onto the Black Isle, heading west to Gairloch fifty miles away. *Black Isle*, noted Chrissa, but she said nothing. Mum was already jumpy, and they hadn't had any sleep. Neither of them had been to bed again. They'd sat in the kitchen arguing, Chrissa increasingly persuasive, Diane less and less certain. 'But Mum, if he didn't even show you on the map where it is, you won't find it without me! Mum, don't you realise I stopped him once already?' And so on until Diane had wearily agreed.

At seven thirty, just before they left the house, the phone had rung. It was the Strathclyde Police. The Volvo (same number as one driven away from a Lancashire filling station without paying) had been found wrecked, rolled over on the shores of Loch Lomond. There were no witnesses; no other car was involved ... and there was no sign of the driver, whose details had been traced through the number plate. Then yet again Diane had been struck by a sense of inevitability, of invisibly rigged odds. Sam was not only still alive and kicking, but very much in motion, possibly not far from Gairloch. Then her last vestiges of disbelief collapsed. So too did her initial calm of the night before. Maybe, she'd told herself desperately, there's still an outside chance ... though of what she wasn't sure. With Chrissa urging her on she hadn't stopped to think. It had been a whirlwind of last-minute credit card bookings, taxis, telephone calls from the flight lounge; then ninety minutes of emotional misery at 15,000 feet. For during the flight Diane had felt all her beliefs falling apart. The horror of what had gone on in the attic ...! And all of it! She felt unhinged! Yet Chrissa beside her, deep in a book, had seemed perfectly calm. Again and again Diane had stolen agonised looks at her daughter, wanting to talk but not knowing where to start. How *did* one talk about what they were going through?

'*Oh Chrissa, when you were talking to thin air last night* ...'

But talking to thin air was only a minor aberration amid so many, and now, driving steadily up the wooded Conon valley past Garve to the bare Ross highlands, Diane had to admit to feeling ... not calm, but fatalistic. At least I'm doing something, she thought. It may still turn out to be no more than a bad dream. We've made mistakes, yes, but surely we can clear them up. So, with Chrissa still quiet beside her, she continued trying to fool herself amid tourist traffic all the way past Achnasheen and through the empty land. Soon, at the top of Glen Docherty's narrow defile, they saw stretching before them the twenty-mile ribbon of Loch Maree, serene in the sun. The busy road followed the lochside most of the way to Gairloch and the western sea: the holiday sensation induced by the scenic splendour was a cruel irony that both of them felt but neither mentioned. For what they saw seemed a thin veil now; pretence was all they had left.

192

Chrissa, though she refused to show it, was beginning to feel panic. What if I have to follow him? she was wondering, remembering those writhing blood-red lights as she gazed at the ancient mountains ahead. What if I never see London or Mum or anything I know ever again? What happens when those burning worms start eating you? Is it like dying? And then again she heard that quiet little voice, *his* voice, the voice that part of her loved but another part doubted more with every passing mile:

There are a million ways to die then live again, sweet child!

'Go away!' she whispered fearfully. 'Leave me alone!'

'What?' Diane jumped at the wheel. 'What did you say?'

'Nothing,' Chrissa muttered, squeezing her eyes shut. Nothing *nothing NOTHING!* What if there's NOTHING?

Well, she thought coldly, then it doesn't matter much, does it?

At the densely-wooded western end of the loch the road narrowed into a series of sharp bends as it climbed up through Slattadale Forest. They slowed to a crawl amid thick traffic. More than once Diane swung out to pass, but it was impossible. Behind them the driver of a yellow Bedford camper was equally impatient crowding them so close that Diane got angry. 'Just fuck off, will you!' she yelled uncharacteristically, waving two fingers up over her shoulder so that Chrissa, jolted out of her dark sad reverie, looked back. The camper's driver and front seat passenger weren't clearly visible because of the tinted windscreen ... but for a moment ...

No, she told herself shakily, I'm just imagining it.

Again she ruffled open the map on her lap.

'Only a few more miles,' she told Diane, dry-mouthed.

'And when we get there, then what? What if he's there already?'

'Then we've lost,' said Chrissa simply. 'But I bet he isn't, not if he had to hitch. We'll have to try and ... and intercept him.'

'Fine.' Diane, with a sense of unreality, listened to

herself being reasonable. 'But he won't go to Cuil-chonich, will he? He'll expect us to follow or be there already. He might start from anywhere.'

Chrissa frowned at the map. It was the same one she'd taken up on the moor, still pulpy from the rain. Only six days ago! she realised as she found the little cluster of Fairy Lochs (they were unnamed) and beside them the triangulation point of Sidhean Mór. 'Mum, the road's closest to the place about half a mile before Cuilchonich.' Her voice sounded faraway. 'It's best to wait up there. We can see him coming without him seeing us.'

'What if he doesn't come for hours yet.' Diane felt increasingly full of doubt and fear. The closer they got the stronger her sense of calamity grew. 'Or what if when he does come he gets violent if we try to stop him going into this place and doing ... whatever it is ...'

'*Vanishing*, Mum.' Chrissa was bleak. 'I saw it last time.'

'Don't play games now!' Diane flared. 'Please be sensible.'

'Maybe Mr Macgregor will help,' Chrissa heard herself suggest.

'But what are we going to tell him?' Diane sounded relieved.

'Whatever you said on the phone. Dad's mental. Anything.'

Diane laughed. 'But he sounded as if he thinks *I'm* mental!'

'Mum, let's just get there first, then we'll decide. Okay?'

They were out of the forest now, crossing the bare neck of land between Loch Maree and the sea. To their left was a large reservoir with another impossible Gaelic name — Loch Bad an Sgalaig — from which the River Kerry tumbled down its gorge to the ocean at Gairloch. Checking all this on the map, Chrissa looked over the placid water and saw, some two miles away, a craggy nub of rock outlined against the sky. She drew in breath with a hiss. That's Sidhean Mór! she realised. That's where the place is! And with a tightness in her chest she stared at Sidhean Mór as if eyeing her executioner, paying no attention as the yellow camper at last overtook, roaring past them with a clash of gears.

'Oh Christ!' screamed Diane, and the car swerved almost off the road before she regained control. 'That's him!'

'What?' Chrissa turned quickly.

'That's *him*!' cried Diane, almost in tears. 'In that bloody camper!'

Chrissa's blood chilled. I was right! 'Mum, are you sure?'

'Of course I'm sure! I've lived with him long enough to know what he looks like!' In a rage now, Diane put her foot down and shot after the camper, which was already overtaking the car ahead. Diane overtook too, on a blind bend, which was nearly the end of them, but they just made it, only to see the camper swerve past a huge timber lorry which was gearing down into a series of tight bends above the Kerry. There was nothing she could do. By the time they reached the Red Point junction they were hundreds of yards behind. At speed she swung left over the river into the little road, which curved for a half-mile over marshy ground to a bend at the foot of the slope leading up to Sidhean Mór and the Fairy Lochs. From a distance they saw the camper stop at this bend; they saw Sam jump out and without delay start up the slope as the camper went on. Only for a moment he eyed them over his shoulder. Then he continued rapidly up the rocky slope.

'I don't believe it!' Diane kept crying as she reached the bend and stopped in confusion, not knowing what to do. But Chrissa had made up her mind. In the last few yards, her heart like stone, she'd pencilled a cross on the map between Sidhean Mór and the heart-shaped lochan. Now, as soon as the car stopped, she opened her door and jumped out, leaving the map.

'Chrissa!' Diane shrieked, 'What are you ...?'

'I've marked the place on the map, Mum. Go and get

Mr Macgregor to call the police, and I'll try and slow Dad down. Go *on*!'

'Get back in the car!' Diane opened her door, but as soon as she did Chrissa was already running, off the road, starting steeply up the slope as Sam, high above, looked down and saw her coming. He didn't wait, he just quickened his pace and vanished over a brow with Chrissa scrambling after him even as Diane reached the start of the slope . . . and stopped.

'Chrissa!' she screamed. 'Come back! Come back now!'

But Chrissa didn't waste any breath, and Diane knew then she'd never catch them. She ran back to the car and grabbed the map, wasting precious seconds locating the pencilled cross and more seconds trying to line up the map with the unruly landscape above. Then she wavered, again setting foot on the slope as Chrissa too vanished over the brow of the hill. At last, her step tremulous, Diane turned back to the car. In a numb daze she drove off to find Mr Mcgregor, already sure that she'd lost more than she could yet begin to imagine. 'I should have followed them,' she kept telling herself in a dull, fearful voice, 'but I couldn't. I just couldn't . . .'

16.
The Gate

Already he heard the music, invigorating him so that his step grew lighter and his mind joyful as he approached its source. 'You won't catch me now!' he sang, leaping up a slide of scree without a slip, 'You won't catch me now, 'cos I'm nimble as a boy again and all my aches are gone!' But he didn't look back or let this levity distract him. He knew exactly how far Chrissa was below him. 'You may follow or you may wallow but this time I won't pull you out!' he called down the slope to her while moving swiftly up difficult rock that the old Sam would have avoided. '*Dad, wait for me!*' her voice came drifting up. '*We have to talk!*' But he laughed as with a spring he reached the top of the slope ... and found himself looking south-west. He was high up the flank of Sidhean Mór, directly above the Fairy Lochs. Then, gazing triumphantly into the emerald depths, he heard the music of the bells ring out loud, shivering sweet and pure in the warm still summer air. There was not a breath of wind, and the place was very, very close. He smiled joyously. 'Why should I wait?' he called out, 'I've waited too long already! Now I'm going home at last!'

Yet in him as he plunged the last few yards through the heather was a bleak cell where the old Sam shivered half-mad, still numbed by the crash, whispering his fears unheard. I should have died! he wailed, alone in his night. It wasn't natural to walk away from a crash like that. Volvos are tough but that was crazy. And hitching a ride all the way! Maybe I *did* die. That's it! I'm dead! This is my body but it's not *me* moving it any more. She's got it, or the stooge she sent. Chrissa, hurry up! — but what can you do? I know you'll follow — but where? To your burning man? Can he help? Can he stop her? Can he teach you what to do? Oh, may you learn what you need to know! May you live and find happiness! And Diane, I'm so sorry but it's too late now — I never knew what I had when I had it!

And all this he took with him like an unseen worm wriggling with doubt and complaint in the darkness beyond the circle of ecstasy he inhabited now. Why listen to that shit? So, seeming to float rather than fall, he leaped from a heathery bank down to the place of the gate where the Old Ones of stone anchored the web she spun through time. 'Here we go, here we go, here we go!' he sang as he entered the place the ring liked, as the music of the bells grew so vibrant it dissolved everything. Almost.

Ian Macgregor was a good West Highlander who always worked hard at his leisure whenever he got a chance, and in a warm sunlit chair in his garden he was doing that this beautiful morning ... until with a screech of brakes a bright red Vauxhall pulled up at his gate. Slowly, reluctantly, he opened his eyes. Her all right. Mrs Joyce. Obviously upset but not showing it. Very English, he thought, getting to his feet as she came straight to him. Maybe now we'll be finding out what it's all about.

Without preliminary, in a trembling voice, the woman poured out a tale that made little sense. Terrible shame what city living does, he observed silently. But I did like that young lass. Spirit there. I'd not see any harm come on her.

'But where exactly is it they've gone?' he interrupted gently. 'It's a big moor up there, and no point going

198

without knowing where to look.'

Diane thrust the map at him, fingering the pencilled cross, and when he saw where it was he frowned slightly. Mmm. There, is it? And he thought thoughts he preferred to keep to himself. 'A half-mile from the track,' he said, scratching his near-bald pate, 'but we'll get the Land Rover up to the top at least. Now just wait a minute. My lad's oldest boy's in the house. He can help, and I'd best tell the wife where we're going.'

'But the police,' Diane protested. 'We must call them!'

'The police. Well, I happen to know the constable's away up to Scourie today,' he told her. 'Be calm now. It'll be just fine.'

But he doubted it. Her eyes said she knew already, and what she knew made him vastly uneasy. It was fifty years now, but he could recall old mad Roderick like yesterday, out at the Point, telling his fairy tales to awe-struck boys like himself. 'I believed those stories then and never since,' he told himself as he went inside his house, 'but now in her look I see what I saw in her lassie's eyes, and I wish I did not!' Yet he called out: 'John! Quickly, lad! There's a job to do!'

Diane was in a sort of trance by the time they got her in the Land Rover and started along the rough track that led up to and over the moors past Loch Bráigh Horrisdale. She barely acknowledged young John who, with his sharp eye, assessed her then squinted at his grandfather. Trouble, said his look. 'Just watch the track, son,' the old man said, 'or we'll have another broken axle.' But he agreed. He agreed entirely, and so, by the way she kept growling softly, did the collie.

Ten minutes later they were on the top. The vast emptiness undulated away on every side, broken only by irregular little sheets of water. The sun was hot. There was not a breath of wind. Not a sound.

'Now we walk,' said old Macgregor. He waved his crook, indicating east to the bare nub of Sidhean Mor. 'Maybe ten minutes.'

But Diane's face was as blank as the land itself. She

199

stared at the wilderness for long empty seconds before, at last pulling herself together, she followed Macgregor and his grandson ... to the place the ring liked ...

Chrissa had to fight every inch of the last hundred yards. The climb up to the ridge of Sidhean Mór was a labour, but no worse than it should have been. She gained no ground on Sam, but didn't lose much either. But all that changed the moment she saw the heart-shaped lochan ahead and below her ... for then she met Madame's defences. Without warning she was caught in an enormous misery, in fear and a sense of failure, and when she resisted this it turned into a storm of hate. 'GO AWAY, YOU MEDDLING GIRL!' voices screamed: invisible mouths blew poison breath in her face, fingers nipped her, unseen feet kicked and tripped her until she could move hardly a step without falling. But worst was the hate. It was like a fog draining her of all warmth and strength. Yet it was counterproductive. Her fear might still have turned her back: this attack awoke her obstinacy and brought *Quant lo bouié* to mind, and with that sweet sad song her strength returned. 'NO, I WON'T GO AWAY!' she cried, fighting closer as the attack intensified until, scratched and bleeding, she was crawling on hands and knees, eyes shut against the bloody phantoms prancing round her. 'GO AWAY YOURSELF! YOU WON'T STOP ME!' So at last she reached the bank above the place the ring liked ... but there a vast lethargy assailed her. A gentle soothing voice sighed: '*Go to sleep now? There's a good girl!*' Yawning wide, she fought this too, staring down into the swirl of ugly light below her ... and when at last she made out what was happening, the sight of it froze her for long, long moments until it was all finished.

For there below her, surrounded by the faceless ones, stood her father — or what was left of him.

He was being eaten alive by the writhing worms of bloody light. They were gobbling him up where he stood like a man crucified, hands clutching his head amid the agony of his dismemberment. The emerald hurled out the slimy-bright sparks that ate him. All over and through him they crawled, gorging themselves. She couldn't move. She couldn't even call out. The lethargy and horror were too great. She could only cling to the bank and wait for the end. It came soon. In a daze she saw how Sam collapsed into a twisting cone of maggoty light that sucked in on itself and was gone. With her mouth open she stared.

He was gone. Her father was gone.

'*Did you think you could oppose me?*' came a soft, triumphant whisper even as Chrissa heard the tinkle of metal striking stone. The sunlight flooded back, the faceless sentinels returned to their stonehood, and the attack ceased. But still Chrissa couldn't move. For long seconds she crouched, staring at what was left of her father. The emerald ring. There it lay sparkling on the flat stone where it had fallen, shining in the sun.

She knew it knew she was there.

Your turn now! it seemed to say. *If you dare.*

Chrissa was transfixed by it. She wanted only to scream in hysteria. She wanted to turn and run, and run and run, and never come back.

Here I am, my sweet child! Don't you want me?

It's laughing at me! She felt rage, but fear overcame it; she tried to turn, to tear herself away. But something curious was happening. The horizon had begun to ... contract. Nonplussed, at first blaming her eyes, she saw the land about in motion like a huge lumpy carpet being rolled in at her from all sides. Then she realised that the bank she clung to was getting steeper; that the blue sky itself was thickening, changing colour, growing darker. Suddenly she found herself slipping and sliding down to the place the ring liked. With a wail she fetched up against the base of one of the stones guarding the place. '*What do you think you're doing?*' it demanded sternly. '*You can't just come here to gawp!*' Then, with a slow crawling fear, expecting to see a faceless face, she looked up at the watcher looming over her. Against the pressing purple of the sky (it had shrunk to a tiny thick circle directly above) she saw robes that were not black but grey, and she saw a face ... of a sort. Yet in that odd half-featured vagueness (like a face seen through muslin, she told herself with one clear corner of her mind) she saw no man, no woman, no cruelty, no kindness: she saw nothing she knew at all. Not at first. For even as she stared, the stone watcher took on the flame-licked features of her burning man ... but the flames were not the flames of an earthly fire, they were the brilliant blazing light of the Shining Ones.

Then she cried with relief, for suddenly she knew what she was doing and where she was going. And it was clear to her that whether or not she went had never been a matter of Chrissa Joyce's personal choice.

'*Use this light, daughter!*' he told her. '*Seek your Shining One and remember who you are! Come to us, we'll teach you how to overcome her dark side and free your father — and more than him, for a world's at stake!*'

Then again she heard the song, the sad sweet song of loss and gain.

'*Yes daughter! The herdsman came home to find his lady Joana dead at the foot of the fire, gone to heaven with her goats! Remember! You must hold this song when you enter here, or you won't come together again!*'

In a trance then she entered that place and approached the ring. The emerald shone radiantly, and at the sight of it she knew her father's fate was not her own. She picked it up. She could no longer see beyond the Watchers at all. The rest of the world was gone. She eyed the emerald depths. What's the fuss? she wondered. You're just a train ticket.

But strictly one-way only, it reminded her.

Are you there, Father Bernard? she called. Are you ready? Of course he is, she chided herself. He always was. I'm the one who wasn't. With the ring in her hand she stood, silent. Mum, she thought, and a sadness began to creep in. No, she realised, it's not like that. You know it too. We all do. It goes beyond our littleness. It's silly to fight it when it takes us anyway, whenever it wants to. Mum, now I have to think about where I'm going.

Goodbye for now.

Then she shut her eyes and called on Father Bernard, filling her mind with the sweet song, the sad song, the song of death and rebirth, doing this until it was strong and sure, shining bright in her. Only then did she slip on the ring ... and agonizing fire leaped through her.

Opening her mouth to scream, she tried to pull it off.

Too late. The world wrapped itself round her, turned her inside out. From somewhere else a scream came twisting into her dizzy vortex as she unravelled and imploded. There was no time for surprise. She was gone.

As Ian Macgregor later tried to tell his wife, it was a hard thing indeed to explain exactly what might or might not have happened up there by the Fairy Lochs that day. True, it had been broad daylight, but the sun was so dazzling on the water, blinding them, that a man could hardly be sure. And young John agreed it wasn't the sort of thing to take an oath upon, though it might be worth a dram or two some night with folk you could trust. As for what Mrs Joyce had told the police from Inverness, well, who knows? Maybe she really thought she saw it happen, her daughter vanishing into thin air over the far side of the lochan. It was sure the dog had begun barking furiously, and there was a moment, true, when himself and John had eyed each other in astonishment. It was then Mrs Joyce had cried out her daughter's name and gone running round the water, distracting them both, so that when they looked again, well, of course there was nothing, and probably never had been. All they could say for certain, they both agreed, was that when Mrs Joyce had got into that place of rocks she'd bent down and picked up something small, something that gleamed in the sun and which she held as if it burned her. She'd cried out in a voice you'd never want to hear again, and hurled that gleaming little thing far out over the water towards them. But before they could really get an eye on it, it was gone, right in the middle of the lochan. Gone with hardly a ripple.

'She said it was a ring,' he told his wife, keeping to himself what once he'd seen as a boy when visiting mad old Roddy Joyce at Red Point, and what he told Jean was what he told the police, the press, the doctor called to sedate the poor woman, and anyone else who thought they had a right to know. 'A ring, and maybe so, and if so it'll doubtless lie there until Doomsday. As for the rest of it, I cannot say, for we did not see them, father nor daughter, poor child. And that's all there is to it.'

Never a trace was found of the two. There were inquiries: suspicions were expressed by some who'd known the family. Samuel Joyce's workmates testified to his recent erratic, disturbed behaviour, while Mona Jackson, colleague of Diane Joyce's at the Park Road Primary School in North London, hinted at the possibility of dark deeds. But nothing was proved, nothing was found, and Mrs Joyce's own testimony (once she was able to make a statement) was discounted as the product of mental disturbance caused by severe stress. So the investigation, though never officially closed, resulted in no charges or conclusions whatsoever.

Diane Joyce sold the house in Berkeley Road and resigned from Park Road Primary. For a year she submitted voluntarily to psychiatric care, then moved north to Edinburgh, where she stayed two years with her (presumed dead) husband's father, caring for the old man. When Mr Joyce died she stayed in Edinburgh, living alone, working as a VDU operator in an arts complex. She developed an obsessive interest in spiritualism, and every year returned to Cuilchonich for a week's holiday, which she'd spend roaming the moors round and about the Fairy Lochs. The Macgregors never charged her for her stay, and always reserved the house for that week.

Fourteen years passed under the shaky bridge of her life before at last she learned what had happened to Sam and Chrissa. That was in a strange time, a time of great and terrible events, and the tale belongs elsewhen, for by then ...

Part Two
In the Former Days

From thence I afterwards passed to another terrific place; where I beheld the operation of a great fire blazing and glittering, in the midst of which there was a division. Columns of fire struggled together to the end of the abyss, and deep was their descent. But neither its measurement nor its magnitude was I able to discover; neither could I perceive its origin. Then I exclaimed, How terrible is this place, and how difficult to explore!

Uriel, one of the holy angels who was with me, answered and said: Enoch, why art thou alarmed and amazed at this terrific place, at the sight of this place of suffering? This, he said, is the prison of the angels, and here they are kept for ever.

I Enoch 21: 4-6 (translated by Richard Laurence, LL.D.)

Béziers

Carcassonne

...oux

Gulf
of
Lyon

River Agly

River Tet   Perpignon

S

River Tech

Map 2

→ • → • → • →
Bernard's journey

Scale in miles
0   5   10   15

17.
The Winter Pasture

Pierre Belot never forgot that wild winter night when Bernard de Laurac stumbled into the cabane he shared with Guillaume Authier and two others on the Catalonian pastures near Flix. For that unexpected visit set in motion the train of remarkable events which in time led him to his fate — a fate which, in his own unlettered understanding, had been set down for him since that primal hour when the angels, or aeons, had strayed from the source and plunged into thrice-damned matter.

Pierre's ostal was in the village of Prades, high in the Sault Razes in the County of Foix. There he'd been born and brought up in the faith the goodmen taught; there as a boy he'd been when Antichrist's creature, Pope Innocent III, had called for crusade against good Christians, inviting the French dogs to seize and devastate the Land of Oc. He could clearly recall that hot summer evening he'd come down with his father from the pastures on the flanks of Mount Tabor to find the village in uproar. News had come of how the crusaders had stormed Béziers and slaughtered all its citizens, both Cathar and Catholic. '*Kill them all!*' the Abbot of Cîteaux was said to have told his knights. '*God will recognise his own!*' It was said that twenty thousand had been slaughtered in one brief, horrible day, and that now the blood-drunk crusaders were marching on Carcassonne. But at the time this had meant little to Pierre. 'Where's Béziers?' he'd asked. 'Is it in the lowlands?' What had stayed with him was the terrible expression on his father's face, and Jean Belot's deeply pessimistic words:

'It's the beginning of the end,' the old man (no older than Pierre was now, but *old*) had flatly declared. 'Now Satan will not rest until he has destroyed us all, for he can't bear to see free men. When he's murdered the Christians of the plains, from Béziers to Albi and Toulouse, then he'll come after the rest of us here in the hills.' And with a sad fire in his deepset eyes he'd touched young Pierre tenderly on the brow. 'I regret my part in bringing you into this world, my son. I beg your forgiveness, for I'll be long gone while this war still rages, and it'll be your generation, not mine, that bears the worst of it.'

So it had proved to be. For twenty-five years now the war had raged, on and off, and there had been many massacres and turnings of the tide, this way and that, but mostly that, so that now even Count Raymond of Toulouse had bowed to Antichrist, had signed a treaty with the King of France and gone to Paris to be flogged in the Cathedral of Notre Dame.

Now we have no protectors left, Pierre told himself sadly amid the dark of that stormy night. Wind screeched round the smoky little cabane: by a smouldering fire he huddled between the sheep that he, Guillaume, young Jacques and Gargaleth the Saracen had brought in from the cortal to keep them warm. Shifting restlessly, he scratched at his tousled, lousy hair and listened to the wind battering the walls, threatening to lift off their insecure roof. And this winter! he thought. The worst I've ever known! Satan's dark wing on all the world — I can't even go home without risking arrest! What sort of miserable stinking life is this anyway? Look at me! Getting on! I'll never take a wife or hear my own children laughing! A stranger in my own land with no place I can lay my head! A wave of misery swept through him; silently he wept in the damp, stinking, unfriendly night ... for the winter was cruel, and not just on account of the blizzards which had raged continually since All Saints, blocking the high passes, blanketing the world in snow and freezing mists. The blizzards will pass, he told himself, sneering at his own misery. Why weep? I'm a free man, lucky compared with many! What of that poor soul, the goodman Bernard's companion they took at Foix? And all those who rot in Dominican jails while I walk free? Those black dogs!

'I was in Toulouse last Whitsun,' he declared with sudden loud anger, not caring if the other three slept or not, 'by the Capitol, near the donjon where that viper de Montfort had his brains splattered by the rock hurled from the machine the women — God bless 'em! — worked during the siege. And those devilish friars came by. Know what they were up to? They were off to burn the bodies of good Christians, long dead, that they'd condemned as heretics and dug out of their graves. Can you imagine it? The crowd would've torn 'em to pieces if not for the French soldiers — and even some of them looked pretty sick. But I saw the face of Arnaud, the maggot who directs that stinking work. What a face! White and bloodless, sharp as a knife — a man who'd see his own mother in flames if she said a word against him!' Pierre spat. 'In the name of God's love, of course!'

Neither Gargaleth nor Jacques Maury nor Guillaume Authier were asleep — who could sleep on a night like this? — but none of them replied rightaway. Pierre could be merry enough when the mood took him, yet lately he'd grown bitter and dour. Jacques and Guillaume shared his feelings: both came from the land north of the passes, Jacques from Limoux, Guillaume from Ax, not far from Pierre's home village. They were safe enough here, shivering amid their sheep, but who knew what the future held? Who knew how their ostals fared? And Jacques, not yet twenty, did not trust himself to speak, for when he was an infant his father had died defending Toulouse, and even now his brother rotted in the Mur at Car-

211

cassonne. Besides, the war was all they ever seemed to
discuss, and it brought no satisfaction.

But keeping silence was too much for him.

'The friars aren't the only beasts!' Harsh, he sat up to
eye the others by the faint firelight — Pierre gaunt and
brooding, Guillaume like a shaggy old bear, Gargaleth
slim and dark with his tattered djellabah drawn tight
about him. 'What of that bishop in Toulouse who went to
the deathbed of an old woman, a believer? He trapped
her into demanding consolation from a goodman, not the
false blessing of Satan's church — then had her dragged
out to the stake, bed and all. What a rat!'

'True enough,' rumbled Guillaume. 'But we should
pity those bastards, not hate them, for they destroy their
own souls.'

'Admirable Christian!' The Saracen Gargaleth, with
one 'wife' in Asco and another in Malaga, laughed
ironically. 'But you lot love suffering. You should thank
these friars for lighting the fires that let you prove your
faith so ardently! They pave your way to paradise, they
. . .'

'You know nothing!' cried Jacques hotly — but Pierre,
leaning over, laid a hand on his arm and hissed at
Gargaleth to keep quiet.

'The goodmen gather at Montségur.' Guillaume
changed the subject. 'Guilhabert de Castres is there, and
Esclarmonde de Foix, and many landless knights. The
French won't take Montségur. It's impregnable.'

'It's a holy place, not a fortress,' said Pierre softly.

'You've been there?' demanded Jacques, almost accus-
ingly, as if to say: *Then why are you here, and not still there?*

'I have.' Pierre paused to scratch ferociously. 'It's a fine
high place, but no good for war. Too remote and difficult
to supply. Queribus or Puylaurens or Peyrepertuse are
better placed. They're at Montségur to bear witness, not
to fight fire with fire.'

'You sound like a goodman yourself,' Guillaume said
drily, yet with respect, for Pierre was widely known —
maybe too widely for his own good — as a man who, though

212

scarcely holy, often risked his neck to lead Cathar priests and deacons out of danger into the mountains where, as yet, the power of popes, kings, friars and Satan had not yet reached.

'I like women and meat too much for that.' Pierre's laugh was sharp, maybe embarrassed. 'I'm a believer, I'm not about to take deeper vows.'

'Women!' Jacques was glum. 'There's a girl in Limoux ...'

Gargaleth snorted. 'You're just a shepherd, son. All you can offer a woman is your cock and your lice, and what can your cock do but help bring more poor souls into this damned world? Isn't that what you lot believe?'

'Pierre ...' — raising his voice, Guillaume threw more sticks on the fire — '... What do you mean, they go there to bear witness?'

'I'm sick of this!' Suddenly Jacques jumped to his feet, kicking a ewe as he did; the beast bleated protest as he stumbled to the wind-blown door of oiled sheepskin. 'What does this gabble do for my brother? Eh?'

'What's her name, lad?' asked Guillaume.

Jacques paused. 'Alais,' he said roughly, 'What's it to you?'

'I wanted to marry once.' Guillaume shrugged. 'Jacotte, her name was. But her mother said: "*What are you? Your family's ruined, you're broke, you're a known heretic ... and anyway, you're just a shepherd.*"'

'So was Jesus Christ,' Jacques cried prompt and aggressive.

At this, Pierre laughed loud, from the heart ... but bitterly.

'Good answer, son! Try telling it to the fat priests!'

'Yes, but Christ too did without women,' Guillaume pointed out.

'Did he, though?' Gargaleth was sly. 'What of the tales that he wed the Magdalene and settled with her in these parts, and that ...?'

'Shut up, you infidel bastard!' screamed Jacques in a fury as he toed aside the rocks holding down the door.

'Shut up!' And the wind blasted in, scattering embers, sending sheep and men alike in a whirl as Pierre cried out: 'Jacques, we shepherds marry sheep and the hills, not women! We know how you feel, but now for the love of . . .'

Then, suddenly, Jacques wailed with fear.

Before him, vaguely outlined against the wild silver-black night beyond the flapping door, stood a tall, dark, snow-rimed apparition.

The youth fell back, trampling another ewe, starting up all the sheep in a panic. Amid frantic bleating the beasts began dashing all round the small dark space, leaping over the hearth and over the other three men, who jumped wide-eyed to their feet. And even Pierre, not a nervous man, found himself shivering at the sight of the tall dark figure in the doorway.

The apparition chuckled hoarsely, weakly.

'I'm not a ghost!' Its voice was barely audible above the wind. 'I mean no harm. I'm looking for Pierre Belot.'

The shepherds simply stared as the sheep tore round them and the bitter wind played havoc with their shelter.

'I'm Pierre Belot,' Pierre admitted uncertainly. 'But who . . .?'

'Thank God!' exclaimed the apparition, swaying on its feet . . . and would have collapsed had not Pierre, at last recognising the voice, leapt forward just in time to catch and hold the bony, elderly, and definitely mortal body of the goodman, Bernard de Laurac.

It was due to his persistent dream that for three days and nights the old man had been trudging alone through the foul weather, all the way from Puigcerda down to Querol and Sainte Croix, then inland to Asco and Flix, everywhere asking the whereabouts of the shepherd Pierre Belot. At last in Flix that cold dark afternoon he'd met a tanner — a believer in exile from Roussillon — who'd seen Belot a week earlier. 'He's in a cabane with three others. See those three peaks?' Standing in the slush of the street, the tanner pointed north-west over the grey

214

rushing waters of the Ebre. 'You'll find him under the middle peak, above the woods.' Eyeing Bernard's scrawny build, the man was concerned. 'My lord, you must stop and rest! It's half a day on foot even in good weather! There's a storm brewing, and ... excuse me, my lord, but you look all in. Rest in my domus and bless my bread!'

True, Bernard was exhausted. Since starting his southward journey he had hardly rested or even paused to eat. 'I can't stop,' he said with a faint smile. 'I need bread, and a dry shirt if you have one.' And when he had these things he blessed the man and went on, over the river bridge and up into the snowbound woods as the wind began rising and the snow and the darkness came again ... and he had little more than prayers to keep him warm.

For a long time he climbed the vaguest of trails through the whirling whiteness until, with day almost gone, he felt his strength going with the poor pale light. The snow still swirled down; he could no longer feel his bare sandalled feet as he struggled on, head bowed, sodden cloak wrapped round the sparse flesh of his half-starved body. His mind began to wander; he concentrated on a text from John: '*I can do nothing on my own authority: I judge only as God tells me.*' But his senses were failing him when, amid the pines, he glimpsed a dim glow, and so came to a woodcutter's hut.

'I seek the shepherd Pierre Belot,' he croaked at the gnarly old man who pulled aside the hairy door. 'Which way?'

Alarmed, the woodcutter held up a smouldering brand. By its light he saw bright grey eyes in a hard-boned face as pale as parchment. To those eyes he made a gesture of respect. 'Sir,' he said flatly, indicating the snow that whirled down, 'tonight there's no way. I own little, but you're welcome to it: for the sake of your life rest here tonight.'

'I must find him!' Bernard insisted. 'Is it far?'

'Not in sunshine! But tonight ... Sir, it is very, very far!'

'Point me the way!' And to the look in the wood-cutter's eyes that asked: *Are you mad?* he said equably, 'Maybe so, but I follow a voice.'

Nonetheless he accepted a warming at the fire and a bowl of bark soup. Then reluctantly the woodcutter pointed the way up into the wild night.

'If God's truly with you,' he cried into the wind as Bernard left him, 'then you'll hear His sheep bleating from the heights you seek!'

There was fearful irony in that remark; Bernard did not turn to wave. Soon he found himself above the woods, climbing a broad open slope knee-deep in snow. The darkness wasn't total; the snow had ceased and a fitful moon gleamed through ragged shreds of quick angry cloud. The chill wind attacked him; soon his mind began drifting and he needed all his discipline to keep going. Pierre Belot, he cried silently, where are you? You didn't snatch me away from Satan's hounds in Foix so I'd perish now! No! This is just the initial test! I won't fail in this! Gaillard, did you die so I should fail? No! There's work to do! God lead me straight!

So on and up he floundered through the dulling whiteness, his mind running hither and thither and back through the years, and the white face of the frantic blue-eyed girl of his dreaming never far from his mind.

'*Father! Father Bernard! If you don't come soon it'll be too late!*'

Who is she, Gaillard? he cried to his lost friend. How does she know my name? Why does she call me 'father'? Do you know, when these dreams began I really wondered if it's possible? A daughter of my flesh I never knew? Oh! — despite everything he laughed aloud into the wind — Gaillard, before the war there was a time when I was young and sang of Grace through Woman! Then I was welcome everywhere, I was showered with gifts and every sort of favour ... heady stuff for a young man, my friend, and it's not impossible that I — he paused, gazing at the fitful moon, seeming to see his lost friend — but of course any daughters of my flesh would

216

be matrons by now, and they'd already have made their claims through easier routes than dreams — I'd know about them! Let's face it, I sired nothing then!

And Fabrisse, he thought on as he climbed. Sweet Fabrisse, you bore me sons but no daughters, and that was long ago too. Twenty years we shared, and no other woman I knew, and no other woman I've known since we renounced earthly marriage. How long since that night Bishop Bertrand laid the Book on our heads? Eight years? It feels like eighty! How have we been since then, Fabrisse? Not fat, that's sure! Lean with running and hiding, thin with disguise and fear of betrayal. Gaillard and I were lucky ... until we got to Foix. And now? It's years since I gave up the sword, and longer since I gave up songs; now I fear I'm giving up my reason in senile dreams of this golden girl who cries for help ...

He was numb and slowing. Keep on! he urged himself. *I am the gate for the sheep.* But where are they? I can only hear this cursed wind! Gaillard, is it you I see, leading me on? And he paused, frozen, peering up through the storm at the cloud-wracked moon. Then he shuddered and groaned.

Only moon shapes and my fuddled old brain, he decided. Forget him! Let the dead bury the dead. But as he moved on, step by painful step, he shook his head. No! he contradicted himself. Gaillard, I feel you here, you give me strength! It's a sin to keep wishing they'd taken me and not you. What could I do? I was consoling that old man when they caught you, and I'd have come, but Bishop Guilhabert sent Belot to hide me in the caves until it was over. Dreadful places! Then he led me to Puigcerda. And for a time I thought I'd gone mad. Did we ever discuss the dangers of dream entities? As soon as I got to Puigcerda it began. At first I thought it a result — a temptation — of despair. I prayed to be rid of it, but soon it was at me every night, and stronger all the time. I'd wake in a sweat, her face as clear before me as yours is now, Gaillard, with the vision of her drowning in a deep black pool, and her voice in my ears — '*Father! Father*

Bernard!' And that song I found — you know the one — every time I saw her I heard that too! I wondered at first: is she a succubus, sent by Satan. Then I thought: what, at *this* stage of my life? So I began puzzling about her drowning in a black pool, in a dark place. The place seemed familiar: I *knew* I knew it, but I suppose I didn't want to know. Yet it kept at me all through Christmas until I had to admit: this girl's in mortal need! She's calling for help, and my vow binds me to help!

But it's more than that, he went on, mouthing thoughts as if speaking aloud as he trudged on up through the freezing wind. I never told you, Gaillard, but once Bishop Guilhabert showed me the secret book that came from the Bogomils, the one that tells what Enoch saw, and of the angels imprisoned in us — and after I'd read it he told me other things, about the Lost Stone, and the gates to the higher worlds. He never said why he told me, and I didn't remember ... until the other night I awoke, but I was still dreaming — I *must* have been, for there before me she stood, all wet and wild. I shivered, I can tell you! Yes, Gaillard, blue eyes and corn-gold hair! *'Father!'* she cried, *'You MUST come soon, or the dark Watchers will triumph!'* I managed to ask: 'Who *are* you?' and she said: *'Your daughter.'* 'Who do you serve?' I asked, and she told me: *'The Shining Ones!'* 'What do you seek?' I asked, and she said: 'I seek what's lost.' Amazed, I asked: 'How is it found?' — and she told me, *'It's redeemed by love.'*

Gaillard, he told his lost friend, groaning with the effort of putting one foot in front of the other, for the slope had steepened; Gaillard, that was four nights ago! There she stood, dripping wet, her hair matted and lank, wearing truly odd clothes — did you ever see a woman in britches? — but shining with the clear light of the aeons! Then I *knew* she called from the worlds out of time! 'Where are you?' I asked, and she confirmed it! *'Not in this world if you can't help me!'* I asked her a second time; I asked her what she meant, but she faded then, and I sensed that black pool again, and realised: I know it! I haven't been there, but the bishop told me! The Gate of the Stone! Deep down in the caves where I hid, deep in the ancient parts beyond the labyrinth where the Old One's snapping teeth reign. Yes, HER! THAT one, black and wise as night, who was banished out of the fields of light to the depths of this dark earth! She who will not lie under man, who kills poets with ecstasy; She of whom it is said: '*She is a ladder on which one can ascend to the rungs of prophecy!*'

Bernard hissed and shook his head. 'But she's dangerous!' he croaked aloud. 'She's full of jealous rage and envy, not to be trifled with and no friend of children — and this child, whoever she is, needs help! That's why I'm here, my friend. An old fool, pinching myself! I can't feel a thing! Maybe I dropped long ago! Maybe I'm dead already! Maybe ...'

It was then through the wind and darkness he heard what at first he thought was that song, the song of Joana he'd found so long ago. Somehow he turned his bent old body towards it ... and before long he knew it to be the bleating of restless sheep. But Joana went to heaven with goats, not sheep, he thought vaguely as further up the slope, in the dim moonlight, he made out the shape of the cortal where the sheep were penned. Beyond it, under an overhang of rock, he sensed the outline of a hut.

Exhausted, with no sensation left in his body, he reached the cabane just as its door was released to flap open. He heard voices raised in anger ... then Jacques Maury saw the apparition of him, and wailed.

You see, Gaillard? Bernard chuckled, though with no clear idea what he found so funny. I must still be alive!

18.
The World of the Aeons

He sat shivering by the built-up fire, kept awake by his will alone. The shepherds stared at him. Bernard de Laurac was tall and stooped, his silver hair thinning, his bony face pallid as alabaster above a sodden dark blue robe. His horny feet, bare but for strapped leather sandals buttoned round the ankles, were frozen blue-white. A leather belt at his waist held two pouches, one for bread, the other for the copy of the Gospel of John that goodmen always carried ... and Pierre, uneasily waiting to learn the purpose of this visit, wondered if, under that belt and next to the skin, Bernard wore the golden girdle that goodmen were said to wear — a girdle like that which the prophet Daniel had seen round the waist of the angel he'd met on the banks of the Tigris; a girdle conferring strength on those who wore it. I could almost believe it, he thought. How else could he survive such a journey? He may be strong in spirit, but in the flesh? And he may be wise, but it's lunacy to walk here without a good pair of boots!

Yet despite the fire, and girdle or not, time passed before Bernard stopped shuddering. Amid the icy whiteness of his face only his eyes held any heat. Yet those eyes, dark and steady, held such force that young Jacques, redeeming his shame by putting warm skins round the goodman's shoulders, could not meet them. Bernard considered him silently before sketching a brief, tired blessing. Then Gargaleth, heating up the mutton broth they'd had earlier, ladled a bowlful of it for their guest.

It smelled rich and appetising. Bernard sighed.

'My thanks,' he whispered, 'but you know I can't.'

'I'm not of your faith and I don't know what you can or can't!' The Saracen looked insulted. 'All I know is it'll do you good.'

'The flesh of beasts is wild and impure, and to eat it is murder.' Bernard shrugged. 'But fish is clean from the sea, so if . . .'

'Fish?' Gargaleth barked a laugh. 'If fish could fly maybe we'd have fish. Instead we have mutton, mutton, and mutton! Plenty of it!'

'Here, my lord,' said Guillaume quickly. Suppressing his desire to genuflect, he offered a stale hunk of bread and a near-empty wineskin. Accepting these, murmuring the Lord's Prayer, Bernard used his own cup for the wine and drew a quick circle on the bread with his knife before he broke it. The shepherds waited in silence while he ate and drank, and as he did his shivering lessened and the blood began to find his cheeks again. At length, with a sigh, he was finished. '*Give us this bread always,*' he quoted with a wan smile, '*For I am the bread that came down from heaven. The bread that I give is my flesh, which . . .*'

Pierre interrupted, apologetically but firmly.

'My lord, I'm glad to see you recovered, and if you mean to preach I'll listen with all my heart, but first, please — why are you here?'

'You're right,' said Bernard calmly. 'I forget myself. Pierre Belot, I need you to guide me to Tarascon. Immediately. It's urgent.'

There was silence. Wind howled. Then Pierre heard himself laugh.

'Tarascon? Is that all? Shall I guide you to the stake too?'

'It's urgent,' Bernard repeated, still calm. 'You're the

only man this side of the passes who knows the way to where I must go.'

'Impossible,' said Pierre flatly, ignoring the voice in him that said: *But you're a believer! You've vowed to do whatever a goodman asks!*

'Oh?' Bernard raised one sparse eyebrow. 'Why's that?'

'Good reasons.' Pierre counted them on his blunt fingertips. 'One, the passes are blocked, the weather is foul. Two, such a journey in these conditions might kill a fit man in good health, and you, my lord — excuse me — are neither. Three, I work for Na Borrel. I guard her sheep here, plus twenty of my own. I can't just get up and go.' With a shrug he met the goodman's eyes. 'And as I said, the black friars won't have forgotten you. Show your face near Foix and they'll have you at the stake with a paper mitre on your head so fast you won't even have time to pray!'

'These risks must be taken,' said Bernard mildly.

But his gaze was not mild. Pierre groaned.

'What is it? Why is it so important?'

'Do you want Satan to inherit everything?'

'At least tell me what's going on!' cried Pierre, upset. 'It's all very well, you turning up half-dead and telling me to take you over the passes now, and I *know* I must serve you, but ...' — gesticulating, he sought justification — '... I've got a living to earn! Who'll hire me if it gets about that I walked out on a job? Anyway, Bishop Guilhabert told me to lead you to safety — he said nothing about leading you back to the stake!'

'That's not your business,' Bernard insisted implacably, and went on without even looking at the other three, who followed the exchange with amazed faces. 'As for your flocks, your friends will look after them. And I recall you telling me Na Borrel sympathises with the faith, so she'll forgive you. Pierre,' he repeated, 'the need is absolute and urgent!'

'*What* need? You haven't explained anything yet!'

'Come outside.' Abruptly, seeming fully recovered,

222

Bernard stood, crooking an authoritative finger. 'Come along!'

Pierre sighed, shrugged, followed him out into the freezing wind. The goodman drew him into the lee of the cabane and said in his ear:

'Remember those caves where you hid me?'

'I wish I did not,' Pierre grumbled.

'Do you remember the talk we had about the invisible treasure called *pecuniam infinitam*?' the goodman asked eagerly.

'You know I don't know priests' language.' Pierre shivered.

'I mean the hidden treasures, the infinite wealth that can't be weighed or measured!' Bernard told him fiercely. 'In the depths of those caves there's a ... gate — a door from the realm of the aeons — and soon there's a messenger coming to us through that gate. We must get there in time!'

Pierre stared at him. High above, the moon rode storm. Inside, the others waited in silence, gazing at the fire. It was again down to embers by the time the two returned. 'I'll do it,' they heard Pierre reluctantly agree. 'But tomorrow you rest here. I'll take my sheep to Asco and look for two strong mules — we won't survive the passes otherwise.'

'I agree,' the goodman said, contented.

'I thought you would.' Pierre sighed as he lay down. 'At least when I die in the snow I'll have a goodman to console me. Now let's sleep!'

'Pray with me first, brother,' said Bernard de Laurac.

'Father! Father Bernard! If you don't come soon it'll be too late!'

Long after the shepherds had fallen asleep Bernard finished his prayers and joined them, huddling by the hearth with shaggy sheep on either side to keep him warm. And sleep came quickly. But later came the dreaming, more vivid than ever before, intense and clear and remarkable.

And it was different this time. Very different.

223

He was burning. He was writhing in a sea of flame, and all around him (he couldn't see them, his sight blazed with unbearable heat, but he heard them, he knew they were there) many others were dying too. He could no longer breathe, his skin was peeling and cracking, the pain so great it was a terrible ecstasy ... yet amid it all he *was singing* the songs of his youth (not aloud; his vocal cords were gone), singing the Song of Joana, using the agony of his dying to seek out one who was far, far away. OH MY SWEET CHILD, I BLESS YOU! he cried from the inferno's heart, HEAR ME, JOANA! And on wings of pain he launched himself, reaching out to the child in need of help; he plunged down a flaming vortex and the fire went with him, a torch she couldn't ignore. For NOW, burning, he finds himself in some great city filled with strange sights and sounds, and there in a bed of a house on a street of that city she lies asleep, yellow hair spread on a pillow, and in her sleep he appears to her — flaming, his roasting flesh stinking — so that she wakes up in terror. Yet again and again, NOW and NOW and NOW, he appears to her, not always in this city, but in other places too, until she accepts him and knows he means no harm. But this girl (and her father too) has another visitor, one not at all welcome ... SHE of the raven hair and the bloody look; SHE who wants something she's determined to get. And as pain murdered itself in him, many scenes of this other world flash past ... until one sticks in his dreaming dying....

For NOW he burns on a bleak watery moor; on a circle of stones. Into this circle runs the girl's father, ecstatic, terrified. On a finger of his left hand this poor man wears a ring set with emerald, in the depths of which he sees the worlds flow. *A piece of the Stone! The Emerald Tablet!* And even as this poor fool enters the circle his daughter struggles after him, fighting the unseen enemy as sparks of light whirl from the ring to envelop him. Then SHE's there, bloody, cruel, her face triumphant. Yes! HER! '*Did you think you could oppose me?*' she sneers at the horrified girl. '*You Weak Ones!*' And then the girl's father, eaten by the foul red worms, is swallowed into ... what? From the pyre where he dies Bernard tries to see, but it's too deep, too far, too hard to grasp. Oh Joana, he cries, you must follow and I must help! And then there's nothing but the emerald, sparkling in the sun as in agony the girl slides down to the stones ... even as he finds himself ... *inside* stone, part of an immeasurably ancient crystal mind. So cool, so quiet! Ahhh! And her face clears, for she sees him, she hears his voice, and so does he, crying from the heat of the flames, the cool of the stone. Or is it the fire blazing in him that speaks? '*Use this light, daughter! Seek your Shining One and remember who you are! Come to us, we'll teach you how to overcome her dark side and free your father — and more than him, for a world's at stake!*' Then again the Song comes welling from him, and the fiery voice: '*Remember! You must hold this song when you enter here, or you won't come together again!*' So she enters the circle and picks up that emerald ring. '*Are you there, Father Bernard? Are you ready?*' YES, SWEET CHILD, I'M HERE!. On goes the ring, and again the gobbling light spills out as, from a distance, a woman screams in utter despair. Gobbling her up as he sings the Song from the flames that gobble up him. 'HEAR ME IN THE LIGHT OF THE SHINING ONE!' The ecstatic terror of dissolution! 'WE BURN WE BURN WE ARE BURNING MELTING OH CHRIST!

And NOW ...

Falling. Fallingfallingfalling...

The round world exploding. Spinning, whirling, plunging through a lightless, ever-tightening abyss without memory or self-knowledge save for the sense of treasure forgotten in the falling and irredeemably lost. NOW constriction, pressure, weight; doors briefly open in the Fall's black mad wall. These doors pass too quick to enter, but through them (NOW and NOW and NOW) the falling one is caught by sensations that'll reverberate in the dreaming of its new incarnation, should it find one — for there's no light, the Song's lost; only hideous mockery, the cruel blood-red face laughing from the void; empty eyes sucking the falling soul into their abyss and crushing it into a point which, though without mass or physical substance, contains potential so unbearably

225

dense that suddenly it collapses, implodes through itself . . . and transforms into an equally unbearable, dazzling light.

Abruptly, without sense of transition or self (yet somewhere there's a watcher, there always is), the unknown one walks in a garden, radiant and bright. A crystal stream sparkles past emerald lawns and flowers of colour that trembles; from a blossoming apple tree an unseen songbird sings:

> *Quant lo bouié ben de laura*
> *Planto soun agulhado*
> *AEIOU!*

Then as it walks it meets one too bright to look upon.

'Daughter,' it says, 'why are you crying?'

'I don't know,' it sobs, 'I don't know!'

'Do you cry for something lost?'

'I don't know! I don't remember!'

'You remember that you don't remember?'

The radiance is dazzling. Rivers erupt: mighty rushing waters burst out. The world swims in tears of flood, in fertility of remembering.

'TELL ME!' cries a sudden strong, hopeful voice, 'WHAT IS FORGOTTEN? WHO ARE WE? WITH WHOM DO WE DANCE? ON WHAT WORLD ARE WE BIRTHED?'

And with the asking come the answers:

'WHAT IS FORGOTTEN IS WHAT WE ARE! WE ARE THE SHINING ONES!'

Then a huge shift, a mighty wrench, a sense of radiant wings beating passage through a tremendous night to the gates of entry into the presence of the indescribable. Here are guardian lightnings, vibrating flames and agitated stars; here's the vast voice answering the third question: 'WE ARE THE THREE-IN-ONE WHO DANCE!' Another shift, new perspective of deeper vision: what could not be seen is now seen and known, for now (WE? US? IT? HE? SHE?) dances in the vast blazing light, golden and violet and silver, whirling and looping in complex spirals and figures of eight, approaching and departing the shifting centre in huge orbit. And of the three, one is searing and royal, a brilliant monarch; the second's a silver dwarf, thick with hidden light and collapsed time; and the third ... the third cannot easily be seen, is as if veiled behind mists. And the music of the dance is the song of the patterns the Three-In-One weave, rippling in waves that bring life, delight, death and pain to the dark worlds born of the fire of the dance. 'THIS IS THE DANCE OF OUR HOME IN THE SUNS BEHIND THE SUN THAT RULES THE DARK WORLD OF TIME AND SHIFT AND SEPARATION! CHILDREN, HERE IS OUR TRUE HOME! REMEMBER THIS WHEN YOU RETURN!' But a fearful voice cries: 'Must we go back to Satan's realm?' Then into the dance creeps instability and imbalance. 'OH, ALWAYS SATAN!' chides the vast voice, 'CHILDREN, SATAN PLAYS HIS PART! SEPARATION, DIFFERENCE, TIME AND DEATH ARE BUILT INTO THE NATURE OF THINGS! THE FIGHT TO REMEMBER WHAT'S FORGOTTEN BRINGS MORE THAN WAS EVER FORGOTTEN TO BEGIN WITH!' 'But ... but ... the Shift!' 'THAT TOO IS PART OF IT. THE ONLY WAY TO OVERCOME IT IS TO REMEMBER IN TIME WHAT'S KNOWN OUT OF TIME! NOW! ON WHAT WORLD ARE WE BIRTHED!'

Then another shift, for here in the dance, lost in the shining light of the Three-In-One, circling the veiled sun, spins a little dark world that wheels about like a child round its mother. Down, down the blazing wings descend, down through successive layers of thickening to a realm of ocean under clouds that never lift, mercifully hiding from physical vision the Shining Ones who dance above. Deep into the ocean plunge these blazing wings unquenched, deep and deeper still past strange constructions that float in the depths; vast constructions that glimmer and twinkle like frost in moonlight, helical and cellular ... and through these buildings (for that is what they are) float great placid beings, smooth and grey, shocking in their familiarity as they greet their visitor.

'Welcome back!' they say. 'Welcome home again!'

'But ... but ...' a voice protests, 'you're WHALES?'

Then the knowledge is absorbed in the light of the Shining Ones, and peaceful among them (WE? US? IT? HE? SHE?) drifts through vibrant halls. So what? asks a guide as huge as Leviathan, its vast rolling eye closing and opening in a wink of unmistakable humour. A shape is a shape, a form is a form! Those hairy two-legs looked odd to us when we made the first contact long ago, and they're odd still, to us! But why worry? There are many odd forms on many worlds; each world has its own peculiarities. The spirit embraces every form, and can take any shape it pleases ... as we can, for we Elohim remembered ourselves long ago when we learned how to overcome the Shift. You must understand and remember: the Shift is not punishment; it's a natural and periodic function of every material world; a process like spring-cleaning. Understand the relationship between organic form and the world that births it — bring that world and its intelligence into the light of the Shining Ones — and you overcome the terror of the Shift! It's a simple matter of taking sane responsibility! But if the natives of any world can't recall their proper business and act accordingly, then things inevitably reach such a pass that the Shift returns with fire and flood, again and again! It's not easy: we know that! You must remember: we Elohim are mortal too, and these are our bodies, deep down in this our world that circles the being we know as the Emme Ya. We've been through all this ourselves! We can't stop others in their self-destruction, all we can do is sing the Song and praise the Light — and try to pass it on! But of course things will go wrong, and often do. Yet now ... see this ...

And into a deep glimmering crystal chamber glide the wings, no longer blazing (now attached like fins to a great grey body), and with a subtle lateral thrust they enter an alcove lit radiantly by a great emerald set like a gleaming eye in a wall of pink and yellow coral.

'Look! Here's what you call the Lost Stone,' *the guide whispers*, 'A fragment brings you back to us. Son and daughter, daughter and son! Do you remember your lives in the dark world, and why you've come here? The Shift can be overcome ... but it's not easy. Now look! See!'

And there in the emerald depths is a warm green glade amid a green sweet grove, part of a great forest stretching to rolling horizon hills. Above it on a high rocky place stands a woman. She wears a birdfeather robe. She has raven-black hair. And the watcher, recognising her, flinches, and everything shudders.

'Careful,' *advises the guide.* 'You see our lost sister ... and yours. Long ago she entered the Dark World to bring the dance to the two-legs, but like others she got caught. Now she's lost in forgetting; she knows only that her memory's failing and that the Shift approaches again. She thinks she'll stop it by opening a gate that's been closed and by violently storming us here. She thinks we stranded her, she forgets entirely that she chose to enter that world and that we can't change fate! What she plans assures the Shift; she fills men with her hate. Now look! See the man she watches — that man in the grove! She prepares him for the rite she'll use to set her scheme in motion!'

And the watcher sees the thin naked man in the glade, the man with the eyes of a bemused idiot and the shock of black hair. Deep red scratches disfigure his left cheek. There's a shock ... of recognition.

'It's Sam!' cries a terrified voice. 'That's Dad!'

In that instant the new world's lost. A cruel dark wing sweeps down, a wall of water strikes, stupid fire blazes, the emerald depths spin dizzily and into them plunged the golden child, all the way down to that glade where the idiot turned and grinned as he saw her, his erection huge.

'Fuckfuck,' frothed the idiot, 'fickyfuck NOW!'

Then in his dream Bernard de Laurac groaned, for the Old One sensed him and saw him, her gaze furious even as the terrified girl now screamed and fled from the fool who'd been her father ... screamed, fled, and fell through a cleft in the rock of the blighted garden. Deep, deep down through the darkness she fell to the place of the Gate of the Stone, tumbling from the World of the Aeons to the place where the Old One's snapping teeth reigned, the Old One in furious pursuit, great wings beating, eyes blazing in hate.

'*You'll not invade my world!*' the Watcher cried in the goodman's dream. '*You'll not upset my plans, and that stupid child won't survive her journey through my gate! I'll see to that ... and I swear you won't stop me, O thin man of chastity!*'

Yet at the same time the golden girl was drowning, screaming:

'Father! Father Bernard! If you don't come soon it'll be too late!'

With a gasp and a start the goodman awoke. He sat up, shaking his head. It was day. The cabane was empty but for himself. His mouth was dry, he raged with thirst, and in his head was a high-pitched singing that would not go away, not even after he went out into the brightness of the morning and rubbed snow all over his face. And he was afraid, exalted, perplexed, impatient ... but there was nothing he could do but pray, and wait for Pierre Belot to return from Asco ...

19.
The Journey North

Now I know I'm mad, Pierre told himself glumly four nights later as he lay shivering in a snow-bound wayfarers' hut in the mountains north of the Porte-Puymorens. I've sold my sheep and broken my contract; now I risk my skin to help this old man hunt his dream-child. He's mad too. The whole world's mad. Well, that makes sense! Satan created it, didn't he?

For Pierre the madness had begun the moment he'd agreed to Bernard's demands. Since then, lunacy had made great strides. Down to Asco next day he'd gone with his twenty sheep; back he'd come with just two mules, and not happy about it either. And as soon as he was back the agitated goodman was at him to leave immediately. 'We must go now! Now! The storm's over, there's no wind, we can't lose time!' I'll get no sleep anyway, Pierre had realised, so we might as well. Thus at dead of night under a sulky moon they'd gone, trekking down the slopes and through the woods to Flix, the goodman like an eager boy ahead, Pierre tired and sullen in the rear. Dawn saw them starting up the banks of the Sègre towards Puigcerda. Amid foul weather they climbed steadily that day and the next, but Pierre had chosen the mules well; they were strong, equable beasts, so good progress was made. The second night Pierre insisted on staying at Berga, in the morning to visit his employer Na Borrel and tell her what was up. The old woman clucked and tutted. 'You left my flocks with who? Who's Guillaume Authier?' But of course she knew Guillaume, and the goodman charmed her so that, as predicted, she was not unsympathetic. Yet as they went on Pierre couldn't help grumbling about the damage to his reputation. 'I'm supposed to be a shepherd of sheep, not goodmen,' he muttered, not quite under his breath, at which Bernard smiled a pale smile and held his peace.

The third night they spent in Puigcerda, where Bernard had been since All Saints, and where surely the Inquisition had informers. They'd planned to avoid the town but the weather made it impossible; wind was howling down from the invisible, storm-shrouded mountains, blowing snow into deep drifts and making the approach to the town so hard that the tired mules frequently balked and had to be goaded. There was no avoiding the place; it was on the main route and they needed shelter. But before they entered the narrow streets Pierre reined in. 'There's no point in taking silly risks,' he said sourly. 'Take off that goodman's robe and dress like me!' He tossed a bundle at Bernard, who did not protest, so that it was two shepherds who came to the inn at Puigcerda that night, both hooded against winter, and it was Pierre Belot who did the bargaining. They got a room cheap, but it meant sharing a bed with two other travellers. 'Please don't get up in the night to say your prayers,' Pierre begged as they went up to the room where their unknown bedmates were already snoring. Bernard assented with a nod, noting that Pierre had stopped calling him 'my lord'. Just as well, the goodman thought before falling uneasily asleep, no false deference. He's like a mule himself, but I think I've judged him well.

Yet in his sleep he dreamed, and tossed and turned, mumbling strangely about a lost child, not waking even when Pierre dug him fiercely in the ribs. One of the other men, a tanner from Sant Julia de Loria, complained. 'Can't you keep him quiet?' Pierre whispered: 'You must forgive him! He lost his only child last week, he's deranged with grief!' Whereupon the tanner grunted and settled back, stuffing cloth in his ears. Yet even so, Pierre silently promised himself: If the weather stays bad I'll insist we stay here tomorrow. There may be spies, but spies don't kill as fast as a freezing storm. I'm in no hurry to die. I'm the guide, I have the say.

But when they awoke at dawn the world was still. The wind had fallen, the sky was a clear pale blue, the freezing air as crisp as a slap on the cheeks. The rising sun turned the high peaks snowy pink; by the time sunlight reached the streets the two men were fed, provisioned, and off again, the mules carrying them up an icy track through an ever-steepening gorge. Below them rushed a swollen river, ahead loomed mountains like a virgin but deadly army. To Bernard (hugely relieved to escape Puigcerda unrecognised) this massive range was truly God's handiwork, expressing in minor key the glories and terrors he'd dreamed in nights past. For as he followed Pierre he saw peak upon peak soaring above him, sharp against the sky's pale infinity. Despite his worries he marvelled, and a text from the first letter of John sprang to mind. '*God is light*,' he cried at the sky in a joyous voice, '*and there is no darkness at all in him!*' He began to preach on this text for the sheer pleasure of it, keeping himself warm by exhorting the rocks and snow, the shepherd being too busy following the trail to pay heed. Yet it was so bitterly cold that soon Bernard had to admit that the warm woollen shepherd's gear of hooded smock, jerkin, boots and strapped leggings made good sense. So they continued climbing through the vast, silent whiteness, hour after hour ... until it was all he could do to restrain himself and not be calling out that they should be making more haste. What he'd learned from his dreaming in the cabane had troubled him deeply; he knew things now that he couldn't tell anyone, save maybe Bishop Guilhabert at Montségur. Speed was vital, yet he held his peace, and so it wasn't until noon, when they paused on a dazzling high slope to break bread and rest the mules, that he let himself ask how much longer the journey would take. Pierre glowered at him.

'That depends,' the shepherd said.

'On what?'

'On whether your prayers can keep the weather good. If so, by tonight we'll be near the Col de Puymorens, by tomorrow night we may even be over the top and at the head of the Ariège, and by the night after — if these poor beasts don't drop dead — we might get to Ax.' Pierre allowed himself the briefest of grins. 'There you may sleep and dream of your golden girl, and I'll visit the whores. I may as well allow myself *that* much!'

Realising the shepherd teased him, Bernard kept a straight face.

'And after you've wasted seed in the whores?'

'Then we'll reach Tarascon and your caves the next afternoon.' Pierre jutted his jaw. 'And why is it wasting seed if I pay to sleep with women? I work for my pleasure, the women work for their money — the arrangement should please everyone, including God and all goodmen.' He shot Bernard a sharp, brooding look. 'So I've promised to receive baptism in the spirit, and so I shall — but not until my deathbed when I'll need it! Now, since you're in such a hurry, let's stop chattering and be on our way!'

So they went on without meeting any other travellers. The mules took them high through dense forest of snow-laden larch and between the great, gloomy walls of the Gorges de la Faou, where all sight of the huge peaks enclosing them was lost. Later, as the setting sun cast long rosy beams over the snowfield, they mounted a series of steep bare switchbacks and entered the Col de Puymorens. The silence was vast and awful; they didn't break it until, after nightfall, Pierre brought them safely to a wayfarers' hut he knew. It was empty and ramshackle, but the last occupant had left firewood neatly stacked. So soon enough, having fed the mules and made an oatmeal porridge, Pierre sighed, said a few words on the subject of getting a good night's sleep, kept his thoughts to himself, and (using the flank of a mule as a pillow) curled up by the fire. He was asleep in seconds.

For a while Bernard watched him sleep, and then, weighed down, the goodman went out into the still quiet night. Knee-deep in snow he stood gazing at the frosty heavens shining far above the peaks that towered black on every side ... and then again he heard the Song. Out of the night itself it flowed through him like a sad subterranean river: his eyes were wet as he sought out the Virgin. There on high she lay so calm, the Cup to one side of her, Bootes the Herdsman dancing on the other. Is she translated entirely into heaven? he wondered. Or will she find a vessel here on earth again? Please God let us reach those grottoes in time! And give me the wit to endure the maze and the trials that lie beyond those snapping teeth!

Then from the sky's southern quarter a brighter light drew him, and as he turned to Sirius his breath hissed out, his hands leaped up to shield his eyes as if he were blinded — *and so he is, for a shift seizes him, and radiant wings beat in him, and high above him in the heavens blaze three incandescent pillars of flame, golden, violet and silver, whirling and looping in their colossal dance, drenching the sky with their light. 'WE ARE THE THREE-IN-ONE, THE SHINING ONES WHO DANCE BEFORE THE HIGHEST SEAT!' cries a voice from the vibrating flame, a voice that makes his very flesh shiver. 'WE BRING LIGHT TO THE LOW PLACES WHERE THE WATCHERS CLASH IN ENVY AND FORGETFULNESS! CHILD, WHEN YOU GO DOWN TO FIND OUR DAUGHTER, REMEMBER THAT DRAGON OUR SISTER CANNOT BE SLAIN BUT ONLY REDEEMED! LIKEWISE THOSE WHO FELL WITH HER, SATANEL AND SHEMYAZA AND AZAZEL OUR BROTHERS, WHO BREED CONFUSIONS AND LUST AND INVENTIONS OF WAR! FOR THEY'RE SEEDED IN YOUR NATURE, AS WE ARE — SLAY THEM AND YOU SLAY YOURSELVES IN FIRE AND FLOOD AND FORGETTING. THEY MUST BE REDEEMED, TAMED, ORDERED AND BROUGHT TO BOOK!*

'YET IF YOU GO DOWN TO THAT PLACE WITHOUT LIGHT OUR SISTER WILL SWALLOW YOU! BEWARE OF HER! SHE'LL

NOT LET YOU TAKE OUR DAUGHTER FROM HER WITHOUT A FIGHT! AND BEWARE OF THE BLACK ONES WHO OBEY HER, THINKING THEY LOVE THE CHRIST! SAVE THE CHILD! FOLLOW YOUR DREAM! MAKE HASTE! BRING HER TO THE LIGHT, TRAIN AND PROTECT HER, AND WHEN IT'S TIME SHE'LL KNOW WHAT TO DO!'

And as this great voice reverberated in him the goodman fell to his knees, his mind reeling with simultaneous visions: *of the terrible fire in which he burns; of that ocean world in the depths of which the Lost Stone shines and where the great grey ones glide; of that glade in a grove where the naked idiot froths and reels and SHE watches jealously from her high place, preparing the rite that restores her power . . . and of the golden girl falling, falling to the dark place where she drowns in terror, crying out:*

'Father! Father Bernard! If you don't come soon it'll be too late!'

Then the Shining Ones were gone. But a long time passed in that chill starlit night before Bernard recovered his senses and was able to get to his feet. With the voice still ringing in his mind he staggered into the hut and, without really knowing what he did, shook the shepherd awake.

'What? What?' Pierre cried furiously. 'For the love of . . .'

Then by the last light from the nearly burnt-out fire he saw the terrible exaltation on the goodman's face. His anger at being awoken died. Stiff and alarmed he sat up.

'My lord,' he said in an awed voice, 'what happened?'

Numb, the goodman trembled. Tears squeezed from his eyes.

'We can sleep no more,' Bernard whispered. 'We must go on at once!'

And so on they went, though dawn was still distant. And all next day the goodman neither ate nor spoke, but rode behind the anxious shepherd, head bowed deep with eyes tight shut, or thrown back with his eyes wide in the deeps of the sky. Perhaps he was praying. If so, his prayers must have been effective, for that day the weather held. So through the vast snow desert they rode, winding back and forth to the summit of the pass. There the wind was vicious, sculpting the dazzling whiteness into fantastic shapes and knife-edged dunes, stinging their faces with whipped-up snow so fierce they could hardly see. On and on they pressed, as if driven by some external force, until at last they were over the top, each huddled on his beast, and the mules must have been given heart by that same unknown power, for they did not drop, they went on without complaint.

Next night for a few brief hours they rested in rough forest shelter at the head of the Ariège. Still the goodman would not eat or break silence, and Pierre feared for him. 'What is it? What happened last night?' But Bernard just shook his head and stared through the shepherd. By dawn they were moving again, so that before darkness fell they were far down the valley, following the tumbling ice-green waters of the Ariège to a point which gave them their first sight, through tall white-boughed trees, of Ax-les-Thermes with its lepers' baths and prostitutes.

Pierre had become ever more depressed, affected by the goodman's pain, but when he saw the village ahead he brightened visibly, perhaps because he thought himself about to spend the night paying tribute to the ladies of the Bassin des Ladres, but also because Ax marked the beginning of his own native territory. It was here the people of Prades brought their corn to be milled and their sheep to be sold; here that those with ringworm and hookworm came in hope of cure. This journey's mad! he told himself. And risky, here ... but I'm glad to be home! And then, urging his reluctant beast to go faster, in a soft but deep bass voice he began singing a song that the goodman, following some way behind, heard with a shock:

> *Quant lo bouié ben de laura*
> *Planto soun agulhado*
> *AEIOU!*

237

Planto soun agulhado
Trobo sa henno al pé del foc
Tristo descounsolado
AEIOU!

Tristo descounsolado
Si n'es malauto, digos oc
Te farei un potage
AEI...

'Why sing that? Do you know what it means?' Bernard interrupted in a very agitated voice, riding up alongside the shepherd who, with mouth still agape, eyed him in complete bewilderment. For it was the first time the goodman had spoken in nearly two days and nights.

'It's just a song!' Pierre said. 'It's about a herdsman who comes home from work to find his lady Joana dead by the fire! She's gone to ...'

'And who is the Lady Joana?' Bernard demanded angrily.

The shepherd was perplexed. 'A woman, like any other!'

'Then,' said Bernard, with a wild, awful look about him, 'I found that song in vain, I have lived in vain, and this journey is in vain!'

'What?' Pierre's jaw dropped still further. '*You* found that song?' Then light dawned; he snapped his fingers. 'You're *that* Bernard de Laurac! The troubadour!' He eyed the goodman with a new but uneasy respect. 'But why did you stop singing? And ... who *is* this lady?'

'She is our faith.' Bernard was harsh. 'I found this song before the war began. I stopped singing because when the war began I vowed I'd sing no more until it's won. Now let's move on. We have far to go tonight.'

He dug in his heels and urged on his exhausted mule, leaving Pierre dumbfounded. Why's he so upset? the shepherd asked himself. What is it?

The sky was deepening into night above the white slopes when Pierre caught up with the goodman on the outskirts of the town. 'Aren't we stopping here tonight?' Pierre asked anxiously.

'No.' Bernard's expression was remote. 'We are not.'

'At least let me stop long enough to find a woman to delouse me!'

'And more than that, no doubt. No. Your lice can wait. The one I seek cannot. Use your thumb.'

'Oh!' cried Pierre, his resentment spilling over at last. 'I suppose you never touched women ever, eh?'

'I fathered three sons,' said Bernard briskly. 'And before I married I knew many women. It took me years to learn that a fire too often fed is no fine flame but only habit.' He shot Pierre a fierce look. Poor huts now lined both sides of the track; there were people about, but the two tired men hardly noticed. 'Listen, my friend, the purpose of Amor is not to lock up more poor souls in tunics of flesh. True love of woman is the same as true love of God. It exists on its own tension; carnal release diminishes it. Is it for love of the soul that you want to stop here and fornicate?'

'I'm not holy like you,' Pierre grumbled, disliking this austere tone, thinking: He's an old man. He's tired. The journey's too much for him, and it's about to become too much for me! 'What's the use of fire if you don't cook with it and warm the body with it?'

Bernard sighed impatiently. His face was haggard and pale. '*Even gold, which can be destroyed, is tested by fire,*' he quoted, '*and so your faith, which is so much more precious than gold, must also be tested.*'

'Oh, fine!' cried Pierre, forgetting there were people about. 'Then why did you marry? Isn't it said marriage is an inferior condition, a contract of mutual bondage?' He eyed the goodman obstinately. 'How can you talk to me about faith when YOUR gold has already been melted down in the inferior fire of marriage? But of course you're the perfect one. I don't know anything, I'm just a shepherd!'

'A shepherd with a loud voice and little sense.' Bernard looked sharply about. 'Good friend, I have no objection whatever to your desires; it's just that we can't afford to stop. We *must* press on!'

'So we can find this lovely little girl of yours? Eh?'

Bernard reined in. They were in a narrow street by a tavern. Against its wall a man leaned, watching them. 'Very well.' Shrugging, he met the shepherd's eyes. 'Godspeed and farewell. I'm sorry to lose you. May your star shine, and may the heat of your balls not bring you back as a goat!' And as Pierre gaped he nodded, heeled his mule, and continued on his way.

'But I haven't even *touched* a woman since harvest time!' Pierre roared after him, 'And my lice are driving me crazy!'

The goodman did not pause or even look back.

'And that's my mule!' Pierre cried furiously.

Bernard reined in, dismounted, and began walking.

'For the love of God!' the shepherd muttered, uneasily aware of the man at the door. People here know me, he reminded himself. With a curse he followed, snatching the reins of the goodman's abandoned beast as he passed it. He caught up with Bernard by a house from an upper window of which a woman gave him a smile that made him groan. 'Mount your *mule* and let us continue in peace!' he hissed. 'And no more argument! I *hate* argument!'

Mildly but with difficulty, for he was exhausted, Bernard remounted.

'I believe the lady we seek will thank you,' he said.

The *lady*! thought Pierre, glaring at the laughing woman in the window. But according to you she's a virgin girl, not even budded. *If* she exists at all! Yet he held his peace as they left Ax-les-Thermes and continued into the fast-falling night towards Tarascon, exhausted men on exhausted beasts entering dangerous territory into which the persecutors had lately extended their arm. For now they were only a few hours from their goal, and Pierre had to acknowledge, though grudgingly, the sense of travelling this final stage under cover of darkness. The Upper Ariège was remote, and had not been devastated to anything like the same degree as the plains to the north — it was said the madman de Montfort had wiped out over four hundred villages during his decade of murder and violence — but even so, times had changed. Roger-Bernard of Foix still held these lands, at least in theory, but he'd been forced to surrender his strongholds to the French boy-king Louis IX. Now foreign mercenaries and Dominican friars were everywhere. Nobody was safe. From here on, Pierre thought grimly, I keep my eyes open and my mouth shut. And so above the tumbling river and through the still cold night he rode, fighting hunger and sleep, coaxing the beast that bore him. 'I'll never say another word against a mule again,' he promised it grimly, thinking of women as he scratched behind its ears.

Behind him along the riverbank Bernard followed, dozing on muleback as the lamps of the Virgin wheeled high in the fields of God above his nodding head, and many half-formed thoughts and visions disturbed him, keeping him awake as the sweet sad song flowed through him, the river of it whispering what he'd learned of the trial that lay before him. The eternal war has caught me up in it, he knew ... and as he dozed he was *there* again, *there* in the ocean depths ... *there* in the great dance ... *there* in the green and fertile grove where a naked idiot played; where the Enemy watched and waited ... and *there* in the deep dark place where the golden girl drowned ...

'*Father! Father Bernard! If you don't come soon ...*'

And so they continued towards the confrontation ...

20.
The Black Friar

At dawn the mules went on strike.

All night they'd kept on over the hard-packed snow of the riverside way, tracking dark forest slopes through silent unlit hamlets where not even dogs barked, until in time they'd carried the two men almost to their destination — the caves entered from the slopes high above Ussat-les-Bains, south of Tarascon. But before they got there, with first light edging the high, pine-spiked eastern ridges, the mules stopped.

Bernard was first to snap out of his doze. The two trembling beasts stood side by side, heads bowed, feet firmly planted in the snow. He nudged the shepherd awake. 'It's a wonder they got us this far,' Pierre yawned, stiffly dismounting to piss against the trunk of a tall cypress.

'What do you mean, "this far"? Won't they take us further?'

'When a mule decides to stop,' said Pierre, 'it stops.'

'Maybe if we feed them …' the goodman suggested anxiously. In the grey pre-dawn his face had the pinched look of a man living entirely on his nerves. Certainly he had not eaten for two days and nights.

'Maybe.' Pierre grumbled. 'But lacking human brains they have no will-o'-the-wisps to keep them going against all good sense.' Clumsy with cold, the shepherd unlashed the remaining sack of oat fodder. The beasts ate hungrily, and so did Pierre, offering Bernard half a loaf which the goodman refused. But after they'd eaten the mules still refused to budge.

'We'll have to abandon them and walk,' said Bernard philosophically.

'Abandon them?' Pierre was outraged. 'I'll do no such thing!'

'Then carry them on your back!' the goodman snapped, then immediately calmed himself. 'My friend, there's no time to lose. There's a safe house in Ussat; I must arrange for a message to go to Montségur, and there are supplies I need for the caves — ropes, flint, clothing, pitch for torches. And you'll need bread while you wait?'

Pierre eyed him askance. 'I'm not going down there with you?'

'The outer caves, if you wish.' Bernard dismounted and without ado began to walk. 'But the deeper parts are forbidden to you.'

'Thanks!' Pierre cried, furiously pulling the halters of the obstinate brutes as Bernard left him again. 'I give up everything to lead you here and now you tell me I'm not good enough for the last leg! And talking of last legs, what happens if you fall down and break yours, eh? Who'll rescue your dream-child then? And who *is* this precious child anyway? Where's she coming from? Heaven?'

'Without her,' Bernard called back, 'what's lost won't be found!'

'And what in the name of God is that?'

'What's the meaning of your name, Pierre?'

'My name? It means what it is. It's who I am!'

'Pierre, you're a lost stone!' Bernard cried back ironically. 'I can't wait. Meet me before noon at the entrance we used before.'

And off he went like a young man who'd had a good night's sleep. More amazed than angry, Pierre watched him vanish among the trees. Daylight was strengthening:

243

with a shiver of apprehension the shepherd looked up over the valley at the mountain to the east ... the massif the goodmen called *Tabor*, their mountain of the spirit. Its distant ridges, sharp and dark against the early light, pointed the way to Montségur, high on its great precipitous rock in the wilderness beyond. Pierre scratched his itching scalp uneasily. A messenger to Montségur? Why? Again he pulled at the mules. Again they refused to move. He couldn't blame them.

'Shift, you stupid beasts!' he urged them wearily. 'I feel the same as you do but we can't abandon him now. He may be a goodman, but he's an old fool too. What if there's soldiers about, or worse, friars? *Come on!*'

But the sun had risen high enough for its light to be dancing on the river's fast green waters before at last he persuaded them to move again.

'That took long enough!' he scolded them. 'Now let's get to those caves. We might even get there first and rescue his dream-nymph for him! I'd give ten years to see his face! Anyway, we'd be doing him a favour — he's not meant to have anything to do with women at all. Now COME ALONG!'

Perhaps Bernard's months in exile, far from the constant danger he'd known during the eight years since he'd formally renounced Rome's harlot superstitions, had bred in him a false sense of security. Perhaps he was too anxious to get quickly down to the Gate of the Stone in the dark depths beyond the labyrinth ... or perhaps it was something to do with the Enemy's desire to stop him. Whatever it was, before that morning was out he was nearly in chains on his way to a dungeon in Foix like Gaillard before him.

Easily and soon enough he reached the hamlet of Ussat with its baths for those with the goitre, an old man in shepherd's gear, and if his face seemed too pale and ascetic for a shepherd's, the roughspun woollen hood hid it, and anyway there was nobody about on the road. Near the hamlet he crossed the river by a swaying rope footbridge and climbed a slope that should have tired him but did not. The spirit is with me today, he told himself, surprised by his energy and physical lightness as he came at last to the forest clearing where lay the isolated ostal of Sicard the Weaver.

Sicard, a little dark man with crooked teeth, a believer who'd received the *convenientia* that (like Pierre) bound him to accept baptism on his deathbed if not before, raised his brows in surprise when Bernard revealed himself. But he said not a word to the goodman until he'd sent his wife out of the kitchen — the only stone-walled room in his flimsy little house.

'Braida, go for water,' he said sharply, 'and don't come back too quick!' And only with her gone did he genuflect and ask for blessing.

Yet before she went she stole a quick look at the visitor's face, so that by nightfall it was an open secret — at least among Ussat's believers — that the goodman Bernard de Laurac had returned from exile.

The two men sat at the rough-hewn table by the hearth, under hams suspended from the rafters out of reach of the cat.

'Why are you here, my lord?' Sicard sounded respectful enough, but Bernard didn't like the fearful look in his eyes. 'I wish Braida hadn't seen you. If it gets out that you're back ...'

'I can't explain.' The moment Bernard sat down a great wave of utter weariness flooded him; it was all he could do to keep his eyes open and his voice firm. 'And the less you know the better. Friend Sicard, I cannot pause even to preach. But from you I need a good strong length of rope, at least thirty body's-length. I need bread, a warm cloak, flint for fire and pitch for brands ... and I need you or another to go immediately to Montségur with a message for Bishop Guilhabert.'

Sicard gripped the edge of the table. He gulped and nodded.

'My son will go. He knows the way. What ... what is the message?'

'*What was lost is found beyond the Gate!*'

Sicard blinked. 'My lord, may I ask the meaning of this?'

He goes to the caves where the goodmen hide treasure, he thought.

'You may not,' said Bernard. 'Call your son and send him, now.'

'These are dangerous times, my lord,' said Sicard in a rush. 'There are friars about. We need luck and keen wit. Please, bless my ostal.'

'Will you do these things?' Bernard asked impatiently.

'My lord, of course!' Sicard rose. 'My son will take the message, the other things are yours. But you'd best be gone quick. I'm sure my woman recognised you, and secrets with her are like water through a sieve.'

Ten minutes later Bernard was on his way again, swinging down to the river with a pack on his back and his energy returning. Of his hunger he was hardly aware. Regular fasting was part of his life, and since that night of vision in the Col de Puymorens he had vowed not to eat again until the girl was found and safely delivered from the darkness. He knew he'd need all his wits for the approaching battle with the Old One: food in his belly now would only dull his spirit.

Troubled, Sicard watched him leave, then went to find his son. Later his wife demanded: 'Why was he here? Where have you sent our son?'

Sicard wouldn't tell her. 'And if I hear you've been talking about this,' he warned, 'I swear I'll beat you black and blue!'

'You'll do that anyway!' Braida jeered.

He ran a few paces after her, but she was faster. He sighed.

Bernard too was anxious as he reached the bridge again. *Something's wrong there,* he thought. *Sicard stank of fear. Is that what persecution does? Turn good men into cunning beasts? If his woman talks ... perhaps I was rash to go there. But this gear's essential. Especially the rope. I hope it's long enough. I'll measure and knot it* once I'm up there. Did the shepherd get those mules moving again? He's a good man, but ... Bernard shook his head despairingly — a lost stone indeed!

So that as he crossed the bridge and returned through the trees to the road above he was paying no attention to the world about. He was gazing up at the steep snowy slopes, assessing them, trying to work out the easiest, least visible route up to the mouth of the caves ... and his old man's ears and eyes did not alert him to the armed patrol's snow-muffled, tree-hidden approach until it was already round the bend and on top of him ...

The patrol wasn't looking for anyone in particular. It had been sent out at dawn by the Count of Foix's bailiff in Tarascon; a routine measure to remind people that Church and King had an eye on them despite the severe winter and the remoteness of the area. The mounted soldiers were local men, most of them secretly sympathetic to the heretics, who practised what they preached where the official clergy did not. Nor was their sergeant wanting to arrest anyone that morning: it was too cold to stand about questioning casual wayfarers. So that when they rode round the bend just as the stooped old man with the pack on his back stepped onto the road, there would have been no problem — save for the unwanted presence among them of Brother Jean d'Aubigny of the Order of Friars Preachers, otherwise known as Dominicans.

A northerner, Brother Jean was an ascetic of the new breed, young and ferociously dedicated to the utter extirpation of heresy, his brows always knitted in a scowl and his eyes never still, always shifting, their cold stare piercing straight to the core of every man, woman and child he met. Who knew what drove him? Perhaps he didn't know himself. Based in Foix, where the rapidly-expanding Inquisition had established an office, he had been trained by the blessed Dominic himself, and already his enthusiastic efforts had led to the fiery salvation of over seventy heretics, including a certain Gaillard de

Capvern. This number of souls saved might have been enough for a lesser man, but Brother Jean was (as he himself confessed to God every night) a glutton for the Lord's work. So this morning, as he happened to be visiting Tarascon, he had insisted on riding with the patrol, and so far had caused nothing but trouble and delay.

Now he caused more.

'STOP!' he cried, for the moment he saw the old man that still cold voice in him, that voice of the Lord he feared and trusted, whispered: '*THIS is one of them! I smell it!*' He reined in sharply. 'STOP!'

The sergeant groaned. 'What is it this time?' he complained. 'Must we waste time and freeze to death questioning every poor peasant we meet?'

'The serpent's face is always innocent,' the friar replied crisply, erect in the saddle, stark in his black robe and white habit with the scarlet cross on the breast. Keenly he eyed the hunched old man.

'You! Old man! What's your name? What's your trade, if you have one? Where do you live? Why are you out on the road? Do you believe in the Holy Catholic Faith and in the True Cross?'

Bernard stood silently, hooded head bowed. I'm done for, he realised, staring at the snow between his feet. The beauty of the sparkling sunlit crystals amazed him. I cannot lie, I'm bound to answer truthfully. Why wasn't I more careful? Everything's lost! This is one of those who sniff us out like a dog sniffs meat. And for an instant, remaining silent, he seemed to see a woman's face mocking him ... the Enemy's face.

'Answer me!' demanded the friar, cold and careful as the sergeant and his men hunched impatiently round the goodman on their fretful horses; as Bernard thought dismally, Gaillard, soon I'll join you, — 'Why won't you speak, old man? Do you claim this world was made by Satan? Do you say Christ our Lord was never incarnate? Do you deny the Eucharist, the Cross, and the Virgin Birth? Look up, old man, meet me in the eyes!'

'Leave him alone,' cried one of the soldiers. 'He's just a

stupid old man who doesn't know what you're saying. Can't you see that, friar?' And there were rumblings of agreement from the others as Bernard remained silent, still gazing at the snow as the friar turned angrily on them.

'You're all heretics,' he warned them softly. 'My superiors will hear of it.' He swung back to Bernard. 'Old man! Answer my questions!'

It was then that Pierre Belot came round the bend, riding one mule and leading the other. He understood the situation immediately.

'Oh-oh,' he murmured to his mule, his heart freezing. 'I told you the old man couldn't do without us.'

Not yet noticed, he kicked the mule forward.

'Sir, of course I'll answer your questions,' said Bernard humbly, his head bowed still deeper, 'but you ask so many all at once. I'm confused. Could you perhaps repeat them one at a time?'

Soldiers laughed, though the sergeant hushed them. The friar stiffened angrily. 'Lift up your face, throw back your hood and let me see you!' he commanded. 'You're not the fool you sound. I think you're a . . .'

'Father!' Pierre shouted loudly, but as he rode up his heart leapt into his mouth, for he recognised the sergeant as a man from Prades the moment the sergeant recognised him. *Raymond Benet, if you don't keep quiet* . . . his quick look both threatened and implored, and the sergeant, without any expression, shrugged slightly as Pierre's momentum carried himself and the mules between the friar and Bernard. 'Father, I *told* you to stay at home!' he scolded the goodman. 'What are you doing? I've been everywhere!' He turned to the scowling friar with an apologetic grin, meaningfully tapping his head as he did. 'Don't worry yourself with my old dad. He's a good Christian, but it's years since he knew what's what. Ask him questions and he just gets confused.' And he shrugged, man to man, grinning confidently.

Meanwhile the sergeant, hiding a smile behind his hand, had waved his men on, so that suddenly Brother

Jean found himself alone and abandoned.

Realising he was beaten, the friar gave Pierre a look that pierced the shepherd's heart like a sliver of ice.

'I'll remember you!' the friar whispered, then spurred his horse.

'Thanks, brother!' Pierre cried cheerily after him. 'I'll remember you too.' But neither he nor Bernard moved until the patrol was gone. Then he dismounted and the goodman at last raised his pale and bony face.

'How did you get into that?' Pierre demanded angrily. 'You really do need looking after, don't you? The trouble with you goodmen is you can't lie even to save your lives. It takes sinners like me to do that. Now we'd better move fast before that red-hot pimple of Satan persuades them to come back and arrest us both. You realise the sergeant knows me? We grew up together. He stayed quiet. If he hadn't we'd both be cooked.'

'Your arrival was opportune,' Bernard admitted drily. But his heart was pumping harder than he cared to admit, and his mouth was tight at the thought of how his carelessness had endangered so much.

'Oh, come on!' Pierre, feeling a sudden rush of affection, seized the goodman's shoulders. 'You're in a hurry, aren't you? So let's get into the caves and find your dream-child!' Showing blackened teeth, he grinned happily. '*And* your lost stone you think I'm too stupid to know about!'

They started up the slope with Bernard mounted and leading the other mule, Pierre on foot behind with a fir bough as sweep to wipe out their point of departure from the road. Then slowly they trekked up through the deep snow, keeping to the cover of the fir woods, Pierre hauling the by now resigned mules past limestone outcrops that burst from the pristine whiteness like huge distorted heads. From time to time he eyed the goodman anxiously, but Bernard seemed none the worse for his near fatal experience. Indeed, after they'd reached and passed the great dark gaping mouth that gave entry to the main cave system, Bernard dismounted and went ahead on foot, his stride eager and his eye hawk-sharp. The Shining Ones are with us! he told himself. Hold to their light and all will be well! That friar is the one they warned me against, but they saw to it that the shepherd came in time to save me from my stupidity. Now! Now! Now!

Bernard had only once been up this way, and only once down, and there had been no snow, but now without error he came to the narrow, shrub-hidden cleft which was the entrance to the secret system. From only a few feet away it remained invisible: even when sunlight fell full on it there was no reason to suspect a door to the depths. Yet he felt like a fish pulled up the slope on fate's line. I'd have found it with my eyes shut at midnight! he realised, the shining energy pouring through him as he stood there, Pierre and the mules still labouring up through the trees below him. For this day I put on the flesh of mortality again! What I do next is more important than anything I ever did or will ever do again! Christ give me strength to overcome her weak ways and release her love on the world!

With Pierre still cursing at the mules below him the goodman removed his pack and set to work. First, remembering what Bishop Guilhabert had told him about the maze, he uncoiled the rope and carefully knotted it to specific lengths. Then he took an axe he'd also begged and, by the time the shepherd reached him, had already selected, cut, and gathered together the lengths of pine which, pitch-smeared, would serve as torches to light the utter inner darkness. He had also cut two staffs. 'Where does your strength come from?' Pierre gasped, finally reaching him. 'Did you really need me to lead you here?' But Bernard said nothing, continuing to make the brands as the shepherd got his breath back. It was near noon now, the sun blinding on the snows as Pierre eyed the shrub-shrouded gloom of the cleft. Grimly suppressing a shudder, Pierre hobbled the mules and hitched them to a tree with fodder set down within their reach.

'Don't think you're leaving me out here,' he warned. 'I haven't come this far just to sit and whistle in the sun!'

Bernard pointed. 'Can the mules be seen from below?'

Pierre looked down. Through a gap in the trees and far below he saw the patrol riding back towards Tarascon. *What if they spot where we left the road?* He watched anxiously ... but the patrol rode on and out of sight.

'That cursed friar's too busy looking down at those he condemns to look up to God,' he commented harshly. Yet he led the mules to a deeper stand, and took the further precaution of muzzling them loosely. 'They can still eat,' he said, 'but they can't bray.' Bernard, still smearing pitch on wood, said nothing. Compressing his lips, Pierre eyed the dark cleft.

'Do you still deny you need me?' he demanded pugnaciously.

Bernard had to smile. 'But you must remain outside the maze.'

Pierre scowled. 'Didn't you tell me you'll be going deeper than you went before when you hid here? To get to this maze, and so on?'

The goodman, winding measured rope over his shoulder, nodded.

'If you've not actually been that far,' Pierre objected, 'how do you know how to get through this maze, to the ... Gate, and everything ...?'

'I've been instructed.' Bernard stopped what he was doing and eyed the shepherd grimly. 'Now, if you're coming, carry these brands for me.'

'But that means you don't know much more about it than I do!' Pierre grinned. 'So why can't I come all the way with you? I warn you, you're going to need me again.'

Bernard sighed. What a mule of a man! he thought. 'Forgive me, good brother, but you don't understand,' he said quietly. 'It's not just the danger to the flesh. Pierre, listen! Beyond the maze is a dreadful place! The mouth not only of the underworld, but of other worlds too!' *Should I tell him of the Enemy, of what we're about?* Deciding

252

against it, he went on: 'Down there are ghosts that drive men mad — phantoms, Pierre, demons! — and for this reason entry is forbidden to those not baptised and trained in the spirit.' He eyed the shepherd and saw him unconvinced. 'You're a brave man, Pierre, I wouldn't be here without you. I owe you the truth. Enter that maze and your own terror will kill you. I've been trained. I must risk it on my own, and you must wait outside.' Hoisting the prepared pack onto his shoulder, he eyed the shepherd sternly. 'You won't find even that easy. You'll have to wait in utter darkness for hours, maybe even for days.' The goodman grimaced. 'I can't tell how long in world's time this will take. You'd be happier waiting out here in the good light of day.'

'I'm not scared,' announced the shepherd, gazing slack-jawed at the gap in the mountain, his body clearly saying that, like many men who love the high open places, he had a horror of being buried alive in the utter dark.

Bernard appraised him, then nodded.

'Very well. Let's go.'

With an unlit brand in his hand he turned and ducked past the shrubs into the narrow cleft. Pierre, with an apologetic look back at the mules, at the sunny glorious outside world, picked up the bundle of brands and followed him through the door into the land of eternal night. Several steps he took, then again he paused, looking back at the sun. Pale, framed between black walls, it penetrated the mists of rising vapours, and suddenly he realised how much he depended on it for all he knew and loved. Will I see you again? he wondered, terror hidden in his heart. And for an instant he thought he saw a raven-haired woman in place of the sun, her blood-red lips opened in a mocking smile.

He shuddered. He fought the fear in his blood. He turned his back on the light of day and followed the goodman into darkness. Into the past.

21.
Fool's Paradise

Shem was happy. It was moon of hawk and willow, moon of nesting, sun warm on bare back as he splashed in brook running so sweet past the hazel-fringed mouth of his cave. Bright new life, springing up everywhere! Her blessing and bounty! Emerald-sharp blades of grass sparkling with last night's rain; yellow clusters of barberry flowers; slow budding of oak and elm; hawthorn and apple unfolding tremorous purity of blossom! And little birds singing with all their heart as Shem, ragged black beard dangling in crystal water, bent to heave smooth big stones and sods of turf into place against a lattice of pliant hazel rods. He was building a dam across the brook, and he was singing too, in harmony with all the warm fresh world, a delighted smile on his worn thin face as he played at work.

Faraway, deep in the womb-hall under the Whole Place, She gazes into the emerald depths. Forgetting afflicts Her. Though the plan ripens there is danger. She sees the Weak Ones entering the caves. 'So they're not so weak!' She mutters. 'But I'll stop them at the gate. That girl must die! She MUST!' Angrily She watches Her Fool in the grove, and those guarding him ... and for one of these guards Her sudden sharp smile is taut with mad hope, feral regret. 'You'll do my will, Hoel!' She whispers. 'But I

254

can't show you any mercy. I must be as hard as the world to save it.'

Hoel shivered. For a moment he'd felt an icicle touch his heart. Then he heard the Fool's happy song and smiled sourly. Seated on a rock where the brook left the grove's tangled depths, he gripped the bronze-tipped spear over his bare brown knees and thought: Only She knows the meaning of his song. If there *is* any. Building his dam again, is he? The women say that's what he does. Every morning building it up, every night tearing it down. They say he's been at it ever since the Battle, ever since She put him here, and that's a fistful of years! Yes, hard at it, until She ...

There he stopped. Dark, squat, curly-haired, clean-shaven in his white linen tunic and kilt, he eyed right then left. His neighbours in the guarding circle of men were in sight. He felt reassured. But that cold touch ... Forget it! he told himself, trying to ignore the Fool's hateful happy song. Think too loud and She'll have my blood bubbling in Her Cauldron. Grinning with fear, despising himself for it, he recited mentally: For She's the Red Lady of Battle who brought us here and won the Whole Place; the White Sow who eats Her own farrow; the Green One with the herbs that increase us and make us strong! Take care, Hoel! Remember: Owl sees for Her; Fox hears us talk by night, and Old Mother Riann with her Nine Daughters — he scowled — rules us in Her name.

No! He bit his lip. Don't think of Ailma! Not now! Not today!

Discomfited, he looked away from the grove, past the longhouse with its cooking smoke pale against the sky, past the pig pens and horse corral and the barley patch where men worked at the far edge of the clearing; his eye roamed over greening forest tops to the distant slopes of rolling hills. He sucked nervous breath. Beyond those hills the Ancient Ones lived in their forts and under-ground raths. Driven back but still dangerous! Shape-shifting degenerates! Hissing, he let go his spear; with crooked fingers he threw up horns either side of his head. Ancient Ones whose faces shine — *like Hers!* he thought fearfully. Surely She's like them! She too is of An and El. It must be! How else could we beat them? She never told us anything. She came out of the rising sun and brought us here. Oh! And despite the day's warmth he shivered, gazing up into the great blue bowl of the sky, remembering tales of how, long ago, An and El had descended from the invisible Whirling Castle ... remembering, more recently, that terrible battle for the Whole Place.

Stop! he thought, close to panic. Why do I think these things?

But ... from what world did She pluck the Fool? Why?

For still the Fool sang as if the world were happy. Hoel clenched his teeth, his spear. Anger seized him. Who *is* this idiot who speaks no known tongue, this Fool that the birds and beasts all love? Listen to his stupid song, and us in Her pot if so much as a hair of his stinking lousy head is touched! His grinning, ugly head that never even turns to see the women who bring him his bread — or so *they* say! Even Ailma says it! What is he? Not a *man*, that's sure! We men should take steps to ...

Just in time he checked it. Appalled, throwing himself on hands and knees, he ducked his head in the brook. With a gasp and a shake, droplets flying from him, he glared at his broken reflection.

'Don't think these things any more!' he muttered hoarsely. 'Why let his song upset you? So Ailma ... yes, but *don't think of it!*'

But that happy voice infuriated him. He couldn't stop the thoughts. As soon as he rejected them they pounced again. He knelt, gripping his spear so hard his knuckles whitened. 'That battle started it!' he told himself frantically. 'She made us cross the narrow sea and marched us to the Whole Place ... and they met us.' Tears sprang to his eyes. 'There my brothers and my mother's brothers died horribly! And I ...'

Memory! Oh Gods no! Over mounds of twitching corpses stumbles the terrified boy, aware only of death and pain and fear

256

as lances of wild bleeding light stab the mists hiding the high
place for which they fight — lances exploding the bodies they
strike, filling the air with flying gobs of flesh, with the stink of
spilled entrails, with . . .

He shook his head violently. 'No!' he groaned. But the
Fool still sang, and a fury filled him. Yet for all Her power
we were losing, he recalled coldly. Nobody denies it! Just
in time with that Beast at Her throat She somehow
plucked this Fool from the fog, and down among us he
came staggering and babbling so that *everyone* fled in
horror, us as well as the enemy! So, he won us the day,
for if he hadn't appeared those devils would have killed us
all, sucked our souls, for they're degenerate, they chose to
take form in this mad world! Did they not descend
lusting for the bodies of us they'd filled with their fire-of-
knowing? So they bred with us and taught us but now
they're worse than us! And She . . .

A mocking female voice broke in on him.

'Hoel, always scowling! Did the wind change and fix
you for ever with that face? You look as if you've lost
something you never had!'

Taken unawares, Hoel whirled, and as he leapt up saw
first the bare brown feet then the slender green-gowned
body and finally the lovely oval golden-haired face of
Ailma, Riann's youngest daughter — and at the sight of
her had to recognise why he was so angry today. For
Ailma had refused him for the third time last night.
Though named after the silver fir, the birth-tree, she'd
publicly declared she wouldn't increase the clan until she
met a *man* — a *real* man. She was headstrong, self-willed,
and Hoel was not alone among the young men in feeling
insulted. 'Yes, Hoel!' she'd told him bitingly last night,
adding bitter spice to her refusal. 'But you're always
ready to take offence. You think too much of yourself.
Why should I give myself to you?' Now at her mockery
his scowl deepened, and deepened again to see the wicker
basket she carried. He knew it held fresh bread — Fool's
Bread. With her own hands she'd baked it so that Shem
should eat, should continue to sing happily; should

continue to build his stupid dam every morning and break it every night. Of course, Hoel knew as he stood glaring at her that it wasn't necessarily her choice to bake bread and carry it to the Fool, deep in the grove from which, by Her order, all men were excluded ... for it was also Her order that all ripe but unwed girls in the clan should take turns to bake Fool's Bread. The girls did not necessarily have to like it, any more than the men had to like Her command to guard the grove, day and night. But Hoel was sure that Ailma did like it ... and now, in his certainty that her presence here, at this point *he* guarded, was a deliberate taunt, his sense deserted him.

'Why do I scowl?' he cried passionately. 'I scowl because I want your love for me, not for a Fool you're forbidden to touch and who doesn't even know you exist, however much you comb your hair when you take him bread!'

She regarded him coolly, hiding her anger at his attitude.

'You're a new kind of man,' she said in a quiet voice, 'to wish to stop me entering the grove to serve She who rules us. If you feel so strongly, maybe you should go deeper into the woods and make an appointment with the Wild Women who suck the marrow from the bones of too proud men.'

He stood gripping the spear, his face flushed. 'Things will change!' he declared, unsure what he meant or unwilling to say it more boldly. Yet the misery in his eyes was so plain she almost took pity on him.

'You're a fool too.' She smiled with prim condescension. 'But not foolish enough. Let me pass to take the Fool his bread. Do Her will!'

Burning, he stood aside. She smiled sweetly as she passed him with her basket of Fool's Bread, stepping delicately in the clear bright knee-deep brook. 'It's a lovely day, Hoel,' she said. 'Take more pleasure in it.'

'There are a dozen easier ways to enter the grove!' he burst out. 'You come this way just to taunt me because you know I want you!'

'I like to walk in the brook,' she said softly, not turning, and there was nothing he could say; with a fever in his crotch he stood watching her hips sway as she ducked past the spiky hawthorn that flowered over the deep-shadowed brook. Hawthorn! A deliciously sensuous fury caught him as he watched her rump vanish into the depths from which men were excluded. White virgin flower! Ach, I'll not bear this much longer! Abruptly he reversed his spear and drove it down hard into the soft and flowering turf.

Why do we men let Her rule us? Who *is* She anyway? If we can beat Her magical brothers and sisters, then why not Her? Why must we obey women?

He was appalled by the rash arrogance of these thoughts, but such questions — and the frustration behind them — did not leave him, not on that warm day, nor on any of the days and nights that followed.

And in Her dark place She watches them through the emerald. 'You both do as you must,' She mutters. 'You rebel as I did. We taught you Lullu well! Thought and war — and rebellion!' But, rising from moon and horns, She frowns. Something's wrong. What? The war? Shem's awakening goes well, but ... And She remembers the Weak Ones. NO! Not now! I'll deal with them soon! 'You do as I want,' She promises Hoel, smiling fiercely, Her head hurting, 'but you'll be punished ... as I was! That's fate! You'll get your wish, you'll become what you must!' Then, trying to recall what's lost, She goes to paint Herself with the blood of life and death ...

She says we mustn't touch him! Ailma quickened her pace up the clean pebbled brook to the place where the Fool sang. Excitement tingled in her body. We're not to talk or approach or touch him. But what's the harm in it? How could She know if I — if *one* of us — just ... *touched* him. On the arm maybe. How could She know? She's far away, She can't know everything. Would he tell her? I doubt it! He's the Fool, he doesn't even have a mind of his own. He is a man, after all. Probably as bad as Hoel, if he wasn't a Fool! Men! Just good for hunting and

259

fighting and filling our bellies!

She sighed. Of course I think like this whenever I bring him bread. We all do. But none of us is going to touch him, not really! How can Hoel be jealous? It's just exciting to imagine, that's all!

So, ducking under a final branch, she entered the sunny glade in the middle of the grove; the glade where Her Fool lived.

And there he was. Singing as he worked, playing as he sang.

She stood behind him, eyeing him just as she did every eight days when it was her turn to bake Fool's Bread. Licking her lips, she eyed his thin, bony body, his wild shock of grey-streaked black hair, his worn thin face with the mark of Owl scoring his left cheek. So unlike any of the men in the clan! Oblivious of her, he went on building his little dam, creating a deep and placid pool, and she imagined, giggling at the idea, how perhaps that afternoon he'd lie in it, submerged save for his nose and straggling beard, letting the trout and minnows swim among his private parts ...

But that's not why he does it, she told herself. He does it in winter too, when it's too cold to bathe. And every night he tears it down again. Maybe there's no reason to it. Why should there be? He's the Fool.

And his song! She shivered with fascination at the mysterious, alien sound of his song; the song with words that nobody could understand:

> 'Daisy, Daisy,
> Give me your answer, do!
> I'm half crazy
> Oh for the love of you!
> It won't be a stylish marriage — '

Then abruptly he stopped singing, stopped working, and turned, his male member waggling, to stare blankly in her direction. The shock of it made her gasp. She stepped back into shadow, wondering if somehow he'd sensed her gaze. Maybe so. Who could tell? Men are so sensitive, so intuitive, she thought, just like animals. She waited, but soon he forgot whatever had disturbed him and turned away looking for a suitable stone to place on an unfinished corner of his daily dyke. I'm here to bring him his bread, she reminded herself, an odd disappointment nibbling at her. And so, just as she'd done a hundred times before, she left the brook and carefully laid the leaf-wrapped loaf down on the grass near the mouth of his cave. By this time he'd started singing again, his back to her, but her heart still beat hard and, truth to tell, she felt irritated. Why did he turn away? I could swear for a moment he actually *saw* me!

No, she told herself practically. That's not likely at all. He never saw me before, so why should he start now? He never sees any of us. We're like ghosts to him. He doesn't see anything but the brook and his silly dam, and the trees and flowers and birds until ... He probably just heard one of his *friends*. He wouldn't notice even if I did touch him!

But her heart pounded and her palms were sweaty.

Maybe, she thought, if I walk just a *little* closer ...

Quietly, the grass warm between her toes, she did just that. Closer and closer she crept, a few feet at a time, and the small birds chattered, but Shem didn't notice. He went on singing, making his dam, placing sticks and lumps of turf with care. And again his ignorance provoked her. He *must* know I'm here! He can't be that much of a Fool! And so on she crept up behind him until she was closer to him than she'd ever been before, closer surely than any of the other girls had been, close enough to smell the earthy smell of him ... and still she came on, until her feet slid into the brook underneath his dam ... and now she was close enough behind him so that, had she wished, she could have reached out and touched him. That's enough! she commanded herself, but her excitement had mounted; she found it hard to control her breathing ... and maybe that was what he heard. For suddenly and once again he stopped singing and swung round, this time facing her directly.

Their eyes met.

In his, she saw nothing she knew. Nothing at all.

But perhaps her eyes told him something that cut through the fog of his foolishness. For, though he made no move, simply standing there in the brook behind his dam with the water up to his thighs, something happened.

The emptiness of his stare disturbed her. She dropped her gaze.

And saw his ... his *thing* erect, stiff against his stomach.

From then on he was no longer simply the Fool to her, but something else, not only mysterious but exciting and dangerous.

Shem seemed totally unaware of his condition. He just stared emptily at her as she coloured, turned and fled.

It wasn't embarrassment or outrage that made her flee, but fear, and not fear of him, but of Her, their ruler, the Lady of the Nine Heights, She of the Long Sight and the Far Ear.

I nearly broke the taboo! Ailma realised as she stumbled away from the grove, not following the brook, for she didn't want Hoel to see her in her confusion. *Maybe I did! I didn't talk to him or touch him, but ... in a way I did, and he answered, because his thing stood. What came over me? He's the Fool, but he is a man, and maybe something in the way I ...*

She couldn't work it out, not least because her guilty fear vied with a sort of gleeful pride that she'd got such a response from him. Before she left the grove she stopped and tried to compose herself. *Nobody must know!* she told herself fiercely, *I mustn't give anything away!* And when she come out of the grove, she seemed her usual casual, assured, beautiful self.

But that night in the longhouse, unable to sleep, she touched her gate, her door, her nest which as yet no man had visited ... and was horrified to find that the Horned One, who for three years now and thirteen times a year had visited her with entirely dependable and foreseeable regularity — and who of course was intimate with their ruler, their Green Lady of Fertility, whispering all the clan's woman-secrets in Her ear — had come a full three nights early. Then Ailma knew she was no longer in rhythm with the other women of the clan, and she wept silently, fearing that soon all the world would know what she'd done. Certainly she knew she couldn't talk about it to anyone, especially not Old Mother Riann. So her pretence deepened.

Hoel slept no better. Long after the hearth fire died at the sunset end of the longhouse, where men without wives had their inferior place, he lay wide-eyed on the platform he shared with his friend Olo, staring at nothing that could be seen. For all the rest of that day Ailma had kept to herself, avoiding company (particularly his) — but he'd noted the dreamy look on her face; he'd drawn his own conclusions. So now he began to hate the Fool. Formerly Shem had seemed insufficiently human, insufficiently a man, to be worth bothering about. Now that was changing. Now, to Hoel, the Fool had become a rival. All that night the mad rebellious thoughts seethed in him. They scared him, but he made no attempt to drive them out. Not now. He had no idea what to do about them. But he would. The fire in him told him that soon he would.

In the heart of the grove, on his cave-mouth bed of heather and moss, the Fool slept as the new moon sank. He had forgotten all about that odd encounter with one of the creatures who brought him daily bread. As usual he'd eaten, and as usual that afternoon he'd pulled down his dam, singing as he did. Night had fallen; Fox and Brock had paid a visit, as they often did. They hadn't stayed as long as usual, though he didn't know why. Now in his sleep he groaned, twisting and turning, as if his dreaming told him things his waking mind couldn't contain. An unfamiliar tension came on him and was released. At dawn he awoke with a sticky stuff dried on his belly and chest. It meant nothing to him. He went down to the brook to begin making the dam, and in due course this substance washed off. He paid no more attention to this than he did to the fact, as he sang, that the emotion of his song was changing. There was a new note in it.

But others, outside the grove, heard the difference and wondered.

Old Mother Riann was one of them.

22.
Shem's Seed

Eight days later it was again Ailma's turn to bake Fool's Bread. Outwardly she approached this duty as usual, joking and giggling about it with the other unmarried girls. She had convinced herself that nobody had noticed anything. Uneasily she told herself that nothing had changed.

She was wrong on both counts.

For three days she had successfully (as she thought) hidden the Horned One's premature visit. It had been hard to act lightness of mood with the broody time already on her, but she had acted well. Just once or twice Old Mother Riann (and others) had eyed her oddly, but nobody had said a word, and she had avoided Hoel. Only when her usual hour arrived had she gone to the dark quiet woman's house, set apart in the wood beyond the edge of the clearing. Normally she found this time special, given to private silence beyond reach of light and chatter. This time it was difficult, for the God, having come early, left early. After two days in the lodge she was chafing to spring out into activity again ... but her act demanded otherwise. So she moped in solitude, nursing sullen storms and thick strange dreams until her usual time was over. Thus it was only on the eve of the day when she was again due to bake Fool's Bread that she returned to the longhouse, unaware of (or unwilling to see) the signs that others had noted.

One sign was the subtle change in the Fool's song since her last visit. Since then he'd sung as much as ever, but with a disturbing new note in his voice — a plaintive, reflective note, no longer unthinkingly happy, as if something had made him look at himself and realise there was a lack in his life. And all the other girls who brought him his bread each morning had noted, each in her own way, that he was no longer quite so unaware of them. His back was still turned as they crept into the glade, but no longer so carelessly. None of them said anything, not even to each other. Each wished to believe that this change in response, real or imagined, was due to herself alone, and treated it as a personal secret, fondly imagining that they were behaving just as they always did.

But none of these subtle changes escaped the older women, especially not Old Mother Riann.

Riann had been waiting a long time for this. The Old Mother knew that the taboos She'd put on Her Fool were of a sort which one day, given human nature, had to be broken. Indeed, when She'd chosen the clan to guard Her newly-arrived Fool immediately after the Battle of the Whole Place, She had spoken privately with the Old Mother, calling her into the dark womb-hall below the Whole Place, and there (as usual masked to hide the brilliance of Her face), She'd given Riann specific instructions. 'Old Mother, you will keep this to yourself,' She'd commanded. 'When the time comes you'll know what to do.' And so Riann had long since reached her own conclusions as to what She intended ... yet feared Her reaction to any breaking of taboo ... and feared it even more now it seemed her youngest daughter was involved. For since the start of the war against Azazel's horde, since the taking of the Whole Place and the Fool's arrival, She had grown cruel, inconsistent and demanding. As to what She wanted, no one knew, not Riann or anyone.

Yet for eight days now Riann had held her peace, giving the other women their lead, while few of the men (save Hoel) seemed to have noticed any change, being more concerned with horse-breaking and the hunt.

But that morning when Ailma again baked Fool's Bread and left for the grove, Riann followed discreetly, and her heart sank when she saw that Ailma did not take her usual path into the grove at the point Hoel guarded.

'Child,' she sighed as the girl furtively entered the trees at a place where no man stood, 'you don't know what you do, and until you talk to me I can't tell you. I fear She has you marked.' And she shook her white old head as the Fool's morning song rose, wondering if she should act now. No, she decided, but today will make it plain, one way or the other. Hear how he sings! Whoever heard words like that? Who *is* he? One of those She sent through the Whirling Castle, and now brings back in the flesh? Then, angry at herself, she murmured, 'Oh Riann, it's not your business!' And she bit her lip in distress, resisting the urge to follow her daughter.

Instead she circled the grove to observe Hoel, a slight figure slipping through shadow without letting sunlight touch her. Her heart sank further when she saw how grimly Hoel stood by the brook, a wild hot light in his eyes as he looked about, obviously waiting for Ailma to come. Then the Fool's song abruptly stopped, the bird-song too, and Riann saw Hoel's lips twist as his face darkened with hate. He turned and glared into the grove from which he was excluded, and even made a half-move to enter, then with an effort checked himself. And by the time she slipped away, very deeply troubled, the Fool still had not started singing again. Nor had the birds.

Hoel stood, eyes shut, gripping his spear tightly. I'm right about them! he thought miserably. But what am I going to do?

He still didn't know. His heart was like a heavy stone, the rage was building up in him. Later that day, when the Fool had begun this jagged new song, by chance he met Ailma outside the longhouse. She would not speak or meet him in the eyes ... but in her face he saw a new knowledge, something that suffocated his reason, so that with a cry he turned and ran off into the woods, and did not return until late that night.

This time, Ailma assured herself as she entered the grove, I'll just put it down and go at once. Yes, I will! Yet, though the day wasn't hot, she felt stifled and on fire; she could hardly breathe as she went deeper in by the unfamiliar route; she heard the Fool singing as she came nearer, and the new note in his song made her flesh tingle. On she went, feeling faint and clumsy as she forced her way through bushes that tore at her. Then a sudden crash; she started with shock as a roebuck burst away through the undergrowth. She stood wanting to weep with guilt. It ran away from me! It knows! The birds have stopped singing! Everyone knows! And a terrifying thought occurred to her, not for the first time. What if She knows? What if She watched me last time and watches now? I swear this time I'll do nothing to offend Her, nothing at all!

But the Fool must have heard her noisy approach, for even before she reached the glade he'd stopped singing. And when at length she stepped nervously into the open space, just feet from where he stood thigh-deep in the water behind his dam, she saw him standing, hands empty at his side, staring in her direction with a puzzled look as if trying to remember who she was. She eyed him quickly. His member hung limp, water-shrunk. She felt giddy. Her gown constricted her; she opened her mouth to breathe as with haste she detoured round him and over the brook to set down the bread in its usual place by the cave. Not thinking, she tugged at a loose upper fold of her gown. Her heart was pounding and a strange, thick sweet cloud was descending on her, occluding her reason. Don't look at him! Just go! She turned to leave. But some inner force, sweetly violent, made her look back. And yes, he was facing her! His eyes were definitely following her, and ... *it* was getting bigger, beginning to rise. She panted for breath, so dizzy now she could no longer think. The glade, the grass, the trees on every side had started pulsating, throbbing, emerald-bright. The air itself was turning into a jelly she could not get into her lungs. Now its swollen purple tip quivered high enough to cover his navel. Now, not even realising what she did, she started towards him, step by trembling step, gasping as she pulled her gown fully open, exposing her breasts, touching her hard nipples as the wet heat spread in her nest. Another step closer. And another. The world was coming and going in huge slow pulsations, dark and light, dark and light. Another step. It was huge! She was bursting. Closer. Still he didn't move from where he stood behind his dam, though he was quivering all over. Now the brook kissed her feet, licked her ankles, her calves, her knees; the water as jellified as the congealed unbreathable air; her body expanding, taut, huge with the unbearable demand, big enough to swallow the entire world and take it all inside her —

Close enough to reach out and touch him — *it* — she stopped.

A belated flood of sensible terror poured through her.

His eyes — no longer the eyes of an unworldly Fool, but the eyes of a man in heat as hot as hers — were fastened on her breasts, her full bare breasts that she'd been lifting and squeezing with slow, circular, kneading movements of her hands.

What am I doing?

She gasped, stifled, as her hands dropped, as her eyes fell —

To his sword, his club, his tree, his pillar, his post, his —

Through the air's bright throbbing jelly her left hand crept out —

No! wailed her trapped reason. *Touch him, especially there, and She'll kill you! Your blood will bubble and boil in Her Cauldron! She knows, She MUST know, She's bound to know, because he's stopped singing, the birds have stopped singing — EVERYONE knows, the whole world knows! SHE KNOWS!*

She shut her eyes, stopped her hand, her fingertips trembling inches from his burning spear ... and it was then he boiled over. It was then, with his own eyes tight shut and a look of agonised bewilderment on his face, that his body convulsed, his spine arched, his dam broke and his glands flung out their load in three great spasms as he grunted, groaned, cried out in pleasure and pain. And the sticky wetness struck her — first on her trembling hand, then higher, between her breasts, and the third time higher still, on her face, so close to her mouth that automatically, not knowing what she did or why, she flicked out her tongue, licked, swallowed.

So she drank the knowledge of his seed.

She opened her eyes. So did he. She stared into his eyes. She saw storms. She saw the delight and dark pain in store for her. Swaying where she stood she looked down and saw the white globules of his seed, trickling between her breasts and from the back of her hand. Her head roared and she saw a swirling abyss of every colour. Almost she screamed out loud, but in the nick of time caught herself. Instead she whimpered, then turned and stiffly tore herself away, leaving him shivering behind his dam, staring at her. She splashed down the brook a safe distance before bending in terror to wash herself clean. First her hands and then her breasts, hastily covering them when she was done. Then she washed out her mouth, but the salty taste would not go away. Fearfully, not looking back at the Fool, she eyed the sky. High above circled a hawk. Moaning, she rushed for the cover of the trees. It's Hawk! He spies for Her! She sees everything! I'm lost! I've broken the taboo! Through the trees she went stumbling with no sense of direction. I swallowed his seed! Will I grow a child? And from the back of the grove into the deeper forest she fled, her face bright and hot, clothing and hair in disarray, the basket left behind.

By chance no man saw her leave. For a long time she wandered in the forest before at length calming herself enough to return to the clan, her gown in place, her hair combed out, and with the beginnings of the belief that perhaps, after all, she hadn't *really* broken taboo. Yet behind the thin mask of this persuasion she was in a state of terror ... and already, before she returned, it was clear to everyone in the clan, even the men, that something serious had happened between Ailma and the Fool.

For the Fool had not sung since she'd entered the grove, and Ailma was very late returning. And the birds were not singing either.

Worse still, when the girl did return, her eyes were wild and distant, and with her right hand (apparently unaware she did it) she kept rubbing at her mouth, between her breasts, and at the back of her left hand, as if trying to wipe something off. She wouldn't speak to anyone, and Riann saw how, when Hoel encountered her by the longhouse, she could not meet him in the eyes. But Hoel saw something in her face that made him cry out in fury and distress; the Old Mother saw him turn and flee into the woods, running as if his heart would burst. This has gone far enough! she thought. Time we talked! And in front of everyone she took her daughter firmly by the arm. 'Come along, my girl,' she said, 'we're going for a walk.'

Then the Fool began a new song. Riann heard it even as she brought the dazed girl to a secluded place in the forest, and it set her teeth on edge, for this new song was not happy, not even reflective. It was jagged with pain; an ululating howl that cut into the heads of all within range. Full of apprehension, the old woman made Ailma sit with her on the mossy root of a gnarled old oak. The girl, staring down at the sun-dappled forest floor, shivered, wringing her hands together. Riann laid a tense, gentle hand on her shoulder. Ailma flinched. 'Well,' asked the Old Mother, coming right to the point, 'Did you break taboo? Did you touch him?'

'No.' Ailma was barely audible. 'I did not.'

'Then why can't you meet anyone in the eyes? Why does he howl like that now? Before She learns, *tell me what happened!*'

Ailma shook her head. She wanted to weep, to admit

271

everything, but her heart felt as dry and cold as stone, and there was anger in her. 'Nothing happened!' Suddenly loud, she stamped her feet. 'I didn't touch him!'

Maybe not, my girl, but it's not the whole truth, Riann decided, and without warning the old woman grabbed Ailma's chin, forcing her head up and round so that their eyes met. And still the Fool wailed from the grove.

'You wanted to touch him though, didn't you?'

'You're hurting me!' But Ailma blushed scarlet. 'I'm not the only one! We all want to touch him, just to find out if ... if ...'

'We all want what's forbidden,' Riann agreed drily, not releasing the girl's chin. 'So you didn't *quite* touch him, is that it? But you made him see you. Did you ... show yourself to him ... as a woman to a man?'

'I was tempted, Mother,' the girl admitted miserably.

Riann hid a smile she could not afford. Yes, she decided grimly, it's time to send word. 'So did *he* touch you?' she persisted sternly.

Ailma hesitated, biting her lip, trying to look away, but Riann would not let her. 'Did he touch you?' Riann repeated ... and the girl smiled in unconscious self-betrayal, obviously thinking she'd found an answer that didn't involve a direct lie. 'No,' she said, 'but he ... he *spat* at me.'

'Oh?' Again Riann had to hide a smile. 'With his mouth?'

Caught in confusion, Ailma simply scowled.

'Did he spit with his mouth?' the old woman persisted.

'No,' the girl admitted with the utmost reluctance, 'not his mouth.'

'Ah,' murmured the old woman, bright-eyed, 'I see what you mean!'

Then Ailma's reserve broke and her tears came as she cried out: 'Have I broken taboo, Mother? It was his ... seed, it spurted and hit me!'

For long seconds Riann considered her terrified daughter. Her heart wanted to melt, but she could not let it.

'Have you considered Hoel's feelings?' she asked at length.

Ailma didn't seem to hear this. 'Mother,' she asked tentatively, 'if you swallow a man's seed, does that mean you ... get a child?'

'No.' Resisting her mad urge to laugh, Riann shook her head. 'It means you tasted what would be better coming from Hoel or another young man of the clan. Now listen, daughter!' she said, at last releasing her grip on the girl's chin, and Ailma did not look away. 'I don't know if you've broken taboo, but you've certainly bruised the spirit of it. The Fool's no longer the Fool he was. Hear him wailing? Know what it means? It's the sound of a man disturbed by a woman. Maybe *he* doesn't know it yet, but we all hear it, and surely She does too.' She nodded fiercely. 'It may or may not be too late. Either way, next time you bake Fool's Bread you must be very careful. Who knows how She'll judge?'

'But I couldn't help it!' Ailma burst out, her eyes round with terror. 'Mother, I told myself not to go near him, just to put down the bread and go, but something came over me and I couldn't stop myself!' And between shaking shoulders she buried her head in her hands. 'What can I do?'

'Start by smiling on Hoel,' Riann said sharply. 'The Fool's forbidden, so give yourself to Hoel and forget the Fool!'

'Is that your best advice?' Wet-cheeked, suddenly furious, Ailma leapt to her feet. 'Give myself to *Hoel*? — Hoel who never smiles, who thinks men should rule women? I'll never *ever* do that!'

Without waiting for an answer, Ailma fled into the forest.

For a time Riann sat alone, listening to the Fool's wail. It sounded as if he was howling his name, over and over and over again:

'SHEM! SHEM! SHEM! SHEM! SHEMMMMMM!!!'

Nobody was working when the Old Mother returned.

273

Not even the children were playing. In grim, silent little groups the men and women of the clan stood gloomily listening to the Fool's new song, and when Riann appeared several anxious matrons immediately surrounded her, but she waved them all away except for Isylt, whose hair was almost as white as her own. 'There's something I must do,' she told Isylt as she put on her travelling cloak, her face unreadable. 'I'll not be back until the Horned One has set. When Hoel and Ailma return, make sure there's no trouble. Tell Olo to calm Hoel down. And tell the people not to fear. Despite everything I believe all will be well ... if I do what I go to do.'

Without another word she left the longhouse and struck deep into the greenwood, continually changing direction in case anyone followed to see where she went. The sun reached its zenith and began to decline, and as she went she muttered continually to herself. 'Yes, it's Ailma. It has to be. Now I see what She meant. The third time is *the* time. Of course She planned it, she means it to happen — what use is a Fool to Her? Yes, and She must have foreseen his arrival during the battle — perhaps that's why She brought us to this island, to take the Whole Place where he appeared. But why the rest of it? Why continue the war? And why the Fool? Why *is* he a Fool? Perhaps he journeyed too far through the worlds and got shocked into foolishness; perhaps all this has been her way of waking him gently back to sense so he can play whatever part She plans for him. And how can full awakening be won save through a woman? There's no other way. So I doubt She'll judge Ailma too harshly. But Hoel ... oh, She has no love for men! If he does anything rash She'll have him straight in Her pot. I'll talk to him when I get back ...'

She had far to go. In time it was dark. The waxing moon sailed high above the forest amid pearl-soft cloud; the woodland came alive with its night creatures and Riann knew she was watched. At length she came to a deep dark place of water where willow tangled. Here she stopped and gave out the lapwing's call, again and again, then waited until there was a rustling in the night. A dark naked creature slipped quietly up to her.

'What do you want, woman from beyond the edge of the world?' hissed the creature, not letting herself be seen even by moonlight.

From round her neck Riann removed a small glass amulet, green and waved with a spiral pattern. This she gave to the creature of the wild wood, who snatched it. 'Take this to the Lady of the Nine Heights,' the Old Mother said, lifting up her hands against the moon to show five fingers of one and three of the other. 'These are the number of nights remaining.'

'What's in it for us?' the creature cackled greedily.

Riann sighed. 'The marrow-rich bones of a strong young man fed on milk and oats and blood-red meat,' she told the wild woman, as the ritual she hated required. 'The well-boiled bones She'll toss from Her pot.'

Smacking her lips with a hungry giggle the creature went without another word. Then Riann left the place of the Wild Woman and started home. She was tired and went slowly, conserving her strength, keeping an eye and ear open for wolf or boar, but not really concerned, for she could feel Her watching presence. Why play with us like this? she found herself wondering. You already know what's happening. So why? Why?

But there was no answer, and the moon had set by the time, near dawn, she got back to the longhouse ... the longhouse where few slept.

In the grove, Shem was asleep ... at last.

23.
The Awakening

For much of the night, and for the first time ever, Shem had found no sleep. In turmoil he groaned on his cave-mouth bed of heather and moss, full of conflicting new sensations — hope, fear, memory and desire — for which he had no names. The lopsided, senile moon eyed him coldly as he sweated and shivered and hissed through clenched teeth. A sudden futile rage seized him: he sat up, shaking his fists at the still, silent silver darkness of the grove. 'Fox!' he cried in pain. 'Hawk! Hare! Brock! Where are you all? Why won't you come and talk to me? I'm all alone, I'm cold, I can't sleep, I don't understand what's happening!'

Not a leaf, not a bird, not a creature stirred. Yet his need was so great that out of the corner of his eye he imagined movement and turned towards it. He smiled, fooling himself he saw Fox there, watching him sardonically, long red tongue lolling. 'At least you're here,' he said in a small hurt voice. 'Thank you for coming to see me.'

'Don't kid yourself.' Fox grinned. 'You know it's over between us. You smelled all right before, but since that two-legs bitch started getting you hard you've started smelling just like all the other men.'

And Fox began to fade into the shadows.

'Fox, wait!' Shem cried in panic. 'Please stay!'

'You know I can't,' said Fox. 'You're not the Fool any more, you're a man, and men can't be trusted. If I stayed, you'd forget about friendship, and next thing I'd be a skin round your sweet lady's neck. No thanks!'

Shem was horrified. 'I'd never do anything like that!'

'Of course not!' Fox gave him a red, ironic eye. 'Listen, I don't blame you. It can't be easy, being a man and having to betray all your friends. You probably can't help it, and I get the same with a hot bitch myself. So don't take it personally, it's just that I want to keep my fur where it is — on me. I'm *warmer* that way, see? So long, pal.'

Then Fox was gone. Fat tears rolled down Shem's gaunt brown cheeks.

'Hawk!' he called in a broken sad voice. 'Where are you?' And as he gazed into the clear night sky he imagined he saw black wings silhouetted and hovering against the moon. 'Hawk! Is that you?'

'I saw what happened today,' screeched Hawk from his height. 'I've heard your new song and I know what it means. You're no longer a Fool, and we can no longer be friends. If I landed on your shoulder now you'd hood my head, bind my claws and clip my wings before carrying me proudly to your lady as a gift — that's the sort of thing you women-besotted men will do.'

'I'm not like that!' Shem protested. 'And I haven't got a woman!'

'Now you're just an ordinary man-fool!' screamed Hawk. 'Remember, I see everything! Goodbye, man! I won't let you trap me — and don't let Her trap you! Do what that old White Sow wants, and it's worse for all of us!'

Then Hawk was gone too, but the cut of his final warning threw Shem into the depths of pre-Shem memories. They made no sense, yet, but they were so urgently appalling that he panted in agony to find himself drowning in the fire and flood of them. He staggered dizzily to his feet, unable to accept the memories, waving arms round his head as if attacked by a swarm of furious bees, and howled in a voice that petrified sleepless listeners beyond the grove. Still howling he lurched down to the brook and splashed through it; with stubbed toes and sore feet he ploughed blindly in among trees suddenly become obstructive, their sappy branches whipping him into a maze of brambled undergrowth that tore his ankles, his legs, his thighs and belly. At last, bewildered and hugging himself against his fear, he was forced to a shivering halt.

'Brock?' he called timidly. 'Are you there?'

He thought he heard a bad-tempered grunt.

He thought he saw Brock, silver and black against silver and black.

'Brock, we have to talk,' he moaned, blundering forward straight into a blackthorn thicket. 'Brock!' he wailed, recoiling from the cruel spikes.

'I'm busy,' grunted Brock. 'What do you want? Is it important? Any useful information? News of the world? New philosophical movements?'

'Nothing like that!' Shem sighed. 'Brock,' he said sadly, 'terrible things are happening to me. I don't understand, but it looks as if I'll have to leave. Fox and Hawk don't trust me any more, and ...'

'Of course they don't!' Brock grumbled. 'You're a man again, and that makes you capable of anything. You sound miserable, but it's probably just a man-trick so you can catch me and kill me.'

'But why would I want to *kill* you, Brock?'

'How would I know? I'm not a two-legs. You tell me.'

'I'm sorry, Brock.' And there under the moon Shem stood, exhausted in defeat, beginning to understand and wishing he didn't. 'I don't belong here any more. But I enjoyed your company ... when we were friends.'

'That's very civil of you.' And just for a moment the badger showed himself more clearly. 'For a two-legs you're not so bad. Watch you don't get like the worst of them. And look out for Owl — She's watching you.'

Then Brock slipped away, and Shem returned listlessly

to the brook. With lowered head he knelt in the cold running water, letting it numb his scratched and aching body, afraid to look up in case he saw Owl.

'Hare,' he murmured sadly, 'I won't even ask after you. You'd say you can't stay because I'm a man, so I'd kill you and skin you and cook you.'

'Yes, that's right!' And in a flash of motion between cave-mouth and brook Shem glimpsed Hare, who paused only when safe in cover to turn and giggle. 'I'm m-m-mad but not *that* mad, not mad like men and not mad about m-m-men who kill the m-m-moon-mad like me!'

'Hare,' said Shem without hope, 'I'm not going to kill you.'

'Maybe you should,' Hare giggled, 'because I'm going to Her now to tell Her if She wants you m-m-moon-mad instead of m-m-men-mad or womb-mad, She'd better come quick. She won't l-l-like it, or maybe She will — who knows?'

Then Hare giggled again and was gone.

'But I've been your friend!' Shem roared angrily.

Back came the already-distant, high-pitched, Hare-mad response:

'Friend-Shem! Sham-friend-Shem! Shem-the-Sh-sh-sham! Shem-the-son-of-a-Sa-Sa-Sam! Sam-Shem-Sham, not friend-Shem, Sam!'

At this Shem began howling again and didn't stop, the bees of memory buzzing mad in his mind, so that nearly till dawn he staggered about in the grove, alarming the guards who didn't know what they'd do if he came too close or tried to break out, slapping his head with his hands and wailing in agony. At length he fell down, exhausted, and slept where he fell.

Not long after that the Old Mother returned.

Many did not sleep at all that night. The clan was too taut already; had been tightened further by Riann's mysterious disappearance, and wound up further still by the tension between Hoel and Ailma after their return soon after nightfall, within minutes of each other but from far opposite directions. Things were bad enough even

279

before the Fool began his savage, lonely, wolflike wailing. Few slept, and those who did were plagued by dreams of spectral armies sent against them for their unknown sins by She-Who-Shakes-The-Bleeding-Lance, She-Who-Boils-Souls-In-Her-Silver-Cauldron. Those who slept awoke with the dawn wishing they had not slept; those who had not slept wished they had.

And all of them, led by Hoel's grim looks, blamed Ailma. From that dawn onwards they put a silence on her. Nobody spoke to her, and when she walked in front of them they did not see her. Likewise when they looked at the Old Mother there was suspicion in their eyes, and a fear they'd not known since the battle for the Whole Place. There the clan, distinguishing itself, had been chosen by Her to guard the mysterious Fool. Other clans had stayed to die in the front line of Her war against the Ancient Ones, pushing the shape-shifters steadily back through the mountains towards the Western Sea; the sons of other mothers had died, not the sons of this clan. But now the Fool howled his strange new song, and nothing seemed sure any more, and they were certain that the Old Mother and her too-proud youngest daughter had more than a little to do with it!

Next day Riann took Hoel aside and spoke with him.

'I'll not forgive her unless she smiles on me,' the dark young man said flatly, his eyes flashing, gripping his spear so tight that in his tension Riann saw the future, black and hard with deadly metal. And Hoel grinned at her expression without humour. 'Why should I care what She does to me so long as Ailma will not smile?' he demanded.

And to this the Old Mother had no adequate reply.

In the days that followed Shem no longer woke and rose with the dawn, no longer went singing down to the brook, no longer spent his mornings making the dam and his afternoons dismantling it. All that was over, for the clan as well as Shem, for She had made him the centre of their lives: a change in him was a change in them, and his new condition terrified them. Yet until it was again Ailma's turn to bake Fool's Bread, life went on with the appearance of normality. Meals were cooked, baskets woven, pigs were fed and the barley patch weeded; children played or helped their mothers; men off guard duty hunted or sat in the sun with their gossip and ale-skins as usual. And when every day the Fool's harsh new name-song sounded from the grove, people pretended not to hear, just as they pretended that Ailma no longer existed. But they heard. Riann saw their frightened, covert looks. And each morning, when the girl baking Fool's Bread that day went into the grove, people stopped whatever they were doing to watch and wait until she emerged safely with no taboo broken, no crime committed. And each day the latest news went from friend to friend, group to group:

'Briga saw him sitting on the grass by the brook, crying his heart out, making daisy chains to wear round his neck!'

'Maeve says he wears an apron now, of leaves and vine. He knows he's naked! And the animals are leaving; they can't stand his wailing . . .'

'Little Bocan saw him standing in the brook, stabbing his finger down at his reflection as if trying to poke holes through it.'

'When she came near with the bread Glaisti thought he'd attack her, so she dropped everything and ran, and from the trees she saw him trampling the bread into the ground then howling with rage as he tore up the basket! That's the howling we heard. Then he started bellowing his name again!'

So the tension grew, and was not lessened by rumours beginning to filter from the west: that the Ancient Ones had won a battle against Her forces; had taken back land formerly assumed to have been conquered. It was unclear if these tales were true or not; strangers and passers-by reported them, but always it was: 'Somebody told me that . . .' or: 'I was going to trade in the hills but a man I met warned me that . . .' Nothing clear. Nothing sure. Yet these rumours from the world outside fitted the new uncertainty in the clan; a sense of doom was growing, and at heart everyone sensed it. But what would She do, and when? Who could tell. Best to pretend nothing had changed; best to say as little as possible and hope.

But soon there came a bright warm morning with everyone thinking: *Tomorrow it's Ailma's turn again!* The dread was palpable, even though now all the green world was blooming with life. It should have been a time of joy, preparing for the Fire Festival and the Wild Night after it; it should have been a time of betrothals and happy songs ... but still Ailma, ignored by all (including her sisters and former friends), would not smile on Hoel that morning as her ex-friend Morwen took Fool's Bread into the grove ... and even the toddlers were grave and unsmiling as Morwen went with her basket.

Pale and nervous she went, a soft-faced girl with chestnut hair who had been crying with fear in the night. Now, creeping on tiptoe into the green tangled depths, her fear grew. The Fool was utterly silent. He might be anywhere — behind her, stalking her, watching her, preparing to pounce! Deeper and deeper she crept until, with pent breath parting boughs, she looked into the glade ... and saw him.

He stood in the brook, gazing uncertainly at his aproned reflection, studying his ugly Owl-scored face. 'Sam,' he was saying experimentally even as Morwen behind him plucked up her courage and entered the glade, 'Shem. Sham. Sam. Sam!' Then, suddenly, when she was exposed in the open and halfway to the cave-mouth, he lifted his head and roared in agony; he began waving his arms round his head and staggered out of the water. For now the memory-bees were driving him mad even during the day, stinging him with voices and faces he could not bear to face. '*Chrissa!*' he cried, and '*Diane!*' — then, in hideous pain, with Morwen behind him frozen in fear, he started bellowing his name-song again:

'SHEM! SHEM! I AM SHEM! SAM-SHEM! SEM-SHAM! SHEM-SAM!'

Morwen cried out in terror. He whirled and saw her, saw the two-legs, smelled her fear, started towards her where she stood trembling. Dropping the basket she tried to flee but his hot dark eyes gripped her. She could not move, could not even cry out again! Contradictory emotions chased like clouds across his thin dark face. Closer and closer he came, his right arm reaching out. She screamed silently. *The taboo —*

He stopped just short of her. His arm dropped, his face creased with disappointment, he gestured disgust and eyed his apron. No bulge there. This two-legs wasn't the one who stirred his now-hidden thing, that thing at the root of all the sensations for which still he had no name, the thing that brought the memory-bees and drove away his friends. No. Not the one. He turned away, forgetting her as she fled. 'SHEM!' he bellowed. 'SAM!'

He knows I'm not Ailma! He was looking for Ailma! Morwen splashed along the brook as fast as she could, ducking the hawthorn sprays, excited now that she'd escaped, fearful in case he chased her. Yes, Ailma *must* have touched him! she told herself breathlessly as he continued roaring his name behind her, and there was envy, fear, relief and disapproval in her all together as she rushed out of the grove ... at the point Hoel guarded.

His face was an angry question. Still from the grove Shem bawled like a beast-man. Morwen seized Hoel's arm and cried impulsively in his face: 'I'll never bake Fool's Bread again, Hoel! Never ever again, because it's all changing so fast there won't be a next time, not for me! Hoel, he's no longer the Fool! He wears an apron, he knows what women are, he nearly touched me, Hoel! He's no longer the Fool!'

'Even we men realise that!' Hoel snapped sarcastically.

Morwen snatched back her hand. 'It's Ailma's turn tomorrow!' she said without thinking, wanting to prick Hoel's sour thin skin. 'That's why he didn't touch me. He knows I'm not Ailma. Maybe tomorrow it'll be her name he sings, Hoel, not his own! Then what'll happen? When She comes?'

Hoel flushed; his body knotted with the rage in him.

'So? I should crawl to Ailma? Beg her on bended knee?'

Laughing, Morwen spun giddily away, pursued back to the longhouse by Hoel's glare and Shem's harsh song, aware only that she'd escaped. Back among the women she burst into tears. They gathered round to comfort her. Ailma tried to approach, but was kept out by a wall of backs, by the web of silence that all save Old Mother Riann spun round her. Dry-eyed, with a new determination in her, she went and sat on her own, and when the Old Mother approached and once more tried to persuade her — for the good of all the clan! — to smile on Hoel, the girl simply shook her head and ran off into the woods again.

Riann, watching her go, sensed fate closing rapidly in. Perhaps She's here already, the old woman thought grimly, and decided once again to try persuading Hoel to make the healing move ... but her hopes were not high as she approached the grove from which the mad song still came:

'SHEM! SHEM! SHEM! SAM-SHEM! SHEM-SAM! SAM! SAM! SAM!'

24.
The Hunt

Like a rock Hoel stood, arms folded round his spear, its point deep in the ground. In silence and without expression he heard the Old Mother's pleas. 'Hoel, I cannot order you,' she said urgently. 'I can only beg you! For the good of all. And I do! I beg you: talk to her!'

So long he stared silently at her she thought he'd never reply. But at length, his face still blank, he said: 'Very well, Old Mother. You never condemned me. I'll try. But only once.'

With that she had to be content. Wearily she left him. At noon, relieved by another man, he set in motion a plan he'd worked out. Round every guard he went, and into the ear of each man he whispered:

'Tonight the moon dies and women are weak. Tonight's a night for men to hunt in pack, far from the eyes and ears of women!'

Then, taking a deep breath, he went to find Ailma.

If she'll just give me a smile, he promised himself, then by the Unknown God I swear I'll not do it. But if she won't...

After a while he found her sitting alone on a grassy bank behind the longhouse. Every eye but hers followed his approach. She didn't even look up from the flower chain she was making as his shadow came and fell on her.

He stood, feet apart, arms akimbo, as usual frowning.

'Ailma, I must speak to you!' he declared harshly.

By no sign did she betray awareness of his presence.

'I said I will speak to you!' he declared more forcefully still.

Lips pursed, she threaded one daisy through the stem of another. Hoel wanted to kick her. Instead, sighing, he squatted down on his haunches.

'Ailma,' he said more gently, 'Look, I ...'

Her eyes shot round and locked with his.

'Look at what?' she demanded crisply. 'At you? Hoel, for seven nights you've led a silence against me. All but Old Mother turn from me, and you were the first. Every eye like a blank wall to me! Why should I see you? Why should I talk to you? Tell me that!'

'You were first,' he protested, 'in rejecting me!'

'Yes, but I did not lead the whole clan in it!'

'I did not ask them to follow my lead! Anyway,' Hoel went on as mildly as he could, 'we have both now broken the silence we put on each other.'

'Not by my choice!' she flared, tossing the daisy chain aside, her eyes flashing. 'And another thing! Every night at mealtime I've been juggled and jostled into sitting down near you! While being ignored by all I've been forced to look at Hoel, listen to Hoel, and admire Hoel! I assume the idea is that I should fall down and open my legs for Hoel!'

'Never mind that!' Fighting for patience, fighting the heat in him, Hoel gripped her elbow and held it tight. She stiffened but did not try to pull away. Aware of watchers, he lowered his voice and tried to smile. 'Don't blame me for your faults!' he said roughly. 'People fear you've broken taboo on the Fool ... and tomorrow you bake Fool's Bread again.' His eyes narrowed on her impatient face. 'Now I swear, Ailma, if tomorrow you do anything to bring down Her wrath on this clan, then I'll ...'

286

Abruptly, sensing an abyss, he stopped.

Her eyes widened. 'You'll ... *what? What* will you do?'

But in his eyes, in the spear he held, she knew what he meant.

'Nothing,' he denied brusquely. 'You make me unhappy so I say things I don't mean.' He grimaced, his face naked, shorn of its usual contemptuous look. 'All I ask is that you smile! If you'll only smile on me, then ...'

'You make threats to get a smile?' she asked incredulously, eyeing the spear, feeling dull and as far from smiling as it was possible to be.

'So!' Hoel's patience snapped. He tensed into a springing position, facing her. 'You'll smile for the Fool but not for me?'

'How can a woman smile on a man who talks like you?' she cried.

He made a last effort. 'You make the clan afraid,' he told her softly. 'If tomorrow you break taboo and bring Her down on us ...'

She stared at him in disbelief. '*You* make *me* afraid!' she exclaimed, and stood up quickly. 'We've talked enough, if you don't mind!' Then she turned and walked away into the trees, swift and distressed and nervous.

Watched by many, Hoel stared after her with freezing eyes.

So let it be, he thought. So let it be!

It was after supper time when Ailma returned. Night was falling with no moon in prospect. The Fool still cried his name-song from the heart of the grove, but all the men were gone save for those on guard. The corral was empty, and so were the spear racks, and gloom drenched the longhouse.

Before the girl even reached the door, Old Mother Riann appeared and peremptorily drew her away, back into the dusk where shadow thickened.

'You refused Hoel again today,' Riann said coldly.

Ailma shuddered. Her confusion and fear had grown intense. For hours she'd walked the woods knowing she might never walk them again.

'Yes!' Her voice trembled. 'Gripping his spear he made threats to get me to smile! Can I smile on a man who demands love with threats of death?'

Riann grimaced. This is truly out of control! she thought.

'So you won't smile on him, not even for the good of the clan?'

'What good will lies do the clan, Old Mother?' asked Ailma bitterly.

'You know that Hoel has led the men on a hunt tonight?'

'So?' Ailma shrugged. 'He'll visit his killing lust on some helpless creature then spend the night drunkenly boasting about his bravery!'

'You've wounded him in his own eyes and in the eyes of the other men!' Riann scolded her. 'Girl, don't you sometimes *fear* men?'

'Fear them?' Ailma toed the earth. 'They're only men.'

'And the Fool? Only a man?'

'Who knows what he is?' said the girl defiantly.

'*She* knows. And She watches. And She prepares to act!'

Rabbits scampered away through the gloaming. Ailma paused at the edge of a darkening glade. 'Old Mother,' she said listlessly, 'in the morning I bake Fool's Bread. I'll do it. And what happens will happen.'

'You're my last-born!' said Riann with fierce love. 'You haven't yet touched him! The taboo is not yet finally broken! Don't kill yourself!'

Ailma sighed, her shoulders slumped; suddenly she turned and hugged her mother. 'I've thought of nothing else!' she said wildly. 'Mother, I've had days to think, with nobody speaking to me! And what I think is ...'— in the last of the light her eyes gleamed — '... that the taboo's *meant* to be broken! Why else does She tempt us? She needs me to wake up Her Fool!'

'What?' Riann drew back, startled to hear her own thoughts.

'Old Mother, you heard me!' Ailma cried in her face. 'The taboo is made to be broken, it *has* to be broken! And I know you know it!'

'Yes,' Riann admitted in a whisper, 'perhaps I do.' She turned away to hide her face, gazing into the moonless night. We must do as we do, she told herself sadly ... and then she took her daughter's arm. 'Come,' she said gently. 'You're tired and hungry and afraid ... but tonight at least no one will trouble you. I'll see to that. You have to be up early to bake Fool's Bread. Get a good night's sleep. Be strong.' She paused, trying to make out Ailma's eyes. 'You must play your part as She wishes.'

'I know,' said Ailma, quiet and sad. 'I'm ready now.'

Still weakened by winter, the stag fought hard. Brought to bay in the last light at the head of a ravine where a waterfall plunged down grey faces of gleaming slate, it turned and charged the baying black dogs with lowered antlers, scattering them. But it couldn't deal with all of them at once. The men, picking their way up the ravine on their horses, found the earth churned up and three hounds dead, stamped or gored. But the stag was tiring. There was froth at its muzzle, its head was low, blood ran down its narrow flanks from the slashing teeth of its tormentors. And Hoel made the killing thrust, though Olo his friend could have got there before him.

'We're not going back to share this with the women!' Hoel cried at the men, standing with his foot on the carcass. 'This is man-magic! We men have slain a great magician here! Yes, this is one of the Ancient Ones, unable to shift his shape in time! Here we'll cut him up and roast him and share his power among us! We men shall have the best cuts, and the hounds shall have the scraps! So let's set to!'

The men all approved this fine idea so that, much later, eyeing stars like petals above the firelit trees, they lounged greasy-lipped round the warming blaze, content as the ale-skin went round. But Hoel was not at all content. Scowling at the fire-red faces he said:

'We men should not fear Her!'

There was no reaction, not even from Olo beside him.

I spoke too soft, he told himself, and why? Because I'm afraid, that's why. On clear nights like this Owl and Fox can see and hear everything. But a man must speak his mind! What's the worth of my word if I don't dare speak it aloud? Breathing deep he grinned; bloody juice ran down his chin as he tore the last of the meat from the bone in his hand. Stag-magician, I eat your courage into me! May your ghost approve what I do! And when he had eaten he spoke again, this time in a voice loud enough to alert the most stuporous:

'Why do we men obey the woman's order of things? Why are we spellbound by Her commands, by the stupid song of a stupid Fool!' He laughed harshly, glaring challenge about. 'We should invade the grove and kill that stupid Fool! Just as we have killed tonight! With the hounds and then the thrust of a good sharp blade!' Shaking his spear, he laughed again. 'Of course we wouldn't eat him. Who needs to eat foolishness, eh?'

But nobody else laughed. The men stared at him, most of them so drunk or perplexed by what they heard that they couldn't take it in. A few, more discerning, were horrified.

'Are you out of your mind?' Olo beside him hissed.

'Maybe,' muttered Hoel, 'but I must act — on my own or otherwise.'

'You'll bring destruction on us all! Hoel, listen!'

'Men!' Hoel cried again, his voice ringing through the dark woods. 'We don't forever have to do as women tell us. Their ways are their ways, and ours are ours! We make their ways too strong if we believe in them at the expense of our own! Listen! We men have an Unknown God, the God of our ways which we have not yet seen apart from Her ways that She puts on us. Now it is time to invoke our Unknown God and seek a new direction!' And he stood, thrusting his spear at the sky. 'For we are men! We do not bury our faces in the earth, we look to the bounding, boundless hunt of the sky! We hunt, we act, we kill, we take and make and do! Men, hear me! Our ways and our God will be stronger! Have we not slain a magician here tonight? We'll forge new weapons of power that women could never imagine, then we'll dismiss the Ancient Ones and drive them from our lands and our minds! And soon there'll be a day when the women obey us and the Ancient Ones are no more than ghosts crying in the wind. Then *we* will make the rules! All this I have seen!' he cried. 'And that is why I, Hoel, say that if taboo is to be broken tomorrow then we men are the ones to break it.' At last he paused, breathing hard, looking round his shocked companions. 'Now you have heard me! Who is with me? Who will enter the grove with me tomorrow when bread is brought to the Fool by Old Mother's youngest daughter?'

There was utter silence. Anxiety was palpable. Men eyed each other in fear, scanned the heavens for sign of Hawk or Owl. Olo said harshly:

'Hoel, you're upset, you can't mean any of this!'

'Upset?' Hoel grinned down at him, face twisted. 'Oh yes, I'm upset! Upset enough to start thinking — which is another thing we men do better!'

'*Thinking?*' Olo was incredulous. 'You call this *thinking?* Ranting a challenge to Her in the middle of Her woods? Brother, stop this!'

'If we cut down Her woods,' said Hoel bitterly, 'would they still be Her woods? Cut down Her woods and we cut down Her power!'

Olo flinched, aghast, and men who heard it protested as they stood. 'I'll not stay to hear the Lady insulted like this!' growled the greybeard Joss, stamping away to his horse. Others followed, calling up their dogs.

'Owl!' one youth bawled, backing off in horror. 'I call you to witness before Her that I, Mog, want no part of this! Do you hear me, Owl?'

Soon only the dead drunk and Olo were left with Hoel who stood unmoving and silent, his face a storm in the night.

'It was a fine night until you began this blether!' Olo

scolded. 'Now speak up again, beg Her forgiveness before it's too late!'

Hoel eyed him with sorrowful contempt.

'Beg forgiveness for what? For being a man? For wanting a woman who goes to a witless caterwauling creature instead? Olo, I swear to you,' he insisted in a rapid, trembling voice, 'I'll stay my hand only so long as they don't touch, speak, or look at each other. But if they do any of these things I'll kill one, or the other, or both!' Then an agony broke out in him and his legs grew weak, he sank blindly to the support of his friend's shoulder. 'Olo, Olo my brother, can't you see? It's time we men stood up for ourselves, no matter what! The rest are gone, they're all cowards! But *you* — *you* will come with me?'

Olo was so appalled he didn't even hear the final question. 'You're crazy, Hoel!' he exclaimed, rolling quickly away and up to his feet as if a mere touch from his friend might infect him with madness. 'You'll break taboo by entering the grove to kill others if *they* break taboo? This is nothing but a madness of jealousy — and that's the name of your Unknown God — Jealousy! Hoel, just sleep it off, then wake up and see sense!'

Then Olo left him too, left him slumped and staring into the embers. I'm on my own! he thought fiercely. They're all scared of Her vengeance. All but me, and Ailma, who's blinded by lust. A curse on you all! And he spat into the fire, yet as he did he saw Ailma's unsmiling face in it.

'Soon you'll smile on me, Ailma! I swear it! In a higher place, if need be. For I'll do as I say and take the consequences!'

He stood and left the fire to the drunks; he took his horse and his spear and wandered through the dark woods until near dawn, following faintly shadowed tracks beneath the high bright stars. 'Is that where you came from with all your clever powers?' he cried aloud at Her, staring at the stars. 'You and your magical cousins, the whole degenerate brood of you! What are we to you but cattle? But you'll learn! You'll learn!'

292

But his challenge, ringing into emptiness, was not answered. It was not until dawn, when with undiminished fever and purpose he returned to his guard post by the grove, that She spoke to him ...

Splendid in birdfeather robe atop the Whole Place as night falls, the Lady of the Nine Heights (She has many such titles, few of which please Her any more) receives a messenger from Her army in the west. A terrified fool gasping of another defeat! What's gone wrong? Her mind's not on it; other matters preoccupy Her. Rigidly in the wind against a burning sunset She stands, Her body violent with the red and black of blood, war and death; Her face concealed by a carved wooden mask hiding Her blinding glory from the trembling man who buries his face at Her feet. 'Lady of the Heights!' he gasps, given courage by exhaustion, by memory of the terrible slaughter, his brain on fire with proximity to Her. 'Red Lady of Battle, Your men who still live all ask: 'Why aren't You with us? Why abandon us to the fire-spears of the Ancient Ones? Why let them slaughter us?' Lady, forgive me, but do You no longer mean to conquer to the Western Sea? You said that was the plan, You said You need these lands! Lady, if You have another scheme now, why not tell it to those who die for You?'

Silently She regards this poor fool. If he could read Her thoughts he'd leap off the crags immediately. With an effort She controls Her face beneath the mask. 'Go back, tell them not to doubt!' She orders him in an oddly weary voice. 'All this is part of the plan! Tell them to fall back as if beaten! Azazel and his death-worshippers think us weak, they'll pursue us too confidently — then we'll close the trap on them!'

But we ARE beaten! the fool's mind cries, and Her hand, shooting out, seizes him by his stinking, bloodstained collar. Thinking of snapping his neck to punish he disbelief She decides, No! Life is the worst punishment for these creatures! In disgust She drops him. But how much longer I've lived! And how much worse My punishment! 'Take care!' She scolds. 'You forget I know your mind! What's the loss of a few short lives with so much at stake? But what can you know about that! Go and tell them that soon I'll loose a new power that turns defeat to victory! Go now!'

And only after he's gone, leaving Her alone again with the clean winds and bloody sky on this high, holy place, does She sigh and gaze dully into the depths of the emerald ring. Past moon and horns, through time, through space, and so much angry sadness in Her. Why did I take this people here? She wonders. I know My plan, but I forget so much! But Shemyaza's son is almost ready! When he awakens he'll remember, he'll seed Me with Last Days knowledge and I'll remember what I need to know! We'll persuade Azazel to help us to the Western Sea, and when the Sometimes Isle rises again we'll be there! The Starchamber! To the Emme Ya! I'll do it! I'll remember!

But — and She hesitates, for now in the depths She sees those two Weak Ones pressing deeper into the caves in that southern land from which one short Lullu-generation ago She led the Children; where long ago She built the Gate the Weak Ones call the Gate of the Stone — She hesitates, a storm in Her; for a moment seeing the golden-haired blue-eyed child who threatens Her, who still spins without anchor between the worlds, and those shining eyes disturb Her with a soft melting sense that She abhors, hurting Her, so that, wrenching Her eyes from the depths, She faces instead the mountains, the woods and lush valleys of the rich land all about Her; land She took from her brothers and sisters of the Nephilim who held it before Her. But instead of calming Her the sight bemuses Her with a sense of vast mystery.

Why do we fight? We've forgotten so much. Why can't we agree? When the Shift comes we'll all go to the Source; we'll cease to be! The Shining Ones have it sò; if we can't break out we're lost! We must meet as friends — weren't we friends once? — and discuss My plan! We must act now before we fall apart so thick in time we have no power left at all; we'll just be ghosts denied by the new man-mind! Behind the mask She grinds Her teeth. But the fools won't listen! They fight Me and say I do it only for Myself! They judge Me by their own debased standards! Even Azazel who was once so bright! Azazel! You too! Yet I followed you here!

Then — and it appals Her — She weeps.

Just like a Weak One, She weeps.

The weakness enrages Her.

East over rolling green ranges She glares towards the place

where Her Fool awakens. Time to go! Down from the Whole Place She looks to the camps of the Children. She sees the messenger shrug in terror at men who ask anxiously what She said. You Lullu! She cries in silent exasperation. Stupid two-legs! Why did I take this flesh of yours? Why can't I swim in the oceans of light again? Am I tied into this weight of time for ever?

And again come the dreadful, treacherous tears, filling Her with hate against Herself, against this entire green world in which She's trapped.

'I'll not give in!' Furious, descending to the place where the Wild Women wait, where once the black bull was penned, She gazes into the emerald depths . . . now to see Hoel leading the men on a hunt in the woods.

'I know you, Hoel!' She breathes. 'I know your fate. The time of men who hate women, eh? You'll get what you want, you'll do what I want and never know it. Tomorrow you get your start! Sweet scowling Hoel, killing Hoel, I'll plant you right! Even if they beat Me at the Gate and get that wretched child safe in their clutches, that's not the end of it. They'll have to do a lot more with her before she knows enough! Her father's mine; he's ripe to pluck . . . but they don't even have her yet! And they won't get her! I'll see to that, Hoel . . . won't I? Eh?'

And muttering under Her breath She glares at the two Weak Ones who trek deep into the caverns towards the maze and the Gate beyond . . .

25.
Into the Depths

Soon Pierre was wishing he'd taken the goodman's advice and stayed outside in the sweet, wonderful, life-giving daylight.

Once they were both in the narrow passage twisting into the mountain, Bernard struck fire and lit the first of the pitch-smeared brands. It flared readily, showing slick black rock above and on either side. Then began a steady descent that went on for a long time. At first Pierre was not troubled; he'd been some way down this and other passages in the cave system before, though only far enough to call out goodmen in hiding. And to begin with the way was easy, the flat cracked roof well clear of their heads, though here and there they could only slip through sideways. But the air, dank with a stench of beasts, grew steadily colder, and Pierre felt panic begin to blossom in him. Digging cracked nails into his palms he swallowed grimly and refused to let it overcome him. The old man isn't frightened, so why should I be! he told himself — and true enough, ahead of him Bernard did not pause, but marched firmly down, his guttering torch throwing off an oily smoke. So tautly the shepherd followed him — down, always down — until, quite suddenly, the walls widened then fell away.

They found themselves in a vast draughty cavern, its

broken walls and high roof in darkness beyond the torch-light, and all around the sound of dripping water. The goodman stopped, and Pierre bumped into him.

'Remember this place,' said Bernard, his voice echoing and hollow, his face a white, flame-tinged mask. 'Remember it in case I fail to return and you have to find your own way out. Two other passages descend into this cave, one to either side, but both are dead ends. The passage you must take — the one we've descended — is the middle one. Now look here.'

The goodman searched until he located a slick and bulbous rock on which water dripped continually. It looked like a huge pale mushroom. On it, as Pierre saw when Bernard held up the torch, was scratched a symbol. 'Do you see that?' the goodman demanded. Pierre nodded, swallowing hard. He bent closer and saw that in fact there were three symbols. At the bottom, an equal-armed cross within a crude circle. Above it, the equally crude image of a cup, and above that, as if leaping from it, a dove in upward flight.

'These are signs to lead you out of darkness,' the good-man murmured. 'When you come to partings of the way on your return, seek these signs, and they'll point you back to the light.' Without warning he thrust his face close to the shepherd's, and Pierre flinched. 'Do you want to go back? I won't hold it against you. This is no place to be if you lack faith!'

Yes! Pierre cried silently. *Let me out of here!*

'No!' His voice trembled. 'Lead on. But ...'

'But what?' Bernard peered sharply, his face all bone and eyes.

'If — God forbid! — it comes to what you say,' Pierre stuttered, 'how will I find my way back without any light?'

'I'll leave you brands and a flint.' Bernard shrugged, turning away. 'Now come along. We have far to go.'

They did. Through that great and eerie cavern they trudged, always sloping down, past rugged limestone walls gleaming wet in torchlight, under the invisible roof from which calcined spears hung suspended, and always the water — dripping water, running water, gurgling water — echoing and so hypnotic that the shepherd found his teeth chattering to the rhythms of the dripping. O Sweet Mother of Life! he wailed soundlessly, by now far deeper than he'd ever been before. I didn't know! This is a dreadful place! And he wants to go where it's even more dreadful? Madness! He seeks a virgin girl down here? What sort of girl? More likely a demon! This can't . . .

'Look here!' Bernard interrupted.

He held up the half-burned torch. The flame, flickering in a strong cold draught, showed that they'd reached the end of the vast cavern. They stood ankle-deep in running water amid a giant's playground of slimy green-stained boulders, each the size of a house. Half-blocked passages snaked off in various directions . . . and again, at the entrance of one such passage, Pierre saw the multiple symbol of cross-in-circle, cup and dove. 'Mark it well,' advised Bernard crisply, thinking, Shepherd, I could tell you that this is as far as I've been myself, but I won't, for you're scared enough already, and so am I, so am I!

So they continued, deeper and deeper, always descending, following ways that wriggled and squirmed through the dripping rock, once wading chest-deep through a silent lake in which — as Pierre saw by the torchlight, and wished he hadn't — blind albino trout preyed on blind albino shrimps, and on and on, past dreary forks and crossings, the route always marked by the multiple symbol scratched by unknown hands in some ancient time, until the shepherd was stumbling in weary terror, scarcely conscious of anything save that flickering light the goodman carried. Two brands had burned down, and a third almost so, with Pierre certain that many days and nights must have passed in the sweet lost world outside this place of horror, when at last they reached a cave with no apparent exit. Here Bernard stopped, and with a sigh, handing Pierre the brand, dumped his pack on the cold rock floor.

Pierre's jaw dropped at what he saw in the torchlight. For the smooth cruel walls were covered all over with bizarre paintings; paintings in red and black, of bulls and deer and stick-men hunters hurling spears, and many unknown creatures, massive, tusked. He stood, no longer sure who he was, and as he stared the blood roared in his head, bringing a welter of images that had him nearly fainting in fear. Meanwhile Bernard had calmly sat down at the foot of a wall. 'Don't drop that light!' he said in a mild, unconcerned voice, coiling the length of knotted rope round his body and over his shoulder. This done, he brought a loaf of bread out of the pack and broke it in half.

'Here I leave you,' he said simply, sketching a blessing on the bread and giving the shepherd both halves. 'If phantoms terrify you, return to the light. You're not obliged to wait here.'

'Aren't you eating anything?' asked a trembling voice, and it was only after a while that Pierre realised it was himself who had spoken.

'*I have food to eat that you know nothing about,*' the goodman said, quoting the Gospel as he bowed his head in prayer, and for a time he was completely still and silent. The shepherd remained standing in front of him, holding the brand in one hand and bread in the other, not knowing what to do or what was about to happen. But shortly Bernard exhaled, and stood, and took the torch, raising it over his head so that Pierre saw how, above the strange paintings, at head height, there began a narrow ledge that went curving away to a hole in the wall. Within this hole lay deeper darkness; Pierre sucked in breath at the sight of it as Bernard, adjusting the rope around his neck, tucked a spare brand into his belt and took up his staff.

'Here is flint.' The goodman pressed a coldness into Pierre's clammy hand. 'Now help me up, and God preserve you, my friend.'

'And you,' Pierre managed to whisper, and did as he was told, heaving the old man up on his shoulders until

Bernard got a hold on the ledge.

Then the goodman crawled away into the maze and left the shepherd on his own in the utter darkness of that place with the painted walls.

For a time all went well enough with Pierre. He sat with his back to the wall, chewing bread (he found it hard to swallow), feeling the pack and the brands that lay on the cold rock floor, assuring himself that he could strike a light whenever he wanted. Soon enough he was telling himself that he was better off down here than in the outside world, where people killed each other for no reason at all. Then, getting bored, he began telling himself the tale of the Fall, the way the goodmen taught it. Of how the aeons, or spirits of light, had been lured into Satan's creation, falling through a hole in heaven down to the fiery, smoky, time-trapped and flesh-bound earth. But this tale-telling proved to be a bad mistake.

'At first you didn't notice, did you, God?' And as he spoke, again he began to wonder who was speaking. 'Then you were surprised, and got angry, and put your foot over the hole, but too late: many spirits had already fallen to earth and into bodies. They were trapped, and that's how it all began, with the lost souls being reborn time and time again; the worst as snakes and insects, the not-so-bad as horses and pigs, the better ones as people, and the best of all as believers in the true faith ...' — the voice quavered — '... as goodmen and perfected ones who ascend again to heaven. And when at last everyone remembers the truth, then evil's beaten and the world will end! The sky will fall, the sun and moon will go out, fire will consume the sea and be consumed by it ... and there'll be nothing left for the Evil One to rule but a lake of pitch and sulphur!'

Having thus succeeded in terrifying himself, Pierre sat shivering in the darkness, in the utter silence, resisting the urge to light a brand. Here in this place there was not even the dripping of water. He sensed phantoms crowding round him and tried to ignore them, talking to himself. 'How long have I been here?' he wondered, increasingly fearful. 'What if he doesn't come back? He said I could flee. But I mustn't! Please God, don't let me be a coward and run away! But I can't just sit here. Could I follow him? Should I? He told me not to, but maybe that was to save me from the terror that he endures. Maybe he *does* need me but wouldn't say. Maybe . . .'

No, he couldn't sit. He stood. He felt his body. Am I still here? Unable to bear it, he struck blinding fire, lit a brand. The fire shocked him. He stared at his hand. Four fingers and a thumb. I'm still here! He eyed the ancient paintings on the wall. His fear was by now so great that his mind seemed scarcely to work. He gazed at the leaping figures of man and beast . . . and it was only when he came across the symbol — cross-in-circle, cup and dove — that his curiosity was aroused.

For etched in the rock above the symbol was another symbol.

A circle, open at the bottom, many lesser circles inscribed in it, each of them broken and opening up passages which . . .

Is this a picture of the way he took? To the Gate of the Stone?

And as he eyed the design more closely he began to shake so hard that the torch nearly went out. Try as he might he could not hold it still.

He told me not to! I'm damned if I even think it! But I *am* thinking it. God forgive me! Turn and run, shepherd, turn and run!

Instead he found himself rubbing a forefinger into sticky hot pitch running down from the torch-head. On the back of his left hand he began smearing a copy of the labyrinth design, trembling so violently it took a huge effort to make the image accurate. But suddenly, amazing himself, he began to laugh. 'What have I got to lose?' he demanded. 'Perhaps I'll die, but better men than me are dying all the time!' And a strange deep calm came over him as he studied the design, memorising the twists and turns needed to bring him to the centre. To the Gate of the Stone.

At last, smiling a crooked mad smile, he looked up and measured the distance to the ledge. Then, in a hurry in case he backed out, stuffing bread into his pouch and still clutching the torch, he stretched and found a grip. With all his strength he pulled himself up. Groaning with effort he got his chin onto the ledge, then his elbows, and finally his knees.

Pausing there, again overcome by the enormity of his intention, he reminded himself of the goodman's warnings ... but they hardly seemed to matter now. In deciding to face this peril he had woken up; he felt more completely himself than ever in his life before. It was as if in response to the challenge a power had welled up in him; a power that answered fear with exhilaration. Grinning, he extinguished the brand and tucked it into his belt. He made sure of the flint and dry tinder in his pouch, and the bread there too. Then, licking dry lips, he began to crawl through the darkness, hugging the slick damp wall until his questing left hand found the tiny entrance to the maze.

Against his face he felt the cold dead draught.

'*Go back now, you fool!*' hissed a furious voice. '*It isn't God's power that moves you, it's Satan's pride! Go back or you'll be destroyed!*'

For a long moment, frozen, he panted with terror. Then he bit hard on his knuckles. 'I said that!' he told himself fiercely. 'The coward in me! Ignore it, Pierre. Go on, now, or you'll be a coward until you die!'

So, on hands and knees, not knowing if his eyes were open or shut, he crawled into the labyrinth leading to the Gate of the Stone.

The entrance was tiny, and the passage within no larger. His nostrils flared in a fresh attack of fear. For a moment he thought he heard piping, mocking voices; thought he felt fingers pinching him. Deliberately he reminded himself of what the goodman had said about the phantoms that drove men mad, the phantoms of the mind. That's all they are! he told himself sternly. I may not be trained in the spirit ... but if his miracle-child does arrive, how will he get her out without my help? He needs me! I knew it all along! Go on, shepherd!

Heart thumping, he crawled all the way into the tunnel, and the first discovery he made encouraged him, for his searching left hand encountered, tied securely to a spur of rock at the side of the tight little passage, the end of the rope the goodman had taken with him. That's why he needed it! So he won't get lost, so he can find his way out again! And Pierre laughed to himself. No fool, my goodman! This makes it easy!

Soon he knew it wasn't so easy.

For as he crawled along the rope — past one junction, up another — the ever-curving passage got tighter and tighter, squeezing his shoulders until they were hunched in against his ears. And suddenly he realised: What if I get stuck? I won't be able to turn round or go back at all!

The phantoms had been waiting for this. Terror flooded him; he felt the fingers pinching as ghosts of those long-dead came to mock him. *What are you?* they cried in thin, painfully whining voices. *Who are you?* And with laughter that shrilled through his skull they answered their own questions. *A Pierre Perdue! A Peyrepertuse! A Lost Stone! You're dead, shepherd! You're dead as sure as we are, you'll never see the light of day again, for you're in Her grave-womb now, and here you stay for ever and ever and ever, because She loves you so much She won't let you go, not ever!*

All but overwhelmed, he bit his tongue and fought the assault, fought to bring to mind all the faces of his youth, fought to summon the voices of Guillaume and young Jacques and Gargaleth, tried to recall songs he loved the best — and somehow, moaning in pain and fear, he crawled on, aware with a thin edge of remaining self-control that Bernard had already come this way and must have survived this same attack. The rope in his hand was proof. Coarse hemp fibre, scratching his skin! — all he had as the mad voices went on hissing, crackling, driving out all clear memory of his life. The rope — sanity, his lifeline, his only sense of direction, and without it he'd be mad already. He clung to it, to himself . . . until soon he knew that his eyes were open, and that worse lay ahead.

For gradually amid his delirium he became aware of a ghostly green light emanating from the passage ahead, always round the curving corner. It was growing brighter, and as it did he became aware too of a curious singing, or vibration, that set his teeth on edge and hurt his head. It was changing pitch up and down in rhythm with the now discernible ebb and flow of the hypnotic, strengthening emerald light; and as he drew near the source of it, a detached part of him watching as if from far above knew that his terror was again close to overwhelming him. *Pierre, if you don't find your precious goodman soon you'll die of terror!* commented a voice, calm amid the madness. For now amid the emerald light he saw half-formed faces (there was a woman, raven-haired, her eyes twin black gulfs sucking him in) of grimacing demons fighting each other to get their teeth in him: blinding bright they shimmered as the terrible singing mounted in pitch like damned souls screaming. He moaned in agony, crawling on with closed eyes, but the light by now was so powerful that it penetrated his closed eyelids; he felt his body burning up in it; he felt a howling wind whip him, whirling into his heart, tearing into the marrow of his bones, ripping his soul from the poor weak flesh which had housed it for such a short time —

Then amid this agony he heard something startlingly familiar —

A song. A song he knew, a song he'd sung himself . . . when was it?

'Quant lo bouié ben de laura . . .'

Amazed, he rallied against the agony, the madness. He opened his burning eyes, his dry cracked mouth; he tried to lift his head . . .

Then the madness did take him.

For there She was.

304

Only feet away.

Waiting for him.

The giant red woman, stark naked, crouching there before him, ready to swallow him, and him helpless on hands and knees.

He stared, his mind glazing as black wings beat in his head. For Her legs were hairy and Her feet were webbed like those of a goose ... and in place of Her female organ there gaped open before him a huge mouth lined all round with sharp, spear-like white teeth ... and it was through this frightful mouth that the flood of emerald light pulsed on the waves of the soul-stripping wind amid a scream that went beyond all hearing ... and also through this deadly birth-mouth that the song, the Song of the Herdsman, the Song of Joana, came pouring, sung in a voice that ...

But Pierre no longer heard. He could no longer think. The voices babbled as She tore his wits from him, her abyssal eyes mocking him.

You Weak One! She jeered. *You stupid, stupid Weak One!*

Pierre began wailing like a demented animal.

It was a long time before he stopped.

26.
Fruit of the Tree

Meanwhile Hoel wandered the woods ... and Shem
dreamed. In the dream he wasn't stupid *Shem* who lived
in a cave, but *Samjoyce*, a man whose body was rarely
naked, empty, dirty or cold; a man who lived in a
bewildering hard place of squared stone where no trees
grew, a place of foul air and baleful thunders. And so
many two-legs scurrying about, their pale faces anxious
and grim! What's this? he asked in the dream. Where am
I? What happened?

Then She's there.

*Down an abyss he plunges, nothing left of him but a point
that wails, but She's there, a column of blazing violet fire
towering from the heights to the crushing depths; and Her hand
snatches and carries him through a sudden door in the black wall
of the abyss. 'Here you are at last!' She greets him tenderly. 'I've
waited so long! Soon I'll put you in a sweet warm garden where
you'll rest and get better! But first I need your help; I'm having a
little trouble with some relations of mine ...'*

*And without warning he finds himself sprawled witless and
shrieking on a high rocky fog-bound place, a pandemonium of
battle raging all round and below him. Bursts of deadly light split
the fog; enormous half-human faces twist and writhe about him;
without knowing what he sees he sees Her, naked in red and
black on Her back, pinned down by a chimerical monstrosity — a*

306

hairless blue giant with the head of a cockerel. 'Shem!' She screams. 'My Fool! Here! Quickly!' And as he stumbles towards Her the cockerel-headed creature turns to glare with eyes that freeze him, but She laughs. 'NOW do you understand Me, Azazel! I've done it! I've done it! He believes in ME where you're just a ghost, a myth, a lost legend!' Then with a twist and a shift the power comes upon Her, She throws off the monster and towers above the pandemonium ... and Shem, howling in terror, turns and flees the battle, scrambling from the heights down to fields of twitching human corpses where horrified faces confront him for delirious instants, where the lances of dripping light explode the bodies they strike as he stumbles through the charnel house and goes running for the woods. 'SAM!' he wails, 'SHAMSAM! SHEMSAM! SAMSON, SHEMSON, SAMSHEMSAM! SHEM! SHEM! SHEM!'

It was then, wailing his name, he awoke without knowing it and sprang to his feet, ducking the deadly spears of light as he ran from cave-mouth to brook before he stopped, confused by the water and splashing. He stared wildly round at the peaceful dawnlit trees, his senses dizzy and ruptured.

'SAMJOYCE!' he cried at the grove. 'SAMJOYCE! SAM-JOYCE!'

But no birds sang. No voice answered.

'Where's this?' he asked bemused. 'Where am I?'

'... *I'll put you in a sweet warm garden where you'll rest* ...'

Her voice! That's what She said! This is the garden! I'm Samjoyce! I came! I'm here! And then at last, shivering near-naked and staring at the misty grove, his discontinuities began to knit; his eyes brightened as bees came humming from the memory-hive. 'Sting me, bees!' he cried. 'Go on, sting me hard!' And they did, swarming through him until he couldn't bear it. *The Last Days before the Shift! London! Diane! Chrissa!* Moaning, he forced himself to take it. GO ON! STING ME! 'I *was* asleep, I've got to wake up!' he babbled. 'I've been a Fool, but ... now I remember! She put me here so I could get over the shock of the Gate. I was Samjoyce! And before that,' he panted, staggering, clutching his head, '... I don't know — STING

ME, BEES! — but I'm more than Shem the Fool who doesn't know what to do when a two-legs ... when a *woman* comes and makes me hard. I'm Shem, I'm here to help Her remember how to stop the Shift!

In sudden exhilaration he clapped his hands and laughed, then tore off the apron of leaves he'd been wearing.

'Where are you?' he bellowed in Sam's tongue, in a voice that rang from the grove to be heard and understood by all beyond it. 'Where are you, bread-bringer? It's time you came again; it's time I left this place, but first I need the key to unlock the gate — and you have that key, you *are* that key, as I'm Her key! So come, unlock me, set me free to do Her will!'

In that moment, with Hawk's warning forgotten by the Fool, even those out on far pastures felt the fear of their kin and sensed the great beating wings of Her presence. *And She sees it all as She prepares to act ...*

As soon as Hoel returned from his night of angry wandering he knew men on the hunt had talked, for the guard he relieved at the grove, Urig, eyed him with furtive anxiety and made off as quick as he could into the mists. 'Rabbit!' Hoel spat after him. 'At least take my horse to the corral!'

But Urig was gone ... while from the glade the Fool roared like a lion. Uneasily Hoel eyed the tangled undergrowth. Don't weaken! he told himself, gripping his spear tight. I'll do what I must! O Unknown God, if I die at Her hands, take me! Send me to the time of free men!

Then breeze stirred the trees; an eerie voice spoke.

'Hoel! Hoel! Hear me, Hoel!'

He whirled, spear raised against hawthorn flower and spike.

'Who is it! Show yourself!'

'You see me well enough, Hoel — and I see you, stupid boy!'

It's Her! He trembled violently, but held his ground ... for though the voice was muffled and strange, it was also oddly familiar.

'I don't see you at all!' he sneered. 'I see only the grove!'

'Ailma bakes Fool's Bread,' whispered the voice from the grove, 'and soon she'll bring it. Wake up, Hoel! I heard your drunken boasting last night, so be warned! I'm kind to those who love Me, but if you disobey My orders, the Wild Women will tear your living body to pieces!'

Somehow Hoel laughed, and shook his spear.

'I hear you, Old Mother!' he jeered. 'You speak through Her mask in Her words, but it's you just the same!'

'Rage and lust fuel your pride, Hoel!' hissed the voice. 'Invade My grove and I'll not be kind; after I've dealt with you I'll turn the men of this clan into fat soft gigglers and make the women look elsewhere!'

'I'll do as I must!' said Hoel grimly. 'Strike me down and boil my bones, for I'm dead and boiled already if Ailma will not smile on me. If you'd stop me, get the other men to tie me down. You know they would!'

Then, behind her carved wooden mask, Riann knew it was no good.

'I can't do that,' she cried sadly. 'Force won't alter your desire and I'm not a *man*, to use force against the Fates. Do as you will, but we'll reap your bitter harvest and you'll die a terrible death!'

'Death!' Hoel sneered. 'The Whirling Castle invites the brave!'

'Hoel, you'll die only to learn you're less than you think!'

He turned his back. 'Old Mother, I tried. She would not smile. Now my mind is made up. A man must stand, or be nothing.'

'But your stand is completely upside-down!' Riann snapped, pulling the mask off her face. 'She's here now! Everything you do is seen!'

'I know.' He gazed longingly at the brightening sky. 'I wait.'

'So do we all,' agreed Riann wearily as she left him, turning deeper into the grove as the bloody sun began its rise through the mists and the Fool bellowed his mad expectant excitement. Hoel! she mourned. Oh Hoel!

And Fool's Bread was coming out of the oven again.

Silently in the night by unknown ways She comes, the Wild Women with Her. Now about Her in a hidden place they crouch, waiting impatiently as She watches. In the emerald depths She sees Her Fool strut, Ailma waiting by the oven, Riann speaking to Hoel. And She tells Herself: Spilled blood will speed awakening! Ailma's fruit will spin our way to future time when few remember Me. Future time! In sorrow She closes Her eyes. I've lost strength already; how much worse can it get? Will this be enough? They'll cut down more than My woods ... what if Hoel's kind have the last laugh? She shudders, and promises: Hoel, you'll fight those Weak Ones for me. That golden-haired child! I feel her hovering! What if she touches her father again and stops us reaching the Starchamber? I MUST speak to Azazel! He MUST understand! Why does he oppose Me? Why won't the Shining Ones hear Me? In fury She eyes the depths, and groans, for now one of those Weak Ones is into the maze and resisting Her phantom guardians. If they can get through My teeth ... ah, but how can they? They don't know enough!

Yes! She decides. It's going to work! It is!

But Her masked smile is oddly tentative for One so powerful.

'Be ready,' She warns the Wild Women. 'They come. Watch; stop only murder by the man Hoel. If you want his bones, take him before he kills.'

And through the grove they creep, seen only by Her.

So Ailma took Fool's Bread from the oven; wrapped it in leaves and put it in the basket, then in a daze she went to the grove. And all who saw her go knew she carried their fate with her, but nobody tried to stop her; it was her duty to do this. Nobody stood in her way but Hoel, and he only because she chose to enter the grove by the brook where he stood on guard. Why, she didn't know: other forces operated in her now; forces taking her beyond personal calculation, moving her in a dream. *Child!* a soft voice in her said as she approached him. *You'll live to bear the fruit!*.

Hoel tensed as she drew near. Harshly he said:

'So you're going to greet your Fool!'

'I bring Fool's Bread.' She met his eyes without emotion.

'I know what you bring! Again, will you not smile on me?'

'I can neither smile nor frown on you,' she said calmly, and in his anger saw the opposite of the power she served. 'Let me pass.'

Only for a moment he obstructed her, then stood aside.

'Go in!' He held the spear with its point at her. 'But I warn you: you'll be watched! Swift punishment will strike down any mischief!'

'Hoel, as usual you state the obvious,' she said sadly, but she did not wait: she ducked under the hawthorn and vanished into the grove.

Then Hoel hesitated. His eyes widened in fear. He looked round. 'I'm dead if I step even a foot along the way she takes!' he muttered. 'But a life of shame is worse. I'll do it! The Whirling Castle will take me and heal me and return me; I'll be a king among men! Breaking Her taboo will bring me power to overcome any death She inflicts on me!'

And having encouraged himself in this desperate way he took his fatal step. A giddy terror seized him; he spun forward and crashed full-length into the brook under the white and spiky hawthorn bushes. After a little while he got shakily to his hands and knees. 'No,' he stammered in a dire voice, using his spear to help him stand, 'you don't put me off so easily! I do as I must!' So, shaking his spear, he started into the silent grove — for now even the Fool was silent — to meet his fate. But his teeth were chattering; he knew he was watched. He could feel eyes on his spine.

Old Mother, he thought, his flesh crawling, I hope it's only you!

My son, Riann thought back sadly, I'm afraid not.

For where she lay nearby the Old Mother felt the Wild Women creeping about, unseen and hungry. She had seen Ailma pass along the brook, that fated dreamstruck look on her face ... and now here came Hoel, prowling below the hawthorn only feet from where she hid. She saw his haunted face, his glazed eyes, his strong white teeth bared wolfishly as he fought Her taboo; she heard his gasping breath as he penetrated this place no man of the clan had ever dared enter before.

I'm wrong, she realised. It's not just rage and lust that fire him. They'd not help him fight the barriers here. Oh, Hoel, it may be the power of the part you play. If taboo's not broken, how can taboo exist? And how can taboo exist unless punishments for breaking it are ...

She could not continue with this.

You're no son of my blood but you're my son all the same! she told him silently ... and it was then, as he vanished from her sight, that she wept, and for her own sake wished to be dead and gone from this world.

Not yet, Old Mother, came Her sardonic voice. *There's more yet!*

So Riann joined those closing in on the glade in the grove.

And so it came to pass. *Daughter,* breathed Her voice through the tops of the trees as Ailma neared her goal, *you'll bear the fruit of his tree, but first you must plant his seed in your earth. Do it well! Balance your fear with compassion and you'll see him as he is, you'll know what to do.* 'Oh Mother of Sowing and Reaping,' murmured Ailma, not even knowing she spoke, 'Oh Mother of Death and Rebirth, I've baked his bread, I'll give him earth for his seed. But the harvest is in Your hands ...'

So it is, whispered the trees. *But you must do it right. Don't fear! Be joyful and give yourself! My Fool needs you to complete his awakening!*

Then came a warm wind bearing a fiery emerald brightness that shone in the grass and flowers, in the leaves and bark of the trees; and a perfume came on the wind — languid, sensual, sweetly potent in those who breathed it, like a shaft of sudden sun after weeks of black cloud. Into the glade blew this sparkling wind, bringing the birds with it, so that by the brook Shem looked up with a smile; he breathed deep as the glow pulsed through him, dissolving his pain and stiffness so that he stretched, he yawned, he laughed in delight, and like a boy jumped up and down on his toes. Then he whirled and ran into the brook, and the water greeted him. 'Now it's time, now it's time!' the water babbled breathlessly, and from the trees the birds agreed. 'She breathes on us, She breathes on us, and look! — look! — Here she comes! Here she comes!'

He turned, and there she was, green-gowned under hair like a cloud of floating gold as she came running into the glade with her basket of bread, her face giddily transformed, her body flowering and quickened as the perfume, bubbling like birdsong in her veins, overwhelmed her senses. She was laughing out loud as she brought the Fool his bread. Yet outside the grove, and elsewhere in it, there was no laughter at all. And when she saw the Fool she stopped running, she stopped laughing, for he stood utterly still, his happy smile turned to a look of urgent, desirous inquiry. His gaze cut her to the core. Her delight fled. Her eyes fell.

She saw the proof of his desire, and anxiety seized her.

Look at him! A naked beast! And look at that thing! How will I find room for that? It'll hurt! And where's Hoel? He's mad, he'll kill both of us. This is all mad! I'll just put down the bread and go, quickly!

Go where? asked the wind. *To Hoel?*

In a panic she spun round and round, seeking escape. There was none. The trees crowded her blankly. The birds had stopped singing; the perfume now smelled rank and overblown. She felt faint and about to fall.

Daughter, don't fear! Give yourself joyfully!

She sighed and shut her eyes, in great gulps breathing the air of Her grove. Shem, still standing in the brook, simply stared. He could not move. Every nerve in him strained, he was on fire, but he could not move. 'What is it, what is it?' sparkled the brook. 'Why do you wait? Why do you wait?' He didn't know. He was baffled, his earlier certainties fled. Obscurely he wondered if she had to do something before he could move. He pleaded with his eyes, but her eyes were still closed as she shivered.

Compassion, girl! See him as he is, not through the fog of fear!

Slowly she opened her eyes. Again she looked at him, and this time saw a man whose entire body was a question mark.

I have the answer! she realised. But do I dare?

With another deep sigh she broke the spell. With difficulty, as if wading through glue, she carried the basket to the cave-mouth. Setting it down, she took out the bread, lifted it, and held it out to him. Then, in dreamy terror of a spear in the back, she broke the taboo on speech.

'Here,' she whispered huskily. 'Here, Fool. Your bread!'

At this tremorous sound Shem shook his head violently. What's that? She speaks to me! She's calling me! And fear rose in him too as he found he could move. On awkward legs, a huge stiffness between them, he went to her up the emerald slope, slowly, his eyes questing. Yes, she's the one with the key! But how is it turned? What do I do? Trembling, he stopped. The sparkling air and her eyes encouraged him. Yes! Yes! Come on! Yet her hands too were trembling as she held out the loaf. Still he hesitated. 'Go on, go on!' the brook behind him sang. So he took another step. Then another. Again he paused. She beckoned, brushing hair from her eyes, and something about that gesture pained him, fired him. Who is she? And for a moment he remembered ... golden hair ... *who?* ...

'Come on!' Ailma said fearfully. 'Fool, come on, *quickly* now!'

With his eyes fixed on her, he took yet another doubtful step.

'Come on, Fool!' Holding out the bread, she too moved closer.

They were face to face, close enough to feel each other's breath.

With a sudden grab he overcame his fear and took the loaf.

Their fingers didn't quite touch. Not quite.

Shivering, he stared at the bread, at her, at the bread. Then with sudden violence, not knowing why, he tore the loaf in half. With the two halves in his two hands he stood. What now? his eyes beseeched.

Slowly she extended her trembling hands, and at this invitation — taut, intent, erect — he offered her a half of the loaf. Unsmiling, with hot eyes and wondering look, she took it.

And their fingers brushed. That was all. Just touched.

The shock jumped through them both. He flinched. She gasped, again fearing Hoel's spear as the taboo on touch was broken. Where is he? She began to look aside, behind her, breaking the moment with her fear.

Forget Hoel! I've got an eye on him! Take my Fool now: make life!

Then Ailma released herself and released Shem too, though first she seemed about to flee, for with a hiss she sprang back — not in flight, yet giving sufficient impression of this to draw him on after her. Her mind swam and roared, but her fingers knew what to do as they untied her gown and let if fall green to the grass.

And with another sigh she shut her eyes and lay down on her back.

Shem's own eyes widened. He took a step to her, uncertain.

'Fool!' Beckoning urgently, she opened her legs. 'Here!'

Shem stood transfixed and gaping. Her thighs opened wider. With hot impatient fear she beckoned again. 'Come here, Fool! You *are* a Fool! Give me your thing!'

She pointed at his erection. 'Put it *in* me! Now!

With sudden explosive amazement Shem realised:

I am the key! And there's the lock in the gate!

Then down on her he went with clumsy joy and nervous haste, and to begin with he made a mess of it, nearly breaking the lock by trying to force the key, so that she cried out in pain and drew away from him, and in his fright he nearly gave up. But the warm wind breathed on them so that their juices began to flow again, and at last they found the way, Virgin and Fool ... and taboo was truly shattered when they began to move as one.

It was then that Hoel attacked.

He'd seen it all. He saw nothing. He saw blood.

With his senses enflamed and transported by Her perfume he'd stumbled from the brook to crouch behind an oak at the edge of the glade, spear trembling at the ready, his breath shuddering out in quick gasps.

He saw Ailma run into the glade. He saw the Fool, naked and erect for her. Fiery hate poured through him; he tried to jump out to kill them, but could not. His body, seduced by Her perfume, would not obey him. Worst of all, his mind was still his own. I'm dead already! he cursed. And from some high shelf of mind the essential Hoel looked down, watching him ... as others watched him. Like a brute awaiting slaughter! What's my crime? Wanting a woman? But I'll kill before I'm killed! For the Unknown God!

Yet even his fine pure hate felt remote. Even as Ailma spoke and broke taboo he felt remote. So You own my body! he cried at Her. It's a joke to You. You think You can jerk us on Your string forever. But I'll do it! I'll kill them! And he stood, straining against the langour of his flesh as the Fool came to Ailma and took the bread from her ... as the two of them touched. He snarled. He gripped the spear, he ...

Wait! Too soft, too warm, She soothed him again. *Why so angry, Hoel? Your passion's strong, but you can still stop. Don't make Me destroy you!*

I'll wait! he told her bitterly. I'll wait generations if I must, but my time will come. I'll remember this!

Oh, poor Hoel! She chided. *You've been so hard done by, poor boy!*

At this the fire shot through him. 'Never fear!' he cried aloud, distracted, for now Ailma's gown had dropped and the key hunted for the lock, but he was looking up and round at the trees and concealing bushes, his face haunted by fright he strove to suppress. 'I'll remember, and so will my Father! He and I will see you beaten back and buried deep down where you belong — underground, in the bowels of the earth!'

Even as he howled this he felt Her leave him; he felt Her huge sense of shock and dislocation, of pain and mortification. With Her hold broken he turned with a roar to see the Fool already through Ailma's virgin gate. This filled him with such fury that he wished to destroy the entire world that allowed such things; Her world and all things green and growing. 'Father, give me strength to aim true!' he howled as he leapt behind from the tree and charged the sweet coupling couple, spear poised by both hands above his head, meaning to kill both with one clean pure thrust.

'What's this?' She cries, snatched back by crisis from the Gate of the Stone where another crisis took Her, too late realising the trap in which She's caught, the trap of simultaneous battles in two places, two times . . .

27.
The Return of Joana

'Father! Father Bernard ...!'

Bernard had forgotten not only the shepherd but everyone and everything else from the world beyond the gate, the maze, the mountain. His purpose was the only thing left. He had no idea how long it was since he'd crawled into the maze ... for what was time itself but another of Satan's clever but false creations of spirit thickened into matter, birthing trials of flesh? And without a sense of time he had no memory of his struggle through the labyrinth, of the pain and assaults he'd endured.

Yet there had been such a journey, one without much chance of gaining its goal, for the maze was complex and the attacks severe. Even so and at length in the utter darkness he'd reached a point (for the third, fifth, maybe tenth time) when the rope — one end tied to the spur at the entrance, the other round his waist — had reached its full, measured length from knot to knot. And on this occasion, unlike the others, his searching hands had found the interlocking teeth that announced the mechanism of the Gate.

I'm at the door, he told himself, quite dazed, and crouching there he rested, breathing deep and slow until the fevered phantoms and taunting voices lost their hold on him. Then, his mind a clear pool again, he summoned up what Bishop Guilhabert de Castres had told him years before, one cool misty day atop the pog of Montségur.

'She's old and Her ways are wild,' Guilhabert had said, his chubby nut-brown face for once unsmiling as they walked the narrow path outside the walls above the precipices and fog-bound valleys far below, 'and the false church of Rome and Rex Mundi has tried to deny Her, moulding an image of woman as meek and obedient. Deadly folly! They exalt their ignorance as virtue by damning Her nature; She has Her seat in our hidden heart and does not forget. One day She'll have Her revenge! Until then She maintains her power in dreams, in night-secrets and the mysteries of madness. She waits in the deep places of this world and our minds. So if ever you come to Her teeth at the Gate of the Stone, take care! Approach Her in fear and Her bite will destroy you! Calm yourself before you act, pray to rid your mind of Her shades. They're not just ghosts, but defences put there long ago! So! Calm yourself, then let your right hand explore Her teeth — lightly! You'll find the upper dog-tooth on your right and the two either side of it missing. Grip the lower dog-tooth that spears up into this gap, again with care, for it pivots. Imagine this tooth is the dog star, Sirius — once Her home and that of those who fell with Her! It stands vertical. Imagine it points to the pole star. To open the Gate, twist it to the right in a thirty-degree arc across the gap, so when you let it go it points at the Seven Sisters, in the sign of the Bull in whose Age this Gate was made.'

Guilhabert had paused to toe a star chart in the dust of the path. 'She made this Gate — and that great zodiac in the landscape embracing Rennes and Bugarach! — in an effort to guard Her wisdom and open a way back to the realms the Shining Ones closed when Plato's Atlantic isle went to the depths. There was a Gate there through which the Shining Ones freely came and went. That Gate's lost now, and so is Her power — and if the false church succeeds in destroying us, then knowledge of all these things will also be lost, as the False One desires ... but don't worry about that now!

'So,' he'd concluded, 'turn the tooth precisely and She'll have to recognise your right to enter. But make a mistake and you'll die.'

'What is Her name?' Bernard had asked.

'She has many names. You as a poet must know some. But no calling of names will help. The ancients who served Her made this machine exactly; what we call sorcery was knowledge to them; magic was a deeper knowledge of things than we have now. They knew and feared Her as one of those of whom Enoch speaks in that book I showed you: the Nephilim or Watchers, shape-shifting aeons cast down by their lust for flesh, trapped in time, fearing mortal death, always seeking to return to the realm they lost.'

'Why tell me this?' Bernard had asked.

'Who knows?' The bishop's smile was remote. 'Maybe once, twenty years or more ago, I heard a singer sing a song at the court of Lombez. He sang of Joana, who has gone to heaven. Maybe Joana will return one day ...'

And there they'd stood, looking out over the great massif of Tabor, the breeze echoing Guilhabert's words. *One day ... one day ... one day ...*

Now, in the darkness at the Gate of the Stone, Bernard prayed, ignoring the phantoms, fixing his mind on the golden-haired child who, spinning and lost between the worlds, had called him here. And when his mind was calm he reached out to grasp and turn the tooth, all in one smooth motion.

He did it. For a moment nothing happened.

Then there was a grinding. A terrible gnashing.

'Oh please God!' he murmured fervently. 'Please God ...'

Then he felt the cold draught on his face and knew Her mouth was open, knew he was still alive. 'Thanks to our Father who rests in the Ocean of Light!' he cried aloud in the enormity of his relief.

For a little while he relaxed himself. Then, with the

utmost caution, he hoisted himself over the deadly teeth into Her innermost sanctum, onto a smooth, downward-sloping stone floor. Carefully, his hands protecting his head, he stood in the utter darkness. Then at last he lit a brand. The flare of light almost blinded him ... and the first thing he made out as his eyes adjusted was its reflection ... on a glimmering pool of black water at the foot of the brief slope on which he stood. The black pool! With heart in mouth he raised the brand and looked about.

The grotto containing the black pool was not wide or deep, but its roof was high. Even by torchlight he couldn't determine how high. On every side, jagged pillars of uncarved rock rose into impenetrable darkness. The smooth slope on which he stood was ebony black and formed a floor like a shallow basin, sloping evenly down on all sides to the circular pool of inky water that occupied the centre of the grotto — itself at the centre of the maze. The pool measured some twelve paces across and was probably not deep, as from the middle of it rose a flat table of rock — a mysterious little black isle with smooth rounded sides.

With caution (for in the chill draught from an unknown source above he felt Her outraged breathing: She was not pleased at being forced to let him in) he stepped down to the edge of the pool. With the tip of his staff he broke the surface of the water and, as he did, flinched, for a shock burned up the staff into him, bringing with it the clear image of Her furious face and the frigid, distant wind of Her voice:

'So you've found your way into My secret place, O man who worships God the Father in the heavens beyond My Gates!' She hissed. 'You tear Me away from important business! So you think the Shining Ones will protect you, eh? You've come for that stupid child! Well, you shan't have her! Leave now, or I promise you'll never return alive to the Fields of Light!'

Nodding in sombre recognition, having seen and heard all he wanted, the goodman snuffed out his brand and sat down at the edge of the pool, legs crossed under him, staff vertical in his right hand and earthed on the rock beside him. Ordering his breathing, which was ragged again, he called on God's light to banish the terror She sent against him ... and when again his mind was as still as the pool below him, he began to concentrate his will, visualising it as a staff as sturdy as the one he held — a living staff, green and budding, with power to confer life on whoever it touched. This staff of his vital will he extended over the pool to the centre of the black islet where (Guilhabert had explained) this particular Gate was aligned with others through the space and time of this dark world. And when (Her ghosts and face and voice locked firmly outside the circle of light in him) he had established this connection firmly, when he felt the passion of the world begin to flow out along the staff, then he began the Calling, sending his burning prayer into the dimensions beyond the Gate, calling the lost, lonely child who'd beseeched him in his dreams:

'*Our Father, which art in heaven, hallowed be thy name.* CHILD, YOUR FATHER IS HERE WITH A ROD AND A STAFF TO COMFORT YOU AND BRING YOU SAFELY HOME! *Thy kingdom come, bringing the salvation of Christ to the pure ones.* CHILD, TAKE THIS BRANCH I REACH OUT! *Thy will be fulfilled on earth in the Christ, for He said: I am come to do the will of my Father.* COME, CHILD, TAKE HOLD OF THIS BRANCH OF THE VINE, FOR ITS FRUIT WILL SUSTAIN YOU! *Give us this day our supersubstantial bread through which this earth takes daily shape and form.* COME NOW, DRINK THE FRUIT OF THE VINE: DRINK WINE FROM THE CUP OF LIFE! *And forgive us our sins as we forgive those that sin against us: let us not fall to temptation, but help us to deliver ourselves from the Evil Ones that falsely rule this world.* CHILD, TAKE THIS STAFF, DRINK FROM THIS GRAIL, COME TO THIS PLACE OF THE STONE! TAKE SHAPE AND FORM IN THE FLESH! MANIFEST YOURSELF, LET YOUR FATHER LEAD YOU OUT INTO THE LIGHT OF DAY! *For Thine is the Kingdom, the Power and the Glory, and Christ the Bread and Wine of it, for ever and ever, Amen!* JOANA! HEAR THE SONG! HEAR THE WORD OF LIFE! JOANA! COME TO ME NOW!'

Over and over he called without any response. Yet as he called a light began to glow, at first faint and uncertain, glimmering deep in crystalline veins embedded deep in the black rock of the walls. Gradually, like a host of fireflies vitalised by the intensity of his chant, this fine light began to dance out of the walls, vibrating ever more strongly and taking on an emerald hue as he continued his exhortation without slackening or pause, as if despite Herself She grew excited by the wilful energy he'd brought into Her secret place. Her walls began to throb and pulse, croon and sing, and this quickening of rock-life the goodman felt as a mounting flood of fire in his heart ... though, had he thought on it, he'd have known that it was beginning to drain him of life even as he extended the ever-brighter staff of his will more urgently. It was beginning to burn him up, yet he did not feel this immolation as an agony, for the fire of it was flowing through him, fuelling the flinging forth of his intention, increasing in him the single-pointedness of his concentration and taking him out of time.

And NOW he sees her!

He sees the lost, confused, blonde-haired girl!

He sees her plunging towards him, towards the staff he holds out!

He sees her in his mind's-eye as she plunges back towards time and flesh from the world of the aeons; he sees her desperate eyes fixed on his burning frame as she hunts for a firm grip on the world, and any weak self-consideration of pain that might be wailing in his flesh is absorbed in the cry he now sends out along the staff of his will (and now the staff of wood too) that he thrusts over the black pool, over the black isle amid it — and that's when he breaks his vow never to sing again until the war is won (yet maybe now the war *is* won) — for the voice of his will roars forth with all the love of life he ever expressed as a troubadour in his younger days: roars forth, echoing through that glowing, throbbing, enclosed subterranean space ... roars forth and bursts out into the wider realms beyond space and time and matter *(So that*

She, distant amid another crisis, is torn away from the glade, distracted from Hoel at the crucial moment, for THAT crucial moment marries THIS crucial moment: the synchronicity's precise) —

'HERE I AM! I AM FATHER BERNARD! TAKE THE STAFF I HOLD! DRINK THE WINE OF LIFE FROM THIS CUP! HEAR MY SONG AND TAKE FORM, FOR I AM HERE!'

A mighty rushing wind bursts into the grotto, and the goodman, like a parched husk yet unaware of it as he sings out joyfully again, opens his eyes to the blinding emerald light. The singing of the rock climaxes, the waters of the pool swirl from black to ruby, ruby to emerald ... and from emerald to scintillant diamond.

'COME, DAUGHTER! JOANA, RETURN! AEIOU! AEIOU! AEIOU!'

Then as he cries out, as She struggles to resist, the waters of the pool gather themselves up into a blinding vortex of light above the black isle, spinning round and round, whipped by the wind of the spirit pouring through the Gate into that tiny deep dark secret place. Now the extended tip of the staff burns in the vortex, and into the goodman pours a flood of images so intense and strange — images from the golden-haired child's own former world; images from the world of the aeons where the great grey ones glide silently through the emerald hall far below the eternal clouds that veil the superphysical light of the Emme Ya; images borne on the frontal wind of her approach — that, momentarily distracted, he almost loses concentration in the NOW. Yet clinging to the staff amid the flames he knows that NOW's the time to sing the Song of Joana again, and he does. '*Quant lo bouié ben de laura,*' he sings in a great voice as the vortex of diamond light spins ever faster, ever brighter; and in it NOW he sees, like a shadow thickening amid the light, taking slim and lissome shape yet ('*Planto soun agulhado ...*') twisted in serpentine agony, the body of the girl, his Daughter of the Gate. '*AEIOU! Aco's la paura Joana!*'

It was then, the far side of the teeth, that *She finds a way to attack* and then that Pierre Belot began to scream.

324

And then that the goodman, startled, lost his concentration.

The vortex with the girl's shape in it shivered, dulled, began to lose coherence ... and Her face appeared before him instead.

'*I won't have this! I don't want her here!*' Blood-red teeth glared out of that white, beautiful, deadly face. '*I warned you, Weak One! You break into My secret place and use it against Me! You don't understand, do you! But understand this: NOW you are going to die!*'

Then without warning the staff in Bernard's hand writhed, thickening instantly with a furious hiss. He found himself gripping not a staff but a black serpent. He gaped, utterly taken aback, as the snake twisted back at him, beady eyes gleaming, poison fangs gaping ... and in those eyes he saw his death and failure, *and so does She, for She shrieks with triumph, but even as She does* ...

'*What's this?*' *She cries, snatched away from the Gate of the Stone and returning to the glade in the grove just as* ...

With a wild, sorrowing cry Hoel struck down.

'One strike for two lives!' he howled at Ailma's opened eyes.

Then Ailma smiled, but not for him ... and even as Hoel struck, the spear in his hand writhed and came to life along its length, thickening instantly with a furious hiss. With the speed of a lightning flash it doubled back on itself and bit the hand that held its scaly, lashing tail. Hoel cried out more in shock and outrage than pain or fear; he dropped the serpent and it returned to a spear even as Shem, oblivious of the attack amid the heat of his rut, climaxed with a huge grunt. And the flood of his coming swept him away even as Ailma took his seed in a spasm so intense it threatened to break her back in two. Then Hoel, realising he'd lost everything, threw himself on them, beating on Shem's back with his fists and crying out in a demented voice. An instant later the Wild Women, taken by surprise by the speed and ferocity of his attack ... and also by Her extraordinary failure to control him ... converged from the trees to attack and drag him off, drowning his cries with their own horrible lusting clamour — all nine of them, naked and filthy with sharp nails and teeth, mud-caked hair swinging from wizened heads in ropes like writhing snakes. There was no stopping them. If angry they'd been before, now they were doubly furious because he'd caught them so unawares. They swarmed over the doomed man ... *as, in a state of frenzy and fearful fury, She flies back to the Gate of the Stone to hear* ...

'OUR FATHER, WHICH ART IN HEAVEN!' Bernard roared, given respite by Her distraction, driving out his will again so that the serpent shuddered back into a straight rod as beyond Her teeth the demented shepherd continued to scream, 'HALLOWED BE THY NAME!'

'*You criminal fool!*' She shrieks, '*You don't know what you're ...*'

'THY KINGDOM COME, BRINGING THE SALVATION OF CHRIST TO THE PURE ONES!'

'*Those you call "Father" betrayed and imprisoned Me! Think they care about you stupid Lullu? Deny Me and the Shift will ...*'

'THY WILL BE FULFILLED ON EARTH IN THE CHRIST, FOR HE SAID ...'

The grotto began to shake; again the goodman's will was diverted as a rock plunged down from the dark heights above, narrowly missing him and smashing to pieces beside him. '*Why should I be invaded in My own place?*' She cries, writhing about him in a multitude of frenzied, revolting forms. '*How dare you tear Me away from My business?*' Another rock plunged down; now the vortex was falling apart in a chaos of pulsating bloody worm-like lights; the girl within mouthing desperately as she dissolved ... and even as he lost her hold on form he heard her desperate cry:

'THE SONG! SING THE SONG! SHE CAN'T FIGHT TWO WARS AT ONCE!'

28.
Hoel's Passion

For as the unformed one plunges through the fields of light, hunting the Song to guide it home, it remains unearthed: its vision embracing not only the Gate of the Stone but the entire hidden world floating below in glories of green and blue through time. Struggling for firm anchorage in gravity the entity is drawn to the glade, and THERE! 'It's Sam!' cries a terrified voice as the thin naked man stirs from the girl below him to gape at the hags swarming over the youth, to gape up at the sky. 'That's Dad!' 'Chrissa?' he mouths — but suddenly then the entity senses She who watches over the murder. Nausea! Confusion! The Enemy! Fear and double vision strike: it struggles in the vortex, for the Enemy's there ... and here too. Serpent there, serpent here: She curses Hoel, She curses Father Bernard, and Her counter-attack is succeeding; the vortex begins to fall apart even as the entity understands how She's divided. The pain of the dissolution is dreadful! Writhing half-formed amid the bloody worms of light the entity desperately mouths advice as its hard-won form dissolves:

'THE SONG! SING THE SONG! SHE CAN'T FIGHT TWO WARS AT ONCE!'

And with his senses leaving him as the entire grotto rocked and swayed amid the howl of green light Bernard heard this distant cry; he fought to retain the staff of his will; he fought for calmness and concentration; he fought

327

for the girl, for the Song, for his voice; and he sang — *he sings* —

> '*Lo cap jous la canelo*
> *tots los romieus que passaran*
> *Prendran aigo senhado . . .*'

— weakly at first, but steadying and strengthening as the vortex begins to regain coherence, and She wails in fury as he sings on —

> '*Prendran aigo senhado*
> *E diran: que es morto ayssi*
> *Aco's la paura JOANA . . .*'

— though NOW nothing's left of him but the Song and his staff that he reaches out to the girl in the vortex; and as he cries out the name JOANA her shape grows stronger, firmer, brighter. Then in desolation like a bird of black night She screeches; great dark wings beat at his face, but now his vision is clear and still he sings —

> '*Que n'es anado al paradis*
> *Al ceu ambe sas crabos*
> *AEIOU!*'

— and with the explosive sound of these vowels the diamond light bursts like a star, banishing the night, filling the grotto with the radiance of the heavens. Briefly, with a furious cry, She writhes before him in weak and shadowy forms to which he pays no heed, still extending his staff into the shining vortex from which, in a jerkily unsure motion, the now solid shape of the golden girl stretches a white, tentative hand. 'COME NOW, JOANA!' the goodman roars. 'TAKE HOLD OF THE STAFF AND JOIN THE LIVING!'

And she does.

With her face as blank and bright as primal creation she seizes the end of the staff in both flesh-and-blood hands as the goodman pulls; she comes staggering out of the vortex, off the black isle at the centre of the pool, her mad imploring eyes fixed on the burning man's face as with the last of his strength Bernard exerts himself. With a wail of huge lamentation She abandons Her opposition *and spins in confusion back to the glade in the grove even as Hoel, spear cast aside, falls under the Wild Women,* even as a spear of fire pierces the goodman's heart and he falls in a dead faint.

Yet even as all strength deserted him the girl came stumbling from the pool, screaming in pain as she pulled herself hand over hand up the staff that still, in his unconsciousness, the goodman held. Reaching him where he lay, she seized the solid flesh and bone of his fist. A groan of relief escaped her; her face relaxed at last as she collapsed beside him.

The shining light ebbed, the singing ceased, the vortex dissolved. Again the grotto was dark and still and silent ... save for the whimpering of Pierre Belot, frozen on hands and knees the far side of Her teeth ...

And the Old Mother made herself watch it all from the edge of the green and sun-drenched glade, her face like a mask of stone.

'I'll see how the Furies of Her Fate deal with you, Hoel-who-was-son-of-my-clan,' Riann said in a precise, formal, and utterly empty voice as the Wild Women, howling in blood-mad glee, dragged Hoel away from the two spent, motionless lovers and set to work with their natural knives, tearing the clothes from his body with tooth and nail. She saw how for a while Hoel struggled and screamed ... but soon he stopped screaming and went limp, and Riann knew he'd given up. He was as good as dead already. 'Now I will see what they do to you and I'll not forget it until I die, and maybe not even then,' she went on in that empty voice. 'We all share in your fate and your fault, I most of all. No doubt it must be done, and now through Her creatures She does it!' A bitterness entered her voice. 'Hasn't She done it often enough since

Her spirit grew bleak and cruel with wars of flesh against the Ancient Ones? Since She came and dragged us here? Who knows, Hoel! Maybe this'll bring you to what you want — a world ruled by men! You poor fool! Yet if so, Hoel-who-was-son-of-my-clan, remember compassion. You're trampled now because you wished to trample!'

If Hoel heard her, he gave no sign. He was in no position to do so. And Riann found it hard to acknowledge the flicker of hate she felt when Shem rolled off Ailma and the girl at last stirred, her face transfigured.

'You goaded him!' Riann cried. 'Couldn't you smile on him just once?'

In confusion Ailma looked for the source of the voice ... and then, very slowly, she realised what was happening. Only feet from where she'd received Fool's seed the Wild Women swarmed over Hoel like a pack of wolves, snarling and tearing with long razor-sharp nails. And with Shem still gazing vaguely about, her hand shot to her mouth, her face suffused with shame and horror as the Wild Women, finding their rhythm, began the keening of their work-song:

> 'First the balls, and then the prick!
> Soft parts first — that's the trick!
> Then cut and slice till what we've got
> Is meat well-diced and fit for pot!'

At Ailma's scream Shem sat up and stared, stupefied, for now the hags were working faster, their bony long fingers already well bloodied:

> 'We'll boil the head and stew the heart,
> Then throw the dogs the stringy parts!
> And when we're done with eating Hoel
> We'll thank him for his tasty soul!'

It was then that Hoel, the sun still being long short of noon, began screaming again, and Ailma buried herself in Shem's arms, hiding her face, but Shem had no idea what to do as the Wild Women went on screeching:

> *'Last the bones we'll suck and lick*
> *Then toss them as foretelling sticks!*
> *We'll prod the liver, scan the lot*
> *And see just what the future's got!'*

What? Shem asked silently, gazing at Ailma's half-hidden face as a terrified voice cried out in him: *'It's Sam! That's Dad!'* And again he looked up at the blue sky as if expecting blue eyes to look down at him. But I turned the key! he told himself, utterly bewildered, gazing back at the drawn-out murder. This body I hold I fill with life, and there they tear life from the body from another ... *man*? Is that a man?

In his confusion he felt the welling-up in him of a sudden pitying tenderness that wet his eyes and had him hugging Ailma clumsily closer. But her eyes were bright and dry as she clung to him. She couldn't look, but it didn't stop her hearing. This is Hoel who dies in agony for lack of my smile! she knew, appalled. Yes, he threatened me, but ... would one smile have cost me so much? What now? *I* deserve to die for this!

Blindly she lifted her head, and over the keening of the hags and the screaming of Hoel she cried: 'Old Mother, did I really do Her will in this? What if Her will is evil?'

And the perfumed breeze whispered through the boughs above Riann's head as the Old Mother, the stone of her heart quite crumbled now, cried back in a broken voice: 'Daughter, you have done Her will!. There's no blame on you for that!'

'Quite correct, Riann,' said a dry, light voice behind her. 'But how and why did you reach the conclusion that I wanted my taboo broken?'

Riann gasped. Instinctively, knowing better than to look up, she sank to her knees and buried her face in the mossy loam. To see the blinding brightness of Her face when She wasn't wearing a mask was usually fatal, even for the strongest, and who knew if She was wearing Her mask now? She has more on Her mind than our safety! Riann told herself with angry irony.

'Also correct!' came Her flat response. 'Your distress is very human, but you still haven't answered My question!'

Hoel was screaming in long cries that trailed off into choking gasps then started again ... and again ... and again ...

'Taboos on youthful nature are bound to be broken,' Riann muttered. 'And the instructions You gave me make it plain You planned all this.'

'Correct again!' But She sounded unaccountably weary. 'Riann, I'm not wearing the mask that protects you Lullu. Now turn and look at Me.'

So I'm to die with Hoel? I'm glad! Riann thought without disguise. Lady, I've seen enough of this. I've done all You asked ... now You'll blind me and kill me with the sight of You? So be it.

She said nothing as Riann slowly turned, but stood waiting as the Old Mother's gaze travelled inch-by-inch up the great height of Her, from Her sandalled feet to Her multi-coloured gown made from the feathers of many birds: hoopoe and golden oriole, kingfisher and green woodpecker, grebe, ruff, redshank and bullfinch; from the sparkling emerald ring on Her hand and up the folds of Her over-mantle, dark as night and embroidered with stars and the horned moon, to the mantle's knot on Her left shoulder onto which tumbled tapering ringlets of Her lustrous raven-black hair ... then at last to Her dazzlingly beautiful ... *but no longer blinding* ... face.

So for the first and last time in her life the Old Mother gaped at the naked face of She who controlled their destiny, and the Lady stared down with ironic sadness, and weariness and fury were there too, but these were not easily read in a face still too bright to look upon easily.

'Lady,' Riann stuttered, transfixed, 'what ... what has ... happened?'

'I've been in a battle that — I lost, Old Mother!' She

said, Her voice dragging under the new weight of time and thickness fallen upon Her since the Weak One had driven Her from Her own Gate. Her eyes flashed to realise how complacent She'd been. Or is it that I forgot too much? She wondered uneasily. I chose to think the Weak Ones weak! I forgot how the Elohim help them! She heaved a sigh, feeling dense new Lullu-emotions — pain and doubt, fear and regret — crowding Her as the wrinkled Old Mother gazed up, her look slack and amazed. Grimly She laughed. 'Yes, Old Mother, I lost a battle, but not the war — not yet!' Tight-lipped She eyed Hoel's agony, She saw Shem and Ailma clinging together, and the sight of Her awakened Fool awoke Her old power. Her eyes flashed with hope, and Riann, still staring at the shining, beautiful melancholy of Her face, was stabbed to the heart by lightnings; by visions of deep starry spaces flickering with blinding shifts of fire and night; of wailing golden faces plunging from fields of light into lurid burning depths. Quickly, gasping, she tore her gaze away and She laughed. 'That's right! Don't look too much, I'm not so weak yet! My Fool's awake, he'll fire Me, I'll carry out the plan! The war will be won, Riann! The Weak Ones won a skirmish but they won't stop me! When the Sometimes Isle rises again I'll be ready! — but you don't need to know about that!' Angrily She gestured at the glade, at Hoel. 'I know you think Me cruel, Old Mother, but I assure you it's necessary!'

'But why?' Riann asked dully, again wishing to be dead.

'Because there's no alternative!' She declared in an iron-hard voice. 'Hoel made his choice; his agony's potent; it'll take him where he wants to go; to the time of men who deny Me as if I never was! In a way it's My weakness that he comes to this, for when I shone bright he'd have loved Me! Now he dissents, and from his pain will grow ugly thoughts and deeds that should never grow in any garden — a time when men, denying all sense, will bring on the Shift again. Disaster for us all! Yet from those Last Days I've plucked one man in the flesh — one

333

man who remembers Me! — and there he is! My Fool who returns to life through the body of your daughter even as Hoel goes to death through his desire for your daughter!'

'And what of Ailma?' Riann demanded bitterly. 'Does she die too?'

'You think me so cruel?' She murmured. 'No, Riann. Ailma bears hope for the future; I bless and protect her.' Saying this She turned away, the trees sighing as Riann felt a huge weariness creep over her. 'Ailma must go away to bear the child, and you'll go with her,' She declared. 'The clan has served its purpose. From now on you people must choose your own gods. But you must disperse. You can't stay here any longer. My final order is that you leave today.'

So you abandon us? thought Riann, but then sleep took her: she slumped to the ground as the Lady left her, and never saw what happened next ...

Unmasked She entered the glade. The Wild Women fell back from their work as Her blood-sweet perfume touched them. Wonderingly Shem looked up; he saw Her tall and bright in Her gorgeous robe, the ring of moon and horns on Her finger ... and at the sight of it his mouth fell open in amazement. Memory-bees stung him, and doubts he could not quite touch as She smiled on him with Her beauty. But Ailma, sensing a horror behind that human form She wore, hid her face as She came to where Hoel lay, still alive in the bloody ruin of his dissected body. From Her height She looked down at him, and he, with the one eye left in the flayed mess of his face, looked up.

Through bloody veils of pain he saw a great red bird of prey, its eyes like spears, blood dripping from its talons and soaking its feathers.

'So you're cut down to size, eh?' Her voice blazed in him. 'Just as you'd cut down My woods! Well, you'll get your chance, Hoel! You'll go to your *Unknown God* and in due course return in your man-time ... but your hate will keep destroying you until you learn better. That's one curse on you. The other is that you'll serve Me without knowing it!' Silently She added: *Go, destroy those Weak Ones who resist Me!* Sharply she gestured at the Wild Women. 'Finish him off! Quickly!' They hissed with disappointment at having their sport cut short. 'Do as I say!' She cried, eyes flaming with Her old power, and they fell back in consternation. 'And no cooking until tonight, and then only in a dark place. Do you want the sun to see too much? Now kill him, and take him, and go!'

They went for his throat even as his ruined mouth moved.

'Ail ... ma,' he croaked, barely audible, 'we ... will ... meet ...'

They tore his throat out. His voice and his life both ended in a gargle of blood. His body bucked, his heels drummed the ground as Ailma screamed. At last, mercifully, he lay still. So Hoel went to his Unknown God as the Wild Women, jabbering, dragged his twitching carcass away. And then, wearily sensing that this victory hardly outweighed the defeat She'd suffered in the grotto, painfully suspecting that the golden-haired child brought down from the world of the aeons would come to plague Her yet, She turned to Ailma ... and to Shem, Her Fool, Samjoyce from the Last Days ...

29.
Out of Darkness

A new dawn, white and clear and calm, came to the mountains.

It was the morning of the Feast of Candlemas, but few were up or about yet in the town of Tarascon-sur-Ariège as the black friar Brother Jean d'Aubigny cautiously emerged from the hillside Chapel of Sabart, his dark face tight with anger. He'd spent all night on his knees in prayer, not so much through love of prayer as fear of sleep, for lately the nights had been worse than ever. Now, before showing himself to the world, he looked this way and that, and only when he was sure nobody was about did he turn and beckon peremptorily. 'Very well,' he told the burly, frightened man who emerged behind him, 'but make sure nobody sees you on your way home, and never seek me out like this again! What use are you to us if the heretics find you out and kill you? Go, and God be with you!'

Scowling, he watched until his informer was out of sight along the track towards Ussat and the caves in the hill above it. Then, turning in the opposite direction, he strode along the riverbank into Tarascon. The morning was freezing, but he was hot with wrath and anxiety. Without any slackening of pace he passed smithies and shuttered windows and came to the centre of town where, near the river bridge, he rapped the bailiff's door.

An old woman opened it an inch; he pushed it wide and forced her back against the wall as he strode in. 'Where's Arnaud Lizier?' he demanded loudly, and her eyes flicked nervously up the stairs of the imposing two-storeyed house. 'But, sir, he's ...'

Without another word he elbowed her aside and took the stairs two at a time. The anger in him went deeper than he could understand. He came to the bailiff's bed-room. Without knocking he opened the door with a crash and went straight in. The room was dark, silent but for muffled snores. With a bang the friar threw open the shutters. Cold air rushed in through the unpaned windows. He turned and shook the bedstead, and two startled heads shot up from under the covers where, a moment earlier, their owners had been happily, exhaust-edly asleep.

'Now I have proof that all your men are heretics!' the friar snapped, grey eyes alight with triumphant fury. 'Or at least that they aid heretics, which in the eyes of Holy Mother Church is the same thing!'

Angry and embarassed, Arnaud Lizier the bailiff sat up in bed. A sharp little man with slick black hair, he tried and failed to stare down his unwelcome visitor. 'How dare you!' he spluttered ... but the friar cut him off with grim satisfaction.

'Never mind that.' Brother Jean gestured. 'Get her out of here.'

The bailiff fought to control himself. In my own bedroom! But the Inquisition was something new, and there was no telling how far it would spread. He shrugged. 'Go on, lambkin,' he whispered apologetically, and the scared girl shot naked out of bed, rubbing her eyes as she did, making no effort to cover herself up. Scowling, Brother Jean crossed himself.

The women are the worst! he told himself, trying yet failing to forget the terrible dreams which had driven him out of sleep to spend his night in prayer. Them and their sly, sinuous ways! But we'll get them all in their place!

A.—15　　　　337

And as the terrified girl fled past him to her gown, her green gown that lay rumpled on an oak chest under the window, he grabbed her plump arm and held her, hard. She gasped and stood shivering, eyes averted.

The bailiff bared his teeth in anger but said nothing.

'Look at me, girl! What's your name?'

'Helis, sir.' She didn't meet his eye. Of course not! he told himself contemptuously. None of them can. Satan owns them all.

'You're a good Christian, are you, Helis?'

'I do try, sir. Please ... you're hurting me!'

'Dress and get out!' he snapped, disgusted as he let her go, eyeing the marks his fingers had left on her flesh. Red marks. Burning marks. And as she struggled into her gown he felt a weary excitement, a pressure in his groin. He didn't take his eyes from her until she'd run from the room.

Expressionless, Lizier asked: 'What do you want?'

You heretic! thought the friar, his composure returning. With a slight smile he stared out of the window at the high white hills as the bailiff clambered out of bed into a fine fur-trimmed robe. 'Yesterday on the Ussat road,' he said in a clipped voice, 'your men stopped me questioning an old man disguised as a shepherd. I saw through him, but they made my holy task impossible. Now ...' — he paused, turning to eye the bailiff — 'Now I hear that the heretic *parfait* Bernard de Laurac was seen in Ussat. Yesterday.' He smiled. 'What do you say to that?'

'Really?' Lizier, who'd already heard all about it from the sergeant, sounded amazed. 'Who told you that?'

'Never mind. The point is, your men obstructed God's justice.'

'Impossible!' On his feet now, the bailiff laughed disbelievingly. Who's the bastard informer? he wondered fiercely. 'How can you be so sure that this old man you met was really Bernard de ... what was it?'

'Laurac.' Languidly the friar turned from his inspection of the snowbound hills in which heretics hid. 'You don't fool me for a moment,' he said conversationally.

338

'Neither do your men. You're all tainted. I'd have had him ... for everyone knows these so-called "goodmen" cannot lie even to save their own lives, since they're all infected with Satan's pride, but before I could make him answer my questions his companion turned up with a lot of evil lies ... and *your* men took the opportunity to desert me. And so ...' — with a cold smile he shrugged — '... two heretics escaped.'

'I'm sure,' Arnaud, began, 'my men didn't realise who ...'

The friar closed his eyes. God give me strength!

'You must realise,' he interrupted softly, 'that now this entire land, and the bodies and souls of everyone in it, has been reclaimed not only by Holy Mother Church but also by the Kingdom of France. You, my friend, are a sworn servant of the Count of Foix, who in turn is a vassal of the king. If you and your men continue to obstruct me, then you are guilty not only of heresey but also of treason. You *do* see your position ... don't you?'

'It's early in the day to be talking politics,' said Arnaud, and very reluctantly he added, 'but yes, yes, I understand.'

'Good.' Brother Jean turned on his heel. 'Call your sergeant. Tell him I wasn't fooled. I know he knew the heretics. Tell him that in one hour I'll be waiting on the bridge. We'll ride out, and we won't return until we have this Bernard de Laurac and his companion safe in custody. And if by any *chance* ...' — he paused to stare hard at the bailiff — '... we should return empty-handed, then I'll have to report to my superiors that the bailiff and sergeant of the guard in Tarascon are unreliable and should be summoned to undergo ... appropriate procedures. Am I clear?'

'Yes, yes,' agreed Arnaud sincerely. 'Perfectly clear.'

Brother Jean left the bailiff's house. In the early morning sunlight he leaned over the bridge, scowling at the icy fast river, clenching his teeth against his fear of the dream which from infancy had terrified him with its bloody agony, its weight of sin. Not love of God but this dream had brought him to these ascetic rigours in the safe bosom of the Church, persecuting heretics, spending bare-kneed nights on chill damp flagstoned floors as far as could be from the deadly delights of women, of soft green grass and sweet woods in the springtime ... the dream he felt torturing him now. And suddenly as he glared at the river he gasped, shutting his eyes tight in agony, and in his flayed mind he focused on visions of multitudes of women burning alive ... for this was his only antidote to the dream ... the waking dream, bending him over the bridge in distress, of nine howling hags dissecting his living body with their teeth and nails.

An hour later, the sun bright, the guard rode out again. And about that same time Pierre Belot began to recover his wits.

Very gradually, frozen stiff and still crouching on hands and knees in the pitch blackness, the shepherd swam out of the panic which had seized him. At first he had no memory and his surroundings made no sense: he thought himself asleep in the cabane above Flix, caught in some nightmare of being buried alive. I'll wake up soon! he told himself uncertainly. But bit by bit it came back to him, and with it came the horror, and he began to weep as with clumsy fingers he felt the tight enclosing walls on every side, as he remembered that dreadful giant red woman and the green scream with which she'd devoured him. Merciful God! he cried silently. How can I still be alive? I'm here! I really am here! Trapped! How can I get out? I can't even turn around! I'M DEAD!

You cowardly idiot! a voice in him scolded. What do you mean, you're dead? How can you be scared if you're dead! She didn't kill you! If she had, you wouldn't be snivelling here! You behaved like a child! And what about the goodman? What happened to him?

His head felt like a tub of mud. Groggily he tried to remember. Yes! That glaring light, the screaming vibration ... and the goodman, singing the Song of Joana amid the intolerable brightness flooding through the thighs of the demon-woman! Then I started screaming, he realised in shame. I lost my mind to the phantoms! But how long? And what . . .?

Laboriously in the dark, achieving a sitting position, he plucked the half-burned brand from his belt. From his pouch he took tinder and flint. After many attempts he struck fire and lit the brand. Before his face he held the guttering, smoky flame . . . and again he saw Her, glaring at him.

Gasping with fear, he shut his eyes. Nothing happened. At length he opened his eyes again. She hadn't moved. She just squatted there with her massive red thighs wide open. Slowly he realised it was no living being he faced, but a painting as crude as those on the walls outside the maze. Yet the teeth ringing the hole — the gate — weren't painted. They were solid, real, carved from stone . . . or were they? Wriggling closer he touched one of them gingerly. No, not stone! More like boar's tusk! he realised. So, shakily lifting the torch, he peered past the teeth into what lay beyond.

There! He saw a . . . a *body*? It lay huddled on a dark slope below him, curled up at the dimly-reflective edge of what perhaps was a pool of water.

Panting, he sought courage to pass the fanged door. At last, ready to make his move, he was about to grasp one of the teeth to help him over — one that lay askew, at an odd angle — when a voice in him whispered: *No! Don't touch it, Pierre!* And dimly into his mind came the sense of a . . . of a *machine* — something men had made to protect this place, a device to kill those who touched it wrong.

Holding his breath, he crabbed himself over the teeth inches at a time, torch in right hand as he scrabbled for firm footing on the slippery slope the far side. At last, safely over, he crouched in the grotto, so stiff it took him a painful time to straighten up. Then he turned nervously to the somehow-too-bulky shape huddled below him at the edge of the pool. Blood-red torchlight danced on still water as he squinted fearfully.

Is he dead? He can't be! But . . . he has too many legs!

341

Swallowing hard, he fought his horror. He made himself approach close enough to see that he stood above not one body, but two.

With a terrified hiss he drew in his breath.

'*Her! His child! She's real!*'

Like a dead white fish she lay curled on her side, hair like a seaweed shawl over face and shoulders, knee of one leg tucked under her chin, foot of the other trailing in water. Both her hands tightly clutched Bernard's right fist, itself tight around his staff, which also trailed in the black pool. For he too lay curled up and unmoving, seeming oddly shrunk in the flickering light, his face a pale, agonised mask, teeth bared, eyes sunken and shut. He looked as if his life had been sucked out. Pierre's heart pounded. He got laboriously down on his knees and put his ear to Bernard's chest ... and then sighed in relief.

'His heart still beats,' he assured himself.

Carefully he took the goodman's shoulders and shook him.

Bernard did not stir. Neither did the girl.

'Don't panic!' Pierre commanded himself. 'It's up to you now.'

Wet his lips with water! said the voice in him.

Setting the brand upright in a crack of rock, he dipped cupped palms into the black pool ... and flinched, for a shock ran through his hand and up his arm as if a bee had stung him.

'Again!' he told himself harshly. And this time the shock was less. But his hands trembled and seemed to burn as he carried water to Bernard and carefully sprinkled those bloodless lips with it.

The goodman's head jerked slightly, but his eyes did not open.

Pierre sprinkled a little more water onto his mouth. And this time Bernard groaned. And when his mouth was sprinkled a third time, his eyes fluttered briefly open, but the spirit in them was faint. So gently the shepherd (his eyes continually straying to the impossible shape of the impossible golden-haired girl) shook him, whispering

342

his name over and over again until at length the goodman
groaned again, and shifted slightly, moving his head. His
cracked, bloodless lips moved too.

'What ...?' he muttered soundlessly.

'It's I! Pierre! Goodman, wake up! The girl's here!'

Time passed. Then Bernard rasped, hoarse and dry:

'You ... shepherd? Did I hear you?'

'Yes! Yes!' Tears welled from Pierre's eyes.

'She's here? In flesh ... and blood?'

'Yes! Can't you feel her hands on yours?'

'You ... disobeyed me!' the goodman croaked.

'Of course I did!' said Pierre joyfully. 'But ...'

'Just as well.' Gradually, as weak and dry as an
autumn leaf, Bernard returned from the furnace. He
opened his eyes, but all he saw was dazzling fire. There
was no moisture in him; his thirst was enormous, he
panted and gasped as Pierre cupped water to his dribbl-
ing mouth ... and only then he saw how his clenched
right fist was held by two smaller hands. 'Shepherd, lift
my head ... shed light!' he muttered in awe. Pierre did it.
And the two of them regarded the girl's curled-up body
in mutual amazement.

'I didn't believe you,' Pierre admitted. 'Is she ... like
us?'

'Enough like us so that ...' — Bernard shut his eyes,
dizzy with trying to think — '... if she's not fed soon, and
clothed for warmth ... she'll die.' Sadly, recalling his vow
never again to touch female flesh, he prised his hand from
her grip and raised himself on an elbow. In her unconsciousness she moaned as he said with arduous clarity:
'Shepherd, you nearly ruined it by screaming ... but now
you're her only hope. Forget me and get her out of here!
I sent word to Montségur, they'll have men out looking.
Get her to Bishop Guilhabert because he'll ...'

'I'm not leaving you,' said Pierre flatly.

'You'll do as I say!' Bernard barked.

'No.' Pierre shook his head. With no idea how, he
said: 'I'll get her out of the maze and wrap her up warm,
then I'll be back for you.' Bernard began to protest, but

the shepherd said rudely, 'Don't argue! You may be wise and holy, but you're just a man like me, and for once *you* will do as *I* say!' He grinned, hugging himself in terror and delight, rocking on his heels. 'I *told* you: you can't do without me!'

'Very well, shepherd.' Bernard fell back. 'The Shining Ones ... with their help you'll get us out. But ...' — he sighed in exhaustion — '... as you go, please don't touch those teeth at the door ... if you do, Her mouth will shut on us and never let us out. Then the Stone *is* lost!'

'A voice warned me about that as I came through,' said Pierre.

'Oh?' Bernard relaxed. 'Now I know we'll succeed.'

The girl groaned, shifted, mumbled in an unknown language as her hands, seeking something to grasp, found the goodman's staff. And with a pitiful whimper she wrapped her body round it. Both men stared.

'But *who* is she?' asked Pierre, wanting to weep again.

'Joana.' Closing his eyes again, the goodman smiled slightly. 'Or so I'll think of her. Shepherd, I know little more than you ... but God willing we'll learn more ... if only we can get out of here.' Strenuously he fought to sit up. 'Maybe you won't have to come back!' he grunted, his will to fight beginning to return. 'Have you any bread?'

'Yes.' From his pouch Pierre fished half the loaf Bernard had given him ... so long ago. The goodman took it, blessed it and began eating with difficulty, needing copious draughts of water to get the dry stuff down.

But eat he did, slowly, deliberately, with relish.

Pierre grinned. 'I thought you said you had no more need of earthly bread!' he said impishly. 'You said you have food to eat that I know nothing about! Clearly it's not true!'

'Be quiet!' said Bernard grumpily. 'Just let me eat in peace!'

When he'd eaten every last crumb he had strength enough to stand, at first with Pierre's help, then without. Without speech they removed their jerkins and wrapped them round the unconscious girl, securing the wrapping with their belts. Then they left that dreadful place.

She dreams.

She dreams without memory, without knowledge of herself.

She dreams of falling. Fallingfallingfalling. A bright place flashing by, great voices booming amid shining fields of light, a pandemonium of falling from the bright place to a dark place, a terrible crushing place where everything burns, everything hurts, so now everything's forgotten but the pain of bright and dark amid the dream of a strong rough-smelling man (Not my FATHER, not my FATHER! a voice insists incomprehensibly) who carries her on his back through interminable underground passageways. Yet even as she's jolted closer to realising that in this dream she's imbedded and embodied, she keeps hearing voices of whatever's forgotten:

('Chrissa!' screams one. 'Come back! Come back now!')

('Dad, wait for me!' cries another. 'We have to talk!')

('Why should I wait?' calls a third. 'I've waited too long already! Now I'm going home at last!')

There are faces too. Many faces, men and women and other beings (some bright, some dark, some both), drifting, shifting, swimming together from landscapes of utter desolation to sweet fresh gardens. Peaceful she floats before an emerald set in a coral wall; its bright depths carry her into a warm green place, some-how familiar ... and there, the thin dark man with the scarred face, and a golden-haired girl asleep on bloodstained grass ... and another one, THE other one, SHE in the gorgeous feathered robe, a stolen fragment of the emerald on Her finger, human but not human, for Her face and body drip red, Her legs are hairy, Her feet are webbed like those of a goose. Sensing her watching She glares with eyes that freeze, so that on the back of the man who carries her through the darkness she writhes in fear ... and in her dream she cries out to that thin dark man:

'Dad?' she cries. 'Remember me? Chrissa? Dad, it's not all lost! The Shining Ones will help, so don't let Her use you or fool you!'

Then dark, furious wings beat her away and set her shrieking, twisting in her sleep, so that amid a wet splashing commotion the man carrying her curses as he nearly drops her; she shudders in her

soaked confusion. Then by firelight she sees an old man, his face
shining wet, wild, yet gentle, and she sighs, knowing with him
she's safe. 'Father,' she mumbles, 'Father Bernard!' Gasping, he
splutters words she doesn't know, but his voice is kind, and she
relaxes back to deep sleep.

Later, suddenly, light invades and overcomes the dark.
Wondering, she opens her eyes to see faces too brilliant to look up
at, in particular the dazzling countenance of a Shining One.
'WHO ARE WE?' this being asks, and in her sleep she murmurs,
'SHINING ONES.' She feels a cool, healing touch of fingertips on
her forehead, 'YOU'RE SAFE WITH FRIENDS NOW,' murmurs the
voice, 'YOU'LL WORK TO REMEMBER WHAT'S FORGOTTEN.'

Then in a rush of white wings the Song pours through her,
stirring her from sleep, so that she opened her eyes and
looked up, her vision blurred, past two faces, past snow-
laden trees to a pale blue winter sky, cloudless, infinite. A
deep voice spoke from one of the indistinct faces; from the
other face (equally vague) came (but so faint!) the voice of
the kind old man who'd sung the Song when she was lost.
'Father Bernard!' she murmured, smiling sleepily at the
delight in his voice. But the other man didn't sound so
happy. She heard argument. She heard an animal bray-
ing. Then a horn sounded, distant, peremptory ... and
life became confusion again ...

Their escape taxed Pierre to the utmost. Alone he got the
girl over Her teeth, then cut rope to pull her after him
through the maze, Bernard crawling behind and cradling
her head with shaking hands. Inch by arduous inch they
tracked their way through the maze towards the place of
painted walls, and at last emerged from the dreadful
wormhole. With a gasp Pierre dropped from the ledge
and heaved the girl gently down after him on his broad
shoulders. They rested. Then, wrapping her in the cloak
Bernard had begged off Sicard, Pierre heaved the unconscious girl onto his back.

He endured it. For unknown hours, sobbing with
effort, he carried the girl, supported Bernard, and tracked
the symbol of cross-in-circle, cup and dove. From the

place of painted walls he trudged up dripping narrow ways to the lake where blind life ate itself; there Bernard stumbled and nearly drowned. At this the girl writhed and shrieked in a dream-fright so fierce he almost dropped her. Cursing with exhaustion, seizing Bernard, somehow he got them both to shore: there Bernard, still spluttering, took the torch and stroked her brow; from her sleep she murmured his name. Too tired to be amazed, Pierre staggered sullenly on past slick mammoth rocks, through caves where calcite spears dripped from unseen ceilings, muttering how he was doing all the work and wasn't it his luck to be dragged away from the whores in Ax to find himself here with this bizarre female creature on his back! 'Am I just a beast of burden?' he mumbled resentfully, scenting her virgin sweetness, her lips against his neck. 'Is this punishment for my sins?' And as they reached the vast hall from which so many false trails diverged, Bernard kept quiet. We'd be dead if not for him, the goodman reminded himself, we'll die yet if he can't keep going.

Yet in time, the last brand spluttering and nearly out, they ascended a passage down which vague greyness came stealing. A dream! thought Pierre. But it strengthened. *Daylight!* Nervously he increased his pace ... and the moment came. Rounding a corner he saw, scant feet ahead, beyond the jagged bush-fringed cleft, the pale bright blue of a sunny sky. Crying with utter disbelief he staggered the last few paces, leaving the goodman behind as he burst into the living world and fell face-first into crisp white snow — so bright, so cold and pure! He let the girl roll off his back, buried his face in the snow, and wept. As the goodman tottered out Pierre rolled onto his back and lay with tears pouring down his face, gazing past snow-laden firs at the infinite mountain sky. Time passed before he remembered the other two. At last, grinning madly, he turned his head.

And was shocked by what he saw.

Bernard had aged since they'd left the light. His hair had turned as white as the snow; he looked desperately frail, his face cadaverous, eyes sunk deep in bony sockets with dark unhealthy circles round them.

But those eyes, gazing down on the face of the girl where she lay, were as tender as those of a newborn lamb, mild and full of love. He looks like a woman who's just given birth! Pierre thought amid his shock.

Weakly the goodman gazed up to meet the shepherd's troubled face.

'Look!' His old man's voice trembled. 'Pierre, my friend! Look!'

Pierre looked, and for the first time saw the girl clearly.

He saw a pale round face framed in a dishevelled tangle of golden hair. He saw half-open blue eyes — wondering, unfocused eyes gazing at the sky. Grimly he stroked his jaw, studying this child who'd arrived so strangely and caused so much trouble. She looks just like any other girl on the edge of maidenhood! he told himself, amazed by her lack of remarkable features. Two eyes, yes, and a nose, a mouth, a body about to bud; two hands with four fingers and thumb on each of them; two sturdy legs with five-toed feet — he felt almost cheated! But blue eyes and golden hair? German? Saxon? Certainly not from hereabouts. And wherever she's from she's never had to work. Look at that complexion! Those teeth! Those soft white hands! An angel maybe, but no peasant! She doesn't look to me like Joana, whatever the goodman thinks! She's never been near goats in her life!

Bewildered and unhappy he eyed the goodman.

'Whoever she is, I hope she's worth all this trouble,' he said without enthusiasm. 'If you could see yourself! I've seen corpses in better shape than you! Goodmen dead after weeks of the *endura* look healthier ...'

'But she *lives*!' Bernard's paper-thin voice was vibrant. 'That's what counts! God has blessed us! The Stone's not yet lost for ever!'

At his voice the girl, smiling sleepily, mumbled in her unknown tongue. In her mumbling the goodman's name was clearly audible, and Bernard clapped weakly, giving thanks to God. But Pierre scowled, feeling unaccountably jealous that the miracle-child smiled for the old man but not for him.

'I'm glad God's happy!' he said sharply. 'But what now?'

Bernard's eyes clouded. 'We get to Montségur soon, or she'll die.'

'And you?' Pierre stood. The effort made him dizzy.

'I keep telling you not to worry about me!'

'If I didn't, we'd never have got this far!'

Angrily Pierre stared through the trees and over the deep valley of the Ariège to the giant heights of Tabor that lay between them and Montségur.

How can we do it? he wondered, gazing at the distant snow-thick ridges. We're exhausted. I could sleep for a year.

Without looking down into the valley he began trudging heavily through the snow to the place he'd left the mules tethered. They'd been waiting over a day and a night; their fodder was long since gone, and now, at the approach of their provider, their hunger so excited them that one of them, lifting its head, burst its muzzle and let out a strident bray.

The sound echoed down the slopes to the riverside road far below.

The shepherd looked wildly down. And even as the lingering echoes of the mule's bray were stridently answered by the blast of a peremptory horn he saw the Enemy ... and the Enemy saw him ...

30.
High Places

So Hoel's carcass was dragged away but Shem gaped at Her as Ailma hid her face in terror against him. She was irritated to see them clinging to each other. 'Daughter,' She said as gently as She could, for She did not feel gentle, 'you've done My will. Sleep now. When you awake you'll leave this place and your clan; you'll go with the Old Mother among strangers to bear My Fool's fruit and keep My name alive. Now, sleep!'

Then Ailma, looking up, shrieked with horror, for above her she sensed no fine beautiful Lady of the Nine Heights, no protector of her clan, but something foul that aped human form; something red and writhing with no warmth or love in it at all. With her eyes tight shut she threw herself back into Shem's lap, hiding her face against him. Shem felt bewildered. Automatically he held her. Many different memory-bees were stinging him but none of them quite made sense, and his feelings were in a riot.

'Lady,' he started to protest.

'Quiet, Fool! Ailma, look at Me!'

Her eyes flashed angrily. Her finger shot out, pointing at the girl. A force she couldn't resist made Ailma raise her head. Fighting every inch she looked up ... into a glowing field of warm, soothing colours that filled her

350

with such a beautiful weariness that she yawned, smiled sleepily, and slumped back against Shem, unconscious already.

Disturbed, Shem gazed up at Her.

She sighed. Her shoulders slumped. I'm dizzy! She realised, appalled. I've used too much strength; I was never this weak before! Was I? And She laughed harshly. I can't even remember everything! Soon I'll be bound as thick and deep in time as the Lullu-That-Live-And-Die! Then what? But — and again She laughed without joy — of course I forget! I *knew* I'd forget, but I forget that too. That's why I planned all this. Fool, you bring Me what I need, the man-knowledge from the Last Days, the belief in Me that brings Me life again! And with fond, glowing eyes She studied him ... but then She frowned, for still he held the sleeping girl, and there was doubt in his gaze. 'Set her aside!' She gestured impatiently. 'We have no time for sentiment. Fool, you've awoken, and it took you long enough! We have battles behind us and battles before us, and you resisted My call until it was almost too late. Now set that girl aside!'

Slowly, reluctantly, he did as She told him.

'Do you know who I am?' she demanded, harsh with foreboding.

'My death and my life,' he whispered, dark face still dubious.

'Death of one. Life of many. And who are you?'

Perplexed, he eyed Her emerald ring.

'Fool, who *are* you?' She repeated.

'S-Sh ... Samjoyce?' he asked.

'Yes! Yes! Him! Who else?'

Clouding, his gaze strayed back to Ailma.

'Forget her! Who else are you?' She demanded, furious in Her anxiety. What if he can't remember and I can't either! 'How were you sent to the Last Days? How did we seed you into this ... this ... Samjoyce?'

Licking his lips he began to shiver, for above him now She swam in Her many forms, shining bright. But not as bright as She was before! a voice in him jeered, confusing

351

him, for *it's his voice, but a voice in him he's never known before
... or do I know it? Yes!* And the emerald on Her finger
sparkles before him, drawing him into its well-
remembered depths, into past and future, what was and
will be ... and amid a multitude of scenes spinning in his
mind there's one in particular demanding remembrance
... driving from London to Gairloch with the scorpion
ready to sting. *Remember that cavern under the whole place
where She led you? Yes, I do!* And for an instant he's there:
the box on the tripod astride the fuming chasm, and the
bells, and their beautiful, beautiful music. Lost in sadness
he lets the Volvo swerve, and in sudden shock he wakes
up to pull it back on course. *And do you recall what happened
next?* the familiar unknown voice demands. *The last part of
the rite by which we prepared this connection with you now?*

Shem gasped. *For there he stands on the Whole Place, the
Horned One rising as night falls on the deep woods and moun-
tains; there he is, facing the Red Woman, She naked but for
Blood of Mother, himself likewise but for the horns of Bull-That-
Roars! And no Weak Ones there to distract them as they couple,
fusing the seed that ensures the future and marries the past with
NOW — Serpent and Earth, Apple in Garden! yes, there he fills
Her Cup, Her Grail, Her Womb; they fling their will and prayer
through all the heights and depths to find this lost Sam-self, this
man of Last Days with his cock that crows, to steer it safe
through the gate, to fertilise ghosts back to flesh and recover
what's lost! But She demands more! He's seized by Her women,
dragged underground to the bottommost chamber where he heard
the bells. Up to the neck he's buried in the soft red earth ... then
they open the gates and ...*

THEY LET IT OUT AT ME! AND SHE WATCHED! LAUGHING!

In horror, lashing out desperately as if trapped, his
eyes bulging at the sight of the horned black bull charging him, Shem staggered to his feet and ran at Her in
wild-eyed fury. And only the steady coldness of Her gaze
stopped him from hitting Her. 'Now I remember!' he
howled, his entire body trembling. 'I remember, *My
Lady!* You had me gored to death! You watched! You
laughed!' He flung his arm at the bloody turf where Hoel

352

had been murdered. 'Even worse than it was for him —
that's what you did for me!'

'Not so!' She cried grimly. 'He chose out of hate, you
chose out of love! You chose it, Shem! We agreed it was
the only way! You chose it because you knew it was
necessary for My plan; because you knew it was what
your father would have wanted! And yes! I laughed! I
laughed because I knew we'd succeeded — that much I
remember!' Passionately She stared him down. 'But once
you were gone I was driven from this land and away from
the Whole Place for many Lullu-generations! But the
plan works! Because when I returned you returned too:
we took the Whole Place back, we have it now — and
now you're with Me again! You're with Me, bringing all
Samjoyce knows from the Last Days! And we need what
you've learned!' Urgently She thrust Her hand at him,
made him look into the emerald depths beyond moon
and horns. 'Look! Look! Do you know what this is and
what we're about?'

Panting in angry confusion — *My father?* — he eyed
the depths and went swirling through visions he couldn't
understand. But the chief thing he saw was a huge con-
vulsion, a great isle sinking into foaming, lava-red sea, a
planet lurching on its axis as global storms ripped entire
civilisations to pieces. 'Yes,' he muttered, breathing hard,
fishing elusive memories from oceans of pain. 'I remember! You *borrowed* it from the ... Emme Ya world when
You came on your last mission after the Flood. A fragment of the Emerald Tablet — Azazel persuaded You,
didn't he?' Tearing his eyes from the depths he glared at
Her. 'You knew what You'd rejected! You'd made your
choice! *This* world instead of paradise — and us Lullu for
Yourselves!' he muttered sarcastically. 'Poor stupid
beasts, cast back to barbarism by the Shift, and You tried
again, mixing Your blood with ours, when to begin with
your blood wasn't *your* blood at all, but ...'

'Never mind that, Fool!' She insisted. 'We have more
important ...'

'Oh yes!' cried Shem, furiously gazing at Ailma. 'More

353

important to *You*, no doubt! But You asked if I remember who I am, and I do, so let me say it!' And he laughed at Her. 'I know! I'm one of those *lucky* ones You bred on Lullu women to make us more like *You*! But instead You became more like us!' he taunted. 'You went rotten: the Elohim shut the main gate and locked You here so You can't get out again! And my *father* — if that's the word for his ... contribution of seed — he was the worst of the ...'

'It's not like that!' She cried angrily. 'Yes, we entered this world to teach you Lullu what we knew! Yes, Shemyaza and Azazel and myself and others came down once too often, and now here we are, *more and more like you*, fighting for our lives! Listen!' She insisted, eyes blazing. 'This is one of many worlds we dealt with, but always the most seductively difficult — folly always stalked us here! Shem, the last Shift wasn't the first, and yes, we were at fault, for those who fell before that Shift encouraged you Lullu in the crystal power which ... well, the Lullu that survived forgot everything! Yet we decided our work here merited one more chance! Just one! If blindness prevails, then the next Shift is the last. No more saving missions! We of An and El locked here perish with the rest of you! The final Forgetting! Everyone back to the Source! The Elohim have an economic view of things,' She went on, excited and bitter. 'They won't try again. We must persuade them! If we can't, we must force them!' And She pouted fiercely. 'Why should I die to satisfy their exalted requirements! What did we do that was so wrong? No ...' — She held up a hand to forestall his interruption — '... Hear me out! Certainly we were told not to teach you Lullu certain so-called 'harmful arts' — but we had to decide things on the spot! Fine for them, high in the light of the Emme Ya, engineering abstract policies — but we had to do the work and take flesh to carry out those policies — impractical policies! *Don't teach the Lullu how to work metal, how to write, how to dispute! Don't even touch the filthy flesh-thick beasts! Just jog them along gradually! Follow orders!* Nonsense! They don't understand the problems imposed by flesh and time and gravity! Time and again we came down here and got into trouble, and time and again the Shining Ones blamed us for it and abandoned us!'

Shem, suddenly remembering Samjoyce at GRYP, laughed out loud.

She stared at him suspiciously. 'What's so funny?'

'You sound like social workers taking the rap for slum conditions you didn't improve!' he cried. 'Now you're stuck because the council abandoned you. And why? Because you lost interest in improvement, you turned into dealers and crooks! All you want is to keep the game running, yourselves on top. No thanks!' He shook his head vigorously. 'I don't buy it!'

For a moment speechless, She stared at him.

'Is *this* all you learned from the Last Days?' She whispered.

Shem shrugged, his face dark with anger, anger at himself, for now too late he understood, he remembered what was going on, and of a sudden as he stood there in the glade with Ailma asleep at his feet he knew just what a fool he'd been. A *Fool!* Yes! 'You tricked me,' he said with a painful smile. 'You tricked Yourselves first, then you tricked stupid Lullu like me, persuading us You were our best chance, persuading me to die for the cause! What cause! You just want back what You threw away. You didn't have to come down here and slum with the natives. And when you sent Me through to the Last Days, yes, so I agreed — but I'm not just Shemyaza's son now, I'm Samjoyce too! Now you want Last Days information to help You — well! You've got it all wrong!' And as he folded his arms there came to him the image of a blue-eyed, golden-haired girl. *Chrissa?* he wondered sadly, and involuntarily he eyed Ailma, asleep at his feet. *No. Not her, but* ... 'So now what?' he demanded savagely, more Samjoyce than Shem.

It was Her turn to gape at him. What's gone wrong? she wondered in silent alarm. Where's the one I sent? Is the Samjoyce stronger? Another mad *man*? 'LISTEN!' She cried furiously, anger getting the better of Her. Seizing him She pulled him away from the sleeping girl at his feet. 'NOW LISTEN! You can't hide your thoughts! Your little daughter won't help! She's faraway in a man-time where Weak Ones delude her; she can't hurt Me unless she remembers more than she ever knew, so forget her and listen to Me! The Last Days filled you with mad ideas! Think what you like, but ...'

'... You'll kill me *again* if I don't do what You want, eh?'

Wearily She released him. 'Fool,' She said quietly, 'I need you. I have less power than I did. There's war between us Watchers now, for the longer we stay the more we lose our wits. But Azazel must agree to My plan! He took this land from Me after your father lost his form and went into the Hidden Place — after you went to the Last Days. I took it back, needing the Whole Place to receive you ... but now he wins victories. Yet without his agreement ...' — She sighed — '... our chances of opening the Starchamber are slight. Since you left I've opened other gates, but none of them reach far enough. I can move through this world, but not beyond, and the longer I spend here, the less my power ...'

'Entropy!' Shem grinned. 'The Second Law of Thermodynamics, I think it's called. Last Days science! Loss of energy from a closed system!'

'Don't laugh at Me!' She flared, gorgeous in Her robe, the emerald bright on Her finger. 'Listen! The only way out of this sphere is to open the Starchamber ... and it's sunk in the sea! But at times the isle rises: it's on an unstable volcanic ridge. We have to get to it, or when the Shift comes again ... I need you, Shem! I need you to approach Azazel — for I can't, not after the way he's treated Me!' She declared scornfully. 'I need you to plead for this world before the Shining Ones — They won't hear Me, but you're a Lullu! Yet to get there ... Oh, there's so much to do.'

Her voice shook with a strange doubting passion, as if unsure what She said ... and it was then Shem felt a friendly presence. But he hid it as She demanded suddenly: 'You can write?' Misreading his reserved expression, She exclaimed: 'Of course you can! Very well. Start writing everything I say in case I ...' She shook her head, eyed him hard. 'You must obey me,' She warned querulously. 'If not, I can ...' Again She shook Her head; She looked ugly and old, and down at sleeping Ailma he gazed as a distant but familiar voice in him whispered with quiet intimacy:

'Dad? Remember me? Chrissa? Dad, it's not all lost! The Shining Ones will help, so don't let Her use you or fool you!'

But She sensed it. Perhaps his face betrayed it too.

'What's that?' She cried. I'm watched! She realised. That child! Child I've had enough of you! Silently She hurled Her rage like a spear; She sensed a shriek. Shem flinched. She smiled grimly. 'What is it?'

'Nothing,' he said blankly, meeting Her bright, furious gaze.

Not as bright as You used to be! he thought. Chrissa ...

'We go now,' She snapped. 'Don't dare look down at that girl!'

But Shem paused by Ailma. 'What'll happen to her?' he demanded.

'She'll live!' hissed the Lady of Nine Heights. 'Now come along!'

'What do You mean, she'll live?' Shem persisted angrily. '*How* will she live? As a beggar? Are You abandoning her, or punishing her as You did ...?' He indicated the bloodstained grass where Hoel had died.

'Look, Fool!' She thrust the emerald ring under his eyes, so that again past moon and horns he looked ... *and in the depths he sees a white-haired old woman creep into the glade after they're gone; sees this old woman awaken Ailma and lead her out of the grove; sees the lamentations of the clan as they carry out Her will, burning down the longhouse, wasting the fields, dividing the goods and chattels and then, before nightfall, dispersing in their many directions, dazed and saddened by their fate. And he sees how the old woman leads the girl to a foreign land where Ailma gives birth to a boy-child ... then in the depths*

357

sees through time past many generations to the birth of a boy who in time becomes a sea captain ... who near the end of his life finds himself enchanted by the gaze of a raven-haired woman on a quay in a seaport sometime not far from the Last Days ... And he sighed.

So Shem followed Her out of the grove, amazed and doing Her will — yet he knew hope. She's done Her worst, but I'm still Samjoyce, not just mad Shemyaza's idiot son! he thought wildly, struggling with hard memories. In the Hidden Place, eh? Best place for him! And Chrissa managed to follow me! The Weak Ones did it! Her burning man reached her! Good for him! And as he started after Her to the Whole Place he felt privately joyful.

But what now? he wondered. What next?

31.
Escape

'There!' the friar hissed, pointing. 'Gather the men, but no ...'

Behind him the sergeant already understood. Hearing the mule bray he'd quickly looked up to see, dark against the dazzling snow, a man crossing open space between trees high up the western slope. Pierre Belot, you're a fool, but you fight for the faith as well as any, he thought with amused weary respect as he brought the horn to his lips. Yet if I burn for this and you don't escape with your goodman, may you rot for ever!

'NO!' snapped the friar ... but too late.

The horn blast sounded along the road and up the snowy slopes.

Pierre froze. He looked down. Then he moved very fast indeed.

'You fool!' raged the friar. 'You've warned them!'

'You told me to gather the men!' the sergeant replied innocently.

'Without sound! You'll answer for this!'

'I did what you told me,' the sergeant insisted, bleak now.

With an effort the friar controlled himself. But, as he reined in, for an instant he saw nine wild shrieking women, their slime-caked hair flaying his face. Gasping,

359

eyes bulging, he met the sergeant's gaze and his tight mouth said: I'll see you burn, my friend! The sergeant did not back off. Do your worst, dung-eater! said his contemptuous look. Aloud he added: 'You think they hadn't seen us anyway?'

'Thanks to you!' Brother Jean breathed deep as the rest of the patrol arrived in a clamour of hoofbeats and harsh cries. You think I'm a fool! his brooding eyes told the sergeant, and that grizzled man could not stop his curt nod. The friar's lips, as thin and pale as paper, smiled. 'But we're not going up there,' he said silkily, though inside he still raged. 'We'll call reinforcements and post men all along this road at every bridge and ford from Ax to Foix. They'll try for Monségur, which means they have to cross the river. We'll get them when they try it!'

You're right, you godless shit! said the sergeant's scowl, but he said: 'There are other strongholds. They may bear north to Roquefixade, or even south round the back of Ax towards Usson. What do you think, lads?'

And his men added to the confusion, crying different advice, nodding agreement, arguing with each other, throwing in other names and places.

Brother Jean shut his eyes. *Why* do they think me a fool? Don't they know they only delay the inevitable? We'll have them all ... and Montségur too ... when we decide to take it. But when he looked again he caught the sergeant eyeing him so nakedly that then he realised the man knew all this too. You people! he thought, amazed and full of pity (but that emotion he crushed). When will you learn? Must we burn you all before you submit to Christ Jesus? Why perish for a futile belief? You call this world hell, but you make it so for yourselves! And unaware of the chill ecstasy on his face he murmured to the sergeant: 'Don't think God will enjoy punishing your blasphemy! Where would this world be if every man had freedom to decide things for himself? How can we defeat chaos without the loving discipline of the Father and the Son? I will pray for you!'

The sergeant grimaced angrily. The friar lifted his eyes reverently to heaven ... and did not fail to observe how already two mules were angling up snowy heights to the crest of the ridge, with two ... *No!* His sharp eyes saw not two but *three* riders on them.

Who's the third? he wondered coldly. There were only two yesterday. But we'll have them soon. Then we'll know.

Soon he had men off to Tarascon, to Pamiers and Foix. By nightfall a thousand men lined the riverbank, each with a flaming brand, each within call of those either side, and none of them doubting how they'd suffer if the heretics escaped. All night Brother Jean d'Aubigny and others of the Order rode up and down the line exhorting the dubious rogues, reminding them their souls were in mortal peril if the heretics escaped. Yet when dawn came, cold and stormy, no alarm had been raised, no man had claimed any sighting ... and so it went on. Late on the second night there was a false alarm when some drunken peasants raised a hue and cry near the bridge at Sinsat upriver from the caves, crying from the woods that they'd found the heretics. All the guards within earshot ran into the woods, where it turned out that the fools had mistaken a terrified woodcutter and his wife and daughter for the heretics. After that there were no more sightings, false or otherwise, until on the fifth night the friar's informer brought him stale news already known to everyone else in the highlands: Montségur had already received Bernard de Laurac, the shepherd Pierre Belot, and the unknown girl-child they had with them. It was rumoured by excitable folk that they'd snatched this child from the mountain depths, that she was no demon but the living spirit of their beleaguered faith. The informer also said that many who'd been wavering were now reaffirming their faith.

There was even talk of victory against the invaders.

Brother Jean raged. Then he grew calm. Today the dragon escapes, he told himself. Tomorrow we'll burn her. Meanwhile there are others.

The bailiff and sergeant of the guard at Tarascon were first to go, chained up in Foix castle until they died of starvation. And soon came the friar's chance to launch a more general persecution. One morning an ass wandered into Foix. Tied to its back was a dismembered, black-roasted corpse. Tied to the tail of the ass was the corpse's head, mutilated almost — but not quite — beyond recognition. It belonged to the friar's informer in Ussat. For this unsolved crime many poor people went to the stake, including Helis who'd shared the bailiff's bed. But the persecution did not touch Montségur, remote on its crag in the mountains. Nor did it help Brother Jean to sleep any better at night. In fact often he did not dare to sleep at all.

After the horn blast Pierre led his charges south along the ridge to a shepherd's hut high on the slopes of Larnat. He built a fire and left them that night, going out for help. The second night the weather grew worse as they were smuggled down to the river at Sinsat. When the diversion began — the flickering torches, the shouts of 'We have them!' from the woods — and the idiot soldiers fell for it, Pierre waded the freezing river under cover of the bridge, tugging the burdened mules behind him. On the far bank they were met by a guide who led them past patrols and up a mountain stream to the vast open lower slopes of Tabor. In a believer's hut Pierre rested, drying himself and Bernard, the believer's wife taking charge of the white unconscious child, all the while exclaiming with pity. By dawn, the girl strapped still unconscious to mule-back as Bernard's senses began to fail, they were labouring up through fast-falling snow, heading for a pass east of the peak, Pierre still tugging the exhausted mules behind him . . .

They'd never have reached the castle alive had not Sicard the Weaver's son got Bernard's message to Bishop Guilhabert in time; had not the bishop persuaded Pierre-Roger de Mirepoix, the garrison commander, to send search parties out in the foul weather; and had not the

patrol that found them been led by a local man, Arnaud
Domerc. His instinct and knowledge of the hills led him,
as much against the will of his men as against the blizzard, to press high up over the east shoulder of Mount
Tabor. 'We go back only when we've found them!' he
kept insisting until, floundering through the Col de Font
Albe against a gale so violent it could hardly be faced, he
came across the three of them. They lay motionless,
barely alive, half-buried in drifting snow. Only the
shepherd was conscious and able to stand. Only one of
the mules still lived. Belot had killed the other, slitting its
throat and then its belly in order to thrust the wraith-like,
near-dead girl into the wet bloody warmth of its still-
palpitating gut. Otherwise she'd have been dead already,
the goodman too ... for Pierre had pushed the unconscious old man into the mule's gut after the girl, then
covered them with his own body. When the searchers
reached them, tears of rage at his act of murder were
frozen on his cheeks.

*Whiteness. Dazzling white flowers whirling everywhere, the
whole world a sparkling white flower, virgin-pure and beautiful,
caressing her with the freezing heat of extinction. Again and
again the plunge down the dizzy ever darker abyss, hunting shape
and form, hunting the Song and crying out from the fading
heights of the timeless realm: 'Father! Father Bernard! If you
don't come soon it'll be too late!' And his cry amid her agony in
the vortex: 'COME, DAUGHTER! JOANA, RETURN! AEIOU!
AEIOU! AEIOU!' — then desperate battle followed by confusions
of vision and journey, first in darkness, then in dazzling whiteness, and all the way the surly cursing man leading the beast that
carries her, with the old man, the Song-singer, a faint burning
presence nearby. Not yet sure of this world she wanders lost
through other realms and times. Once (the freezing whiteness
abated by a moist, slippery, stinking gut-womb) she reaches a
point of no return, only to find her way barred by a Shining One.
'NOT YET! YOU HAVE WORK TO DO! BACK TO THE WORLD!'
Feebly she resists; but motion jolts her; she hears anxious voices;
wind seizes her hair as the white flowers whirl down again, but*

she cannot move or open her eyes. Not yet. I DON'T WANT TO! a
voice moans. SAFER, QUIETER, NICER HERE! NO PAIN! I DON'T
WANT TO REMEMBER — but another voice retorts: IDIOT! THE
SOONER YOU WAKE UP THE BETTER!

For hours through the blizzard they descended the
wide slopes of the Montagne de la Frau: neither the girl
nor the old man moving, and it wasn't until they were
climbing the last stretch to Montségur that she opened
her eyes, albeit briefly, when the beast carrying her
stumbled. Then, jolted from the deep, her eyelids flickered open ... to see all about, at first in a blur then with
sudden sharpness, a swaying white-and-black landscape
of huge plunging rocks, high ridges, wild ranks of fir and
gnarled old pine knottily clinging to the mountainside ...
and above, over the huddled head of the man tugging at
the mule, through wind-torn veils of mist she glimpsed
the prow of a castle riding the huge crag they climbed.
And even as her eyes fluttered shut again she remembered —

The dream! The burning man! And the dream seized
her:

The burning man! Silently she whimpers, gagging on the
stench as his black, shrivelled hands grope from the flaming
stockade where he burns with all the others, eyes popping from the
cracked, peeled ruin of his face — WHAT IF THEY SPLATTER
OUT ALL OVER ME? — and, worst of all, his dying song:

> *Quant lo bouié ben de laura*
> *Planto soun agulhado*
> *AEIOU!*

He's calling me! I won't listen! I won't go! Tearing her gaze
away she sees instead the black hooded ones, the faceless ones on
their knees, praying to heaven, exhorting the cursing frightened
soldiers to feel no pity as her eyes flee up the crag soaring over this
awful place.

... to the castle looming grey above ...
Then she realised, without any shadow of doubt:
I'M HERE! I'M HERE! THIS IS NO DREAM! OH GOD I'M

Fire consumes her, the world explodes, the song's drowned in
cruel laughter as, gazing from the void, Her bloody face agleam,
the Enemy cries mockingly: 'YES, YOU'RE AWAKE! YOUR
MARTYRS HAVE YOU! I PLANNED IT! SOON YOU'LL GO UP IN
SMOKE AND STOP INTERFERING! BURN, CHILD! BURN!'

Shock seized her: she jerked in a spasm severe enough
to strain the cords binding her to the mule. And had not
Pierre, alerted by the brute's earlier stumble, already
pulled it to the inside of the steep, jagged path, she'd have
taken it and herself over the edge. Cursing, he managed
to counterweight her shift, dragging the mule back then
calming the beast before checking the girl. He hadn't
seen her eyes open; now she seemed completely unconscious again . . . and he mumbled through his frost-rimed
beard at the sight of her, for she looked so peaceful.

For a coolness has touched her brow.

'Joana, hush!'

She sighs and murmurs, 'Father Bernard!'

Her lips fluttered but Pierre missed this too. He had
already turned away, concerned only to get up this
deadly final pitch before daring to relax. Gaunt, he
grinned into the wind. By now he was so exhausted that
his exhaustion had become a detached ecstasy: he
watched his clumsy frozen body drag itself and the mule
up towards safety, towards food and warmth, wine and
song, and maybe, who knew, even a woman! — though
probably not the first night, he allowed with lightheaded
prudence. You may want to sleep, and your root will
need to thaw. And occupied like this he did not notice,
either, how on the mule behind, the corpse-like goodman
moved not at all.

But Arnaud Domerc, attending that mule, watched
Bernard.

'Goodman, are you still alive?' he asked. 'The lady-
healers will draw you back — if you want to return.'

32.
Montségur

Nobody thought they would. Even when at last they were
brought safely into the cramped narrow castle (*perched so
high atop its precipices like the Ark on Ararat!* Domerc
marvelled yet again as he led the goodman up the icy,
winding dangerous final turn to the wide high South
Door), it seemed sure they'd die. The girl lay in a swoon,
her breath imperceptible: the goodman's spirit had all
but fled his shrunken frame. Like corpses they lay as
night came on, she in a room atop the keep, Bernard in a
room above the North Door, his breath too faint even to
fog a glass, and many of those who visited him went away
not wishing him back, for his own sake.

Bishop Guilhabert de Castres came, nut-brown and
chubby, to give him the kiss of peace on each hollow
blue-white cheek. 'May the touching of her not impede
you, my friend,' he murmured ... for Pierre had told him
how he'd found the two of them by the black pool, her
hands clasped round the goodman's fist. Yet without this
minor sin, Guilhabert was sure, the weird girl's trans-
lation through the Gate couldn't have been accom-
plished. How else? he thought with a little smile as he left
to talk again with Pierre Belot, who'd recovered his
customary surly strength. How else?

Then came the Seigneur de Montségur, Raimon de

Perella, a tall middle-aged man, the haugteur of his dark face belied by sad, reflective eyes. He was joined by his strong-jawed wife Corba, now his wife in name alone, for she had put on the black robe of the *parfaite*. Together at the foot of the curtained bed they stood, studying the goodman's face, which stayed as white as the fleeting, cloud-wracked moon. At length Raimon said sharply: 'Well, whatever you've brought us, maybe it's best if you don't live to see the results. They'll use this as a pretext for more killings.' Then he left too, but Corba stayed, soon to be joined by her daughter Esclarmonde, a slender pale serene woman who'd never in her life been out of the hills; and with her was the older Esclarmonde, sister of the Count in Foix, who'd borne many children before receiving her husband's permission to leave him and receive baptism. The older Esclarmonde, grey-haired and emphatic, knew the world well. She had often argued for the faith at her brother's court, and debated patiently with Catholic clergy. Now that was impossible: fire and sword had replaced debate. Now she was permanently at Montségur.

The three goodwomen eyed Bernard de Laurac's earthly husk.

'Still with us, but barely,' whispered the younger Esclarmonde.

'He doesn't need this world any more,' commented Esclarmonde de Foix. 'But maybe it still needs him. And the girl he brought us.'

'But who *is* this girl,' asked Corba, puzzled and doubtful. '*What* is she? What realm is she from? Is she a child of light, or . . .?'

The two Esclarmondes eyed each other sharply.

'We don't know that yet,' said Corba's daughter.

Soon the two Esclarmondes went down to the narrow courtyard and along to the keep at the castle's western end. They climbed steps under canvas awnings where the wives and soldiers' doxies scrubbed clothes and minded children. Some of these women were of the faith and genuflected, others did not. Entering the keep, where the families of Raimon de Perella and Pierre-Roger de Mirepoix had their quarters, the two women climbed dark spiral stairs and came to a tiny cell on the top floor. Here on a cot the mysterious golden-haired child lay, all but her head buried under blankets and furs. Her eyes were shut. There was no sign of life in her pale round face. Her mouth was slightly open. With troubled faces the two *parfaites* studied her. They could see fillings in her front teeth. In fact both had studied the dental work in the child's mouth, but neither wanted to talk about it, for it pointed to questions they were unwilling to consider.

'What do you think?' asked Esclarmonde de Perella.

'I don't know,' the older woman admitted softly. 'I can't reach her. Her soul's in a maze. It may be my own doubt and lack of skill. Is she truly an aeon of light sent to combat Satan? So weak, so pale ...!'

'I've tried the laying on of hands,' whispered the seigneur's daughter, 'but as you say: she's not to be reached. I too think it may be because of my doubt and lack of skill. But I get a sense of her that's ...'

She shrugged, unable to articulate what she felt.

'A sense of ... evil?' the older woman asked sharply.

'Not necessarily. Just ... *strangeness* ...' And the younger Esclarmonde licked her pale lips nervously as she repeated: 'Just ... *strangeness* ...'

'Perhaps we need better skill than either you or I possess.'

'Yes!' Esclarmonde de Perella nodded. 'Who have you in mind?'

So a messenger was sent to the house of women at Fanjeaux, asking the healer Fabrisse de Montréal to come to Montségur immediately ...

'Goodman, are you still alive?' Bernard never heard Arnaud Domerc's question. Near death in the chill storm as they climbed the last stretch, he'd been dreaming, dreaming of his youth before the war, a ghost visiting that night at Lombez he met Fabrisse. *Tall and slender he floats in the firelight of the richly-cultured court, so very serious in his fine*

Moorish gown, the red rose held prominent in his strong delicate hands as he sings; the red rose telling his audience to seek subtle meaning behind the outer face of his lyric. He sings the new song he found high on the slopes of Tabor ... the sad song of Joana. When he's done, he approaches the graceful girl he eyed earlier. Daughter of Raymond de Montréal, she's hardly more than a child, but her eyes are so clear! 'Isn't this world beautiful?' she asks bluntly. 'Why darken it with songs of pain and death?' And, swimming in her eyes, he smiles his funny smile. 'Your beauty's too bright to know darkness,' he tells her, 'but how can I admire your beauty if I can't face darkness? Without darkness, beauty can't exist!' And at the dancing response in her eyes he laughs and knows: This is the one who'll ...

Abruptly from this pleasant dying drift he's snatched by sudden terror, by disorientating shock, by an agony of flame eating his flesh, by vision from many angles at once, by sense of the Enemy glaring and gloating from a black abyss. For an instant amid this he returned to consciousness, his eyes opened and he saw Montségur above; he saw the child Joana writhing on the back of the mule ahead, and knew that the shock and terror which had alerted him came from her. Calming himself, he closed his eyes and returns to the deeper level, picturing her bright blue-eyed face as he whispers:

'Joana, hush!'

And with mental fingers strokes her brow until she relaxes, and as he does this he summons the gentle image of a warm woodland glade where red roses grow, where they sit at ease by a fountain of pure crystal water that sparkles in the soft sweet air before turning into white doves that fly away, healing all sickness and pain. Carefully he plucks a rose and gives it to her. 'Here, child! This is for you!'

'Father Bernard!' she murmurs in her sleep.

'Joana, why are you here?' — and as he asks he senses another presence, the sharp but kindly presence of the one he was dreaming about before the shock. 'Fabrisse?' he asks. But there's no reply.

'Because you called me, Father!' the child dreams back.

'But you called me!' he insists. 'You called me from the aeonic world to save you from the dark Watchers, and I came, and we've *fought the Enemy together! And not done badly! But what's the work? Joana! I must know!'*

'Father Bernard!' But her shock is lessened by the beauty of the place where they sit. She senses an unseen watcher — but there's no feeling of evil or the Enemy. She yawns, breathing the scent of the rose deep as she does. 'If you don't know, who does? Father Bernard, YOU called ME!'

'Please stop "Father-Bernarding" me!' the old man barks. 'What do you think I am? I've clung to your toes and glimpsed the aeonic world; you told me what to do when the Old One had me beaten — why suppose I know more than you? You even foresee my fate! — it seems we both call each other!'

'But . . .' — wide-eyed she appeals — '. . . you're supposed to teach me!'

'Teach you what? What can I teach you? How to die?' She winces at his dry laugh. 'Yes, I see that too!' he explains more gently. 'I recall a dream of reaching you in your world . . . from the fire! Here at Montségur! Well, so be it! But to what end? We trick ourselves all the time! What if these dreams of Shining Ones are the false god's joke? Joana,' he tells her passionately, and it's not a bent old man sitting by her, but a youth, tall and slender, so fine in his embroidered silken gown, and for a moment the water leaping from the fountain leaps from her eyes — 'I'm old and full of doubt. I've seen the world you fled. I call you from a fire that's yet to be lit; here we speak in the aeonic world outside the time that weighs down this false world; I've seen the Old One seduce your father with Her fragment of the Stone, and you come here, begging help. I see all that . . .' — he gazes acutely at her, for now, though still she senses that friendly watcher, she senses something else too — '. . . but do you see where he goes? What time, what land, what state? Show me! Don't be scared!' He pauses, sensing something wrong, but — NO! NO FEAR! 'We beat Her once already!' he insists urgently. 'Now perhaps we'll find your father!'

'I think we're there!' Trembling she eyes the glade, seeing a man and woman coupling as beside them a man is murdered, 'But . . . Oh Father, Father Bernard, I'm so tired, and I don't think we should let Her know that . . .'

Abruptly the Enemy attacks. Only it's not Her, but a blue

cockerel-headed monstrosity, panting with lust as it materialises to seize her and bear her down on the grass, poisoning her with its foul burning breath. 'Help me!' she cries, still clutching the red rose. 'Help me!'

And then again her senses whirled in whiteness as the castle loomed and she went falling, falling, falling ... and Bernard, losing her even as his own senses failed, cried out: 'Fabrisse! Fabrisse! To Montségur! Joana's returned, but she needs your help! Quick! To Montségur!'

33.
Fabrisse

Fabrisse was on her way before the messenger arrived.

The convent she governed lay amid woods and low rocky hills, a day's journey north of Montségur and half that distance west of Carcassonne. The French in the fortress at Montréal nearby knew about the heretic house but had left it alone so far: they had bigger fish to fry than a house full of war widows and orphans. But the time would come. Fabrisse knew it. She had lived with the knowledge for years. It didn't disturb her. She wasn't the sort to be easily disturbed.

Yet that night she was disturbed by the vision which came to her, so much so that by dawn next day she and her companion Braida were well on their way to Montségur.

Her sense of crisis involving Bernard had begun late that afternoon. In the midst of organising dormitory accommodation for refugees from a slaughter in Limoux she'd suddenly found herself thinking of that night long ago at Lombez when she'd met the Chevaliar de Laurac, as he'd been then. It was as if for an instant Bernard stood there before her again, young and handsome, singing Joana's song. Yet even as she saw him in her mind's eye his youth peeled away like a discarded mask and there instead she saw a dessicated skull, covered in snow, a skull in which only the eyes were alive — eyes that burned on her for a moment before the vision faded.

Gripped by chill, the stocky white-haired old woman paused in her work, momentarily feeling faint. What's happened? she wondered. Are you there, Bernard? Are you in this world? But as she asked this an overwhelming sense of shock and terror struck her, making her gasp. Without more ado as darkness fell she excused herself and went to her room to pray for his soul, sure that catastrophe had seized him. Before she got on her knees she went to an oak chest, the only piece of furniture in the room apart from her cot. From a compartment in the chest she lifted out a small stone disc suspended from a silver chain. Inscribed on the disc was an equal-armed cross; set in the middle of it was a small cut emerald.

With a sigh as she knelt she touched her forehead with this disc, and felt the gem's cool light in her. Over and over she murmured the Lord's Prayer until the far sight began to awaken in her, preceded by signs that in her experience distinguished genuine vision from the idle fancies that so easily and often distracted the mind during the long winter nights.

First came the flashing colours, then a high-pitched ringing and a fiery tingling in her body. The colours flowed into the green ray as the ringing became a voice, one she knew well, singing the song she would never forget. And song and green ray together carried her to a place of shape and form — a bright summerland, elsewhere and elsewhen ...

She finds herself in a glade in a wood by a fountain of crystal water which plumes and sparkles in the radiant air before changing into white doves that fly away above the banks of red roses that bloom everywhere. 'Fabrisse?' whispers a familiar voice, and she senses Bernard, wounded and faint in the spirit, but alert to her presence.

She doesn't reply.

She cannot.

For by the fountain she sees a shining golden-haired girl, little more than a child, holding a red rose, and there's talk between

373

this child and Bernard, talk she cannot hear, for as her vision grows clear she senses a shadow, deadly and furious, thickening over the glade round the pair of them, blighting the light, wilting the roses and killing the doves. But Bernard and the child aren't aware of it! She tries to call out, to warn them — too late. The evil materialises! She sees the shining child borne down to the ground by a blue cockerel-headed monstrosity that's sucking the life from her. 'Help me!' cries the child, still clutching the rose, 'Help me!' — and the creature killing her looks round, snarling, even as Bernard, warned too late, cries out: 'Fabrisse! Fabrisse! To Montségur! Joana . . .'

A huge, numbing blow drove her from the vision. Shaken, the old woman found herself alone on her knees in the winter night of her room, listening to wind moaning through the trees. Her head was splitting; something foul had touched her. That cockerel-headed monster . . . 'Azazel!' she breathed angrily. 'I thought there was a stake through your heart ages ago!' She shook her head, tried to rise, found she could not. *Help me!* moaned the wind, *Help me!* And the vision of that golden-haired child tingled in her. For a while longer she stayed on her knees. *Montségur? Joana?* At last, grimly, she smiled. 'What have you found under the rose now, Bernard?' she asked as she stood and went to find Braida. 'An old flame in a new skin?'

Deep in the night the two women put on their shabby travelling cloaks and left the house disguised as tinkers. Dawn's stormy light saw them well down the road from Mirepoix to Lavelanet, and the armed horseman who came from the south would have passed them had not Fabrisse called out:

'Friend! A moment, please!'

The rider was a sergeant from Montségur, Pons Narbona, ruddily in love with the life he risked travelling this road alone. Impatiently reining in he cried: 'Good ladies, forgive me, I can't waste time.'

'You seek Fabrisse de Montreal? Here I am!'

He eyed the tiny old woman in astonishment. He'd

seen only two frail old peasants dowdily cloaked against the wind. Now, leaning down, he met the light in her eyes and belatedly recognised the goodwoman. In a hurry he dismounted to kneel in the snow and make the *adoramus*, for he was a believer. 'Good lady, how did you know?' he whispered as Fabrisse sketched blessing over his head. 'Who told you?'

'Little birds sing in my ear. Friend, your message, please.'

Quickly the sergeant gave it. When he was done she nodded.

'Good. Return and say we'll be there by nightfall.'

'But,' he warned, 'the land swarms with ...'

'Never mind. We'll be there. Now go.'

After he was gone and as they continued along the empty road, Braida, thick and red-faced in middle age, said anxiously:

'Shouldn't we take more care than this?'

'The good spirit helps us,' Fabrisse assured her. 'I believe those frightened children who try to hurt us are all elsewhere today.'

Yes, she thought, that's what they are. Frightened children who lost their mother. Worshipping the false god called I AM GREATER THAN THOU.

On they went, and as it happened they met no soldiers of pope or king. Even so, they skirted the scattered roofs of Lavelanet before starting up the steep dog-leg valley leading to Montségur. By then it was afternoon, grey and cloudy: with wet feet they climbed silently between melting banks of slushy snow from which great firs sprang. They passed through the hamlet of Montferrier and it was there, through a gap in the steep hills, they got their first sight of Montségur, distant on its soaring rock.

Bernard, what have you been up to? Fabrisse wondered again as they continued up through the poor light. With a wan smile she recalled that night she'd first seen him at Lombez. Thirty years, but as clear as if he sings before me now! And that song! I still feel the chill of it! Yes, and I taxed him with pessimism, but he just said something clever. Then he laughed. Such a laugh! I fell in love with that laugh. It terrified me and made me joyful at once. Now here we are, Bernard, amid the horrors you foresaw. You know you're the only man who ever made me admit to love? But you gave me plenty of trouble too, she thought, following Braida up the icy and darkening trail. Her smile faded. You gave me three sons too.

For despite her vows and all the years she'd never quite distanced herself from the fate of her sons. *Their* sons. Mir, Roger, Roland. Hard even now to think of them. Mir long dead, betrayed to the friars. Roger, alive but crippled and witless, crushed by a rock from a trebuchet at the battle for Avignon nine years since. And Roland, for years now in exile in Aragon with Raymond Trencavel of Carcassonne, and never a word of news.

Three sons, all gone. She watched a crow flap through the fading sky. Now what have you found, Bernard? A daughter to replace them all?

Soon after that, riders from Montségur met them.

She wasted no time. Met at the great South Door by Bishop Guilhabert and the two Esclarmondes, she insisted on being led straight to the child. 'They're both alive,' said the older Esclarmonde anxiously, 'so far as we can tell.' But Fabrisse just nodded as they told her what they knew, and removed her cloak only as she entered the tiny, slit-windowed cell on the upper floor of the keep, letting it fall where it would. The cell was lit by a smoky tallow candle. Shadows flickered on bare walls as she got down on her knees to examine the pale face below her. Her eyes softened. Yes, the face she'd seen ... but it hardly shone. 'Poor child,' she murmured, shaking her hands loose, 'so you're the one who's come so far.' Gently, without more ado, she laid her open left hand on the girl's forehead, thumb resting on closed eyelids, while with her right hand under the blankets she felt for and found the rigid fearful muscle of solar plexus.

'She's been the same since she arrived,' said Esclarmonde de Foix. 'Sometimes restless, muttering unknown words, but no awakening.'

'There was a swelling on the foot,' said the younger Esclarmonde. 'We applied witch-hazel and salt. It seems to help.'

'Good,' said Fabrisse. 'Leave me with her.'

And for long, long hours as the wind wailed round the mountain that night, Fabrisse worked with the healing tides, reaching out for the poor lost child until, not far short of dawn, the child's spirit returned, and her eyes opened ... and Fabrisse saw that they were blue ...

Epilogue: The Rose

Hissinggrabbingpumping! Azazel invades the glade and shrouds the terrified child with his cold blue lust, enveloping her in panting stench, beady cockerel eyes wide and wet, forked tongue flickering from quivering beak, knee trying to force her thighs abart as he snatches at something she holds. 'Drop it! Drop it, pretty Lullu! Put it assside, let me tassste you!' he hisses, fingers like icy jelly slobbering over her cringing body, poison breath stifling her. 'FATHER!' she pants soundlessly in terrified agony of suffocation. 'FATH ... ER! FA ... THER ... BER ...

'Therber, therber, yesss dear, but therber's lossst you! Such a pity! Such a pretty little bud, so dimpled, ssssoooo ... oooooh little Lullu, let Dada Azazel look after you ... let it go! Stinking rose! Drop it!'

Rose? The rose? What rose? Father Ber ...

In my hand! she realises. It ... it scares him!

Its rich scent springs in her, driving out the foul suffocation. With a curse the creature backs off, but not far. Clutching the rose tight she shudders, teeth chattering as she stirs from blood-stained grass and finds the breath to cry furiously in her terror: 'Who ... Who ... Who are you? What are you doing, you, you, you stinking sex-maniac pervert pig!'

'Aaaaah!' In huge smooth curves under the cold blue lustre of his skin Azazel's muscles flex. He crouches close, talons digging into the soft green turf of the glade, scarlet comb as erect as his

378

swollen blue one-eyed worm. 'Ah, my little Lullu, so you're the *tassste* of the Lassst Days!' he crows, fondling his comb with long delicate fingers. 'So bitter-sssweet, So ... sophissticated! So crrruel and heartlesss!' Then wringing his hands he crawls to her with imploring, arresting eyes. 'Have you no love for a poor old monsssster who only wants just a littlelittlelittle affection ...?' But, warned by his mocking tone and hard eyes, she sways back as he grabs at the rose; she laughs hysterically in his contorted face at the miss. 'You creep!' she rages, amid her panic wondering: What can I do? Only the rose stops him! 'What are you? How did you find me here?'

'Quesstions, silly quesstions!' He rears back, languidly plucking a thorn from his thin blue hand. 'You scare my sisster, little one, yet you ask silly quesstions.' His little round burning eyes fix on her. 'Don't turn your back on me, child! I might jump again!' She gasps, flinching, her attention seized as the monster croons: 'Look in Dada's eyes! See his nice pictures! Dada Azazel sees his queen-bitch sssister here! Dada sees ssstrange things here! Do we want to see them? Do we want to see our daddy we followed from Lassst Days?' His eyes spin hot and black: seized by them she sees ... brands flaming from the slick black walls of a blood-red chamber. She sees Sam, his face a mask of fearful ecstasy, on his back on Her bed as dripping naked She rides him, doing things that ... 'My sweet sissster! Insatiable!' Azazel declares, smacking his lips. 'Diss-gusting! With Shemyaza's brat too. Hah! If the sad old fool only knew!'

'Dad!' she screams, turning Sam's head as foulness whistles too close. Just in time she sways back, but Azazel, snatching a petal, throws it away and sucks burned fingers, his eyes fixed on her. 'So quick, my sssweet! I thought I had you! Do you know what they're up to? Sisster Tiy hopes I'll agree to her mad plan to stop the Shift! She'll send your daddy to talk to me soon! Yesss, Shemyaza's brat! Do you know Shemyaza, sweetnesss? He led us here! The Elohim blamed him when we disssobeyed their orders. It wasn't hisss fault — it was mine, sweetnesss, and Sisster Tiy's. Now he's lost in the Hidden Place, his power is gone completely, and she needs me to get to the Starchamber! Look, sweetnesss, I'll show you the Starchamber!'

Abruptly she's plunging deep under the sea (it reminds her of

379

another sea, but she can't quite . . .) past the looming black cliffs of a drowned land — and again the foulness snatches: another petal's gone as she jumps back. 'What do you want?' she cries. 'Why are you so horrible?'

'I'm a little bored.' Abruptly, whimsically, Azazel shifts shape, and she gasps. It's Father Ber . . . oh no it isn't! 'Beauty can't exist without ugliness,' murmurs the elegant young man lounging before her in his fine Moorish gown, his smile dazzlingly sincere. 'Sweetness, I LOVE beauty!' Smilingsmiling he sways closer. 'To sssuck your sweetnesss!' he groans, still smiling. 'Oh, why do I let you torment me? — you must not wither like other women! Seize the opportunity . . .' — again he lunges; just in time she sways back; but again he snatches a petal, and she feels her strength dwindle a bit more with the rose now half-stripped — '. . . to find joy!' Rocking back, his eyes plead with her. 'Lovely child, I've watched you since you met my sisster — I watch her all the time, though she doesn't know it. She doesn't know much now! She even let you watch her — I sssaw you here, and I've seen you in your nice little house in the Last Daysss. Oh,' he sighs, 'your poor mother! You've forgotten her, haven't you!' And painful memories flash through her mind, of Diane asking: Have you clean knickers? Where's your bus pass? Tears well — but again that foul burning breath; another petal goes. He crushes it, smiling triumphantly. 'But you haven't ever ever seen me . . . except in video nasssties and on telly!'.

'Never!' she mutters dully. 'Not even in the worst nasty!'

'Child! Of course not in the flesh!' he giggles. 'Christ and Science throw me out then forget me, thinking me dead! But I'm the virus invading the cell; the fear breeding the Bomb; the greed that poisons the world and prepares the Shift! I hide in the dark and spawn sick ideas — puritanism, free sex, romantic love. My Country Right or Wrong! I encourage anything that AIDS the Shift! — ha! Get it? Get the joke, child? AIDSSS!'

'What are you on about?' she asks faintly.

'Even Tiy with her mad ideas can't stop the Shift! Look!'

The world foams and flames in her mind. She sees metal camps belching fire, gleaming silver eels soaring into the sky leaving plumes of smoke, then . . . with a gasp she sways back again with two more petals gone and the remains of the rose rapidly wilting. 'What's mad about wanting to live?' she implores through a haze of weakness and fear. And Azazel laughs.

'I'm the lussst that undoes itself,' he declares with melancholy self-satisfaction, sucking his fingers with fastidious care. 'I'm the worm to blight your rose — if you'll let me! What's beauty without ugliness to enhance it? Child, your beauty's too pure, you need help. See!' His hand starts fondling the huge stiff bow of his lust. Shivering with fascination that both fires and chills, she stares. 'You think me a beast!' he sighs, and with a tired gesture shifts shape again: 'Maybe. But in the Last Days I find many hosts! The Shift will come and all will end!' The blue youth squats on weary haunches. 'But it takes so long and I'm tired of waiting. When I came to this world I took sssolid form. Now it's hard to hold form for long ... yet even if I discard form I can't die!' Tears trickle down his cold blue cheeks. 'Death is the climax of all desssire ... but for us of An and El it's not easy. We were shut up here for bringing you knowledge and we're not allowed easy Lullu-death. We must wait for the Shift, and if the Shift's overcome our torture goes on! And why?' he groans, inching closer again. 'Only because we fell in love with sweet little Lullu like YOU!'

With a roar and a leap he shifts again and the monster's back on her, the poison stench of him suffocating, his fingers like slobbery electric eels feeling her frantically. 'GIVE UP YOUR ROSE, CHILD! MY PATIENCE ...'

'Father!' she shrieks, 'Father! Help me! HELP ME!'

'DROP IT, YOU OBSTINATE CHILD!'

With all her remaining strength she concentrates and finds a shining space, a distant vision, and through the swirling foulness flies a blazing arrow, a sound, a song, a wrinkled old face, a white-haired old woman —

'A good spirit guards you!' a soft voice whispers. 'Find the Song!'

'AEIOU!' she screams. 'AEIOU! AEIOU! AEIOU!'

Azazel bellows with rage and ...

She floats. She floats namelessly, ignorant of herself, without care save for something too terrible to touch. In a bright place she floats by a pool of clear water round which oak and hazel bloom. 'Chrissa!' cries a despairing voice, 'Chrissa-Chrissa-Chrissa!' Her brow wrinkles but she doesn't really hear or recognize the name: she just floats in warm golden light, needing it after the chill of trials forgotten, watching duck and moorhen glide in reedy shadow under drooping cool willow. Reflections of massy oak and high-sailing white cloud glimmer on the water, entrancing her as a peewit calls piercingly . . . and mirrored sky and piercing call together — so sharp and pure, slicing veils of blindness — lift her on radiant wings through huge night to the diamond lightning-guarded gates where (WE? US? IT? SHE? HE?) dances in vast blazing light, whirling amid They from whom time and forms are born. Deep the ecstatic spirit dives into the ocean world circling Emme Ya's veiled light; there it joins the great grey ones at council in the hall where the emerald's mounted in a coral wall. 'FOUND US AGAIN, HAVE YOU, CHILD?' a voice inquires gravely . . . and all about it the awed soul senses rank upon rank of great grey ones, radiating nose-to-tail into illimitable distances of ocean beyond this hall — a vast motionless dance, a flower in the deep. 'BUT HAVE YOU COME TO STAY?'

For there in the emerald, like a nugget of darkness clenched against the light, the hidden world floats. YOU CAN'T GET AWAY FROM ME SO EASILY! it whispers . . . and without warning unleashes a flood of dreadful images. The burning man straining from the flames! Azazel swirling like furious smoke! Sam gazing longingly up from his love-struggle with Her whom the cockerel-headed one calls Tiy; Tiy with her snaky, bloody black hair like slimy shroud-growth over the face of the world, blank-eyed like two zeroes as she climaxes in gouts of flame and black smoke. I SEE YOU, CHILD! She cries, exploding. YOU GOT AWAY THIS TIME . . . BUT YOU WAIT! YOU WAIT!

Ecstasy flees in a silent scream, in a teetering on the brink, in a desperate pulling-back to remain this side of the emerald depths.

'YOU MUST GO.' The quiet voice emanates from all the great grey ones: the voice of council sounding as one. 'YOU CAN'T RETURN HERE TILL THE JOB IS DONE! YOU'RE NOT CHRISSA FROM CROUCH END ANYMORE. YOU'RE NOT ALONE: MANY OF YOU LULLU BEGIN TO REMEMBER AS THE SHIFT NEARS. CHILD,' the serene voice goes on as the lost one senses the presence

of others like itself; others recruited from the occupied territory to join the company, *'IN YOUR WORLD DUNG BREEDS HOPE, BUT YOU DON'T REMEMBER ENOUGH YET! YOU'RE STILL CAUGHT IN OUR SISTER'S WEB! GO BACK TO THOSE WHO'LL HELP! HEAR THE SONG!'*

In turmoil, fighting the Enemy-held depths, the confused one looks to the great one alongside, and again (What other time is there? Am I always here?) sees that vast rolling eye close in a wink of unmistakable humour.

'But why make me do this?'

'MAKE YOU? IT'S YOUR CHOICE. LOOK AGAIN!'

Again the world calls, its song drawing the unwilling one with hope and fear, horror and desire. *'YOU SEE?'* murmurs the voice of the Elohim, *'YOU MUST WORK WITH THOSE WHO REMEMBER US TO REDEEM OUR SISTER BEFORE SHE BREAKS THE GATE WE CLOSED! IF SHE OPENS THE STARCHAMBER THE SHIFT IS ASSURED, AN END IS SURE, FOR THAT GATE CANNOT BE FORCED! SHE'S YOUR PURPOSE; SHE AND THE ONE YOU FOLLOW: YOUR FATHER, SHEMYAZA'S SEED WHO MAY YET FIGHT FREE OF THAT CURSE! IGNORE AZAZEL! OTHERS DEAL WITH HIM! NOW HEAR THE SONG! GO!'*

And she goes. Again, knowing the time of awakening has come, she wings down, down, spiralling back to the world, to the snowy mountainous world, to a castle perched atop a huge forested crag ... to find herself lying on a cot in a cold bare room, a wooden shutter on the unglassed window. Her eyes are closed, her face is pale, she's covered by mounds of furs, a woman in black watching over her touches her with tingling fingertips, drawing her closer to the surface. *'I heard you call and here I am,'* a soft voice whispers. *'Can you hear me, child? Can you feel my touch? Take my love. Take my strength. It's all for you — winter never lasts for ever — you're beginning to wake up! And when you do we'll take you into the deep healing woods where you'll knit together again! Can you hear me, child?'*

She can, and the curious thing is that though this voice speaks in a foreign tongue, it's not foreign at all. *'... Quant lo bouié ...'* — like a wraith of sound it touches her; she senses Father Bernard drifting weakly but alive somewhere close. Feeling safe at last, on the edge of awakening she drifts again to a green place, to *a glade in a wood where a fountain plays, its plume of water sparkling in the sun. Everything dances there, the foulness is gone, the light is clear, and there's someone speaking to her, a little old lady with a bright-eyed, wrinkled, friendly face ...* and again as in her sleep she smiled at this old woman she felt the touch of fingertips and heard the old lady whisper:

'Joana! Joana! Wake up, girl! Now!'

Slowly her blue eyes opened. Above her in the flickering candlelight of that winter night she saw the bright-eyed face of Fabrisse de Montréal.

So Joana came to Montségur in January of the year 1234.